COPYRIGHT ACKNOWLEDGMENTS

CONTENTS

ACKNOWLEDGMENTS

Priya Sharma, for suggesting organizations that might take an interest in Alice.

To my contributors, for their enthusiasm.

To my editor, Liz Gorinsky.

MAD HATTERS
and
MARCH HARES

Introduction

There have been many books written about *Alice's Adventures in Wonderland* and its companion volume *Through the Looking Glass and What Alice Found* by Lewis Carroll, exploring their meaning—psychological, political, mathematical; and about their author, Charles L. Dodgson (1832–1898), a mathematician, logician, Anglican deacon, and photographer, and his relationship with the model for his heroine, Alice Liddell.

I've loved Carroll's two classics since I was young. I wouldn't say I'm obsessed, but I've been a collector of illustrated versions for many years, especially appreciating the enchanting illustrations of the books by fine artists such as Mervyn Peake, Arthur Rackham, Barry Moser, Ralph Steadman, Lisbeth Zwerger, Salvador Dali, Rodney Matthews, Anne Bachelier, Maggie Taylor, and so many others, some relatively unknown.

But I must admit that my vision of "Alice" herself has been subverted by the 1985 movie *Dreamchild,* in which the adult Alice Liddell, who is visiting New York, flashes back to her childhood. There we see the dark-haired little girl who inspired the tales as she was seen in photographs, very different from the long-haired blonde image created in John Tenniel's ubiquitous illustrations. In that movie, which is very much about the relationship between Dodgson and Liddell and how his creation of her fictional counterpart might have influenced her life as an adult, there are darkly magical, partially animated interstitial sections with amazingly creepy Wonderland inhabitants imagined by Jim

Henson. In fact, it might be the creatures in Carroll's works that are even more likeable than Alice herself, bringing readers back over and over again to the land beyond the looking glass.

Everyone is familiar with Walt Disney's 1951 animated musical version of *Alice in Wonderland,* which took about twenty years to get off the ground, and made an indelible mark on childs' psyches with its colorful renderings of the Cheshire Cat, the Mad Hatter, the White Rabbit, the March Hare, the Hookah-smoking caterpillar, and one of my personal favorites: Dinah the kitten. In 1971, Czech filmmaker Jan Švankmajer made a short animated film based on the *Jabberwocky,* and in 1987 made a full-length feature, the darkly surreal *Alice,* which in its original language was called *Something from Alice.* Its tone was entirely different from the Disney. In 2010 and 2016, Director Tim Burton interpreted the two volumes in his own inimitable way. Love them or hate them, they did create a whole new set of images that one can savor. *Then She Fell,* a marvelous immersive performance piece created by the theater company Third Rail Projects, has played continuously in New York City since 2012. The ongoing popularity of all of these disparate visions demonstrates how strongly Carroll's work continues to be loved.

So how did this anthology come about? I was being interviewed at a convention a few years ago, and someone from the audience asked me what anthology idea I hadn't yet done but would like to. I mentioned that I adore the Alice books, and after the event, I was encouraged by several bar companions to try to sell such an anthology. So reader, I did. And this is what you now hold in your hands (or are reading on your screen): eighteen stories and poems inspired by Alice, by Lewis Carroll, by the critters of Wonderland. Some of the entries are fanciful, others are dark indeed. In either case, I hope you find as much enjoyment in these works as you have in the original books.

GENTLE ALICE

Kris Dikeman

She
sifts
among
the dirty
plates and
shards of
shattered
mirrors piled in
splintered mounds.
Searching for a
single cup still
sound and whole
amid the chaos of the
table, spread before
her like a field at
battle's end; strewn
with bent spoons,
ruined pawns,
crushed petals
white and red.

I watch from my perch above the table, invisible beneath the moon.

At last she finds the one gilt-edged survivor. She pours in tea, cold and thick with dormouse fur. Her reflection in the dented pot is a stranger to herself: the Red Queen's bloody crown heavy on her brow. She swirls once, twice, thrice, flicks her wrist, leans forward to read black dregs against bone china. What future is written there? She's weary now of games and trials, knaves, rabbits, riddles with no answers, food that grows and shrinks her at its fancy. But where to go? Home to dreaming spires? Can fairy stories told along the river's edge still keep her heart content? Can any earthly prince amaze a girl who faced a pasteboard queen? She could stay, grow tall, rule this dark, strange world, call for clamor, lopped heads and painted roses. But gentle Alice longs for bedtime. If she can, she'll nod, and sleep, and wake to home; clean sheets, butter biscuits, hot milk in a clean cup and kitten Dinah's sweet soft purr, instead of magic cats that, smiling, disappear.

MY OWN INVENTION

Delia Sherman

Two forward, one across, and I'm in a wood: the seventh square, since I know who I am. My horse is plodding down a path unspooling under her hooves like a ball of wool, only wider, while I think of ways to wake kings or small children or writers, all of whom seem to be constantly sleeping and dreaming of me in the seventh square on a horse with a mind of her own.

My horse's name is Horse. She carries not only me, but also two sets of armor (hers and mine), a saddle, a spiked club, a sword, a mousetrap (*sans* mice), a bunch of carrots and another of onions, a beehive (*sans* bees), fire-irons, and a bundle of reeds for a campaign chair. It will fold and have its own sunshade and turn into a table, suitable for cards or tea. All I need is some string to tie it with. Or possibly glue. It's my own invention.

In the clearing, the Red Knight is climbing onto his horse. Beside a large silver dish, suitable for serving plum-cake or sliding down a snowy hill, stands an Alice. The Red Knight brandishes his club and shouts at the Alice, who looks alarmed, as well she might. The Red Knight has a voice like cold pease porridge.

"Ahoy! Ahoy! Check!" I cry.

"She's *my* prisoner, you know!" says the Red Knight crossly, and we fight. It is awkward and noisy and involves a great deal of Maneuvering and Mountaineering and things beginning with "T," like Tumbling

Topsy-Turvey and Tintinnabulation. I beguile the Tedium by Thinking of a way to make a ladder out of eels so that I may remount Horse without banging my shins on the fire-irons. After a while, the Red Knight and I simultaneously knock each other out of our saddles, and the move is over. We pick ourselves up, shake hands, and the Red Knight mounts and gallops off into the wood. I see the Alice standing behind a tree, wearing a curious expression compounded of apprehension, admiration, and amusement.

There is always an Alice in the seventh square. They are generally yellow-haired, with pinafores over blue dresses, striped stockings, and little black slippers. Male Alices are rare, as are whales and crickets and mice and any non-chess piece over the age of seven years and six months, give or take a decade.

This Alice's hair is shorter than usual, and less golden.

"It was a glorious victory, wasn't it?" I ask.

"It was not a victory, not really," the Alice observes, brushing at her pinafore. "It was a draw. He just gave up and left."

Here in Looking-Glass Land, everyone disagrees with one another more or less constantly—except for the Red King, because he is asleep, and me, because I can never be sure I'm not wrong.

"I'll see you safe until the end of the wood," I say soothingly. "And then you can be a queen."

The Alice shrugs. "And it's all feasting and fun. I know." A sigh, not enraptured. "Come on. Let's get it over with."

We go through the business of getting my helmet off, I fasten it to Horse's saddle, and we set off through the wood. It is getting on towards brillig, and I want to get the Alice disposed of quickly so I can have my tea. I have a fat borogove in my bag that should stew up very fine, with treacle.

Almost immediately, Horse snorts, stops short, and I tumble off her back into a ditch. The trees are like cobwebs against a glassy sky. Or perhaps the cobwebs are like trees. In my present position, it all comes to the same thing.

The Alice's scowl comes between me and the cobwebs or trees. "You do that on purpose, don't you?" she asks as she pulls me upright.

It occurs to me that this Alice, like a mouse on horseback, is not altogether comfortable with Looking-Glass ways. Perhaps she has tumbled into the wrong dream by mistake. "Do what?" I ask.

"Fall off your horse all the time. Nobody could be that clumsy."

"Did you ever wonder," I say mildly, "if a good cure for baldness might not be to coat your head in mud and plant grass?"

The scowl becomes a glare. "What's with you, anyway? Do you have ADD?"

"Alice Daily Demands," I say dreamily, climbing back up on Horse. "Articled Dozing Dormouse. Antique Doily Dolls. No, I don't have any of those."

One black-shod foot stamps dust from the path. "No! It's a syndrome: Attention Deficit Disorder. It means you can't pay attention in class."

"I have been in a box and in a wood and in an order, child, but never in a class."

The Alice makes a sound like an angry cat and marches away, leaving me to follow. When Horse and I catch up: "I don't know why I'm dreaming about you," the Alice grumbles. "This isn't even my favorite book."

I fall off again, into a ditch this time. To my surprise, the Alice pulls me out again. "Are you going to keep doing this? Because if you are, I think I'd rather go on by myself."

"*I* was thinking, too!" I exclaim, "About names. There are all sorts, you know, just as there are all sorts of creatures. Take Humpty-Dumpty, for instance. His name means the kind of shape he is—"

"And a good, handsome shape it is, too," the Alice murmurs.

"Just so. But the rest of us have to make do with names that say what kind of thing we are. The Sheep. The Red King. The Jabberwock. True," I add thoughtfully, "there's only one of each of them, so it's not as confusing for them as it is for us Knights. Still, it's not the same as having a real name."

"Like Alice?"

The Alice's tone is scornful, underscored with melancholy, and so far from the self-satisfied smugness I am accustomed to in Alices that I say, quite spontaneously, "Alice isn't your name."

Another scowl. "If it's not, why am I wearing this stupid outfit?"

"Well, that's it, you see. Here, Alice is what you do. If you flew, you would be a Gnat, or perhaps an Elephant. If you knitted, you'd be—"

"A Sheep," the Alice interrupted. "That's dumb. What you do isn't what you are. I mean it *is,* in a way, but not like that."

Disagreements, it seems, are like boats. Once you are in one, it is impossible to get out again without falling into deep waters. I sigh so deeply my armor rattles and my mustache flutters like eyelashes. "It certainly isn't what *I* am. Perhaps that's why I make such a bad one."

We walk in silence for a space, and then the Alice says, "I feel you."

I am about to ask for an explanation, or perhaps talk about mousetraps, when a furious outgribing breaks out in the distance.

The Alice whirls like a grig. "What's that?"

"Too loud for a mome rath," I say thoughtfully. "Unless there's a herd, but it's unlikely, this distance from a wabe."

The outgribing gives way to whiffling. I unstrap my club. Though it might be large enough to give a Bandersnatch pause, it's like hay for a headache against a Jabberwock. Still, it makes me feel better.

A wind sighs through the branches, wafting a stench of burned toast, and then the Jabberwock is upon us, burbling as it comes. It is clad in a scarlet cap with a little bill in front and a blousy white jacket, trimmed in scarlet and emblazoned with the mystical letters R-E-D-S-O-X.

The torpid mouth gapes, the lantern eyes goggle. I swing my club, miss, and fall off Horse from sheer momentum.

The Alice gives a little scream of absolute fury. "Get out, get out, get out! This is *my* dream!"

"Perhaps it's a nightmare," I offer from the prickle holly bush where I have landed.

"Joshjoshjoshjosh," whiffles the Jabberwock.

The air fills with carrots, onions, and cabbages (alas for my borogove stew!), followed by the mousetrap, an ash-shovel, and a bellows. The Jabberwock burbles and roars, crashing its guillotine teeth, whirling its glaucous eyes. Huge clawed mitts clutch at the Alice, who has gained some inches of girth and height and is brandishing a vorpal blade that looks very like a fire-iron.

"Snicker-Snak! Snicker-Snak!" the Alice cries, and swings mightily.

The iron shears the whiskers from the Jabberwock's chin as neatly as a razor and the monster rears back, tumbling along its long, scaly tail like a lizardly hoop, a look of blank astonishment on its fearsome countenance.

The Alice is nearly as tall as I, now, and considerably sturdier. The hair is shorter than ever and quite dark, the dress and pinafore transmogrified into blue pantaloons and a kind of buttonless shirt with short sleeves.

"Joshjoshjoshjosh," burbles the Jabberwock.

"Go away," shouts the child, who is most certainly not an Alice. "Or I'll cut your head off and throw it to the crabs!"

The Jabberwock swells and gibbers. The not-Alice throws the vorpal fire-iron at it and it disappears like a bun at breakfast.

"That was too easy," the not-Alice remarks, and extracts me from the bush.

"What were we talking about?" I ask.

"Names," the not-Alice says. "You said mine wasn't Alice."

"Nor is it. Will you give me a leg up onto Horse? You seem to have thrown my stirrup at the Jabberwock."

"Sorry."

"Don't mention it."

Horse, unburdened of fire-irons and vegetables, is inclined to be frisky, but the not-Alice is now tall enough to steady me in the saddle. As we progress side by side, through the wood, I reflect how pleasant it is to ride without the trouble of falling off and clambering back up again. I regret the carrots, also the fire-irons and the stirrup. But the saddle is certainly more comfortable without the mousetrap.

The not-Alice flexes a strong arm and surveys it critically. "This isn't right."

"It is, you know," I say apologetically. "Your right arm, that is."

The not-Alice's eyes roll briefly skywards. "Right. But it's not *my* right arm."

"Isn't it attached?"

A sigh. "Yes, it's attached, but that's not what I mean. It's the *wrong* arm; it's not *my* arm!"

Horse stops short and lowers her head, expecting me to dive forward. When I do not, she looks reproachfully over her shoulder at the not-Alice holding me in the saddle, snorts, and walks on, ears at an offended angle.

"What kind of thing would you like to be?" I ask.

"Not sure," the not-Alice says. "Not what my dad wants me to be, anyway."

"And what's that?"

"A real boy."

For a moment, a boy walks at my stirrup. He is strong, like Horse, and his appearance hovers somewhere between Tweedledum and the Beamish Boy, with a touch of Bully and Bore about the eyes and mouth. Then the not-Alice returns, smaller and wispier than before, like a guttering candle.

"You could be an Alice if you like," I say soothingly. "A real Alice."

The not-Alice shrinks a little further. "No!"

"Without the pinafore?"

"The pinafore isn't the point."

Deep waters indeed, and not a boat in sight.

"You are sad," I say. "Let me sing you a song to comfort you."

"No way," the not-Alice says.

"You haven't heard the song yet," I say, stung.

"I don't need to. I've read it. It's dumb. And kind of pathetic and self-pitying." The not-Alice stops, and so does Horse. I fall off.

The not-Alice watches as I get to my feet. "Josh."

"I beg your pardon?"

The not-Alice is smaller now, and wispier than ever. "It's my name. It's short for Joshua, who was a mighty warrior. It's a kind of joke, if you think about it, but it's a pretty lame one."

Smaller and smaller, less than Alice-sized, and shrinking. I cast around in my mind for something to say that will stop the process, but the best I can come up with is, "That's not your name."

"IT IS," says a voice like an avalanche.

The sky is coming on very dark. The not-Alice-nor-Josh looks up and up at the giant bestriding the path. Or at least the giant's foothills, which are covered with black-and-white shoes of no recognizable type, tied up with white rope, with two massive towers rising out of them into the clouds. The towers are pale, like dirty pinkish brick, and one of them is plastered with a shiny yellow banner decorated with what looks to be a giant bat.

"WEIRDO," the avalanche adds.

The not-Alice-nor-Josh is sheep-sized now. In a moment, it becomes kitten-sized, then gnat-sized, then pawn-sized, after which I lose sight of it in the grass. I fear it has gone out altogether, like a candle.

"Quick," I cry. "Who are you? Are you Jack? Are you Jill? Are you Beast? Are you Beauty? Tell me what you are!"

A pause, and then I hear a tiny squeak in the grass at my feet. The next moment, not-Alice-nor-Josh is visible, and visibly thinking hard. I know the look. I have felt it on my own face often enough, although my face is not as round, my mouth as determined, my eyes as dark, my hair as thickly bristling as the not-Alice-nor-Josh's have grown.

The ground groans as the giant shifts its black-and-white shoes impatiently. "I'LL GRIND YOUR SOUL TO MAKE MY BREAD!" it thunders.

I unhook my club from Horse's saddle and hold it in my arms, determined to do or die.

The not-Alice-nor-Josh looks at me, dark eyes glittering like poison, then cups two hands into a trumpet and shouts, "Hey! Giant-face! I have a riddle for you!"

"A RIDDLE?" The avalanche sounds curious.

"I am here and there, neither and both, impossible and present. I come and go as I please, and nobody can pin me down. What am I?"

"LOSER!"

"Wrong!" the not-Alice-nor-Josh cries. "Give up?"

"NO! I GET THREE GUESSES!"

A sigh. "Okay. Go for it. What's guess number two?"

A pause as the giant gives the question some thought. "A CATERPILLAR!"

"Wrong!" The voice is triumphant.

"NOT FAIR!" The giant roars. "THERE'S NOTHING LIKE THAT IN THE WORLD! YOU'RE A DIRTY LYING CHEAT!"

"Third guess!" crows the not-Alice-nor-Josh triumphantly. "And it's wrong!"

The foothills shuffle, the leg towers tremble. I hold my breath; Horse lifts her nose out of the patch of clover she is cropping. Not-Alice-nor-Josh is holding the vorpal fire-iron and looking a little pale.

"Me! That's the answer: Me! I'm Me!"

Three times, as any fool can tell you, is magic, even in a backwards place like Looking-Glass Land.

The sun comes out, the warm wind stills, the foothills and leg towers (and, presumably, the giant above them) have disappeared, leaving simply rocks and trees, with observable tops. Me is swelling with pride, beamish, solidly and uniquely Me-like. "Wow," they say. "That was pretty cool, huh?"

"A glorious victory," I agree, and sigh. "And now I must leave you. You've only a few yards to go. Down that hill and over that brook, and then you'll be a Queen."

"I'm good," Me says gently. "Thank you anyway. You want to sing your song now?"

"No," I say firmly. "I do not. But if you will wave to me until I reach that turn in the road, I would be grateful."

Me nods. "You got it. Um. Thank you. For everything."

"Don't mention it."

With Me's help, I drag Horse away from the clover, mount, and head back along the road. The sky is blue, the air is sweet, the trees cast dancing shadows upon the path. Horse stops short. I cling to the saddle and the bundle of reeds; I do not fall off—then, or when Horse starts up again.

When I am nearly to the turn, I pull on the reins until Horse stops, I suspect from sheer astonishment.

Me is standing by the brook. They are dressed in a blue overall and big, black boots, and waving a scarlet bandana.

I stand in my stirrups. "Me," I shout, "is not a real name, you know."

Me grins like a Cheshire Cat. "I know. It's my own invention."

LILY-WHITE & THE THIEF OF LESSER NIGHT

C. S. E. Cooney

"And 'the wabe' is the grass-plot round a sun-dial, I suppose?" said Alice, surprised at her own ingenuity.

"Of course it is. It's called 'wabe,' you know, because it goes a long way before it, and a long way behind it."

—Lewis Carroll, *Through the Looking-Glass*

"Four buzzards in a storm-belted sky—and someone," Mother said, "has been stealing caterpillar silk again."

Mother did not look at Lily-White when she said it, but Lily-White bridled at the implied reprimand.

She had not kipped a single thread of that ever-sticking silk since she was thorn-high to a vorpal rose—and *that* had been a unique situation. A dangerous venture, denuding a caterpillar of silks. Not only is the Borogovian Caterpillar a gregarious species, she is also gargantuan, a colossus of nature. The last thing anyone wants, especially when that anyone was not a very tall anyone at all, is for an entire sibling society of large larval lepidopterons to aggressively pursue one home.

The "four buzzards" part meant nothing, Lily-White decided. That was just Mother being dramatic. When you were Hetch of the Borogoves, you spoke in riddles from underneath ominously lowered eyebrows, even to—especially to!—your own daughters.

Ruby-Red looked up from polishing her sword. "Which silks were taken, Mimsy?"

"All," Mother replied. "Tents and trellises ripped from their moorings, hunting webs cut down—prey included—and the nursery emptied of cocoons. The caterpillars themselves . . ." She shook her head. "Pierced through. Chewed. Spinners hacked off—those taken, too. Naught much left but blue guts and fuzz."

Lily-White, whom nothing much bothered when it actually happened, remembered waking up that morning awash in forefeeling. (*The Edible Dictionary of Wabish Verbs* once defined the infinitive "to forefeel" as "Suffering the emotions of a traumatic event before it occurs without divining any actionable knowledge about it." The last copy was eaten four hundred years ago.) She had cried and cried, her body wracked with shock, then nausea, succeeded at last by sadness. Now she knew why.

"All?" she asked. "All dead, Mimsy?"

While Lily-White did not like caterpillars (it is difficult to feel affection for creatures who try to gobble you up just for stealing the *least* skein of silk, and that for an urgent cause), they had spun their parasitical palaces back behind Mother's cottage ever since she could remember. And now they were gone.

"*Vidi nihil permanere sub sole,*" Mother said severely, quoting this year's Motto. *I have seen that nothing under the sun endures.* Her shoulders and neck were bull-heavy, perpetually sunburnt, freckled with an exact map of the Looking-Glass constellation (whatever it happened to be on a given night). Her thick arms bore the dagger-deep scars of her vorpal roses, which she had bred and raised to her peril. Just, she often observed, as she had her own daughters.

Ruby-Red wiped a tear away. Unlike her sister, she always cried at the right time.

"There, there." Mother patted her eldest daughter's head. "One did survive after all. Baby-Blue, the newborn. Found him in a basking basket high up in the trees. Sound asleep, sunning himself through the slaughter. 'Twas his snoring alerted me to the rescue. Brought him home. Be in a delicate state till I can procure him some poppy seeds. Cast 'em out back on the shady side of the cottage. Coax 'em to bloom, milk the pods, dry the gum. Then we'll see if Baby-Blue will latch." She sighed. "Little ones don't always latch, you know—if it's not their own mother's hookah. Like I said, delicate. So don't go messing with him, either of you."

She squinted at her daughters through the smoke-black lens of her hexacle, which she wore to protect loved ones from her Evil Eye. Whenever that hexacle came off, swinging from its chain like a bruised pendulum, the girls knew they were in trouble.

"Wasn't you, was it, Lily-White?" Mother asked abruptly. "Did you do those caterpillars in and burgle their silk?"

Lily-White stomped her foot. "I only took that *one skein,* Mimsy! *One time!* I was practically a baby back then! And I never killed anybody!"

"But you've a hardness, girl. Meticulous and methodical as the shadow of Mount Gnomon."

Lily-White bit her lip. That was true.

"And you, Ruby-Red? Innocent or guilty?"

Ruby Red grinned. Her teeth glittered like garnets, as they did when she was angry. "Wasn't I, Mimsy. I'm no thief. Besides"—she tossed her lava-colored hair—"I like to chop things up, not chew 'em. You know that."

Mother knew that. Every so often, she would wake to find all her roses decollated, their petals decorating her parlor so prettily she couldn't even scold. She smiled at her daughters.

"Well, then," she said. "I'm content as ever I was before my tragic walk this morning. And now you girls have a new brother!"

Blowing them a Hetch kiss, which fluttered from her lips in the form of a black moth to brush a benediction upon their brows, Mother swarmed up the loft to check on the cradle. Her cooing voice floated down, mingling with the peeps and mewls and chitters of Baby-Blue.

What hath teeth but hath no mouth
That ne'er shall swear nor be foresworn?
Nor eyes nor ears nor nose hath she
But champs and chaws thee, grates and grinds thee
Gnaws thy flesh to tatters torn?

Lily-White stood a while, rubbing the kiss-pollen off her forehead and pondering Mother's song. She wondered if it had to do with their next Motto. About time for a new one.

One of Mother's duties was to maintain the Motto of the Wabe. The Motto spanned the southernmost part of the Dial where the shadow of Mount Gnomon never touched. Each spring, Mother cut a new Motto out of the tender green grass with a push mower. She filled in the stubble with luminous pebbles so that the words could be read plainly by very high-up things, like giant blond girls and insect swarms and the migratory borogoves who flew down from the north every summer and roosted in tall, teetering columns of themselves just south of the Motto until winter came. The caterpillars always captured a few columns each year, and spun their palaces about them, sucking each bird dry of substance and leaving only stiffened, silk-draped skeletons, which rose in ghostly groves behind the Hetch's cottage.

Mother's song faded.

Lily-White turned to Ruby-Red, who hummed an off-key echo of the lullaby as she polished her sword.

The sword was a thing of beauty, forged of silk and thorn. Could slice a diamond like butter. Lily-White's work, years of it. She owed Ruby-Red her life from early on in her infancy, but when she made a gift of the sword, both sisters acknowledged the debt had gone down some. Perhaps she owed only a quarter of her life now. Or someone else's life, should Ruby-Red require it and Lily-White had the means to deliver.

Lily-White plopped down on the sofa next to her sister, who stopped humming.

"The last time Mimsy grew poppies," Ruby-Red reflected, without looking up from the gleam on her lap, "we had all those wonderful dreams!"

"We also got constipated," Lily-White grumped.

"Well, we know better now," Ruby-Red said. "Drink it, don't smoke it, and never three days in a row."

"Still—a brother?"

And such a brother! Lily-White thought, grimacing. Caterpillars really were insufferable.

Ruby-Red shrugged. "He can keep Mimsy company whilst we go off on adventures!"

"We never have adventures."

"We will, Egg-White," Ruby-Red assured her sister, who wrinkled her nose at the abhorred nickname. "I'll make sure of it—if I have to conjure one up myself! There are wonders amassing wonders out there in the wide green Wabe, and we must quest us a few!"

Suspicious, Lily-White tried again to catch her sister's eye. Had Ruby-Red, after all, slaughtered those caterpillars simply out of boredom? It was not in keeping with her character; she was very fond of animals—even horrible, hairy, opium-smoking bugs. And even if she had, Lily-White reasoned, Ruby-Red would have boasted about it, not lied to Mother.

Besides, what would she need all that silk for? Her sister was no crafter. One had to be very patient and careful to work with Borogovian Caterpillar silk, for it binds whatever it touches, and holds forever. Didn't Lily-White know? The amount of Jubjub oil it took to scrape that stuff off her fingers, after!

She opened her mouth to pester for more information—but then the roses started singing.

When a vorpal rose sang, it meant she was happy.

Which meant somebody was bleeding.

This is Lily-White's earliest memory of the vorpal roses.

She is not yet two. She often cries for no reason. Later, when reason occurs (her four-year-old sister dropping her on her head, for instance, or Mother forgetting to feed her in a timely manner due to some distraction, like a stranger visiting, bartering for boons of their local Hetch, as they often did and still do to this day—this very day in fact, which will bring us back to the vorpal roses of the present, but not yet), later, when any other child would be whining and whimpering and writhing, Lily-White is as calm as winter in Wonderland.

At first Mother is inclined to think her second daughter fussy and spoilt (which she is), but one day she comes to the cradle, and without warning, Lily-White awakens from her nap, opens her mouth, and lets out a scream.

It is a very particular scream. It is the scream of a tiny child, not yet two, who has been snatched bodily from her little bed, thrown out the window, only to break her fall in the tangle of vituperative vorpal roses waiting below.

It is unmistakably the single most awful sound a mother's ears will ever suffer, and it is instantly recognizable.

Of course, there is only one thing to do—and the Hetch of the Borogoves knows just what it is.

She snatches Lily-White from her bed and throws her out the window.

What follows is nothing. Not a shriek, not a whimper. Not what you'd expect from a baby presently swaddled in barbs.

Mother wonders if Lily-White has died in the fall. She asks her eldest (and now possibly only) daughter to check the thorns, just in case. Ruby-Red, her milk teeth turning the color of blood in her fury, dashes headlong into the briary snarl, hollering and cursing and hissing as the roses start to giggle, singing and slicing in retort. A vorpal rose loves when a child bleeds; young blood is beauty's finest fertilizer. At last, Ruby-Red seizes her bewildered baby sister out of the grasp of those terrible raking thorns, and bears her back to safety.

The sisters will bear the scars from this adventure their entire lives. A life that Lily-White now owes mostly to her sister, minus the price of a magic blade.

The blade, of course, is the reason she stole the caterpillar silk in the first place. When she is old enough to creep, Lily-White crawls deep into the grove of borogove skeletons, where the caterpillars live. She steals a skein of nursery silk, whereupon eight outraged aunties give chase. But they are doped with opium; the splendor and delicacy of their highly dressed hookah instruments slow them down. Lily-White escapes exsanguination in a hunting web by the sag of her nappies.

Shortly thereafter, when she gets steadier at walking, Lily-White teaches herself to walk backward. She devotes herself to circling the cottage, over and over, backward and widdershins, as fast as she can go. Everything moves sunwise on the Dial, so moving widdershins at speed has the "tweedling" effect, which you may have heard about, as Lily-White did, in that old song:

"You'll whistle up the sun, my lad
I'll thistle down the leaves
You'll wheedle up the stars, my lad
I'll tweedle down a breeze
And with my leaves, you'll see, my lad
I'll blot the face of day
And with my breeze, your stars, my lad
I'll blow them all away."

And so, Lily-White tweedles up such a wind around the Hetch's cottage that the vorpal roses rattle together. Shiver and shake and shudder together. Squeal and scrape and wail together.

Of course, nothing can slice off the thorn of a vorpal rose but the thorn of another vorpal rose. Thus are roses quite standoffish, and only nod at each other from a distance, gravely and vainly and very much on their dignity, out of sheer self-preservation.

But in that wind that Lily-White whips up, every thorn of every vorpal rose catches every other thorn of every other vorpal rose, and cuts them all to the quick. Fang-sharp thorns the flashing green of certain sunsets fall like hailstones, bleeding sap onto the cobbled path that labyrinths its way through the briary snarl.

That's when Lily-White leaps out of her tweedledance.

She scrambles on her knees and gathers up the thorns in a net woven of caterpillar silk. Later, she rolls this silken net and the thorns inside it flat with Mother's rolling pin (which she has dipped liberally in Jubjub oil, to prevent sticking). She heats the length of this spiky mess on Mother's forge, and pounds it into shape with Mother's hammer, and cools it in a pail of Mother's special Wishing Well water. (As careful as she is, she leaves silk everywhere, and especially on herself. Weeks of washing in that vile Jubjub stuff for her.)

"Voilá!" she cries to Ruby-Red when at last she is done. "A vorpal sword, and all for thee!"

"It's a frumious weapon that can hack the heads off anything!" Ruby-Red exclaims in glee. "Worth at least three-quarters of a life of a stupid baby sister!"

This satisfies Lily-White. Even at the fierce age of four, she hates being in debt.

But she never stands between Mother and a window again.

And she never likes caterpillars.

And though she makes a truce with the roses—who eventually grow back their thorns—they all agree to loathe each other mutually and cordially, and make this sacred vow: the roses will withhold their scratches and jeers from the youngest Hetchdaughter of the Borogoves. Said Hetchdaughter will, in turn, employ her scurrilous winds only for other, less genteel foes.

Which brings us, ten years later, back to the vorpal roses of the present.

The thorns had caught two cheshires, although Lily-White only saw one at first, the other being mostly invisible.

The Cheshire Bear was not invisible, though in bad shape. Once a dapper and debonair bear, with sequin-speckled waistcoat, daintily glittering tutu, and tricorne with a cockade of peonies affixed to the front, now he was shaggy, grayed-out, matted, the yellow of his great eyes suggesting jaundice rather than pots of honey. He gasped for breath, and the vorpal roses had taken no small pleasure in raking his fine clothing to ribbons.

"Oh, how he groans!" cried the Baronne Henriette de Snoy with glee. She was pale pink and carmine, vigorous with petals, and she smelled divine. "Oh, how he moans for his mama bear!"

"A bear should show more dignity!" chortled General Jacqueminot, preening like a butterfly upon her glossy foliage.

A cluster of Jeanne d'Arcs shrilled, "Get him off! Get him off! He's bleeding all over our hips!"

Ruby-Red, who loved animals and hated roses, charged out of the cottage behind Lily-White, blade raised. When the shadow of the vorpal sword fell upon Lady Banks, Lady Hillingdon, and the Lady of Shalott, they squeaked and emitted a strong musk of perfumed terror. Distress furled their yellow and apricot petals to tight buds, which they tried to hide beneath their leaves.

"Put up thy sword, thou viper!" Mrs. Sam Houston scolded Ruby-Red, bristling self-righteously against this imminent attack. "We're only playing! We're naught but little flowers, and he is a big monstrous bear!"

Taking this as their cue, the vorpal roses released the imprisoned cheshires, whipping them out of the briary snarl with thorn-studded vines and decanting them onto the gravel walkway.

The ragged bear sobbed like a Mock Turtle with a bone in his throat, and did not rise. But the second cheshire, reluctantly emerging mouth-first from her vanishment, smiled with relief and patted herself down with tiny hands.

"Why, you're a monkey!" Ruby-Red exclaimed, lowering her sword and sounding half her age. "I didn't think cheshires came in monkey!"

"Pygmy marmoset, if you please," replied the Cheshire Monkey, clearly resigned to being mislabeled henceforth.

"What brings you to the Hetch of the Borogoves?" Lily-White asked. "And what's wrong with your bear?"

The Cheshire Monkey's head-body trembled. "Oh," she cried. "Oh! Oh! Oh! Can't you see? He's been snatched!"

Before either sister could ask what this meant, the poor bear let out another wheezing moan and stretched his mouth into a terrible rictus. The Cheshire Monkey rushed up to him and put her clever little paws on both of his cheeks and squeezed with all her might.

"Empty beehives!" she shouted. "Rotten river trout! Bad berries! Sad thoughts, damn you, Bear! Think sad thoughts! Don't you dare smile!"

But her paws were small; the bear's gaping mouth might easily have fit her whole body, fez and all. The Cheshire Bear rattled his head back and forth. His companion clung as long as she could, but there was nothing she could do; that rictus grin only grew and grew as the rest of the bear's gray body faded out entirely. The mouth went last, as was the way of the cheshires. But instead of that glittering crescent of teeth winking and blinking in the air like a trickster sickle, Lily-White and Ruby-Red glimpsed a flash of empty gums that scattered a few last drops of blood like a passing raincloud.

Then it, too, disappeared.

The Cheshire Monkey lay where she fell and sobbed, tail beating gravel like a gavel.

"Oh, and he will never return," the Cheshire Monkey sobbed. "He will never, not ever return. For our teeth are the first and last of us, and his are gone, gone, gone. He's been snatched!"

"Yes," said Lily-White impatiently, "you said that already. But who snatched his teeth, or what—if it's a what—and why?"

"We don't know!" the Cheshire Monkey shrieked, leaping agitatedly to all fours, and then up and down in place. "We have never seen our foe's face, this night hunter who stalks our village. When we lay us down to sleep, we are smiling fools, Toms and Maudlins all in the lordly lofts of Bedlam. But when we wake, another of us has been snatched. Sans molar, sans cuspid, sans incisor, sans everything! And once the snatched ones vanish, they're gone forever."

"Can't you just . . . *not* vanish?" asked Ruby-Red, weeping red tears in sympathy.

The Cheshire Monkey gave her a scornful scowl. "You try holding your breath the rest of your life! Cheshires are made to fade in and out on a smile. We're a begimbled race, half-whole, half-hole, and that's all there is to it. But so long's we have our teeth, we can come back! That's why we're here," she insisted. "We've come—or I've come, I guess, now that Bear is gone—to beg the Hetch of the Borogoves to seek out our enemy and kill it dead—before it murders us all!"

Lily-White and Ruby-Red took a moment to study each other from the corners of their eyes.

"Oh," Ruby-Red said casually, "we'll go. No need to bother Mimsy about it. She's got the Motto to maintain and a caterpillar to incubate."

Lily-White had already dashed to the cottage, meaning to gather up their things, but found the door locked fast against her. She tested it twice, then looked around for clues; Mother never locked the door without a reason. After a brief survey, she noticed the two packs nestled beneath the stoop and checked the contents: DRINK MEs and EAT MEs aplenty, gauze and theriac for wounds, pads for menstruation, plus one large bottle of Jubjub oil.

"Mimsy says it's okay!" Lily-White called out, settling her own pack on her back. She dutifully trotted the other to Ruby-Red, who slung it over one shoulder, jaunty-style, and sheathed her vorpal sword at her side with an ostentatious hissy-click.

"Lead on, monkey!" she commanded, grinning. "We shall follow! Across the Motto and into the Dial, even unto the very nest of thy Bandit Tooth-Snatch, we go! Off with their heads!"

I really hope, Lily-White thought privately, *it doesn't have more than one.*

Not so long ago, Cheshiretown had been the gaudiest, chaoticest, pranciest place in the Wabe. It was built around the VIII of the Dial—which, as you know, is the number associated with Flimflammers, Frauds, and Fools—and looked more like a carnival than a settlement. Pennants, balloons, colored lights, a House of Love (with swans), a House of Horror (also with swans), even a Ferris Wheel.

All dull now, and silent.

Those of its denizens who had not fled were in hiding, and those in plain sight had already been snatched. Like the Cheshire Bear, these grayed-out and grim victims had not yet surrendered to their inevitable vanishment. The Cheshire Hyena, the sisters noted, had wired her bone-crushing jaws shut, but to no avail. Her spots were disappearing, one by one, from her saffron-piled fur. Her mane a ghost ruff, unmoved by the breeze.

"I must see to my family," said the Cheshire Monkey worriedly, and scurried off to clamber up a Tulgey fir. (The Tulgey fir, named after botanist-explorer Professor Theolodia Tulgey, is the second tallest tree in the Wabe, dwarfed only by the Tumtum tree, which is most notorious for never being where you saw it last.)

The palatial purple trunk of the Tulgey fir, with its bristling cobra nest of branches, was massive enough to host whole colonies of pygmy marmosets, whole generations. Lily-White and Ruby-Red awaited the Cheshire Monkey's return in the undershade. They waited long enough that the VIII of the Dial fell under the shadow of Mount Gnomon, and Cheshiretown took its turn of Lesser Night.

Lily-White and Ruby-Red shivered and exclaimed aloud, delighted. Where they lived on the Motto, they had Greater Night but no Lesser Night, for the mountain's shadow did not touch the southlands.

"Look! There's the Looking-Glass Constellation!" Ruby-Red pointed between a break in the Tulgey needles, where night striped a precise slice of sky.

"And see," Lily-White cried, "the Timeless Rabbit! And the Portal Maid!"

Occupied thus with celestial concerns, the sisters hardly noticed the shadow passing until Lesser Dawn had all but surrendered to the dazzle of IX AM.

When it was light again, the girls got antsy and hungry. No wonder they had breakfast twice up north!

"Where's the Cheshire Monkey?" Ruby-Red asked. "I'm about to eat an EAT ME. Then I'll be tall enough to look down into the tree and shake her right out of it!"

"Oh, save it," Lily-White advised. "Mimsy wouldn't have packed it just for snacking on."

They lingered an idle minute longer. Ruby-Red huffed and stamped. Lily-White re-plaited one of her white braids.

The Cheshire Monkey did not crawl back down.

"I'll holler for her," Lily-White offered, craning her neck and opening her mouth.

But before a single word escaped, she slumped. She stumbled. She fell upon her fundament.

Stunned and sick, she stared at nothing. Pale. Pale. Everything was pale, inside and out. Queasy, squirmy, maggoty-pale.

Suddenly her sister was kneeling before her, tracing the vorpal scars on her face, reawakening the scorch and scrape of them. Memory countered foresight; Lily-White exited the future via the past, and re-entered the present.

Ruby-Red patted her on the shoulder, whispering, "Your eyes got pearls in 'em, Egg-White. Something bad's about to happen?"

Lily-White nodded, mute. Ruby-Red drew a deep breath, and Lily-White automatically did the same, having forgotten, until that moment, how.

"Let's go see," her sister urged. "Right now."

Ruby-Red always wanted the worst over quickly—ever since she had rushed into the thorns. For Lily-White, the worst always happened before it actually happened, and maybe this was better all around.

"All right," she agreed.

Ruby-Red grinned weakly. "At least we're braced for it, eh?"

But she could not be, not really. Lily-White had not been. Whatever it was, there could be no bracing against it. She let her sister go first, not only because Ruby-Red insisted and was quicker anyway, but because Lily-White wanted the phantom pearls of future-feeling to clear from her eyes. Hard to see through all that milky murk.

When Ruby-Red screamed, Lily-White sprang to action. She leapt for the lowest-hanging branch of the Tulgey fir, bare feet scrabbling for purchase on the shaggy purple trunk, and swung herself up.

About five or six levels high into the coniferous purple needles, a carnage of limbs greeted her. Ruby-Red clung to a branch, belly-down, head pressed to the bark, shaking and crying. Her hair spilled like magma across her face

Whatever had snatched the pygmy marmosets had been greeted with a fight. The pygmy marmosets had preferred violent death to vanishment, knowing that if they died before their teeth were taken, their bodies would remain. Poor things. Bravery had not kept their mouths inviolate. Even their tiny teeth had not been deemed too small to take.

Obviously (Lily-White hypothesized rapidly, her thoughts clear and untroubled), the 'Snatch had only just visited. This patch of blood was barely cool. It must have lurked in the highest branches of the Tulgey fir until Lesser Night, then got right to business as the sisters examined the stars.

Perhaps the Cheshire Monkey—whose little fez was nowhere to be found among all these strewn corpses—espying the 'Snatch upon her return, had crept upon it all slithy-like, and clung to its back as her brethren fell around her, knowing her only hope was to see where it fled with the light.

Lily-White shook her head. "She might have cried warning!" she said. "We were right below, vorpal sword and all. But cheshires," she added, "never do the sensible thing."

"Oh, they're so small!" Ruby-Red sobbed. "They're so small, and so, so many. And poor Hyena! And Bear! Oh! I can't breathe! Oh!"

Lily-White scooted down the branch and laid her hand upon her sister's shoulder. She drew a deep breath, and Ruby-Red automatically did the same, having forgotten, until that moment, how.

"I'm going below," Lily-White said, when Ruby-Red seemed calm again. "I think the Cheshire Monkey rode hag on that thing, and I want to see if she left a clue."

Without answering, Ruby-Red wiped her red eyes and dropped straight down. She landed on her feet, as she always did.

Lily-White followed more carefully. When she found her sister pacing and possibly trampling evidence, she gnawed her tongue against remonstrance. Ruby-Red needed a job, a distraction, and Lily-White needed to work in peace.

"You up for a tweedle?" she asked casually.

Ruby-Red lit up. "I'll tweedle you a Borasco!" she cried, executing a fierce pirouette. "I'll tweedle you a Brickfielder! A Brubu! Say the word, and I'll run widdershins around the Wabe, and return with a cat o' nine Cordanazos! I'll have you a Sundowner by sunset, Lily-White!"

Lily-White grasped her sister's arm. "Good. Go! Fly! Tweedle up a herd of hard winds, and drive them before you. Find me. I'll be moving slowly, tracking from the ground." She grinned and quoted her favorite of Mother's Mottos. *"Festina Lente!" Make haste, but slowly.*

Snorting, Ruby-Red retorted, "*Hora fugit, ne tardes.*" *The hour flees, don't be late.*

Then she was off. Ruby-Red ran even faster backward than she did forward.

In her wake, silence.

Lily-White bent down and found her first clue.

A fez.

Mount Gnomon was a hard-edged jut of glass, speckled black and red, cutting the sky with its peak and dividing the Dial with its shadow. If you peered close at the sparkling slabs of the cliff face, you could see the pips trapped inside, like insects in amber: hearts, diamonds, clovers, and pikes.

When Ruby-Red and Lily-White were children, Mother told them how she dug the black glass for her hexacle right out of a chunk of pike. The bargain she struck with the mountain to do so, she said, resulted not only in one but *both* of her pregnancies—but that was a story for when the girls were older.

When they were old enough to request the details of their conception, Mother said they were much too advanced for origin tales, and that they must invent the story themselves if they wanted one so badly.

Sitting in the sparkling red shade of a broken heart, feet tucked up under her and apron rolled in her lap, Lily-White had finished doing just that when her sister came hurtling out of the sky.

Ruby-Red tumbled about in the buffet, her winds moiling and roiling around her like spooked stallions. Breathlessly, she hailed Lily-White, who smiled up in greeting.

"What's going on?" asked Ruby-Red.

"We have two mothers," Lily-White replied solemnly. "Mimsy, and this mountain. Once upon a time . . ."

"Oh, you!" Ruby-Red cried impatiently. "Dreaming whilst I work! Hast thou espied the 'Snatch?"

"Ages ago." Lily-White rolled her rigid shoulders. She had been there all night and all morning, waiting. "*That* was easy, for it won't stop sobbing. The noise led me straight to its lair, then drove me back out again. My ears are still ringing!"

Ruby-Red frowned uneasily. "A sniveling villain will be difficult to kill."

"It'll be hard to kill anyway." Lily-White *tchaw*ed. "That's the whole point."

All those gray dawn hours, Lily-White had crouched under cover of a clover-shaped stalagmite to observe the 'Snatch in its lair. How it had wept and blubbered, burbled and moaned, patching a dozen seeping monkey bites with stolen silk, and sinking the last of the Cheshire fangs root-first into itself.

But before it had made that last repair, Lily-White caught a glimpse of the creature that cowered behind its toothy spikes and misappropriated sticky-silk integument. She knew it for what it was, and why it had done what it did.

At its core, without accouterments, the 'Snatch was a frail and feeble thing. Like that old war song about King Humpty Dumpty—"an eyeless, noseless, chickenless egg." Only it was not an egg.

It was an oyster.

A flaccid, prodigious, soppingly gloppy, slurping, burping, gray-white oyster that had somehow lost its shell. Snot without a nose. Sentient paste. Slouching prey. Every which way it went, it went in danger of being eaten—for the Wabe is full of walruses, you know. Pitiful, really.

Before the 'Snatch had snatched its armor-making supplies from the caterpillars and the cheshires, leaving havoc and hecatomb in its wake, it would not have been hard to find its weak spot. Indeed, it was *all* weak spots.

Which would make Ruby-Red feel very sorry for it indeed.

Lily-White understood that her sister was ferocious and gallant, valiant, vigorous, and indomitable, as brutal as a thunderbolt when roused to ire. She also knew that Ruby-Red had the softest of hearts.

Lily-White, therefore, was prepared to be hard.

She stood. She let her apron unroll slowly, directing the tumble of its contents at Ruby-Red's feet.

"What is it?" Ruby-Red gasped, though of course she knew. The winds muttered and grumbled. "*What is that, Lily-White?*"

The winds began to roar.

"It's the Cheshire Monkey," Lily-White said softly. "She unpieced herself to leave a trail. I collected all the bits. First, her fez. Then, her fur. She snatched her body bare. She snatched her claws, and then her paws. She cast away her arms and legs, her torso, her tail. She chewed the teeth out of her mouth and spat them, strewing a path to Mount Gnomon. At the very end of it, her head. I found it at the mouth of the 'Snatch's cave. She trusted us to follow her. To finish this."

Ruby-Red sobbed, shuddered, hugged herself—but her tears and her teeth were red. Lily-White was satisfied.

This, she thought, *the rage that obliterates pity.*

"Do you have a plan?" her sister demanded.

"I do."

Lily-White stepped aside, revealing the fissure in the great glass heart behind her. A jagged doorway into the luminous depths of Mount Gnomon.

"Ride your winds, Ruby-Red, all the way inside. Brandish high your blade and drive it where you may. I, in turn, will ride your blade," she continued, "and take my opening where you make it for me."

Lily-White removed a DRINK ME from her pack, jiggled it suggestively, and slipped an EAT ME into her pocket. Ruby-Red followed each gesture with feverish eyes.

"But you will be so small!" Ruby-Red said. "What if you are crushed?"

Lily-White countered, "Well, I can't die yet. I still owe you a quarter of my life."

"Don't you forget it!"

Lily-White laid her palm upon the hilt of the vorpal sword. Her skin was slick with Jubjub oil, with which she had anointed herself head to heel after her bout of forefeeling. Ruby-Red covered her fingers with her strong, brown hand.

"Egg-White . . . will this plan hurt you? I mean," she corrected herself, "*has* it hurt you already?"

"Quite a lot," Lily-White replied calmly. She had spent a not insignificant number of hours earlier that morning forefeeling her slow death in the digestive tract of a lachrymose oyster, and knew whereof she spoke.

Ruby-Red grinned suddenly. "Then I will avenge you!"

Her hair lashed her tear-bloodied cheeks like a thousand fiery bullwhips. Her winds snarled and stampeded behind her.

"*Culpam Poena Premit Comes!*" she yodeled. *Punishment follows on the heels of guilt.* "Drink up, Egg-White, and hop on!"

Lily-White opened her eyes wide. The Wabe had never been so clear, her body so much her own, her thoughts so present, as now.

She drank.

The second time Lily-White sees the 'Snatch, she is barely an inch tall—courtesy of the vile DRINK ME she's just downed. She is a pale gem riding the hilt of the vorpal sword. She is utterly and literally in her sister's hands.

Compared to her present size, the 'Snatch is massive—as big as a borogove roosting column, as colossal as a full-grown caterpillar. But then, so too is Ruby-Red huge, the size she always seems when Lily-White closes her eyes and imagines her, and Ruby-Red has her blade and her winds and her forge-scarlet temper. Surely the 'Snatch is no match for such a girl—a Hetchdaughter no less!—however many cheshires it has stalked and murdered in the murk of Lesser Night.

Wrong.

For the 'Snatch has plated itself in splinted mail of a most peculiar nature. It is armed to the tooth (or, more accurately, armed *in* teeth) with illimitable cheshire choppers that barb the silk swathing its soft body. Varnished in vanishment.

When it beholds Ruby-Red cycloning toward it through the relentless luster of Mount Gnomon's innards, the 'Snatch bristles its bridgework, twinkles like a hundred thousand razor blades—and disappears.

Lily-White tenses on the hilt of the vorpal sword, gazing left and right.

"Where did it go?" Ruby-Red booms.

Lily-White cannot even hear the words. Her ears are too small, the sound too vast. It is a whole-body ache, a thunderclap, bones splitting.

She squints. Tricky, in this glassy atmosphere, to make out the telltale diamantine glister of a cheshire's imminent reappearance . . .

Ruby-Red staggers. Head turns over heels. Limbs flail. The sword flies from her hand, Lily-White with it.

While Lily-White watches, her sister is slammed into an airborne somersault by eleven thousand pounds of armored oyster. Only an affronted buffer of angry winds prevents Ruby-Red from smashing skull-first into the unforgiving vitrine of the mountain's inner slopes and dripping down like bug jelly.

Ruby-Red rights herself, rushes toward the 'Snatch, who vanishes again. She has just time enough to scramble for her sword. Lily-White clings grimly to the hilt, thinking about the EAT ME in her pocket. Perhaps it is time to scrap her plan, regain her height—and then some. But it is dangerous to grow inside a mountain. One might get stuck forever: or worse, burst out of the top, destroying the centermost ornament of the Dial, and thus the Wabe entire.

The coward 'Snatch appears again, this time from above. It drops from a red diamond stalactite, aiming to crush, to comminute, to smear.

"Ruby-Red!" Lily-White shouts.

Just as Lily-White can only hear her sister as a thunderstorm, Ruby-Red can only hear Lily-White as a mouse's squeak, or perhaps the quick sting of a needle.

It is all she needs.

She dives out of the way, and the 'Snatch splats down. Lies there, stupefied. Mount Gnomon trembles, tickled.

Ruby-Red strikes.

Cheshire teeth are a powerful magic, keen and cunning, lunatic and lovely—but they are no match for the hard slice of vorpal thorns. The sword pierces tooth and silk, skewers the mucilaginous mollusk within. Right through the worm-pale, tongue-like radula. Not a mortal wound, but still.

It is enough for Lily-White. It is an opening.

She detaches herself from the hilt and slides down the length of the blade. The blade is firmly stuck, of course. The silk cocooning the 'Snatch's softness clings to what it touches, binds fast. But Lily-White, a-slick in Jubjub oil, slips right through. She hops from the tear onto the injured radula. From there, into the digestive system.

Which is just as horrible as it was this morning, except it isn't, because she has already endured it.

It is dark. Slimy-writhy-viscous. Oddly non-muscular. It smells of the sea.

She takes the EAT ME from her pocket, stuffs it in her mouth. Not all. A third will do. She is mindful of Mountain Gnomon, of its importance to the Wabe. Also, Ruby-Red never likes it when Lily-White looms. Not her place, as baby sister, to lord it over her elder, wiser, braver sibling.

But Lily-White has to eat enough—just enough, just so much and no more—to do what she intends.

Please, let this be enough, she thinks. Chewing is difficult while being chewed.

The EAT ME works quickly.

Lily-White shoots up and out, everything expanding at once. She covers her head with her arms, just in case she miscalculated.

Her calculations are true.

The 'Snatch bursts from within.

In the (admittedly gooey) silence that followed the eruption, Lily-White and Ruby-Red blinked at each other. Then Ruby-Red threw back her head, clutched her sides, and howled with laughter.

Lily-White's ears were once again of a size to bear this happy noise, and now that the winds had settled into low-whispering Zephyrs and Kavers and Coramells, Ruby-Red's laughter was the loudest thing inside the mountain.

After a moment's reflection, one corner of Lily-White's mouth twitched.

She started to snicker. Lily-White had always been more of a snickerer than a laugher. She was a duck-behind-her-hand, half-snort, half-hiss-like-a-punctured-balloon sort of person. Rarely did her laughter peal out, and now was not the time to let it. Best to keep her lips sealed till she had a proper wash. Even before today, Lily-White had never been fond of shellfish. Now that one had consumed her, she was fairly certain she would never acquire the taste.

Eventually, Ruby-Red ran out of breath and doubled over, hiccupping.

In the mountain's new quiet, there came a soft, plaintive noise from far away and high, high up.

"Arreow! Arreow!"

"Oh, balls," said Lily-White, who just wanted to go home, and knew that this would never happen until Ruby-Red rescued the beast.

"Kitty!" Ruby-Red squeaked. Her winds picked up again, urgent and ungentle, prodding Lily-White to her feet.

She warned, alarmed, "It may just be the wind through a chink . . ."

"It's a kitty, stupid!" Ruby-Red insisted. "I know a kitty when I hear one."

Despite the gunk depending from Lily-White's every limb like viscid icicles, Ruby-Red grabbed her sister's hand and pulled her into a close embrace. "Up we go, Egg-White! Giddy-up! Calloo-callay!"

Uttering this jubilant ululation, Ruby-Red spurred her winds with a widdershinly kick of her right heel.

Up they went, straight and fast (much faster than Lily-White liked), through the narrowing light. The walls slimmed, slanting inward at velocity. The source of the mewling became increasingly demanding the closer they came to it. Only when they reached the peak of Mount Gnomon did the sisters realized the noise was coming from without, and that they were still within. Lily-White managed to prevent her sister from punching a hole through the pointed ceiling and breaking right through—"You might damage the animal!" she remonstrated—and down they went again, riding the wind tunnel at a gut-plunging plummet, sweeping out through the broken heart, and up the sharp glass mountainside again, this time in the open air.

A tiny, cheese-colored kitten awaited them placidly, balanced on the knife's edge of the peak.

Lily-White could not imagine how it had gotten there—and why, since it had, it did not have the sense to get itself down again. Upon closer inspection, she realized the kitten was a cheshire. Science and sense did not apply.

"Kitty, kitty, kitty, kitty, kitty," Ruby-Red crooned, reaching her free hand out for it. "You're unsnatched! Oh, puss, let me take you home to Mimsy! You are quite the last of your kind!"

The kitten glanced from one sister to the next. He saw that of the two, Lily-White was covered in the stuff of which grimalkind breakfasts are made.

He meeped charmingly and graced them with a glittering grin into which he vanished, only to reappear on Lily-White's left shoulder. Whereupon he began a desperate grooming and/or feasting upon of her forehead.

Lily-White sighed. Ruby-Red was sure to take affront. And since Ruby-Red was the only thing currently holding Lily-White aloft, she hoped something would come along pronto to distract her sister from dropping her. Again.

It did.

Lily-White might have guessed Mother would be three steps ahead of them. Not forthcoming, mind you. But three steps ahead, all the same.

"Look!" Ruby-Red gasped, though Lily-White had already seen. "Mimsy's rolled out a new Motto! What can it mean?"

Three words glowed up from the green lawn of the southlands.

FELES REGINAS SPECTET.

"A cat may look at queens," Lily-White translated. "Well, and so they can. So can we for that matter! But the Wabe doesn't have a queen, much less two of them. What a silly Motto! What was Mimsy thinking?"

"Arreow!"

Thus declaiming, the Cheshire Kitten sprang off Lily-White's shoulder, suspending himself midair by frolicsomeness alone.

Ruby-Red crooned at his cuteness. Lily-White, who did not trust cuteness, scowled.

The Cheshire Kitten stared insolently at both of them, his eyes as large and as golden as two saucers full of buttermilk. He seemed to make some decision, and swam through the air once more to Lily-White's shoulder. There was, after all, a seafood breakfast awaiting him, served up for his pleasure upon her royal pate.

CONJOINED

Jane Yolen

The Tweedle twins were at it again, which meant everyone on the circus train had to shut their doors and lock them tight. It would be another knockdown fight. Happened every now and then, and we had long ago learned to ignore them.

They were easier to handle before they'd been separated. Better draw, too. Even Barnum had given up on them. And when he gives up, it's like a piece of cloth ripped right down the middle. You can hear the tear up and down the length of the train.

Told it to them straight. He might be a whirligig to the marks, but to the family—which was what we were to him, from Jumbo to the Tweedles—he was a real straight shooter.

"Can't make you headliners anymore, lads," he said. "Conjoined, you were a goldmine. Separate, you're just two small, fat, ugly men, with volcanic tempers. And *I'm* the only lava lamp on *this* train."

Mr. B never just minces words. He slices and dices them.

They had another meltdown right in front of him then, called him all sorts of names. Some of them were verbs. All of them impossible to do, even if you're conjoined. Especially then.

But Barnum, he'd heard worse. Besides, it was *his* troupe and *his* dough. They were lucky they weren't just flung from the train right there and then, bottoms first.

Not that they would have been permanently injured. Probably would have bounced until they came to a full stop. Barnum wasn't just kidding about them being fat. *Spheroid* was another word he used. I had to look it up. Took me near an hour perusing my pocket dictionary because I couldn't figure out how to spell it. Being an ape in human clothes is tough enough. But learning to spell . . .

Of course, when the Tweedles performed, they had stretchy bonds, flesh-colored, that looked like the real thing, and most marks never knew the difference. But there was something just . . . off. And since the rest of us freaks knew they weren't freaks anymore, we treated them different. (Or is that *differently*. Grammar rules are tough if you've spent the first month of your life squatting in Sumatran trees.)

Different, that is, till the cops came, called in by some snoopy neighbors in houses along the train line. Then we circled the wagons, as always. Even I knew what to do. Trust me, no cop wants to tangle with an orangutan in full threat mode, even if he *is* wearing a tuxedo. Or maybe especially then.

Once the cops left, there had been the inevitable Barnum meeting in his private car. Meeting may be too kind a term for it. It was Barnum in full-bore mode: shouting, cajoling, scolding, cursing us with his power voice—not the soft sawder he used to cozen the rubes.

But no sooner had the train started up than the Tweedles were at it again. This time, we ignored them, as per Barnum's advice, which was the same as an order. But as my compartment was next to theirs (we three plus The Fat Lady, Mary, needed our own spaces, given how large we were), I could hear every thump and bump as they fought their way from Toledo to Cincinnati.

We stopped outside of the city to sleep. We'd be setting up tents in one of the parks the next day, but it was politer not to disturb the locals during the night. That was one of Barnum's rules.

I don't sleep well in the compartment, anyway. Besides, the entire car in which our individual compartments sat shook with the Tweedles' struggles. They had evidently given up shouting at one another and taken to rolling around on the floor, I assume trying to reach one another's necks with their small hands.

It was the perfect excuse for me to leave the train. Even after all this time with Barnum—fifteen years it is—I preferred finding a tree in which to sleep. I might have been treated as a man, but I was also an ape. "Two souls in a single breast," the poet wrote. As conjoined as the Tweedles had ever been.

Sniffing the air, I not only picked up the scent of trees off to the west, but apes as well. And that meant a zoo was nearby. I left my clothes on the train—you try swinging from limb to limb wearing a tux or those tight pajamas Mr. Barnum had specially made for me. My arms, like all orang arms, are considerably longer than my height when stretched out.

Off I ambled, on foot till I could find the woods my nose had promised. And then maybe a converse with the apes.

The trek to the zoo was easy, mostly unlit meadow, with only a farmhouse around. There were but two major roads to cross, but with no carts or carriages out this late, I had no worries. Besides, though I am big five feet tall and as round—I know how to hide.

The little natures—frogs and small narrow snakes, plus the occasional rabbits—fled. A fox gave me a quick glance, then headed in a different direction. They were safe from me. I prefer fruit and insects as a meal. Besides, Barnum fed his freaks well.

So I came at last to the zoo. It was fairly new. The date carved on the wall said *1875*, which by my calculations made it close to the oldest zoo in the United States, the first being Philadelphia.

When I retire, I think I will ask Barnum to gift me to Cincinnati. Better than a pension. Philly's nice, too. They gave me the keys to the city the last time we were there. I wear them on a gold fob when I am in my tux.

The woods around one side of the zoo was really only a small copse, but it would do. I hoisted myself up onto the largest branches of a native oak and let go of all the encomiums Barnum had invented for me: The Human Ape, The Great Ape That Walks and Eats Like a Gentleman, and the like.

While I sat there, I remembered the Eden that is Sumatra, though it is boring as well. It has no books, no museums, no strolls on ocean-side promenades. It had been fifteen years since Barnum found me there, a six-month-old lying in the arms of my dead mother, who'd protected me from the worst tropical storm Sumatra had had in years.

But of course, even in reminiscence, I was ever alert. You can put an orang into a tux but you can't take the wild out of him. Not completely.

Without warning, something large stirred in the tree next to mine. That was exceedingly strange. For one minute I had no sense of it, the next it existed on a branch nearly parallel to my own.

Since one never knows when a tiger or a large snake might be hungry for ape meat, even in a city like Cincinnati, I shrank back into the cover of the leaves and watched, all senses alert.

Though I wear a veneer of sophistication and have a human stepmother in The Fat Lady, Mary, I have not lost my tree smarts. I waited until there was another ripple in that tree before turning my head and saw—amazingly—a large grin appear above the tree limb. Just a grin, mind you, but neither head nor body. It was an unreadable smile, which made me extremely cautious and ready to either flee or fight.

Just then, a pink tongue as long and sinuous as a boa, swiped the grin's lips. It was even more unnerving. I had no idea what I might be facing. In fact I had no idea if the thing had a face at all.

I tried to reason out from the shape of the lips, the pinkness of tongue. *Possibly,* I thought, *something in the cat family.* But though the great cats certainly can blend in with tree foliage, camouflaged in plain sight, they cannot disappear. Not entirely.

Just as I was thinking this, the smile disappeared and all sense of the cat in the tree next to mine disappeared as well.

I went into full alert. For a moment I thought about my stepmother, The Fat Lady, Mary, her skin softer than any female I've ever met. Her alien smell, both floral and human. And then I banished all thoughts, for they made me an infant again, weak and vulnerable when I had to be strong and smart.

I waited to see or to hear where the invisible cat would land next. I did not descend to the ground for I am faster in trees. But only if I can see who is chasing me and where. I needed to know the size and shape of this cat thing, and if it liked the meat of apes or men.

Suddenly, the limb I sat on bent as if touched lightly. Then two eyes opened close to my head. Too close. The mouth opened as well. The teeth, sharp and shiny, gleamed in the darkness like a warning light.

"Are you a man," a voice purred, "or a mantle?"

"I am an ape," I answered in my thick voice. It had taken Barnum many years to get me to sound reasonably like a man.

"What are you aping?" Again that purr of a voice. Soft as a snake through the bends of green. Or the feathers of an owl on the hunt.

"Sometimes," I said carefully, "I ape a man."

"Do you bow to kings?"

I wondered if there was method in the cat's madness. Or just a kind of methodical tick-tock of a predator. Was the lure set? Had I already taken it? And then—because it is better to keep the hunter engaged than engorged—I answered, "I bow only to queens." The only queen I'd ever met.

"Check," the cat said.

I knew this one. Barnum had taught me how to play. And promised to teach me how to write Shakespeare as well. "Mate!" I said.

The cat manifested fully, giving him—he was quite clearly male—weight as well, and the limb began to sway precariously. He was not as large as I had feared. I stood up on my hind legs, partly to show him my length as well as girth, partly to grab hold of the branch above us in case I had to swing away from the perch.

He didn't seem terrified. Rather he burled around my legs as if trying to bind them with magical unseen threads.

"Well played, ape," he said. "Have you escaped from the zoo? You smell too much of the drawing room, a softer prison. I met a man once named Tarzan who smelled a bit like you."

"And how do I smell?" I asked. Not an idle question.

"Not like dinner," he said. "More like a friend."

"Soft sawder," I whispered. "Have you met Barnum?"

"That bunkum!" he said. "You and I are the real deal."

I nodded.

"Ready to meet Wonderland?" he asked.

I thought I already had.

I followed him into the zoo, but that was not our actual destination, it seemed. We headed off to a dark corner of the zoo, where there was a black hole under the lions' cage.

"Let me go first," he said. "Then they will only smell cat."

"Isn't that dangerous . . . ?" I began, making sure there was no tremor in my voice.

But he didn't answer. It seemed he'd already offered as much of a plan as he was going to. And surprisingly, it worked. No one in the lion house woke, and we didn't come up into their territory, only went into a tunnel beneath it. The floorboards over our heads held, as did the mesh under them, placed there to keep the lions from escaping. Even if they'd smelled us, they could do nothing to get to us.

I relaxed and followed the cat further down into the hole, which canted downward in a kind of slide.

"Is there danger . . . ?" I began again.

The smile turned toward me without the cat. "There is always danger," he said, and disappeared down.

Are you a man or an ape? Scolding myself silently, I stepped off into space.

The hole slowly widened into a tunnel filled with some sort of wind that held me up even as it let me down. I did not so much fall as float.

There were open cupboards on either side of the hole, lit by some kind of phosphorescence. They looked a bit like the ones in Barnum's private railroad carriage, which I know well, for it's there we play chess.

Ahead of me, the cat, with a velvet paw, batted at an occasional object in the cupboards as we floated down: comb, bottle, bangle, even a small book, which he then chased until the next cupboard, where the game began again.

Sitting cross-legged in the air, I let the wind earn its keep.

I have no idea how long we floated down the tunnel, but we came at last, unannounced, to its end.

When my bottom hit the tunnel's bottom, I stood up carefully. Ape erectus once again.

"Wonderland," the cat said with a swish of his tail before disappearing through a door that was only roughly large enough for me to go through as well.

When I finally managed, by turning sideways, I found myself in a massive rose garden.

The cat, though, was long gone.

I sniffed, but all I smelled was a heavy rose scent, which reminded me so much of The Fat Lady, Mary, I sat down amongst the flowers till the memory passed.

I must have fallen asleep because I was awakened by soft quarreling around me, the voices of women—both young and old—squabbling over whether I was a man or a manqué. When I opened my eyes, it took a moment to realize that it was the flowers who were speaking, but I could see their tiny budlike mouths opening and closing, as they turned and nodded on their stalks.

I stood to my fullest height and said, "I am neither. And both."

They immediately stopped their gossip.

"Which way did the cat go?" I asked.

"The Cheshire?" asked one carefully.

I shrugged. "The disappearing one."

"That's him," they said together, and pointed their thorny arms toward a door that suddenly appeared in the garden wall. "He's off to the queen's party. Crashing, we believe. It's what he does best."

"A crashing bore," said a bud in its tiny voice, then tittered. The other roses joined in the laugh, which sent a leafy scent into the air, like a trail of vapor.

"I like parties," I said, lying. We orangs prefer solitary pursuits. Having my hair brushed by The Fat Lady, Mary, and playing chess with

Barnum were the usual extent of my reach. When I had to perform in the Barnum show, I mostly closed my eyes and thought of Sumatra.

I got to the door in three large steps, and was halfway out when one rose cautioned in a wild voice, "Ware the Jabberwocky," which, at the time, was just jibber-jabber to me.

The door opened onto a real forest, trees from northern and southern climes crowding together. I happily swung from limb to limb, and when at last I climbed high, I spotted a bunch of white tents—not unlike Barnum's—with colorful flags flying in different directions as if the breezes couldn't make up their minds.

Did I really want to go down there to the party? To sit on seats too small for my nether parts, drink tea? (Barnum had cautioned me long and hard about drinking anything stronger than herbals, and one blackout night convinced me he was right.)

Did I really want to chatter and chitter and make small talk with strangers? Most humans had trouble enough with my language skills anyway. I write much better than I speak. Barnum's veterinarian says it has to do with the make-up of my vocal chords.

"Seals, walrus, and sea lions," he told me, "pinnipeds, are closer to humans than you apes in the vocal apparatus area."

Though here in this odd, wonderful land, it seemed I had no trouble so far making my wit be known. Perhaps, if roses and cats could talk with ease, I could, too.

But I needed to find that cat.

Right, I thought, *party it is.* And made my way mostly by tree till I reached the meadow where the tents had been set up.

Close-up, those tents were a bit threadbare, the flags faded, the whole looking remarkably like an old, crackled painting, or the palimpsest for the painting.

I was greeted by a rather large rabbit. Almost a hare, I would have said, but he gave me little time to ask.

"You've left it very late," he scolded, glancing at an oversize pocket watch that had some scribbles on the silvered back. In ape count that silver back made the watch quite old. Whether valuable, I didn't know. Barnum had taught me much about the meaning of value, and how to implant it in a mark's mind. "The value," he used to say, "is not what a thing is worth intrinsically but what someone is willing to pay for it." And this he demonstrated time and time again whenever he sold merchandise before and after the shows.

The rabbit was tapping the watch. "No time left. You're on."

"On what?" I asked. It was the most sensible question I could come up with.

"Why, you're the queen's champion, of course," the rabbit said. "No one like you in all of Wonderland. The cat was quite specific about that." He shook the watch again. "Except for the Villain, you are the largest creature here." If a rabbit could be said to beam, he beamed.

I looked around for such a large beast, saw only walking cards, the ghost of a Cheshire smile, a rather odd caterpillar weaving in and out of space like a sailor on a three-day drunk, a man with a top hat that overtopped his head, and a small, spindly girl who was dressed in an out-of-date pinafore and a worried look.

Behind me something roared menace.

Jibber-jabber, I thought.

"What do I get for a weapon?" I asked, flight no longer an option out here in the open.

"What's a *weapon*?" the rabbit asked, shaking the watch a third time.

Which kind of made nonsense of my asking. I bent over and picked up a round cobblestone from the walk. It fit comfortably in my right hand.

The rabbit ignored me and gazed mournfully at his time piece as if he and the watch were only marginally acquainted.

I wanted to know more about the fight—the Villain's real name, his misdeeds. I needed to ask about the queen: what she stood for, how she treated her champions. I wondered if I would have to fight again after this one time.

The rabbit looked over my head, blanched. If a white rabbit could turn any whiter, he did. Then he passed out at my feet.

My questions were not only left unanswered, they hadn't even been uttered. I stepped over the comatose hare, then turned, and looked up and up and up and up at the Villain.

And then I knew. Jabberwocky! Who else could it be?

I am large.

The Jabberwocky was much, much larger. And he was green. Like a giant lizard. Or a dragon crossed with one of Barnum's dinosaurs. I'd seen clippings of Barnum's American Museum in New York City, which had burned down the year before I became part of his troupe, where he'd had pictures of dragons. And when The Fat Lady, Barnum, and I—in my new tux—visited the National History Museum on one of our Eastern swings, I'd seen fossils for the first time. The Jabberwocky reminded me of them.

Barnum had once said, matter-of-factly, "I made monsters, called them history, and was known as a bunkum. They found bones, called them fossils, and were known as scientists." Then he'd winked at me. "But whose name will be both a noun and a verb in the future?"

That made little sense to me at the time. But the longer I am with him, the more I understand.

Here in this Wonderland the barnum is real. So real, I wondered that I didn't have wings. At the thought, there was an itch between my shoulder blades. Only a small itch, you understand, nothing with feathers or flight. Yet. If I remained here in this strange land . . . who knew?

First, though, I had to remain alive. And that meant fighting the Jabberwocky. I squeezed the stone tight. Wings would surely have been helpful in this fight. But I had what I had, not what I needed. So I had to make do. "Mother of Invention," I said aloud, one of Barnum's favorite tags.

The Jabberwocky roared.

I roared back, thinking: *Someday they will make a moving picture show of this fight. Ape v. dragon.*

Whatever this fight was really about mattered little. All that mattered was that it had begun.

* * *

At first all I saw was the Jabberwocky. It filled every inch of my sight. But that way lay fear. I needed to know where I was, how I was situated, and so I took a step back and looked around.

It was then I heard a loud sound. A familiar sound.

It was the sound an audience makes in Barnum's tent, a kind of restless anticipation, part holding of breath, part expelling it. Then a chatter as if a thousand tongues were warming up to speak. And then a roar.

Not like the Jibber-jabber's roar. This was a roar of approval. A roar of anticipation. A roar of delight.

I looked past the dragon-beast, past the green tiles of his skin, past the massive jaws that could bite, the claws that surely could catch. Past the eyes glowing red as if they were banked fires about to flame. Past the odd burbling sound he was now making.

And there, in front of the white tent, appeared a vast number of wooden bleachers slowly filling up with Wonderland folk.

Now I knew the rules. I understood what was at stake. This was *Entertainment.* Blood, perhaps. Death, perhaps. But above all, it had to be memorable.

I let the stone drop from my hand. There were more about should I need them.

And then, without preamble, I leaped.

Monkeys are great leapers. We greater apes, less so. But being larger—we cover more actual space. And when we land, we can shake the earth.

The Jabberwocky took a step back, making a whiffling noise as he did so. He was no longer burbling.

But he didn't step back far enough.

I leaped over his head and—before he could turn around—had scrambled up his back as if it were no more than a tree. There I grabbed his skinny, vulnerable neck with both my hands.

He slammed me on my head with his tail, which had the force of a club. But even dizzied by the blow, I held on.

His huge wings flapped on either side of me as if they could brush me off, but I had survived tropical cyclones in Sumatra we called the Biggest Wind. The wind from the Jabber's wings was small and insignificant compared to that.

The tail was raised once more to bang me on the head, but I let go of the creature's neck. Then *One, two! One, two!* I boxed its ears with my powerful fists, thinking to stun him for a moment, till I could talk to him, tell him my plan.

How could I have known that the dragon's ears were the equivalent of a glass jaw. I had seen such bare-knuckle boxing at the Pelican Club in New Orleans when we had performed in that fair city, its steamy weather so reminiscent of Sumatra. It was Barnum who'd told me about a boxer's "glass jaw" at the time. It had seemed an unlikely thing, yet here it was—though ears, not jaws.

Of course, neither boxer at that fabled fight—Gentleman Jim or John L. Sullivan—had any such thing as a glass jaw. They battled twenty-one rounds before a knockout decided the winner.

The Jabber barely lasted but one.

His ears were his downfall, and indeed down he fell.

The noise of the crowd was astonishing. The queen, all dressed in red—and one-faced as any playing card—put a gold medallion around my neck and a blue sash over my shoulder.

"You shall have the run of the kingdom," she said to me. "But you must come at my call whenever there's a challenger."

Then she turned to her knaves, who were buzzing about the fallen beast. "Carry the Jabber to the woods," she commanded, "where our Red-headed Hero shall have him for dinner. Then come back for our victory celebration."

She turned again to me and spoke softly so that only the two of us could hear. "I can send my royal executioner to cut off its head if that will be easier."

I stumbled through my thanks, and ended with, "I prefer to prepare my meals myself, Highness."

She waved her hand at the wispy-looking child. "The Alice will clean up after you. She seems useless for anything else." Then the queen was away, trailed by her court and their courtesies.

The little girl came over, smiling sadly. She whispered to me in her wisp of a voice, "I rather liked the Wocky."

"I think I might like him, too," I said.

She shuddered, thinking I meant him as food.

I grabbed the Jabberwocky's tail and pulled him behind me into the far trees. The child followed behind.

"Do I have to watch you eat him?" she asked.

"I don't eat meat," I said. "And besides, he isn't dead. Just knocked out."

"What are you going to do with him, then?"

I smiled, thinking about how much Barnum would like the Jabber. Probably call him The World's Only Living Dinosaur. I thought how in exchange for adding the Jabber to our troupe, I'd convince the Tweedles to come down the Cheshire's hole and live in Wonderland, there to be feted by the queen. They'd like being part of a royal troupe. And the queen needn't ever know they'd once been conjoined.

Besides, Alice could become The Fat Lady, Mary's child and free me to be the grownup I now was.

I was thinking about my ace in the hole: in exchange for leaving off performing, I would take Barnum once a year into Wonderland to poach wonders at will. My cards were the Grin Without a Cat, the White Rabbit with a Watch, a Caterpillar the Size of a Horse. And that would be on our first visit together. Who knows what other wonders he might bring back.

Maybe even the Queen of Hearts—if he plays his cards right.

MERCURY

Priya Sharma

The Duchess had a demanding fist. Alice knew she was at the door from the sharp, insistent raps.

The woman needn't have knocked. She had a key. That she hadn't let herself in meant she was on her best behaviour. She'd brought a visitor. When whoever it was had gone the Duchess would be back with an open hand, demanding.

You can't expect me to traipse around for nothing. I'm not at your beck and call. This is a debtor's jail, not a hotel.

The Duchess was a racketeer with stout boots and a bunch of keys. They'd only been in prison for a month but Alice knew her tariff by heart already, from the price of receiving a letter to clean sheets. The extortionate cost of having a room large enough to house her and her father.

How much? Alice had exclaimed when the Duchess had held out her hand. *You expect us to pay for my father's cell?*

It's a room for two. I'm paid to house your father, not you. If you insist on staying with him, then you're robbing me of another prisoner's bed. The woman sniffed. *Besides, you have a view.*

A view of the prison yards and the main prison opposite.

The Duchess' name was Mrs Malfi, but she was called the Duchess by her affectionate husband and by everyone else because of her affectations.

Alice tried to make her face look neutral, if not cordial, as she opened the door. The Duchess was nearly as tall as the man beside her. Mr Selby tipped his hat. Alice recognised it as one of her father's. Or rather, one of hers.

"May I come in?" His grin revealed white teeth in contrast to his face, which was red and full from good living.

Alice blocked his way.

"Father's not well enough for visitors."

"Really dear, don't be ungrateful to the kind gentleman."

"That's quite all right, Mrs Malfi. Thank you so much for the delicious tea." Alice couldn't abide Selby's snideness, which was lost on the Duchess. "I'd like to see him, child."

He sounded anything but paternal, brushing against her. He was always doing that. The Duchess hovered for a moment before realising that she'd been dismissed.

Mr Selby of Selby and Sons, the finest purveyor of hats in England, sat down opposite Theophilus Hargreaves, handing Alice his top hat and gloves without so much as a please or thank you.

"How are you, Theophilus?"

"Row, row, row your boat. I've been on the river. What a glorious day."

Even if Theophilus *could* leave the debtors' prison, the closest waterway was the Manchester Ship Canal and outside was a pewter sky that threatened rain.

Alice gently took her father's hand to stop him picking at the flesh of his forearm. His skin was red and angry, peeling away in strips.

"Make these damn ants stop, Alice. They crawl and bite."

Mr Selby frowned but transformed his face with a bright, false smile when Theophilus looked at him.

"What the hell do *you* want?" Theophilus said, as if he'd only just noticed his visitor. Then he stood, picked up his chair, and turned it to the wall and sat down again.

"I'm sorry. He'll be better tomorrow."

"Perhaps I'd better see the hats."

Alice fetched one. Mr Selby took it, turning it around in his hands. The felt gleamed as if polished.

"I'm deeply saddened to see such a craftsman so reduced. Such a pity he let his affairs go so astray." Mr Selby had a smile for every occasion. This one pretended concern. "I still don't understand how he amassed such debts."

"Pelts are expensive. We had the money but . . ."

Alice had raged at him when she found the tin box where they kept all their money empty.

"I do wish your father had agreed to work solely for me. I'd have been in a much better position to help him. Such a shame that no one else will touch him. Still, I'm here now. If I take what's left as agreed by the courts, then it might help you a little. Unfortunately this hat's a little broader than his previous ones. Stove pipes are the thing."

Tall, narrow hats.

"You don't come to a hatter like my father if you want to *follow* fashion. A man like my father sets the style."

She took the hat back, all reticence and fear gone.

"Look, it's not just wider in the body but the brim too. The curve of the top is more marked. It's less dandy. More sober. The band is the finest grosgrain. *This* is what the finest gentlemen should be wearing this year." She put it on, as if to demonstrate.

Mr Selby leant back in his chair, considering her.

"Hhhmm, I'll take a chance on it. How many do you have?"

"A dozen."

"I'll take the lot. Just to help you."

"The Queen waits," Theophilus slurred. "Knight takes pawn. Poor pawn."

"Pardon?"

"It's nothing, Mr Selby. He likes chess."

Mr Selby counted out the money. It lay between them on the table, reducing craft to filthy commerce.

"They're worth double."

"You shouldn't be so impudent. Not with me." His languid grin was incongruent with his words, the curve of his lips had a language that she didn't understand. "I do business with your father, not you."

"I speak for him when he can't speak for himself. You said yourself how fine his work is."

Her anger seemed to excite him.

"Sell them to someone else if you can. You'll get pittance. His reputation's ruined."

Alice pocketed the money, her hands shaking in defeat. Or maybe it was the cold. It was always cold and her hands were always shaking. Mr Selby put a cupped hand behind his ear, an eyebrow raised in expectation.

"Sorry, sir. Thank you."

"Very good," he beamed. "All's forgiven."

"May I . . ."

"What is it, Alice?" Mr Selby was now solicitous.

"Perhaps I could work for you, like my father did. I can make hats. He taught me. I needn't work here if you don't like the idea. I'm allowed to leave. I'm not a prisoner. The sentence is my father's, not mine."

"A girl hatter? What delicious nonsense!"

"Bonnets, then?"

"I have dozens of girls for that."

All she'd been able to find was piece work, stitching gloves late into the night. Her means to make a living had been taken with all their tools.

"Bless you, girl. Your father's hats are in the past. Beaver pelts are scarce. Soon all toppers will be silk and made in factories. The future marches on us all."

Machined millinery. Outrageous. A machine couldn't understand the anatomy of a hat.

He walked to the door, his hand at the small of her back now.

"How old are you, Alice?"

The question made her queasy.

"Sixteen."

"It's tragic how you suffer for your father's lack of," he paused, searching for the words, "economy and sense."

Alice wasn't sure what he expected of her. It was too dangerous to speak. Her father wasn't a large man but he was bigger on the inside than the out. He could pull all these people from out of himself. He tried to teach her this trick. *Be tiny. Be giant. Adapt to the dictates of the situation.*

She willed herself small.

"Perhaps I *could* help you after all. How would you like a little house of your own with a maid?" Alice slipped her rough red hands into her pockets. "I could visit you there. I can be very kind, when I choose to."

The thought of him smiling at her in the dark was too much.

"I can't leave my father," she whispered.

Dinah, Alice's cat, came from under the table. Alice had brought her with them. She was Alice's one solace even though she was now a grand dame who rarely strayed far from the fire. Dinah stretched and shook herself, scattering tiny silver drops from her fur. The mercury was all that remained of the Hargreaves' hat making. It was the one thing that Theophilus had refused to leave behind. He made such a fuss that the bailiffs shrugged their shoulders and left them the big stone jar.

"Bad girl. You're into everything," Alice chided.

"If the arrangement were to be successful perhaps I could see my way to clear your father's debts."

Alice scooped up Dinah, holding her against her chest like a shield.

"There aren't many gentlemen who'd be willing to pay attention to a girl in your position."

"No, Mr Selby. Thank you."

Gentleman, my eye. Sniffing around like a dirty old tom cat.

"Well—" Mr Selby picked up his hat and gloves. "I'll send my man up for the hats."

He turned back suddenly, the motion startling Dinah, who hissed. "I'll call on you in a month. Give you a bit of time to think over my offer. And Alice? Don't let Theophilus drink so much."

She was about to protest her father's temperance but he was gone. She closed the door. Theophilus twisted around in the chair and called, "What did that infernal smiler want?"

* * *

When Alice was five Theophilus laid a beaver pelt on her knee. She buried her face in it, trying to imagine this marvellous creature floating on the water. There weren't any beavers in Manchester.

Dinah's fur was soft and fluffy. This was thicker than the kitten's and contained the making of her father's craft. Dinah was scant compensation for her siblings but Alice loved everything about her from the tender pink pads of her paws to the notch in her ear from some previous scrap that she'd come off the worse from.

"It's important that you watch and be careful. This is very expensive. We can't afford to spoil it. See these long hairs? They're called guard hairs." He picked up a pair of tweezers and pulled out a few to demonstrate. "They ruin the felt."

Alice took the tweezers from him and set about the task. Her father sat opposite, watching.

"Oh, Theo," her mother chided him as she put down the teapot, "isn't she a little young?"

"No, Maria. Alice has an excellent temperament for this. Look how patient she is." He put an arm around his wife's waist and drew her closer.

"So, is she just to help with plucking or are you going to teach her how to make hats?"

Neither of them mentioned Harry. Alice wished one of them would. Harry would've learnt hats, had he not been swept away on a tide of burning throats and fevers that killed so many the previous winter. Lorina and Edith had died the year before. So many children gone into the ground.

"A lady hatter? Why not?" The idea seemed to please him.

He motioned to the picture propped up on the mantelpiece; it was a soap advertisement that Maria had kept of a boy blowing bubbles. He had curly blond hair. His close resemblance to Harry was never mentioned. The handsomest boy that ever lived.

"Children are cherubs, unless they're poor and then they're stuffed up chimneys or lose limbs to the loom. You're right. Alice should have the means to a decent living."

Maria kissed the top of his head in approval.

So began the apprenticeship of Alice Hargreaves.

* * *

The debtors' jail and the main prison faced one another, their exercise yards divided by a wall, so they formed a mirror image of each other. Alice looked out on it from their window.

"Let's go down and get some fresh air."

"I don't want to. I don't want to. I don't want to. I don't want to." Theophilus' eyes grew large and round.

She wanted to shake him. To shout in his face. Instead she put an arm around his shoulders. "You can sit in the sun with everyone else."

"I don't want to."

He wouldn't be moved. When in this mood he'd sit and stare at nothing for hours, sweating, even though he didn't have a fever.

Alice went back to the window. They were all out there, crowding into the rectangle of light. There was Johnny O'Hare, who sold fruit from a barrow and went into debt when he broke his leg and his wife ran off with all they had. He was talking to Dorian Hamley, a printer who'd been undone by narcolepsy and overindulgence in rare books. Then there was Mr Neil who was driven into debt by patenting his ridiculous inventions.

The prison-proper was over the wall, containing the desperate, wicked and downright dangerous. She could see a strip of their yard.

Even after a few weeks Alice had come to recognise the rhythms of the day inside. At this time there were only a dozen convicts out there, shuffling around in shackles and wearing identical grey uniforms.

One man leant against the wall. A few others milled around him, talking. Occasionally one would look at him to gauge his reaction to what was being said. She'd come to recognise him because he always stood in the same spot.

Alice, four floors above him, forgot caution. She looked at his long face, his fine cheekbones and brow. In the moment that she was gazing at him, he tipped his head in her direction and looked straight at her. Then he did a remarkable thing. He smiled. Not like one of Selby's smiles, but something genuine as though she was a true friend recognised.

Alice stepped back into the shadows where he couldn't see her.

The man beckoned and a warder came over as if he were the man's foot soldier and not a jailor. She recognised the warder because of his whiteness. His hair and skin were like unsullied snow. It was Mr Cotton, the albino, who worked in both prisons. He looked up, red eyes squinting at the light, to Alice's window where the man was now pointing. He said something and Mr Cotton shook his head and started to walk away but the man clamped his wrist and held him fast, talking urgently. Mr Cotton closed his eyes.

Stitching gloves didn't give Alice the same satisfaction as making hats. Each week she'd drop off the completed work to a man on Eccles Road and collect pieces of leather or satin for the next lot. He always complimented her neat stitching. Frustrating work that paid little and wore out her eyes and fingers. She missed the grand architecture of a crown forming under her hands.

The alternative to gloves was a job as maid-of-all-work, but she'd have to live in and there'd be nobody to get her father up and help him dress, to remind him to bathe and eat.

Alice sat close to the candle, attaching mother-of-pearl buttons to a pale blue satin glove. There was a knock at the door. Too late in the night for the Duchess to be bringing visitors.

It was Mr Cotton.

"What's the matter?"

"Nothing. Good evening." He was always kind. He wiped his palm on his trousers, shifting from foot to foot, glancing up and down the corridor. "May I come in?"

When Mr Cotton stepped into the light she saw the bruise spoiling the perfect white skin of his cheek. He turned his face away, embarrassed.

"Who is it, Alice?" Theophilus called from his bed. "Oh, Mr Selby, the hats will be ready tomorrow."

"He's getting worse, isn't he?" Mr Cotton scratched his ear. "Alice. I'm sorry. There's someone who wants to meet you."

"Who?"

"Please, you have to come." He took his watch from his waistcoat pocket. "There's not much time."

"Alice, where are you going?"

"Sshh, Father, go back to sleep." She tucked him in and kissed his forehead.

"Alice, he says I'm to fetch you, whether you want to go or not." He grasped her arm.

"Who says?"

"You'll see."

Alice already knew who "he" was. She could tell Mr Cotton was determined; he'd haul her out if she struggled.

"You're better than this, Mr Cotton, procuring girls for convicts. You should work somewhere better than this."

Tears spilled down his cheek.

"How many people would give me a job? Most spit on me and call me a freak."

"I know." She wiped his white cheek. "You're far too kind for here."

"You don't know what I am," he wept, "and what I'll do to survive. I'm as bad as the next man. Only lock and key divides me from them."

"It's the man you were talking to in the yard today, isn't it?"

"He wants to see you."

"Did he do that to you?" She was looking at his bruise.

"No. It was my colleagues."

Alice couldn't think of an answer to that. The debtors' prison was cast in darkness. She'd never seen it in the quiet of night. Its corridors and stairwell were made of moonlight and shadow. The fancy brown tiles looked grey. There was a door under the staircase.

She hesitated.

"Where are we going?"

"The warren. It's the run of cells beneath the main prison."

What sort of crimes demanded incarceration down there?

Alice hesitated, then followed Mr Cotton down the rabbit hole and underground.

* * *

Mr Cotton's lamp swung to and fro in the narrow tunnel. The bare brick walls smelt damp. Cobwebs brushed her face. He unlocked the iron grille door. Beyond it were the cells.

Mr Cotton stopped halfway along, fumbling with his keys until he found the correct one.

"I'm so sorry. I don't have a choice."

"There's always a choice."

He rounded on her.

"My life's intolerable. You've no idea what it's like to be bullied and mocked. To be apart and unloved."

Unexpected passion from this nervous, twitching man. Then he was deflating, anger ebbing now they were here, but he grasped the last gasps of it. He shoved Alice into the cell.

The cell was dark, a candle throwing light on one corner. The man's face was hidden in a patch of shadow. She could hear him breathing, then a deep sigh.

"I don't mean you any harm."

"Not meaning harm doesn't mean you won't cause me any."

The man laughed.

"Where are my manners?" He stood, offering her his seat, coming into the light. He doffed an imaginary cap. Up close his hair was golden.

"You're the girl that makes hats."

"My father, not me."

"If you insist."

The cold seeped from the stone bench through her dress. She gambled that boldness would protect her more than meekness.

"So what is it you want? A top hat?"

"The last time I wore one was for the opera."

"And I've left my ball gown at home."

"It's true." He talked like a toff, to be fair. "Don't you want to know why I'm in here?"

"That's your business."

He smirked at that.

"You come and go as you please, I understand."

"The debt's not mine. It's my father's."

"I need you to run an errand for me."

"Mr Cotton's in your pocket. Send him. In fact, he can just let you out, can't he?"

"Getting out of here's easy. Getting out of England's harder. Blackmailing rich men is a mug's game. It's made me lots of enemies." He winked. "Luckily I have lots of friends too. There's something Mr Cotton can't be seen doing. And between us, I wouldn't wholly trust him."

"I can't waste my time running errands for you. I have work to do."

"This won't take long."

"And what do I get in return?"

"Some girls would do it just to please me." His smile produced a dimple in his cheek.

"Better ask them then."

"So what would persuade you?"

"Money. Money would persuade me."

Theophilus taught Alice carrotting at seven.

"It's just the two of us now. Would you like to learn the next step to make a hat?"

Death was a familiar visitor to the Hargreaves. It ended Maria with a dead baby inside her and profuse bleeding that wouldn't be stopped when she delivered it.

"Yes, Daddy." She itched to try what she'd only watched him do. She'd have said yes anyway, just to make him happy.

"I'll show you how to make mercury nitrate, but put the cat out first."

Dinah had followed Alice into the workshop and was climbing up her legs. Alice picked her up and the cat became boneless, trying to slide from her arms.

"Alice, keep her out of here or I'll make her into a hat."

Dinah was banished.

"Put one ladle of mercury into this flask. That's it."

Theophilus kept the mercury in a jar. Alice saw just how quick and silver it was as she poured it out, slipping and sliding, separating as if trying to escape.

"Now add the nitric acid that's in this pot."

Her father pulled her back. It made a gentle sound at first. Then it started to bubble and boil. She'd summoned this magic with the tipping of her wrist.

When the mercury nitrate had ceased seething Theophilus passed her a brush and a pelt he'd been keeping back for her.

"Brush it onto this like you've seen me do."

They watched as the fur was transformed from rich brown to orange.

"This process makes the fur rougher so it felts better later on."

Once the pelt fried he taught her to shave the stiff fur off the hide. It unnerved her, this strange matted sheet of orange that kept the animal's shape, long after it was parted from the skin, as if the essence of what it was could never be erased.

When Alice got back to the room Theophilus was out of bed.

"Where have you been? I've been worried sick."

There were times when the fog and confusion lifted and he was himself again.

"To see Mrs Malfi. I couldn't sleep." It was a ridiculous thing to say but it was all she could think of.

"At this time of night?"

"She doesn't sleep either."

"Come and sit here."

She did, knowing this spell of sanity would be short-lived. He took her hand and she felt like a child again. He was in charge and all would be well.

"Alice, I should've done better by you. I still can. It's not too late."

"No, of course not." She kissed his cheek. It was far too late.

Something glinted on his nightgown. Drops of quicksilver ran off him. She held up the lamp, brushing them off.

"Oh, Daddy, what have you been doing?"

"Oh, God, Alice, stop making such a fuss!"

The sudden anger startled her. He turned away and then back abruptly.

"How is a raven like a writing desk?"

"I don't know." She dug her nails into her palms to keep from crying.

"No," he whispered. "Neither do I."

Alice had never been in a public house before, never mind one like The Lion and Unicorn on Silent Street. It stank of men and beer. A loud whoop went up as she pushed through the crowd.

"Come and sit on my knee," called one man.

"Let me stroke your petals," said another, which received appreciative guffaws.

"Are you looking for a unicorn, love?" Another thrust his hips at her, pointing at his crotch.

The landlord thumped the bar and shouted, "Shut it! She's not a flower."

"All women are flowers when you get them on their backs."

"I told you, Carstairs! Keep your hands to yourself or I'll cut them off." The landlord beckoned Alice over. "You shouldn't be in here, sweetheart. What do you want?"

"I'm here to see the Colonel, sir."

"Sir? Bless you." He frowned at her. "You're not looking for work, are you?"

"I told you. She's a pretty pansy awaiting plucking."

"One more word from you and I'll crack your skull."

She beckoned to the landlord and whispered in his ear. "The Knave sent me."

The landlord's face darkened. He ushered her through to the back of the bar. "That man will be the death of us all. You don't want to get mixed up with him. He harms his friends more than his enemies in the long run. Up them stairs, girl. Go to the door right at the end of the corridor and mind you knock before you go in."

The men were banging their tankards. Alice took the stairs two steps at a time. The corridor was painted an oppressive dark shade of green. A woman in a silk wrap was framed by an open door.

"Hello, pretty."

The woman's cheeks and lips were rouged. The wrap gaped to reveal creamy-skinned cleavage.

"Hello." Alice realised she wasn't a woman but a girl with a woman's eyes.

"Shy girl. Ain't that lovely."

"Who is it, Rose?" The voice came from deep within the room.

"A fresh bloom." Rose stood aside.

The woman lay on the bed. A fire roared in the hearth.

"Run, little girl, while you can."

Rose made a face.

"Ignore Daisy. Safer here than the street. Warmer too."

Alice knocked on the door at the end of the corridor.

"Go away!" A man's voice boomed.

"I've brought a letter from the Knave."

"Oh, come in then."

The Colonel was perched, legs crossed, on a pile of cushions. He wore a burgundy jacket and paisley shawl, medals pinned to his chest. His hair was a grey mass and his skin tanned and leathered by foreign suns. A woman sat at a desk, her long black hair shining like lacquer, her eyes elongated by kohl.

"Tiger-Lily, will you excuse us?"

"Of course." Her accent was pure Lancashire. "Remember what I said. You're too harsh with your *R*s."

Alice didn't understand what she said as she swept from the room but the words sounded like tinkling bells.

"Tiger-Lily is teaching me French. And she's my accountant. Robs me blind and shares it with the other girls, but I don't mind. She speaks five languages: English, Russian, French, Persian, and Urdu. Some men come here just to listen to her recite poetry."

Alice had never seen a man so besotted.

"You judge her, don't you? If she'd been born with the Knave's opportunities she'd be prime minister by now."

"I don't judge anyone. I'm only here to deliver a message."

He tore open the envelope and puffed on his hookah as he read the letter within.

"Clever boy. He's calling in all his debts." He got up and went to the desk. She waited as his quill scratched paper. He blotted it and sealed the letter with wax. "Do you know why he's called the Knave?"

"No."

"Our boy, Arthur, is the younger brother of the Fourth Earl of Arlington. For such a posh lad to be bad, he must be truly badder than everyone else. He had an army commission and the chance at quite a career, but the turn of the Knave of Hearts was his downfall. Bad debts and bad business to repay them, including blackmail and kidnap. And I've seen him kill a man in cold blood, although the law's clueless of that."

"I don't care who he is."

"You should, dear. He says I'm to ask you to come back when I'm ready with all the arrangements. I shall need ten days. Can you do that, Alice Hargreaves?"

"We didn't agree on that."

"This is for today." Metal clinked in his hand. "And there'll be double that if you come back."

She gripped the coins so hard that they left imprints in her palm.

"Where did you get all this?"

Theophilus had been busy while Alice had been at The Lion and Unicorn. The table was covered in white linen. It was cluttered with mismatched china laid with a feast: jellies, potted meats, sausage rolls, Banbury cake, Bath buns, and such.

Her father poured a steaming arc of tea into a gold-painted cup. Dorian Hamley was slumped over, asleep, his cheek squashed against a willow pattern plate. Next to Dorian sat Johnny O'Hare.

"Alice, join us."

There was the spark of her father. He seemed as much himself as he'd ever been. She wanted to believe it, but she knew it wouldn't last.

"Where did you get all this? The Duchess?"

Dorian jerked upright, looking like he'd been awake all the time. Crumbs struck to his face. "We were hungry and Theo said he'd fetch us a treat. Try this treacle tart. It's delicious."

"No, thank you."

He shrugged as he cut a generous wedge and shovelled it onto his plate. He smiled at nobody in particular as he chewed.

"We can't afford all this." Alice slumped into an armchair at the end of the table.

"You need to eat something, darling." Theophilus poured her a cup of tea and passed it to her, followed by a plate of bread and butter. "It's tea time."

"No, it's three o'clock. You've got the time all wrong."

Dorian fell forward again, landing on his sticky plate. He started snoring. Johnny leant on him, an elbow on his back.

"Alice, you're a good girl." Johnny wiped his nose with the back of his hand and then on Dorian's coat. "You're always busy. You work far too hard, love. And you're always so worried about time."

Alice picked up the bread and butter and took a bite. She *was* hungry. The bread was dense, spread thickly with creamy butter that tasted of the country. Her father frowned, fingers tapping the table.

"Time time time. I can't kill time but maybe I can change it."

There wasn't any point in crying. She'd cried a pool of tears already, enough to drown in, and it had made no difference. Defeated, Alice finished her food.

Alice learnt the art of felting next.

"It's really just a fancy way for getting the fur to tangle together, so when it shrinks it's a better material."

Theophilus did this work in the back room, which was free of draughts. He'd constructed a slotted table for this himself. He'd made Alice a bow too, a small version of her own that looked like something an archer would use.

"Now follow me."

He worked across the table, plucking at the bow string as he passed it over the fur laid out on the table.

"That's it. A bit more gently, if you can. Perfect."

Afterwards he knelt down, showing her the dirt and tangles from the pelt that had dropped through the slots onto the floor.

"What's left on the table is called a batt. Look through this magnifying glass, the fur's all going in different directions, all evenly spread."

Theophilus showed her how to wrap the batts in leather and then put them on the heated iron plate. She sprinkled it with water while he worked the batt into a loose cone shape that was the beginnings of a hat.

"Let me do the next one."

"Are you sure you're ready?"

"Yes."

So Theophilus swapped places with her and Alice moulded the beginnings of her hat. All traces of the beaver that it had once been were gone. Such alchemy. She coughed and spluttered.

"Heating releases the mercury vapours," Theophilus winked. "You'll get used to it."

Alice worked close to the window, trying to use what was left of the light rather than a candle. Gloves would drive her to madness. She stitched them in her sleep. She could feel the needle pushing through the leather in her dreams.

Theophilus was watching Dinah. Alice glanced up. Then she put the glove down on her knee.

Dinah was playing with something on the floor. She pounced and batted at it in a sprightly manner, not at all like the sedate old lady that she was.

"What's she got there?"

"A rocking-horse-fly. It followed me here."

"You mean a horsefly. And where did it follow you from?"

"I said rocking-horse-fly." Theophilus didn't take his eyes off the cat. Alice put the glove onto the pile in her basket. Dinah's head jerked up as she approached, her cool green eyes large with interest. Then she swatted at the fly but too late because it took flight and landed out of her reach. Theophilus chuckled.

"It's too fast and clever for her."

Alice squatted down to see it better. It *was* a tiny rocking horse, no bigger than a fly. It looked wooden, bright and sticky as if freshly painted.

Dinah leapt at it again, but its wings were a blur and it was gone, up out the open window before she landed. All that remained to prove it had been there were the lines of red paint on the floor from its runners.

Alice woke to cold biting her toes. It was far colder in jail than a home. She missed the kitchen. There was a spot where she'd always sit when she was little. She'd forgotten her mother's face but when she closed her eyes to enjoy the stove's warmth, she could see the outline of her narrow shoulders as she reached to pick Alice up.

She couldn't recall her siblings, Edith, Lorina, and Harry either.

Alice rolled over. Her father's bed was empty. He'd been busy while she slept. He was crouched at the far side of the room. He was barefoot and shirtless. The thin morning light made him look grey. He was losing his hair. She saw him not as her father, but as a man worn down and worn out.

The space between them was unintelligible. He'd refashioned it. The floorboards were covered in white marks. Theophilus' hands were thick with chalk dust. He sat back, hands on his thighs, leaving hand prints on his trousers.

$$x + 2y + z - u + 2v + 2 = 0$$
$$x - y - 2z \quad u - v - 4 = 0$$

"Daddy?"

He didn't look up.

$$2x + y - z - 2u - v - 6 = 0$$
$$x - 2y - z - u + 2v + 4 = 0$$
$$2x - y + 2z + u - 3v - 8 = 0$$

Numbers and letters ran across the floor, curved around furniture legs and climbed up walls. She pulled the blanket off her bed and started towards him.

"Don't. You'll smudge it."

$$\begin{vmatrix} 1 & 2 & 1 & -1 & 2 & 2 \\ 1 & -1 & -2 & -1 & -1 & -4 \\ 2 & 1 & -1 & -2 & -1 & -6 \end{vmatrix} \begin{vmatrix} 2 & 4 \\ -1 & -2 \\ -1 & -2 \end{vmatrix} \begin{vmatrix} 2 & 6 \\ -1 & -3 \\ -1 & -1 \end{vmatrix} \begin{vmatrix} 2 & 5 \\ -1 & -1 \\ 3 & 3 \end{vmatrix} \begin{matrix} |2 \quad 4| \\ \therefore -2v = 4 \\ \therefore v = -2 \end{matrix}$$

His writing was shaky. In places it grew to an epic sprawl. Elsewhere it was small and cramped.

"Daddy, stop."

"I have to finish this while I can still remember it."

$$\begin{vmatrix} 1 & -2 & -1 & -1 & 2 & 4 \\ 2 & -1 & 2 & 1 & -3 & -8 \end{vmatrix} \begin{vmatrix} 2 & 6 \\ 3 & 0 \end{vmatrix} \begin{vmatrix} 3 & 0 \\ -1 & -2 \end{vmatrix} \therefore 3u=3 \;\ldots\ldots\; \therefore u= 1$$

"What is it?"

"Mathematics. Humpty Dumpty taught me."

He carried on writing.

$$\begin{vmatrix} -3 & -3 & -3 & 3 & -6 \\ 3 & 3 & 3 & -1 & 2 \end{vmatrix} \begin{vmatrix} -1 & 0 \\ -5 & -2 \end{vmatrix} \begin{matrix} |6 \quad 6| \\ \therefore -6z=6 \end{matrix} \;\ldots\ldots\ldots\ldots\ldots\ldots\; \therefore z=-1$$

She tiptoed through the gaps to reach him, wrapping the blanket around his shoulders. What did a hatter know about mathematics?

"It's a problem of determinants. The bigger numbers you see . . ." He put his hands through the front of his hair, leaving white streaks. He tried again. "It's the bigger numbers . . ."

"Yes, Father."

"No! You don't understand. I know this. It's the problem with the bigger numbers. I can't work out what *x* and *y* are." He was drooling. "Humpty Dumpty and I were working it out. We did it with this very chalk, on his wall. He's such an egg-head, although he is quite pompous sometimes."

"Why don't you lie down and think on it and I'll get you a drink. It'll help you to remember."

"It's all inside here." He slapped the side of his own head, hard. "Somehow my head is filled with ideas, only I don't know what they are."

She put her arms around him.

"The further and longer I'm away from there, the harder it is to remember."

He wasn't just cold, he was tired. She could feel his body sagging against hers. Within a few moments she could hear the change in his breath, feel the sonorous rise and fall of his chest. She laid him down and piled up the sheets and blankets over him to keep him warm, rather than try and move him and risk waking him.

Alice washed down the floor and when he woke, he didn't notice the writing had gone.

Alice used some of the money that the Colonel gave her to send for a doctor.

"Who are you?" Theophilus shrank from him.

"Mr Hargreaves, it's a pleasure to meet you. I'm Dr Pleasance, a physician."

"I'm not ill."

Alice started forward but the doctor knelt beside her father's chair.

"I know. I've been asked to see everyone here today. Just to make sure that everyone is well."

Alice was glad of the lie. Despite his youth, the doctor was earnest and reassuring.

"May I, Mr Hargreaves?" He held out his hands. They were square-palmed with stocky fingers.

Theophilus complied, putting his trembling hands into the doctor's, who inspected one side and then the other. Theophilus' fingertips were pink and peeling.

"They burn," he whimpered.

Dr Pleasance checked Theophilus' pulse against his pocket watch.

"Where were you born, Mr Hargreaves?"

"Why do you want to know?"

"I was just making conversation. I myself was born and bred in High Wycombe."

"I was born in Daresbury."

Alice shook her head at the doctor. A quick, slight gesture that she didn't want her father to see. Her family were Stockport through and through. She'd never heard of Daresbury.

"I know Daresbury." The doctor didn't miss a beat. "A pleasant place."

"I've always thought so. I had seven sisters and two brothers."

Another bewildering story.

"And how are your spirits? Does being here make you melancholy?"

Theophilus looked around and a tear or two twinkled on his cheek. Dr Pleasance didn't press him.

"How do you spend your days?" he asked gently.

"It's so much nicer on the other side. There's a tea party every day. And a Caucus-race."

The doctor shot Alice a look. She grimaced.

"Now, Mr Hargreaves, may I see you walking?"

Theophilus lurched about like an unsteady toddler.

"Heart and chest now. Let's help you out of that shirt."

Excoriation marks covered his arms and chest, despite Alice keeping his nails trimmed. The doctor listened to his heart and lungs with his stethoscope.

"Cold," Theophilus commented, looking put out.

"Sorry. Can you manage to dress? I'll wait with Alice by the door."

"Thank you, do do. Do-do-do-do," Theophilus stuttered. "Thank you, doctor. Oh, stupid buggering bastard!" He slapped his own forehead.

Alice walked ahead of the doctor, her cheeks burning, trying not to cry.

"I'm sorry, Dr Pleasance."

"No matter, Miss Hargreaves. Shall we sit here?"

"Is it very bad news?"

"Have you heard the term 'hatters' shakes'?"

"Of course, all hatters get them in the end."

"Do you know what else they get?"

"No."

"What was your father like before he became ill? I mean, what was he like as a person?"

"He laughed a lot. He used to love company. Now he can't stand it. And he doesn't care about anything anymore."

"And he forgets things?"

"Yes."

"And sometimes he makes up nonsense to fill the gaps in his mind."

"Yes." It was a relief that the doctor had said it first.

"There are times when he sees things that aren't there?"

She nodded.

"He has mercurialism, Miss Hargreaves. He has all the signs. Trembling, drooling, slurred speech and apathy. I've read monographs from the States. Hatters there are affected too."

"Will he get better?"

"I'll write you a prescription for tonic."

"So it's hopeless then?"

"I'm very sorry."

"I have payment here . . ." Her heart pounded and her hands shook.

"No. I wish I could do more to help." He folded her fingers over the money in her palm. "You see, from looking at you, I think you have it too."

By the time Alice was twelve she'd perfected felting and Theophilus allowed her near the large copper kettles.

"Stand back," he said as he tipped the beer grounds into the sulfuric acid. "Now stir."

He'd made her special gauntlets for the task.

"I feel like a witch casting a spell," she giggled. "What's the matter?"

"Nothing."

"What have I done wrong?"

"Nothing. It's just that I sometimes forget you're still a girl. I've been a

bad father. I should've sent you to live with my sister when your mother died. You would've had a better chance at a childhood. I wish you'd had all the things I robbed you of. Better parents and a nursery, not a workshop." He was crying.

"Don't say that." She started to take off the gauntlets.

"Keep stirring." He wiped his face. "I'm sorry. I got everything wrong. I just don't know how to make it right. I can't turn back time and I can't magic us to a better place."

"You and the hats are all I have. I love you and I promise that everything will be well." Oh, for that time before childhood ends when parents know everything and the world is safe just because they're there. "Come on, Dad, show me what comes next. I've been dying to learn."

She coaxed him from his doldrums. The cones of felt were dipped into the cauldron then worked, dipped and worked. Handling them stung her skin despite the gauntlets.

"It's marvellous." Alice didn't need to feign pleasure. She held up the final cone that had dried to half its size, the fabric contracted to something dense and warm.

The Knave looked cleaner than she'd ever seen him before. He'd even trimmed his beard.

"Did you get everything?"

"Yes."

"I knew it! I knew the Colonel would come through for me!" He slapped his leg.

"Tell me."

"I have a parcel of clothes, a leather bag and a ticket."

"Did you open the bag?"

"No."

"Really?"

"I said I wouldn't."

"You know, I believe you."

"I don't care whether you do or not."

"You're a treasure. An honest girl. You were in that window, Alice, like a star to guide me. I just needed someone to trust. And I trust you, more than anyone I've ever met." He reached out to touch her face. She retreated a fraction. Just enough to stall him.

"My name is Arthur. Call me by my name."

"Arthur."

"Will you kiss me, Alice?"

The cell's cold air moved through her parted lips. What was it like to desire rather than be subject to the desires of others? She was suddenly aware of the rough shirt moving over his chest with each breath and the hollow at the base of his throat.

"Can *I* kiss *you* then?"

She didn't want to learn the mystery of what men and women did on the stone floor of a cell. From her observations that particular secret only brought death and babies. Better to remain a child.

"I want to remake myself, Alice. I can be a different man. One that would hold you above all others. Come to New York with me."

"I can't. My father needs me."

"We could be anything we want. I'd make you a queen."

Queens and pawns. Virgins and whores. Mothers and daughters. Such deficiency of imagination.

His fingers hovered over her face and ran down her neck.

"I'll come in the early hours to collect what's mine."

The plan was for him to put on new clothes and walk out of the debtors' jail entrance, as Mr Cotton would be on duty there that morning.

Alice felt like the Knave was choking her as he stroked her throat. Strange, because his touch was as light as butterfly wings. That Mr Cotton opened the door was a mercy. The man was breathless and pink, if that were possible.

"I should be taking Alice back now."

"Not yet."

"I'm not your servant." Mr Cotton reached for Alice, pulling her from the Knave's grip.

"Aren't you forgetting something?" The Knave blocked their way.

He was as tall as Mr Cotton but broader. Built for fighting, for all his fine breeding. He twisted Mr Cotton's arm, forcing him to his knees. "Give me the key. I'll let myself out."

"I can come do that."

"You're not meant to be on shift. If they see you creeping about there'll be questions. Stick to the plan. You're in too deep now to give me up." He twisted harder and Mr Cotton's face contorted.

"In my left coat pocket."

The Knave pulled out a pair of keys.

"And these won't be missed?"

"The governor keeps a spare set in Mrs Malfi's desk."

"And you'll be there at the gates tomorrow, sharp."

"I will."

"Of course you will." The Knave let him go and patted his head like he was a pet. "I'll make good my word, either way."

Shaping and finishing. By this point in the process Alice was in love with the hat she was making. She understood every fibre of it, coaxing the cone over the lathe turned wooden blocks that were shaped like a man's crown. She rubbed the surface with pumice to make the nap fine.

She'd experimented with beeswax and resin in different parts to produce her own concoction to waterproof the hat, stiffening it with gum Arabic.

Alice ironed and steamed the hat while still on the block, attaching the brim. Then came another round of brushing until her arm ached and the surface was a smooth gloss. Finally she stitched in the lining and the leather headband and trimmed the whole thing with ribbon.

"My first top hat."

Theophilus turned it around in his hands, flipping it over to inspect its innards.

"Truly marvellous. You're fourteen and you've already finished your apprenticeship. Where shall we send it? Selby and Sons?"

"No."

"No?"

"It's for you."

Alice hadn't dared to go out. She prowled around the room, unable to settle to the basket of gloves. Her father was asleep in his chair, his feet shuffling as if wandering through his dream.

On impulse she went to check the door was locked and that the Knave's things were where she'd hidden them. She'd put them all at the bottom of the carpet bag under the bed. She'd bitten her nails to the quick, lying awake and thinking of how she could take it all and leave the Knave to rot. Her father would be cleared and there'd be enough to set up somewhere on their own. But if she repaid the debt all at once, now, wouldn't there be questions? And the man was coming here and he'd be furious that they'd cheated him.

Trust was a fragile cord. Fear was stronger.

She riffled through the rags in the bag. A strangled sound caught in her throat. Everything was gone.

"Father." She shook Theophilus awake. He opened his eyes. "Where is it?"

"Where's what?"

"Oh, God, he'll kill us. Tell me what you've done with it."

She slapped his face. He started at her, touching the spot where the red mark rose on his cheek as if the pain had surprised him. Alice put her head on his knee.

"I'm so sorry. Daddy, what are we going to do?"

"Hush, daughter. I'll fix it. I can fix everything. I'll fix you in mercury. I'll fix you in silver nitrate. I'll fix you with words. You'll be safe. You'll be little Alice, forever."

"I'm not little anymore."

"I know. But if we can be two people, why not three? Or four even?"

She twisted away from him, covering the despair on her face with her hands.

"You don't believe me, do you? I tried to tell Mr Cotton last night, when he came back on his own but he didn't either."

"Mr Cotton? On his own."

"Yes, he came back on his own, after you left."

Mr Cotton. The sneaky bastard. He'd run all the way back after he'd left her in the cell, taken everything and then hid it, then came back for her. No wonder he was so puffed out and flushed.

Alice ran along the corridor to the main stairs. She nearly tripped but Johnny O'Hare caught her.

"You look an awful colour, girl. Are you ill?"

"Johnny, have you seen Mr Cotton?"

"He was here earlier."

Mr Bartholomew was turnkey at the main gate when she arrived. He tipped his cap at her.

"Has Mr Cotton left?"

"He's gone, love, for good."

"Gone?"

"Cleared out. Quit. Funny man. Said he had an aunt in Newcastle he never knew about who died and left him a bundle. He told the Duchess to shove her job and keep the week owing him and not to ever bother him as he was going right away and not leaving a forwarding address. I said I'd have his wages if he didn't want them but I got short shrift. You know the Duchess, hasn't got a funny bone in her . . ."

He stepped out too late to catch Alice as she fainted dead away.

Alice protested that she was well enough to walk back to the room alone. She'd been an honest fool in a world of thieves and liars. She should've cut a deal with Mr Cotton and spirited her own father out in place of the Knave. They could have gone to America.

Now the Knave would come in the dark hours of the morning and cut her throat and then her father's and that would be the end of the Hargreaves.

There was only one option left, provided she could find him in time. She'd have to comb her hair and wash her face first though.

* * *

Selby and Sons had a new factory, its sign newly painted in black and with gold lettering. The yard was full of men loading crates onto carts. She was relieved to see a fine carriage on the cobbles.

"Where's Mr Selby?" Alice asked the foreman.

"The master's inside." He pulled a pencil from behind his ear, wet the tip with his tongue and ticked something off on the piece of paper he was clutching. "That way, love."

Alice stood in the doorway, gawping. She'd never seen a factory before. All she'd known was the small house that was a workshop more than a home. This was too much to take in all at once. There were so many people—at machines, at benches, rushing to and fro. How did they think above all the noise? There were clatters and bangs, the hiss of steam and the occasional call for more ribbon.

"Watch it."

A clerk in an ill-fitting suit barged into her, his arms full of files.

"Where's Mr Selby?"

"Main office, up there." Then he was gone.

A plain wrought-iron staircase led up to a series of offices where the managers could look down on those on the shop floor. From this vantage point Alice could see that there were areas where men were blocking, another where women attached brims to finished crowns. Once done they handed the hat up the line; the woman next to her sewed in the lining, the next attached the band. It was a nightmare. There wasn't a single person able to coax a topper from a pelt from start to finish. And all these hats were silk.

Mr Selby had told the truth. Alice and Theophilus' time was over. Here was the future. The horror of the moment. She'd never forget it. At least her father would never see this.

The outer office doors were open. Alice could hear heavy metallic thuds. Men worked at typewriters or else wrote in ledgers. A man paced up and down, stopping to inspect the work and then cuff some unfortunate on the back of his head.

Alice approached him because he looked in charge. He was bald and gently rounded.

"I need to see Mr Selby."

"Junior or senior?"

She hesitated.

"Come on, girl, I don't have all day." His sharpness belied his looks.

"Neither do I. It's urgent." That earned her a hard stare.

"And you are?"

"Alice Hargreaves. I'm here about a position. And who are you?" She was scared that if she was meek he'd send her away.

"Mr Richard Flowers, the master's personal secretary. What position might that be?"

"It's personal. Mr Selby offered it to me himself."

"That'll be the young Mr Selby then," he smirked. It was contagious, as the men around her sniggered gently. She found it hard to keep her head from bowing with the weight of their collective gaze. She might as well be back at The Lion and Unicorn.

"You'd better come with me."

She wanted to shove this paper despot out of the way but she followed at his heel like a beaten dog. The inner office was different. Luxurious. There was an outer annexe with a secretary's desk. The furniture was heavy walnut and there was a clock that marked the hour with a melodic chime as they entered. Four o'clock. Time for tea.

Alice could hear shouting. Whoever was in there was to be pitied for they were getting a pasting. She heard a rich bellow full of displeasure, catching words like "You're a wastrel and an idiot, boy."

Mr Flowers knocked and went in when summoned. Alice could see the profile of the two men in there. A red-faced Mr Selby sat, head hung, and his father stood over him, a lion of a man with a white mane of hair. That would be Selby senior then. She couldn't hear what Mr Flowers said but they both turned to look at her.

Mr Selby junior opened his mouth to speak but he was silenced by another round of shouting.

"How many women are you keeping? That's it. You're disowned . . ."

Mr Flowers closed the door behind him.

"I'm afraid that position is no longer available, Miss Hargreaves. That's all. Goodbye."

That was it then. There was nothing left. Just the taste of humiliation.

She'd go back to her father and wait for the Knave. There was one thing though. Scant recompense but she'd enjoyed seeing someone wipe the smug smile from Mr Selby's face.

Alice started to giggle.

There was no need to rush back. The Stockport streets were as they'd always been, but the world had shifted sideways. The faces of the street urchins were sculptured and lean, unlike the fat cherubs of popular paintings. The mill workers were so worn out that Alice could barely see their features. And it was funny. All the ruin and desperation was a joke. She laughed out loud, not caring who stared.

She passed Mr Bartholomew at the gate with a cheery wave. Would it be him to find her sticky corpse or Johnny O'Hare?

Alice had decided. While she waited for the Knave she would hold her father's hand and tell him about the trip they'd planned but never taken. She'd wring out every detail for him. How they'd caught the train to Llandudno and walked along the promenade with ices. Why not embellish further? Her mother and Edith, Lorina and Harry were there too and they'd stayed in a house looking out across the water. She'd tell him just how happy they'd been.

When she opened the door there was a pool of mercury on the floor. It didn't bother her in the slightest.

"Alice, look at me."

Theophilus' eyes were clear and bright. Mercury dripped from him like he'd been doused in it.

"I have to explain before I get too muddled. The longer I'm here, away from the other side of the mercury, the harder it is to keep things in order."

"Daddy, it's over."

"I told you I can fix this. I found the way because I followed Dinah through."

He held up Dinah. It *was* Dinah, marked by her torn ear, but as tiny as when Theophilus had first brought her home. All fluff and bones and mewling. Theophilus flicked a globule of mercury from her before she could lick it off.

"Dinah and I have been going to and fro. I wanted to make sure it's safe for you. Dinah's more affected. She's permanently changed. She's young again. I'm not sure if it's because she's small or because she's a cat. I'm a different man when I'm there. I'm better too. Let me show you."

He upended the jar, spilling out what remained of the quicksilver, which ran to join the rest. He reached into it. It had gone soft, like gauze. A mist that he could push through. His arm disappeared up to his elbow, then his shoulder. He rummaged around, pulling out a fistful of white hair in his hand. Whoever it was attached to swung its head and then a twisted horn appeared, followed by a nose and silky ears. The dazzling creature tossed its head and trotted from the pool into the room. It stood, white shadowed with grey along its flanks. Its sensitive nostrils quivered. Its eyes were dark liquid.

"It is real? Is it a real unicorn?"

The unicorn reared up on its hind legs, threatening to trample Alice. Theophilus stepped in front of it, holding up his arms in supplication.

"Don't be distressed. You'll feel yourself again soon, I promise. I'm sorry, my daughter doesn't mean to give offence, she's never seen anything like you before."

The unicorn shook out its mane. Theophilus reached up and patted its neck.

"He's even more remarkable on the other side. He walks upright on two legs and wears buckled shoes, doublet and a hose. And he's a most eloquent speaker." The unicorn nudged him. "I'll let you get back to the lion. Thank you for coming, my friend."

The unicorn trotted back into the pool and was gone.

This is it, Alice thought. *It's the mercury. I'm as mad as he is.*

"The way out's through there. We can have a better life."

"I'm scared."

"The other side's just a wondrous reflection of what's here."

"Daddy, will we know each other there?" There was a strange relief to giving in.

"We'd know each other anywhere, child. The night you were born, I held you in my arms as I stood by the window. You were bathed in moonlight. It was like you were lit from within. I'd know you anywhere. You're mine and Maria's love manifest."

"Daddy, do you promise we'll recognise one another?"

"Yes. Do you believe in me?"

"Yes."

"Good, because I believe in you. Here." They were reflected in the silvery white mirror. A mist floated above it. "Hold my hand."

And they stepped through to the other side.

SOME KIND OF WONDERLAND

Richard Bowes

On a Sunday afternoon Gilda Darnell and I are in her living room, phoning in one last conference call. I tell the host, "We two have been buddies since we were both in Scott Holman's Alice film *Some Kind of Wonderland*, back in 1965. She was the Duchess. I was the Cheshire Cat."

With the show's 50th anniversary/resurrection scheduled for Monday evening, we've chased down every promotional opportunity we could find.

Gilda says, "*Some Kind of Wonderland* came out early in 1966. The *Village Voice* had us on the front page. '**Hippy Alice Hits The Big Apple**!' was how they put it. We got lots of downtown Manhattan attention but *so* many underground films got released around then. And Scott Holman our producer/ director had passed away. But I never forgot about it. A few years ago I managed to buy the rights from the Holman family and got The Film Annex interested in restoring it."

She nods to me and I say, "Scott Holman had this off-kilter perspective—like the Alice books themselves. He caught New York at a certain moment. And he created the cast out of people he found. His Alice was a young model he saw on a fashion shoot."

Gilda says, "I'd been in a couple of off-off-Broadway shows but I came to his attention because I was the mouthiest waitress in all the West Village."

"And what were you, Justin?" the host asks me.

"A street boy who got very lucky," I hear myself say as the interview ends.

Gilda gets a call from a publicist she hired. This one actually works on Sunday. "The approach is: 'It Was Worth the Wait,'" she says.

Things I learned working on *Wonderland* led to my nice gig as a location scout and fixer for movies and TV shows shooting in New York. But Gilda has managed to learn the ways of Manhattan real estate and politics. She's my hero.

While she talks strategy, I look down at the world from her twentieth-story windows in Tribeca. Below is the intense green of Washington Market Park. Late afternoon sunlight bounces off the Hudson.

I love the way she doesn't forget the actual past. Prominent in her living room are framed black-and-white photos from fifty years back and more. They show a stark, corroded highway, a junk-riddled Hudson riverbank, and the wrecked warehouses where this building and other high-rises now stand.

This had been the thriving, sprawling Washington Produce Market. The neighborhood that fed New York until the city abandoned it in the 1960s. Bringing those ruins to Scott's attention was my proudest contribution to the film.

Gilda has a photo of Scott Holman displayed prominently. The writer/director/producer wears black-rimmed glasses and a Borsalino hat like a European auteur. But underneath that you can see a young guy staring intently at something off camera. I want to believe he's watching me.

The editor of an online entertainment site calls Gilda. At the same moment Lucinda Gold comes out of her room and floats through the apartment in dark glasses and a lovely green kimono. Gilda is Lucinda's partner and caregiver. Lucinda was Alice in the film. She's gone a few rounds with addictions and had a stroke a decade or two back. The glasses hide a dead eye and she speaks a bit haltingly.

We go out on the balcony and watch the sun set. I sit on her good side and catch a hint of the lovely kid for whom I once was a body double.

She's kind of excited by the revival and tells me, "Gilda tries to appear so cool and professional. Actually, she's gaga. I hope you invited all the freaks and monsters?"

I start to run down the list of invitees. Then I recall a recent confrontation that I'm not sure wasn't a nightmare and blurt out, "I got asked about Bonibo and how I killed Scott." Right about the time the movie was made, an anonymous chemist achieved the dark marriage of junk and speed. Bonibo was the street name.

"Oh, Justin, I'm sorry." She looks like she's ready to cry. "Everyone who matters knows how much you loved him." I feel bad about having stupidly upset her and try to lighten things.

"He may have loved me but he wanted to *be* you!" I say, and somehow we laugh. With an early spring night falling on the city, I kiss her and wave goodbye to Gilda.

At ground level, the gathering darkness and the absence of pedestrians could give a minor chill. But this is Tribeca, now the safest of Manhattan neighborhoods, not the bombed-out wreckage where we filmed much of *Some Kind of Wonderland*.

On a cobblestoned side street leading away from the river I pass the eighteenth-century two-story townhouse we once used as the White Rabbit's home.

Fifty years back it was on a different street, with faded tradesman signs over the door and shingles falling off. Now it's been moved and refurbished. A light is on in a second-floor window and a figure stands talking on a cell phone. He turns slightly and reveals rabbit's ears.

Someone walking her dog stops and stares. A male couple snaps cell phone shots. The light goes out, and I wonder if this is something Gilda's created as publicity for the revival.

I also remember Scott telling me, "It's a kind of leakage. A story spreads out into the world around it. Even someone who's never read the Alice books remembers a song or once saw a drawing."

As I walk uptown through SoHo and into the Village, I remember thumbing my way to Manhattan from South Jersey when I was seventeen. People back home said I talked and walked funny. Everyone knew my mother drank and did drugs and that my father was nowhere to be found.

On my way to the city, I dumped that prior life.

When the last lonely driver let me out of his car on Bleecker Street, I took one look around and knew this was my place. I wasn't the hottest boy but I wasn't stupid. I used whatever charms I had. And I learned to talk to everyone, forget nothing, and smile a lot. I could be trusted to run errands, keep my eyes open, and be discreet.

One night, I was filling in for the busboy at the Village Gate and caught the eye of a young man in glasses sitting with some other guys. When I paid an unnecessary visit to their table, he said, "You've got a smile like the Cheshire Cat."

Because I'd gotten a really lousy education, I had no idea what he was talking about. The night after that he came alone and met me at closing time.

We went out drinking. Scott was his name. He'd just graduated from Yale and moved into the city. Scott took me to his apartment on the first floor of an old brownstone on a quiet old street.

My trip from Gilda and Lucinda's leads me down that street and into the apartment where I've lived ever since.

Yes, I'm lucky and, yes, it's haunted. There's a mirror over the unusable fireplace. When I flick on the light it catches my favorite Scott photo on the opposite wall. My lover sits twirling his horn-rimmed glasses, smiling at me. I walk closer, kiss his reflection on its lips, then wipe it clean.

On Monday evening at The Film Annex we've turned out a crowd. The theater seats about two hundred, and there are standees. A curator tells the audience how editors managed to reconstruct our nearly lost Manhattan Alice film. She describes the mid-sixties explosion of New York's underground cinema, cites stuff like Anger's *Scorpio Rising, Chafed Elbows* by Robert Downey Jr.'s father, and the rise of Warhol's publicity machine. "It seems *Some Kind of Wonderland* got lost in the melee," she says.

Then it's my turn to stand before the screen in my best suit and talk about Scott Holman. The world has changed for certain when an aged former rent boy is called on to explain a director's work.

The first thing I say is, "When we first met, Scott called me 'the Cheshire Cat.' All I knew was that he was magic.

"For me it was magic that he was able to devote every minute to what obsessed him. And his obsession was a movie about Wonderland, but with New York grit.

"He was shocked that I'd never heard of Alice. He read the first part of *Alice in Wonderland* aloud to me. I read the rest—first book I ever finished. Within a few weeks I found myself immersed in that story.

"Not my first lover or my last," I say, "but the only one who woke me in the middle of the night to wonder how gay the Frog Footman was."

I don't describe Scott's telling me how trust funds worked and my awe at such things' existence.

At the Annex I don't dwell on his downfall. "Maybe Scott Holman wasn't meant for the long haul. He gave everything he had to one dream and you'll see it wasn't in vain."

There is some applause as the lights go down and I step aside. Just before the opening credits, the curators have inserted a tiny clip from the film. The Cheshire Cat (me in mask and costume), all lunatic smiles, pounces upon an invisible mouse.

This gets laughs but I hear a woman murmur in the dark, "The cat must have been on Bonibo." And I freeze.

Scott Holman interspersed the opening credits between shots of Alice waking from a nap on a wicker couch in the living room of our apartment.

He told me early on what caught him about Lucinda. "She was at the center of this chaos of models, photographers, art directors on a fashion shoot. She wasn't twenty but had this expression of amused disbelief. Just the way a modern Alice should react.

Scott came from a well-to-do family that didn't know what to make of a boy who read and reread *Wonderland* and *Looking-Glass*. In his heart of hearts, this thin guy with thick glasses wanted to be Alice. Instead he tried to live through Lucinda.

At moments early in the shooting, with her long blond hair and wide-open eyes, Lucinda combined Tenniel's drawings of a self-assured Alice with her persona as a bright young woman in New York almost one hundred years later.

On screen, Alice arose and parted the curtains. The first thing that caught her eye was a human-size rabbit played by an elegant kid in a waiter's outfit with a white rabbit's tail on the seat of his pants. He murmured to himself about being late.

Alice took one look and slipped on her sandals. She wore a dancer's cream-colored leotard and a long, flowing embroidered blouse over it. Lucinda had designed what would be her costume throughout the film.

The audience saw Alice go out the door, then saw her on the street. She followed the rabbit along that old block, hurried to keep up with him.

Watching this on screen, I remember being across the street with Scott and Jackstone, his cameraman. They caught some good footage of the Rabbit and Alice. But gawkers and passersby did double takes and ruined a lot of shots. This was street photography without red tape or licenses.

What the viewer saw next was the rabbit running down a flight of stairs and through a door with Down the Rabbit Hole painted above it.

Jackstone rarely spoke and never smiled. But he caught Alice following the rabbit through the door really nicely.

Scott had been told about a legendary bar in the Village called Down the Rabbit Hole. Rich kids are used to getting what they want, but nobody could find him such a place.

Over my last couple of years in the city I had learned more than he could imagine about how the Village worked. I knew, for instance, of a beat-to-hell bar located in a cellar on a back street. The owner was always broke.

When I told Scott what I was going to do, he didn't have total confidence in me. But I did get the hundred dollars I said it would take. With that I bribed the owner into painting Down the Rabbit Hole over his door. Scott was impressed.

A bit later he said, "The Cheshire Cat's a small part. Alex quit today and I'm giving it to you." I was terrified. "All you need is that wild smile. I'll coach you."

He then rented the place, which was a dark semi-hellhole with low lights and old, scarred furniture, for a shoot. Much of the newly assembled cast and extras of *Some Kind of Wonderland* were there in costume. Human-size birds and turtles, Mad Hatters and Dodos leaned on the bar. Men dressed as playing cards and women in crowns sat at tables. There's no scene like it in the book. The camera caught me in my Cheshire Cat suit. Gilda as the Duchess had a small guy in bonnet and gown who played her child, sitting on her knee.

On screen the rabbit passed through the room and out a rear door with Alice following. Next we saw them go down a long, dimly lit corridor where she found a small table with a bottle and the note. "Drink me." After debating the idea for a moment, she popped the cork and took a belt.

Back when I stood next to Scott watching her do this, I found it amusing. The bottle was full of tea.

The next scene was shot from the floor up. Alice didn't get giraffe-necked or anything. But Scott had Jackstone somehow make it seem that her head was floating on the ceiling like a helium balloon.

Further down the hall she found a cake on another table. "Eat Me" was written in frosting. Alice was a sensible but daring girl: so she did. Watching her on screen in The Film Annex fifty years later, knowing how fond of strange potions she became, I shivered.

On screen, Alice started to cry. Mice and rats and birds, all human-size, watched a puddle of tears form.

The next moment the audience saw a pool of tears with Alice swimming in it. This was shot a few nights later without too much light in the swimming pool at an old health club. To get us in after hours I'd bribed the night watchman.

That night Scott was drinking and smoking weed. This evoked my mother and my home and showed me a part of him I didn't want to see.

Scott told Lucinda a couple of times: "Alice swam fully dressed in the pool of her tears." Like this somehow meant she should be able to do that. Scott wanted to film her in semi-darkness swimming in tears. Lucinda couldn't do much more than hang on to the pool's ledge and kick her feet.

I saw him having trouble distinguishing the imaginary Alice from Lucinda in the real world.

Jackstone was uninterested in anything not involving lenses. So I was the only one who actually worried about her drowning in the dark. One way sissy boys fulfilled their high-school gym requirement was the swim team. I stripped to my briefs and played lifeguard. When Lucinda had trouble staying afloat, I jumped in and helped her out of the water.

Scott wasn't pleased. But she and I weren't that different in height and my hair in those days was long and blondish. I wore the Alice outfit and the scene was dimly lighted enough that the viewer saw what could well be Alice swimming in tears with her clothes plastered to her.

That night I saw Scott divide people into those who could help fulfill his fantasies and those who couldn't. He relied on me and I was in awe of him. But I remembered that night.

As I thought about it, the audience in the Annex watched the White Rabbit scamper by, talking to himself about his impending execution by the queen. He threw open a door and outside there was sunshine.

Then he noticed Alice all dry and dressed somehow and said, "Mary Ann, quick now fetch me a pair of gloves and a fan," before he stepped into the light.

On screen, Alice in her leotard and blouse, but looking a bit wary followed the Rabbit out the door and onto a street paved with broken cobblestones.

Scott and Jackstone had complained about their trouble shooting in noisy, crowded Greenwich Village. So I'd taken them on a tour of the lost Washington Market neighborhood that I knew about. He was fascinated, and from then on much of the film was set in a world stranger than anything in the book.

Empty brick hulks with faded wooden signs like: *Collin Brothers: Egg Brokers* and *Josephson: Grain Wholesaler* lined the streets. The windows were full of jagged glass and seemed to stare down on Alice or any trespasser, with expressions of shock and horror. At the end of the street was a rusty elevated highway and beyond that the murky Hudson River.

In this neighborhood nothing moved and there was little noise. Most of the abandoned buildings had rusted loading docks.

On screen, Alice and the audience saw something blue move on one of those docks. It was a large caterpillar smoking a hookah. He stared at her and asked disdainfully, "WHO ARE YOU?"

And she answered, "I hardly know, sir, just at present," and told him she had been several different people since that morning.

Watching her on screen, I felt exactly as I had when I saw her perform this scene on that wrecked street fifty years before. She had her lines down and delivered them. But her Alice seemed a bit remote and withdrawn—changed by the world into which she'd wandered.

When Scott whispered to me, "The city's making our Alice tough," I got that when he talked about Alice he was talking about himself.

"EXPLAIN YOURSELF," said the Caterpillar, and took another hit from the hookah.

"I can't explain myself, I'm afraid, sir, because I'm not myself, you see." When Lucinda delivered that line, it sounded like the truth.

But the contemptuous insect again spoke with disdain, "I DON'T SEE."

All this was in the script and the Caterpillar is a satiric creation. But I'd heard the actor playing the part express his contempt for people like Lucinda and me, because he was a professional and we weren't.

Scott let the scene play out. The viewer saw Alice appear to break off and eat a piece of the mushroom on which the caterpillar sat.

Then he muttered, "The scene doesn't go anywhere," and looked at me like he expected a solution. I was in the next scene and was already in the Cheshire mask and costume. Before the second take I said, "I can jazz it."

Scott nodded. When he said "Action," I was moving toward the loading dock. The other thing sissy boys did in high school was gymnastics.

Late in life, a sudden glimpse of yourself when young can be like a flash of sunlight in a dark wood.

Before the Caterpillar even spoke, my Cheshire Cat, with his mad grin, grabbed the pipe from the hookah and drew deeply.

On screen I imitated a cat doing a long, fond inhalation. My eyes crossed and my mad smile seemed to spread all the way to my ears. Later I found out this was called improvisation. On my own inspiration, I crouched down, hissed at something only I could see, and pounced on an invisible mouse.

My shenanigans ended up in the film. Watching in the Annex I was impressed at how catlike and off script I'd managed to be.

The Caterpillar stared at me, affronted, and I was pleased to see how pissed off I'd made him. He was just an actor with a couple of off-Broadway credits. I was the director's boyfriend.

After shooting at Down the Rabbit Hole stopped that day, Scott turned to me and said, "We should drop by Down the Rabbit Hole. The crowd there is amazing."

I smiled and reminded him that he had hired that entire crowd. He seemed startled, but I knew he had a lot of things on his mind.

In the front row of The Film Annex, Gilda sitting beside me says, "Now *my* big moment is here."

On screen the Duchess went into her act. Gilda in the movie wore an enormous, misshapen hat. Flaming ringlets of red hair clashed with a chartreuse lipstick shade never seen before or since. Her dress looked like an orange tablecloth tied around her waist.

During the filming I'd heard about a tired, old restaurant on the waterfront that had suddenly gone out of business and left everything behind. For a price we shot the Duchess's house scene in the kitchen.

On screen a shrill-voiced midget played the cook. She and the Duchess tossed plates and cutlery at each other.

Then Gilda held "the baby" who actually was the very short actor she'd held in her lap at the Rabbit Hole.

Gilda smacked his ass while he pretended to sneeze. On the first take Gilda had felt too softhearted to lay into him.

But when he complained that he wasn't given enough screen time, she got *way* more aggressive.

Scott had paid someone to come up with a raucous tune for the famous song, which she sang far off-key:

Speak roughly to your little boy,
And beat him when he sneezes;
He only does it to annoy,
Because he knows it teases.

The cook, the Duchess, even the "little boy" sang it. Then the Duchess's Frog Footman and the Queen's Fish Footmen, the White Rabbit and a lizard, a dodo, a lobster, and finally Alice and the Cheshire Cat and a dozen others appeared behind them and we all sang. I think it was the White Rabbit who began doing the Twist. That stupid dance was several years old by then. But we all knew it and did our own versions of it. Lucinda was smiling.

Scott too was wide-eyed. I never saw such joy on his face before or after. The next day, he had us dancing on a wrecked street in Washington Market. Everyone who saw the movie in its first incarnation agreed this was a great chaotic moment.

Fifty years later the Annex audience applauds. I turn and watch Lucinda stare up at herself on screen. Gilda whispers something to her and she cracks a tiny smile.

With almost no preliminaries, the Red Queen (a tall, mad-eyed drag) strode on screen. And she and Gilda as the Duchess had a short but vicious croquet game on a patch of dying grass. They glared at each other with genuine hate and used pink lawn-ornament flamingos to whack balls across the lawn.

* * *

Then I watch Lucinda in her Alice outfit and ringlets walk down a Washington Market alley that looked like Berlin after the bombing. This was from the period in the shooting when she wanted me on screen with her all the time.

Unless it involved swimming or somersaults I never was much of a performer. I got reminded of this as I watched myself on screen standing in the shadow of a building. Alice walked by and I was supposed to ask her, "What happened to the Duchess's baby?" Rather than expose the New Jersey accent I was trying desperately to lose, Scott had an actor overdub my lines.

"It turned into a pig," Alice said, and shrugged.

"I thought it would," the actor's voice replied. But his dubbed voice and my lips didn't coordinate. The Annex audience notices and titters.

Then a Jackstone shot silenced them. Scott had him catch me in evening light and the camera made me fade until only the mask and my phony smile were there: a nice effect.

"Well, I've often seen a cat without a grin," Alice said. This was said in the voice of an Alice who had seen quite a bit. "But a grin without a cat! It's the most curious thing."

Just after I'd read the book, Scott told me, "Alice, behind her nice upper-class manners, is kind of a remote survivor." I'd never met people like Alice or like him. I took in what he said but didn't much understand.

Only later did I realize how a kid who never quite fit into his well-to-do family could worship Alice's independent spirit. In Lucinda he created an Alice with the beauty and confidence he could only dream about.

Back then I mostly managed not to think of home. And I tried not to notice how Lucinda at times acted secretively like my mother did when she got hold of a new painkiller prescription.

The morning we were about to shoot the Mad Tea Party scene it was obvious to me. I asked Lucinda what she was on. She just gave me her coldest Alice look ever, turned her back, and walked away.

I wasn't in the tea party scene, probably at the request of Johnny Breen.

On the Annex screen, the March Hare and Mad Hatter are at a long table on a cobblestone street. They were played by Breen and Ted Libber, a duo who billed themselves as a "Neo-Vaudeville act."

Libber, as I recall, was OK. But Breen had spotted Scott, new to the city and just down from Yale. He'd attached himself to Scott as if they were an item. Johnny Breen was there the night Scott found me at the Village Gate.

On screen the duo start crying, "No room. No room," as soon as Alice appears. They run through their routine and yank the dormouse out of the teapot with eye rolls and shtick that was older than *Alice in Wonderland* itself.

They *could* carry a tune. The Annex audience, in a friendly mood, applauds their singing:

"Twinkle, twinkle, little bat!
How I wonder what you're at!
Up above the world you fly,
Like a tea tray in the sky."

I rise and walk to the back of the house. Breen was full of resentment the moment he saw me on the set with Scott. Fifty years after I'd forgotten him, I discovered he hated me still.

One of my tasks for the revival of *Some Kind of Wonderland* had been contacting as many surviving veterans of the film as possible. Gilda had lists of everyone who appeared on or off camera. Certain names were crossed off because of death. Libber was deceased. There were question marks next to those whose status and/or location was unknown.

Johnny Breen was one of the potentially missing and I'll admit, even after all these years, to not having put a lot of effort into finding him.

So encountering him in the evening dusk a few days before the *Wonderland* showing was uncanny and unpleasant. Breen came around a corner near my place as I walked by. Like he'd planned an ambush, he stood in front of me on the sidewalk as ethereal as a puff of smoke and smiling a tight smile. Two old men stared at each other.

"No room, no room," he said in a hoarse whisper. Then he said,

"I introduced Scott Holman to avant-garde theater in New York. I guided him when he babbled about doing *Alice* in dirty old New York. Next thing I knew a certain gutter rat was sleeping with him, appearing in Scott's movie even though he had never acted.

"Libber and I got a few days' work out of that film, and nothing more. We'd hoped for a sequel. But the movie flopped. Then Scott was dead. Everyone knew you'd given him an overdose but somehow you didn't get touched. We wondered who you bribed, how much you stole."

I made myself smile and said, "No one killed Scott. He still lives. Come to his show and see for yourself." I stepped around him. Breen tried to block me and it seemed like I walked right through him.

Standing at the back of the theater, I'm still not sure if that meeting was real or a dream. Breen couldn't imagine any motives on my part but theft and murder. That was his stupidity. But I think about Scott and how lost and innocent he was. I could have saved him if I hadn't been so young and in awe.

When I turn my attention back to the film, Alice with a fixed smile wanders with the Cheshire Cat under a corroded highway and down to a junk-filled beach. A tugboat pulls a bunch of barges up the Hudson and sunlight comes through layers of good, old-fashioned New York smog.

On the shore the Gryphon and the Mock Turtle, in full costume, dance a pavane and sing "Beautiful Soup," while Alice and the Cat watch.

As that scene ends, a voice that's somehow familiar whispers in my ear, "Remember when we were shooting on that stinking beach infested with truck tires and rats. The only way to get there was by walking under that expressway, hoping all the time it didn't collapse as you did."

I turn and recognize the face. Carson is the name. She was the Gryphon. Her girlfriend, Shep, was the Mock Turtle.

Today they wear modified versions of their movie costumes. I recognize Gilda's hand in this. Carson says, "For that four-minute scene, I had to stand under the sun flapping my wings and wearing a bird mask. Shep had it worse. I think her shell started out as a bathtub.

"Scott began OK as a director—a sweet guy. But when he did our scene he was less than half present. By the time he and that Golem cameraman found a take they liked we were dying for a drink.

"There was nothing open in that hellhole. But you led us out of the neighborhood and trekked across Canal Street. There was actual life there, including a little deli that sold beer and wine.

"I'm wearing this bird head and wings and Shep's got the turtle shell on her back and they don't let us in. But you're a smiling pussycat and they welcome you, tickle your phony ears and sell you six packs and cold bottles of cheap wine. I love you for that still!"

The two of them are headed out the Annex doors when Shep looks my way and finally speaks. "Watch us on the news!"

The grand finale is the Knave of Hearts' trial. It was shot amid the mirrors and red velvet of an old-fashioned strip club that I'd found for Scott. Wonderland lizards, rabbits, lobsters, pigs sit in the jury box. The Red Queen and the Duchess glare at each other before a backdrop of a couple of dozen extras dressed as playing cards.

On screen Jackstone made it look like the human playing cards are being shuffled, riffled, and fanned. Viewing it I saw how, when the film got released, Jackstone was on his way to Hollywood.

Scott assembled this whole scene, acquired the costumes, supervised the lighting, assigned lines to the performers, and arranged them around the location. When the last take was shot, Scott slumped against me and whispered, "It's over."

What I remember about the end of shooting is getting Scott home after the wrap party. On his desk (the one I still use) I noticed a bill for costumes. It involved the kinds of numbers I'd never even thought about. Scott grabbed it. "This is an investment," he said.

In the Annex, the credits roll and my name pops up on the screen as Alice walks up the stairs of Down the Rabbit Hole with a slight smile that says she knows whatever is worth knowing about this town.

There's nice applause and the lights come up. A woman in a devastating suit whispers in my ear that she's from the Tribeca Film Festival, a prestigious event run by Robert De Niro.

That evening, Gilda gives what she calls "A Survivors Party" for those connected with the movie who have made it to old age.

She lets me announce that the Tribeca Film Festival is very interested in showing *Some Kind of Wonderland*. It's ironic that it was filmed in Tribeca before that's what this neighborhood was called.

Gilda knows how to garner publicity. We watch social media display photos of actors she dressed as playing cards standing at attention in front of The Film Annex.

New York One interviews Carson and Shep in their personae as the Gryphon and Mock Turtle as they sing while strolling down the Hudson River Park.

Someone on radio calls the film "As surrealistic as *Alice in Wonderland* has always been." It's getting more and better attention than almost anything got fifty years ago.

Gilda says, "We're here to celebrate a young man who came to New York with a dream and died bringing it to life. Holman went for something dark—Carroll's characters in a ruined city and an Alice who gets tough in ways he couldn't.

"That young man's gone but his better half lives on." She points to me and my eyes tear. The party is running down when I kiss everyone and go out the door. As the elevator opens Lucinda slips in beside me.

"I'd like to visit Scott" is all she says, and we walk through the lobby and onto the side street. The upstairs light goes off in the rabbit's house as we approach. "Gilda's doing?" I ask.

Lucinda shakes her head. "She was upset because the Rabbit Guy tried to follow her home. Remember Scott saying a great story had a kind of leakage. Bits of it get out and lodge in peoples' heads? There's plenty of that hanging around right now."

The townhouse door opens. The White Rabbit, in a jacket and slacks that display a white tail, steps out and walks away briskly. Lucinda and

I look at each other, nod our heads, and follow him uptown along dark Hudson Street. People on a corner smoking outside a club do double takes as the rabbit passes.

"It's not just us: ordinary people can see him," Lucinda says.

Unable to stop thinking about Scott, I talk to her compulsively, saying stuff she already knows. "After he'd shot the film, when it was being edited, then shown to distributers, he kept spending money on booze and grass. But I thought it was from his magic Trust Fund. As a kid, I'd learned not to notice things I didn't want to see.

"Then I discovered checks were bouncing. The rent was way overdue and his family didn't want to know him. He mainly just lay there smashed out of his mind. Even I knew he was doing narcotics, but I somehow couldn't talk to him about it."

The White Rabbit has led us into the West Village. He turns a corner, and facing us is Down the Rabbit Hole. "Oh, my," Lucinda says. Without the slightest hesitation, we follow him down the stairs. The bar has, like everything in the Village, been gentrified almost beyond recognition. The rabbit walks past the yuppie clientele, opens the door he opened in the movie, and disappears.

On occasion nostalgia has led me here over the decades. I know the door leads, not to a tunnel and a pool of tears, but to a closet full of cleaning equipment. Still, I open it to make sure. The bartender says, "Guy, the restroom's the other way."

Lucinda takes my arm as we exit. Suddenly, on one wall of the bar, we see the whole crew: life-size playing cards, birds, beasts, Duchess and Queens. She and I, Alice and the Cheshire Cat, are there. It's not a photo but a kind of living mosaic all alive and nodding to us. We do a double take and they're gone. The bartender and a couple of patrons who were looking our way are blinking and rubbing their eyes.

"Talk about leakage," Lucinda says when we get outside.

"Scott created all that," I say. "I feel like he created me. I even learned to talk like him. To support us when he was down, I ran dirty errands, worked late shifts at clubs, anything short of peddling my ass.

"Around then, Jackstone came by. He was showing New York producers this reel of his camera sequences from our film. This was just before the studios brought him out to Hollywood. He saw Scott and just shook his head. But he connected me with a couple of guys about to film a cop TV movie, told them what I could do.

"I gave them a tour of the waterfront; they gave me a few hundred bucks. Not a lot, but it would pay the rent. So, I gave the money to this guy who'd changed my life. The clients wanted me the next day too. So I compounded my stupidity and left him alone in the apartment. When I came home and found him on the floor, I called for help but it was too late."

Because it was drugs, cops were called. Because I was a gay kid I got arrested.

Lucinda knows this story but we need to tell it again no matter how it hurts. Tears come out of her good eye. "I'll never forgive my addiction," she says. "After *Wonderland,* the Warhol crowd and a couple of shock fashion photographers got interested in me. Bonibo was speed to keep you going and then junk to knock you out. I looked like the goddess of death, as you must remember.

"Scott was doing Bonibo," she says. "He told me he needed more, said he had to travel. So I furnished his suicide."

We reach my place and she's patting my back and I'm patting hers as we go inside. She calls Uber on her phone. I turn on the light and there's Scott watching us from the photo.

"Justin, you knew I'd dealt him the drugs. You could have told them and you didn't. I still owe you."

"I used my one call to phone Gilda," I said. "Even back then she was connected. Knew a crusading lawyer who got me released. He even found out Scott had put my name on the lease. Made it possible for me to survive."

A horn beeps. I see Lucinda's car in front of the house. She goes to the glass and says, "Oh, Scottso, with you, there was never a regular day. Thank you." She kisses the reflection and me before leaving.

Then I kiss him as always and tell him, "*Some Kind of Wonderland* had a great day. I know you can feel it."

ALIS

Stephen Graham Jones

A guy on hiatus from grad school gets a call from his aunt to house-sit for the week, and ends up having to watch his best friend die on the floor in the living room.

Stop me if you've heard this one before.

A grad student uses the last pre-paid minute on his cell phone to answer a call from his lovely aunt Cyn, and he says yes so fast that she doesn't even get all the way to the question mark.

We're talking about me, here.

I took the bus over for the big key hand-off ritual. It was a Thursday. In spite of all my assurances over the phone, I hadn't visited my aunt once over my three years in town, was just seeing her wide ranch-style house for the first time. As for the why of that—I don't know. It was probably that I could never tell if she felt sorry for me or if she was regretting what I was doing with my life. Not the grad school or brief infatuation with math—those were supposed to be me getting back on track. Everybody said so. No, what she was disappointed with, I have to figure, it was the general slouchiness I probably expressed, to her generation. Cigarettes, hair I didn't feel the need to compulsively brush, some scruff on my chin, a fine braiding of careful scars above my sleeves and pants legs. Four- and five-day jeans. Better living through chemicals.

Thing was?

In secret, I shared her estimation of me. Her judgment. Or, I could imagine the sightline she had to have on me, and it kind of made me crinkle my nose, too, look away.

Just because I could see myself like she did, though, that doesn't mean I finger-brushed my hair on the bus ride over. I even smoked a cigarette between the stop and her front door, to be sure I smelled like the ashtray she'd expect.

She squealed my name over the welcome mat, then rose to—her words—"hug that neck."

I narrowed my eyes over her shoulder like already taking stock of her living room, let her say what she had to about who in the family I was looking more and more like, and how she remembered this thing I did at that one reunion, and soon enough we were to the walkthrough part of this: three bedrooms two bathrooms, shoes off at the door, dishwasher needs a push on the door right *here* or it'll run and run, just leave the mail in this paper bag, master bed and bath are off-limits, and emergency phone numbers are there by the phone in the dining room. Do I still know how to use a landline? Oh, and be sure not to leave the doggie door open, as raccoons will make themselves at home in the kitchen.

And of course there was no smoking inside—drapes like these are an absolute *sponge* for smoke, go yellow at the slightest *hint* of nicotine—and no parties, but "it's not like you're fifteen anymore, right?"

Right.

If I smiled here, she didn't see it, anyway.

The next night, Aunt Cyn's extra key folded into my wallet because I couldn't locate my keyring, Lewis and Tabby and Alice showed up.

I'd known Lewis since the smoking circle at high school—his post-grad stipend was my life support—and Tabby was his sometimes ex, and Alice, she was Tabby's miniskirted chaperone, I guess.

I was pretty sure I remembered her from my first year in the program, and she might have even been in Number Theory with me for a few weeks. As far as I knew, she was still advancing through her coursework, was probably cleared to teach pre-calc to undergrads now. Anything I taught undergrads these days, it was by example. By cautionary tale.

We slouched instinctively to the back porch, to the wire patio furniture that was all built on springs.

All four burners of Aunt Cyn's stove were currently bubbling pots of Tabby's made-up-on-the-spot hybrid of lasagna and spaghetti, which she assured us was probably going to solve world peace.

"You don't solve peace, you achieve it," Alice said. It was her first contribution.

"Have to agree with her," I said, not immune to her careless way with that miniskirt.

"It might solve some world *hunger,* though," Lewis chimed in, rocking so deep in his chair that I had to suspect my aunt felt a shudder of concern over her patio set.

Were the neighbors keeping tabs over the fence? I had to think so, yes. To them we'd be four floating embers by the sliding glass door. Four floating embers finally rising, crushing themselves out in a cascade of sparks that fall through the wire tabletop. Then the shadows coalescing around those embers, they slide the glass door open, they slouch inside, away from prying eyes.

As best I can remember, it was the last time both Alice and me were outside the house.

When Alice had stepped back to a bedroom for a phone call, Lewis and Tabby, our matchmakers here, told me her story.

Apparently it *had* been Alice in Number Theory lo those three years ago, but higher math had turned out to be more of a romantic notion for her. Number Theory was fun to show off at the coffee shop, and zero and infinity and exponentials were difficult enough to conceptualize that the effort left you spent in a way that felt like it mattered, but unless math was your chosen fulcrum with which to leverage the world up on its end, well: it tended to leave you with just a handful of slippery numerals, each more variable than the last.

This coming from two people deep in mathlandia. Lewis and Tabby hadn't fallen into bed again yet this month, but their minds still had sex on the chalkboard, and probably left them, I don't know: pregnant with knowledge? Or maybe math's an STD, one they'd be passing back and forth for the next decade, until one of them inoculated themselves with a big Russian novel.

It's what Alice had done. She was a humanities major now—had become a folklore major, of all things.

"So you saying I shouldn't ask her if I can borrow any money?" I said.

Lewis and Tabby chuckled like they were supposed to—like studying math was the path to financial security?—and I registered that their pinky fingers were already touching on the couch between them. It was kind of sickening.

When Alice breezed back into the house she caught us up on the drama in her department—no, I finally figured out, a couple minutes into it: she was talking about the drama involved with a class she was teaching for a prof, out with some emergency but always calling to micromanage. The class was folktale morphology and dissemination of urban legends, and the prof, while she'd been there, had assured the students this could all be gleaned through tattoo culture, through the semiotic codes being passed from arm to arm, shoulder to shoulder, below the radar of the rest of the uninked and uninitiated.

"Tats?" I said, looking around to be sure I'd heard right, then turning sideways on the couch to show her the back of my calf. "What's this mean, then?"

"Mountain lions were on blue light special?" Tabby said.

"More like well shots were a dollar per," Lewis chimed in.

"That a house cat?" Alice said.

"It's a panther," I said, rotating my leg back around, barely catching the ash from my cigarette.

"I'm calling Aunt Cynthia . . ." Tabby sing-songed.

"Tell her I left the doggie door open last night, too," I said back, opening my hand, letting the ash I'd saved drift down onto the carpet.

Alice smiled.

Lewis picked up on her and me, and on his way to the bathroom did his usual crude hand gesture, for my eyes only.

"Real subtle," I called after him.

"What?" Alice said.

"So tell us a folktale," Tabby said, redirecting her.

Alice sat back in what my aunt had assured me was her favorite chair. It swallowed Alice's starved-down frame.

"A *scary* one," I added.

"I'm just first-year," Alice said. "Technically."

"We're zero year," I said back. "Practically prenatal."

She liked that too.

"You already know it, sort of," she said. "Everybody does. From the movies?"

"Jason Voorhees was a folktale first?" I said.

"This is before that," Alice said. "Lewis Carroll."

"Wonderland's not a folktale," Tabby said. "That's just a story he made up."

"But what if he didn't?" Alice said.

I had to admit, it was a good lead-in. At least until Lewis ruined it from the arched doorway to the hall: "So . . . Alice is what you're teaching to the kiddos, *Alice*?"

Tabby chuckled and blew smoke up and to the left, as if there were some air intake in that part of the living room that could scrub our breath clean.

"It's not my born name," Alice said.

At which point Lewis hauled up what he'd scavenged from the hall closet: an ancient dinosaur of a video camera.

He held it up to his face, aimed the bulging iridescent lens at us each in turn.

This is where a good nephew would have protected his dear aunt's valuables, defended the homestead, all that.

There weren't any of these good nephews in the immediate vicinity.

"So," Lewis went on, tracking into the room like a real cameraman, "so if your name's not really Alice, then Alice in Wonderland *is* a legitimate research focus?"

"Who *were* you in Number Theory?" I said.

"Doesn't matter," Alice said, her eyes suddenly full and shining.

Because of Lewis, sure. But also because of herself.

She wasn't long for humanities grad work either, I suspected.

I wanted to tell her I'd save a stool for her at the bar of broken dreams, but instead it came to me all at once, her real name. I said it out loud: "Marly."

At which point Alice ran from the room, slammed the door to my aunt's bedroom, that was supposed to be off-limits, and still would be if Lewis hadn't known how to jimmy a lock.

Tabby glared at me and chewed her gum with her mouth open.

"This where one of us go after her?" Lewis said, setting the camera down on the coffee table, its red light blinking.

"One of us, yeah," Tabby said, thoroughly disgusted with us, and rose, leaving Lewis and me with all the wine and smokes. It was like we were in Charleton Building's math-basement again, my first semester here, all of grad school spread out before us, still. All of academia.

The world, right?

That's what we were going to apply ourselves to, conquer forthwith.

Right after this cigarette.

Right after one more cigarette.

My turn at the stove sat us down at the table over what I was calling a taco sandwich lunch. It was the next day, whatever that was. Saturday?

Alice walked into the dining room like nothing had happened the night before. It made me wonder what I'd been expecting. For her to be demure and guilty and apologetic, like serving penance for the eggshells she'd left all around the house for us to tiptoe through?

Tabby had already explained to us that "Marly" was someone Alice had *used* to be, clear? Someone who dated the wrong guys, fixated on unhealthy things, and maybe cut herself in weak moments.

Serving lunch, I tried not to study any folktale major's legs for lines or x's or triangles—whatever her thing had been. Also, I made sure to keep my inner arms from being the center of any attentions. At least the left one, since I'm right-handed.

We've all got a history, I figure. And none of us are those same people we used to be. Some of us even have certain tattoos to help us forget. To cover up.

I was getting defensive about Alice, at least on the inside.

On the outside, Lewis was already going for her.

"So, *Alice,*" Lewis said in his professor-y voice, his fingers even steepled under his chin. "Not you, I mean. Her."

Alice took a hesitant bite and flashed her eyes up to us.

"Good," she lied about that bite, guiding a stray spaghetti noodle the rest of the way in.

"Thought I got all those out," I said, eeking my mouth out to the side.

Alice swallowed what looked like a lump and said, her voice hovering at some register that felt more like a persona than a real person, "With undergrads you want to start with defamiliarizing what they know."

"And they all know *Alice in Wonderland,*" Tabby filled in.

"It's a famous exercise," Alice said. "Not mine. But it works. What you do is ask them to tell the story from the other side."

"Of the looking glass?" I said, because, come on: one of us was going to.

Alice nodded. "Not what it's like for Dorothy, say, to get whisked off to Oz. But for some random munchkin to get pulled up into the storm, deposited into the middle of Kansas. Our colors would be just as Technicolor. Our customs just as alien. Our songs just as corny."

"They are the same, aren't they?" Tabby said, squinting like seeing deeper into this line of thought. "Dorothy and Alice."

"Mirrors everywhere," Lewis said, using his spooky voice now.

"Bloody Mary," Alice said, keeping right up. "Say her name into the mirror three times, then she's standing behind you."

"Only if you turn the lights off," Lewis said.

"No," Tabby said. "You're supposed to close your eyes at the end."

"Same difference," Lewis said.

"Are they related?" I asked. "Bloody Mary and Alice?"

"Then Snow White would be, too," Tabby said. "Not everything with mirrors is going to be the same story—not that I'm the expert, of course."

"I did find one story," Alice said, kind of quieter. "It wouldn't print, though. The PDF wouldn't resize down for our machine."

"Do spill," Lewis said, reeling his fork toward himself, like urging more from Alice.

The taco sandwiches weren't as bad as I'd feared.

Neither was Alice's story.

What she'd unearthed from the library was pulp. A thirties story from a thirties magazine, which was when Wonderland was only a couple of generations old—so recent that "Alice" had been spelled "Alis," likely to avoid litigation, or carve down to the truth under the cartoon characters, the story before the fiction, something like that.

"Sounds like this is going to be high quality, timeless, and bulletproof," Tabby said, picking up on Alice's hedging.

"And you can cite that kind of stuff?" Lewis asked.

"Popular outlets often distill what's circulating out in the world," Alice said back to him so fast it was a practiced line, practically. I was starting to like her. Whoever she was. Already I could feel my fingertips getting sensitive enough to read the braille-work of delicate scars she might be keeping secret.

"Let her talk," I told Lewis, and, judging by the way his back straightened, Tabby must have clamped a hand onto his leg.

"It was somebody doing this exercise back before folktales was really a class," Alice said. "He flipped the story around, like."

"Like—to Bloody Mary?" Tabby said.

"Bloody Mary wasn't a thing yet," Alice said.

"Snow White, then," I said.

"Which one?" Alice said. "There used to be two. But—in both of them, there's an entity in the mirror, like? A different intelligence? When you say 'mirror, mirror,' you're talking *to* someone. Someone other than yourself."

"You're making them real by addressing them," Lewis said, impressed. "I like it. What do they call that? A performative utterance?"

We ignored him.

"Remember," Alice said. "For a long time, mirrors, the old silverback ones, not polished tin or whatever, they weren't everywhere. So associating lore with them would really come down to a class-thing, as the victims of that mirror lore would of course be those privileged enough to own and use these fancy mirrors."

Listening to her, I could imagine her at the front of a classroom. The undergrad in me was falling in some sort of love, and the grad student I wasn't anymore was wondering when her office hours might be.

Tabby rose, poured wine all around. We all toasted her thanks. She was just sitting down when the dishwasher fired up again. It had been on continuous cycle ever since Aunt Cyn had left. I didn't have the knack for where to push with my knee, evidently. It was kind of soothing, though. Like a surf, surging up onto the beach at regular intervals.

"This is also the early days for photography," Alice went on. "Not everybody had cameras, either, but it was a technology that was out there. And, like with any new technology, 'scary' progress gets warned against by demonizing the tech. Same way cell phones are sapping our brains of brains, or sterilizing us."

"Demonized how?" Tabby said.

"Set a camera up parallel to a mirror," Alice said, holding her hands up. "Aim it right into itself, straight on. What's it see, right? Itself. Then itself being itself. Then itself seeing itself seeing itself. In this story, that infinite reduction makes a tunnel something can crawl up through."

"An Alice," I said, then, holding my hand out like stopping traffic: "Not you, I mean. Her."

"I wouldn't say *infinite* reduction . . ." Lewis said apologetically—but more like what he was sorry for was her poor choice of words.

At which point started The Great Argument of How Many Reductions Would Fit in a Camera Lens, and whether that had to do with the *laws* of optics or the fineness of the optics, and did this correspond to that stupid bar trick of only being able to fold any piece of paper evenly nine times? Or was it eight?

Luckily Aunt Cyn had some copy paper in a kitchen drawer.

Seven folds was easy, eight took some doing, and for nine you had to either cheat or have the kind of muscles none of us had, even with the next bottle of wine and a second round of taco sandwiches.

This took us up until dark, about.

And then we had to settle the other argument. The one about the mirror.

Since it seemed like providence that we had the video camera, we elected to use it for this experiment instead of our phones.

Also, of course, neither Lewis nor Tabby wanted their phones to end up haunted, and mine already was, by a lack of pre-paid minutes. So we single-filed it down to the off-limits master bathroom.

While Lewis—of course Lewis—was getting the camera aimed and steady, I watched Alice's reflection. What I didn't say anything about was how she never really looked at herself in the mirror.

Reason I noticed, though? I wasn't looking in the mirror, either. It's not something cutters really go for, right there in front of other people. It's like our eyes might flash different or something, give us away.

"How does it end?" Tabby said to Alice. "That story?"

"It was a horror story," Alice said, leaning back on the vanity.

"So, what?" Lewis said, tapping one of Aunt Cyn's 1978 barrettes under one side of the camera. "Chainsaws, machetes?"

"Something did crawl up the tunnel," Alice said, shrugging like it didn't matter. "Something always crawls up the tunnel in these kinds of stories."

"Let me guess," Lewis said without looking around. "No one saw it at first, right?"

"When she—and it *was* a she—came through," Alice said, "she was kind of . . . I don't know. She walked through the house after the people were asleep but her feet didn't make any noise. And then she reached into some sleeper's open mouth, found something to hold on to—a memory, I think it was a memory—and she pulled herself in. That was the first step. She'd been living behind the mirror so long, watching everybody through the glass, that now she wondered what they were like on the inside."

Now we were all staring at *her.*

"She already knew their outsides, I mean," she added. Like that would make it better.

"So after that it was just run-of-the-mill possession stuff?" Lewis said, finally satisfied with the camera.

"Pretty much," Alice said, leaning over to look directly into the camera lens. "There were some more steps or something. Like a ritual, or rules. No—like *instars.* That's insect stages of life, right? Larva, pupa, all that? Doesn't this freak y'all out just a little?"

"Fermat's Last Theorem," Lewis said. "The Riemann Hypothesis. That Collatz bullshit. Now, that's scary."

"It's all just numbers underneath," Tabby said. "After everything else."

"My God, it's full of numbers," I misquoted. Nobody smiled.

"So do it, then," Alice said, about the record-button.

Lewis started to but I brushed his hand away, positioned my middle finger above what felt like the right button. "Here?" I asked.

"Three, two, one—" he said, and I hit it.

We all looked to the mirror. For some shadow spider-crawling up a series of wider and wider frames.

There was just us, though. Three stupid, drunk grad students packed into an old woman's bathroom. And a fourth, looking into the hall, like—and I say this with retrospect—like she'd seen something scuttle past.

I make it sound like a photograph itself, don't I? That moment.

That's what it is, in my head.

When the camera's playback in the little eyepiece was about fifty times too small to count the reductions and settle the argument for us, we had to eject the tape, slide it into Aunt Cyn's equally-antique VCR. It was so old it still had the kind of tray that rises up from the top.

The television wasn't much clearer than the camera—it was still cathode-ray—but it was bigger, at least.

"Eight," Lewis said, sitting in front of the screen, rubbing his hands together in anticipation. "Eight" was his ante, his bid, his gamble.

"Prime number," Tabby called for herself.

"You?" Alice said to me.

We were on the couch. The *only* ones on the couch, with Lewis sitting on the floor, Tabby leaning in the doorway to the hall, her arms crossed.

The air changed subtly. Like somebody'd dialed the thermostat back to "high school."

I instantly forgot what to do with my hands. They were just these lumps of mechanical possibilities, these fumbling appendages I knew were going to betray me the first chance they got.

"Infinite," I said—my gamble. "Not a tunnel, but a bottomless well, straight to Hell."

Tabby shook her head, said, "You can't claim resolution failure, you know? We have to reach consensus on how many rings of *this* particular hell there are. And none of us can count to infinity."

I bolstered that with Zeno's Paradox.

Lewis laughed while looking around, corrected me to *Dichotomy* Paradox—the one where you can never reach a point because first you have to get halfway to that point, and halfway to halfway to that point, and on down finer and finer, until you're never moving, are just stuck forever in that event horizon, not quite *to* the black hole, but not ever going anywhere else, either.

"Yeah, that," I said, maybe playing up the wine a bit. Then, to Alice, my eyes fixed on her bare knees, "What's the humanities major's wager?"

"One reflection," she said. "Just, a thousand times."

"I don't know what that means," Lewis said, but didn't want to argue it, probably because he already assumed he was winning this thing anyway. These other bets were all just formalities, to him.

He rewound a half second, hit Play.

It took a moment for the tracking to dial in through the static, and for the vertical to hold, but finally our image of the bathroom shook onto screen.

Lewis, being Lewis, had lined the camera up perfect, looking right into its own soul, right through the heart of reality.

We all leaned in, holding our breaths. I don't know about everybody else, but I wasn't counting yet. I was looking for the hint of a shape down that smaller and tighter tunnel.

At the very smallest reduction, though, either the last or the first reflection, depending on where you started, in this world or in that one, the image just blurred into darkness, and then was suddenly replaced by the comparatively monstrous-large face of Aunt Cyn.

She was either teaching someone how to knit or stashing that knowledge here, on tape, for if she ever forgot.

"Think she can see us?" Lewis said, not expecting an answer, just leaning in to cue the tape back to where we needed it, in order to count.

Twenty-three diminutions.

A prime number.

Tabby wouldn't have to do dishes for the rest of the week.

Not that any of us were anyway.

A discreet amount of minutes after Lewis signed off, saluting us all goodnight then rotating slow on his right heel like falling back into the hall, Tabby fake-yawned onto the back of her right hand, said she'd better hit it as well.

"Take your winnings and leave?" I said.

"Know when to walk away," she said, "know when to run," and then she was gone into the more private parts of the house.

Not that we couldn't hear their desperate operations in the master bedroom.

"They've got some certain math problems to work through, I guess," I said to Alice without quite looking over. I could see her in the black screen of the television, though.

She hissed a laugh out, crossed her legs the other way than they had been. "She told me to stay away from you," she said.

"Who needs friends when you've got friend's ex-girlfriends like her, right?"

"No," Alice said. "I mean, she said that, but I think she said it to like push me toward you. If that makes sense."

"We've got to be fast," I said, using my fakest voice. "My parents'll be home right after bowling."

Alice laughed. It was a good sound. It was honest.

"Marly would have fallen for that 'stay away from him' tactic," Alice said, kind of in apology.

"But you're not Marly anymore," I said for her.

"Ask me who I am tomorrow night," she said, then leaned over, pecked me on the cheek, and stopped to pick her shoes up before making her exit, careful to point her knees mostly at the other wall than the one behind me.

Mostly.

The sounds of Lewis and Tabby's various attempts at solving their complicated equation didn't help my abandonment on the lonely couch in the lonelier living room, an intense spot of heat practically glowing on my cheek.

I rose like a puppet on a string, followed my hand to the kitchen, to the counter, to the wine bottle, and took it with me to bed, the dishwasher coming on like a tidal wave for a moment, then pulling its water back into the unknowable depths of the house.

Only after I was ensconced in the sheets did it occur to me that we'd left that image shuddering on the television screen, trying to hold in place.

Would the tape, stretched to its limit, finally snap?

I shouldn't have been worried about the tape, though.

I should have been worried that we hadn't posted a sentry there on the couch. One who knew to stay awake. To not look away, even for an instant.

* * *

The next morning was one of those where ten o'clock came and went without me. Eleven probably would have, too, but there were pans clattering in the kitchen. Alice was scrambling eggs.

All around her, the kitchen was a mess. Every box plundered, every bowl turned over.

"I could have told you where the forks were," I said, impressed.

"Raccoons," she said.

I sniffed the air like I knew what a raccoon might smell like. Musty and fetid, I supposed. And, evidently, quieter than the mess accounted for. Either that or I'd been somewhere deeper than sleep.

Alice set a plate of the eggs at the table for me, leaned against the counter with an ice cream bowl of them.

I probed the yellow with my fork.

"Just eggs," Alice said.

The dishwasher was surging and thrushing, louder than usual.

I speared a bite, held it up to her in thanks, and sent it down the hatch.

"They still trying to figure where that last integer plugs in?" I said, pointing down the hall with my fork.

"Tab left an hour ago, said Lewis must already be up there."

"There?"

"The office, the department."

"Ah," I said. "Back to the math mines . . ."

Alice shrugged, was watching the doggie door like a small furry bandit was about to peek through.

"You have any dreams?" she said, still watching the door.

It took a moment for me to think this one through.

"I mean last night," she said. "Not, like, in general."

"You?" I said back, just to stall.

She shook her head no, but you don't ask about somebody's dream if you're not still suffering from one.

"I turned the television off this morning," she said, like that was going to be my very next question.

I forked another bite of yellow in.

"Weird morning," I said, kind of obviously.

"It's just because of normal food," Alice said, and set her bowl down into the sink with the rest of the crusty dishes. I don't think she'd eaten any of the eggs she'd made. We drifted to our own naps and television shows and reading and wine and staring at nothing for the rest of the afternoon, and on one of my trips back through the kitchen I noticed maggots wriggling up through the yellow eggmeat. I'd seen exactly this happen with a series of roommates, but had, for no real reason, kind of imagined Aunt Cyn's house would be cleaner, or better, or immune.

Nope. The maggots were massing up, blind and ravenous. It was only four or five o'clock then. How long does it take for an egg to hatch?

I ran the hot water onto them then ground the disposal, imagined them screaming down there, then imagined their fly mother watching me from the side of the refrigerator, that image of me fractured into sixty-four hexagonal panes at once.

Alice sat in the backyard on the chaise lounge in her miniskirt, sunning her legs. I think if I hadn't been there, she'd have stripped down some.

Tabby finally made it back for what would have been dinner, if we'd bothered to cook.

Lewis wasn't with her.

At first Tabby was confused, thought for sure Lewis had just beat her home, slipped into their room for a nap or a shower.

His phone was still on the nightstand in the master bedroom. Dead.

In a fit of hopefulness, Tabby plugged it in, yelped from the blue spark that arced from the prongs to the outlet.

Nothing was making sense. Including Alice. The dream she finally told us about when the three of us reconvened in the living room, she qualified it by saying that she didn't think she was exactly asleep. That she did that sometimes.

What we hadn't considered at breakfast, we considered now: that raccoons had surely had their greedy little hands on everything in the kitchen. Our solution wasn't to wash the dishes, it was for Tabby to come back from the corner store with two boxes of cereal and a half-gallon of milk. Plastic spoons from the condiment counter by the deli, bowls from the clearance rack. We called it dinner, and while we ate, Alice told us what she remembered. That's how she phrased it. Not what she said she'd dreamed, but what she *remembered.*

All it was was a sense, upon waking, like a fact she already knew but was now thinking about for some reason. That fact was that we were five in the house, not four.

The way she just said it flat-out like that, it made my elbows pull into my sides without me telling them to do that.

Tabby wasn't so easy a mark.

"That's your big scary dream?" she said, trying not to smile around it.

"There's only four of us, though," Alice countered.

Tabby stared into the living room like seeing us there two nights ago, smoking and drinking and laughing.

"We're a field experiment for you, aren't we?" she said. "You've got a closed system here. A social scientist's wet dream. Introduce a little folklore, trick us into participating in what we think's an experiment, then watch the results—watch us reduce to our superstitious medieval selves. Tell me I'm wrong."

"I'm not a social scientist," Alice said.

Which wasn't the same as denying Tabby's accusation.

"Is Lewis in on this with you?" Tabby asked then, fixing Alice in her suspicions. No, I could tell from her eyes: Fixing "Alice" in her suspicions.

"Are we sure it was raccoons?" I said, trying to break the awkwardness.

They both looked over to me.

"Lewis wouldn't mess up a kitchen," Tabby said.

"It was like this when I came in," Alice said.

"I mean—no," I said, using my hands to emphasize my words where my mouth was failing. "What I'm saying is, wouldn't a cat fit through that door as well?"

"Great," Tabby said, standing all at once, spinning away from the table in a grand gesture. "You've infected us all, *Alice*." Then, to me: "A caterpillar would fit, too, wouldn't it? Did the smoke detectors go off? Should we check all of Aunt Cynthia's hats for mercury? Are we having a tea party later?"

"We don't know what happened to Lewis," I said. It was the best defense I could muster.

"Don't say it like that," Tabby said. "We don't know where Lewis *is*."

And now I tuned in to the waver in her voice, the sheen to her eyes.

Shit.

Everybody knew she and Lewis were on the long road that ended under a wedding arch. Everybody knew that they'd end up together when grad school and first teaching posts and last flings had all been traipsed through in proper fashion. It stood to reason that she'd know that, too. And now that probably seemed to be falling apart, to her.

I stood to, I don't know, *stand* with her, be concerned alongside her—Lewis was practically my brother—but she gave me her shoulder, ran down the hall, slammed the door of the master bedroom behind her.

Whoever starts crying gets the big bedroom, I didn't say.

"Sorry about that," I said to Alice. "That's kind of why Lewis is always breaking up with her."

"I think those eggs were bad," Alice said.

Already I could see myself in ten minutes, vomiting into the toilet. Watching the scummy surface of the water for wriggling motion.

But not yet. Don't let it rise yet.

"He'll show up," I said. Mostly for myself.

"I dreamed—" Alice started, then backed up, tried again: "I was watching the fingertips of her right hand," she said. "I don't know why her fingertips were so important."

"Her?" I said, already wanting to reel that question back in.

Alice just shook her head no, nothing.

It didn't do much to settle my stomach.

* * *

The screaming woke me.

I was on the couch again. The glass of wine I'd had balanced on my stomach spilled onto Aunt Cyn's beige couch, the one with that kind of suedey fabric you could fingerwrite your name in.

The scream had come from the master bedroom, I was pretty sure.

I rose, lurched across the living room, and stopped in the doorway to the hall, suddenly aware I was at one end of what could be construed as a dark tunnel. At the other end, there could be the dark shape of a woman with matted hair. Just standing there, fixing me in her stare.

I kept one hand to the wall all the way down to the open door of the master bedroom.

It *was* Tabby who had screamed. I knew because I could hear her jerky breathing, like she was building to it again.

I stepped in as carefully as I've ever done anything. The bedroom was dark, the bed empty, the air musty. Skirting the bed, since arms could stab out for ankles, since eyes could be watching from under there, I made it to the bathroom.

Tabby was pushed up onto the sink, her back to the mirror in a way that made me want to pull her back, keep her from falling through.

What she wasn't looking away from was Alice, in sleep pants and a sports bra, bare feet. She was standing in the bathtub, facing into the corner, a kind of hoarse moan coming from her slack mouth. Her scars were a filigree of pale ridges, coming around almost to her spine—as far as her pinching fingertips could reach a razor. Meaning her front side would be worse. Her front side would be deeper, more intricate, a map to her true self.

No, she hadn't wanted to look in the mirror.

"She's not there," Tabby said, clamping onto my shoulder.

Alice *wasn't* there. She was asleep. Or something.

"Turn the water on," Tabby said, stepping forward to do it herself now that I was here.

I held her back. If we flipped the water on, then Alice would turn around, fix us in her blank stare. And she'd still be moaning that creaky sound. And there would be that instant shame, on all our parts: her, for doing this, and us, for seeing her do it.

I led Tabby out by the hand, clicked the door shut behind us.

"We should leave the light on for when she wakes up," Tabby said.

"She's just sleepwalking," I whispered, hating the way it sounded: like we were cutting her loose. Abandoning her. No, like *I* was.

But I didn't even know her, shouldn't be the one responsible for her. It wasn't on me, was it? Was she Marly, or was she Alice? Had she made that stupid story up, about someone living in the space behind mirrors, just waiting for a tunnel out into this world?

We'd just accepted it, too. A secondhand, out-loud PDF. When we're supposed to be better than that. We're supposed to be grad students. If you don't set your research criterion up to "stringent," then you're just asking to get played. There's proofs and there's *proof,* one of our math profs used to say.

Not that your heart knows the difference. Not in the dark. Not at two in the morning. Not with a tranced-out sleepwalker who's ninety percent stranger anyway.

"I think she did something to Lewis," Tabby said, gripping my hand tighter, more meaningfully. "He wouldn't just leave."

"We should," I said back. "Leave. Now."

"Without Lewis?"

I closed my eyes, felt myself falling.

What we finally did was that TV thing where you chock a kitchen chair under the master bedroom doorknob. We held hands like ten-year-olds all the way back to the couch.

Hardly any minutes later, something thunked solidly in the master bedroom end of the house. I pictured Alice, collapsing like a rag doll into the bathtub, lying there with her eyes open. Or her running fast from the bathroom, tripping, catching her forehead on the edge of the bed frame.

I didn't know which I wanted, really.

Moments later Tabby's phone buzzed in her hand. She flipped it over. Lewis's goofball face smiled up at us from her screen.

She answered without thinking, pulled the phone up to her ear.

She passed it across to me.

It was . . . maybe Alice? Lewis's phone *was* on the nightstand in the master bedroom, anyway. But this voice was deeper, creakier. Like Alice's mouth was a puppet mouth. Just, saying nonsense. Not even people words.

Tabby took the phone back, said into it, "*Alice.*"

The mumbling stopped, like this had worked, like Tabby had woken Alice up at last. But then there was a soft chuckle, there and gone. "She never told you about the third part," the voice said.

Tabby hung up, kept her thumb there, pressing where the red had been. I cast around for a blanket, not because we were cold but because a blanket can be a shield from horror, if you need it to be. There wasn't any blanket, though. And Aunt Cyn was old, should have had blankets everywhere for her thin blood. Maybe she'd put them up for my visit.

"What does that mean?" Tabby said. "Third part?"

"When she was telling the story," I said, rising. "Didn't she say that, that something was the first step?"

"When she, that girl who crawls through, when she reaches into your mouth," Tabby recited. "She reaches in for a memory. But, shouldn't there be a second part before a third part?"

Maybe this is it, I didn't say.

What I also didn't say out loud: Alice had called herself "she."

"Come with," I said, pulling Tabby up from the couch, and together we made our way into the hall again. The linen closet. Where normal people keep their normal blankets.

I needed some normal.

The chair chocked against the master bedroom door was still there, still secure.

"What are we going to do?" Tabby said, watching that chair.

"Not answer your phone anymore," I said back, and pulled the closet door open for the blanket we needed.

I was reaching to a high shelf for what looked like an afghan—Aunt Cyn had passed through a crochet-frenzy a few years back—when something clumped out from the storage space under the shelves, latched on to my knees.

It was an arm. A pale hand.

It was Lewis.

He was trembling, his shirtfront wet with saliva.

We hauled him to the couch, laid him across our laps.

He couldn't speak. His breath kept hitching.

"Water," Tabby said, so we tried that.

It ran back out his mouth.

We gave him what body heat we had. He was clammy, wrong.

"Where were you?" I said to him.

"He's here now," Tabby said. She had his head cradled in her arms.

"We've got to leave," I said.

"Just let him warm up," Tabby said back. "We'll go anywhere."

"The hospital."

"The hospital," she agreed, holding Lewis tighter.

I was breathing too deep. It was making my vision swim.

Tabby's phone buzzed again with the healthy version of Lewis's face. I threw it clattering into the kitchen. Tabby didn't go after it. Her chin was trembling.

"It's not her anymore, is it?" she said, because I guess one of us had to.

I wanted to argue, to defend Alice or Marly or whoever she was or wasn't, but Tabby was right: that voice on the phone, it hadn't been the Alice we sort of knew, the Alice I thought I was getting to know, through the scars we shared.

"Alice isn't Alice," Tabby went on.

I shook my head no, for her to please stop doing this to us, and then Lewis mewled, trembled all over. His forehead was damp with sweat. I went to wipe some of it away, keep it from stinging his eyes, and his left hand jerked up all at once, pushing his shirt up, so his fingernails could pinch and scratch into the slack skin of his stomach. Like he was trying to pick through it.

I stilled his hand but Tabby guided me away.

"He's telling us," she said, watching, rapt.

"What?"

"You saw her cuts," Tabby said, looking to the other end of the house. As if in pity.

"She doesn't do that anymore," I said, no give to my delivery.

Lewis was still picking at his stomach, making blood blisters. Next would be the blood.

"She's Marly again," Tabby said finally. "Alice might not be a cutter. But Marly was. We can't—we can't leave without hiding everything, right? She'll get out after we leave. She'll hurt herself."

I studied Tabby in the dusty green reflection of the television screen. She was patting Lewis's hair down.

"And then we're gone?" I said.

"Hospital," she promised.

Shaking my head no, that I hated this, I policed the kitchen and the dining room and the living room, commandeered a wicker basket to hide all the sharp objects in—sharp objects that could have been triggers for me, years ago. Triggers, licenses, invitations, it's such a slippery slope.

But I steeled my eyes, set my jaw.

There were the usual handfuls of knives, and there were also two razorblades in the sewing drawer, one corkscrew with the wine glasses, and what we almost missed: Aunt Cyn's wrap of knitting needles.

"There," Tabby said, pointing from the couch to where I should tuck this basket: under the counter, closer to the hall than I really wanted to leave it, but it was a good hidey hole. I covered the open top of the basket with a placemat. It looked like a picnic, forgotten in the corner.

"Now?" I said back to Tabby, kind of bouncing on the balls of my feet, the back of my calf itching like the tattoo was still new or something.

"Just let me get—" Tabby said. When she couldn't push Lewis off, I came over, took his weight onto my lap. Tabby wormed out and up, hesitated about braving the hall from the living room.

"Nothing's that important," I said, trying to keep Lewis's arms from spasming too much.

"I'm not leaving it with her," Tabby said, and stiff-legged it through the living room, to come at the hall from the kitchen, so that light could be her welcome mat—she wouldn't be stepping onto darkness, at least. I couldn't see her right at the end, but she was safe as far as I could track her anyway. "Keep talking!" she called back.

I did. What I ended up saying was multiplication tables—the fives. It was all I could think of. Maybe fifteen seconds later, Tabby was back.

"Get it?" I said.

She shook her head no, looked about to cry.

"What was it?" I asked.

"His cell," she said. "I thought he might—" She didn't finish but she didn't need to: she thought Lewis might call. When he was right here with us. Or, when his body was. But getting the phone would mean going back into the master bedroom.

I didn't blame her for just standing there. But I wasn't going to offer to get it for her, either.

"Now?" I said, and exactly when she nodded yes, Lewis seized. Like, *double* grand-mal. All that was touching the couch was the back of his head and his heels, like he'd tapped into some line of current, and that current, it was cooking him.

"*His tongue, his tongue!*" Tabby said, coming across, sliding on her knees to jam the heel of her right hand against his teeth, to try to force his mouth open.

Lewis's eyes were rolled around to the whites, his fingers crooked and hard. I'd have sworn they had an extra joint to them somehow, except that's impossible.

Right at the end of it, Lewis looked over to the hall doorway. It stilled him. In that quiet, we all heard what he'd sensed: the chair down there, its wood back scraping slowly down . . . *some*thing.

"The master bedroom door opens inward," I said aloud, like the announcer for this evil game. Neither me nor Tabby had ever tried to block a door, evidently.

"It always works on TV," Tabby said.

"We've got to get out of here," I said, crabbing out from under Lewis.

Tabby stayed where she was, bringing her other hand around to cradle his head. Just as her fingers found the base of his skull, his lips creaked open, and it was just like someone had their hand behind his face, was moving his mouth for him.

"The second step is migration," he said tonelessly, and then coughed once, twice, and the third cough was a bubble of dark blood, followed by a runny thread of vomit.

What was in that frothy red vomit was shards. Of mirror.

So that's where he'd been. Back there.

One mystery solved. A thousand more opening up.

Tabby pushed back from him, covering her mouth with her hand, but Lewis's trembling right foot had just given up the ghost. Along with the rest of him.

I had my hand to the inner doorknob of the front door when Tabby registered for me. She was grabbing my pants leg.

"We just going to leave him?" she said, about Lewis.

"He's not him anymore," I said. Not like I was tough, or heartless. Like I was collapsing on the inside. Like I was begging her.

She hugged her knees and sobbed, her hand falling away from my pants leg.

"Police," I said, my big compromise here, then cast around, trying to remember where Tabby's cell phone was.

Oh, yeah: I stared over the dining room table at the refrigerator, the sink, the window, all so many impossible miles away. Tabby's phone somewhere over there. Where I'd thrown it.

Every action has an equal and opposite reaction, right?

More like every action comes back to bite you in the ass.

But hesitating wasn't going to save any days.

I stepped across Lewis, held my hand out for Tabby to wait.

Four steps later I was standing beside the dining room table. It felt like I was in the calm eye of a great storm. Like this was a little moment out of time. No—like the world had calmed down special so I could cue into something.

What?

I scanned, studied, did it again, and . . . no. Please no.

There was an empty place under the counter, by the doorway to the hall. Where the basket of blades and knitting needles had been. It made the back of my calf itch even more.

We wouldn't have heard feet on the carpet of the hall, would we have? We wouldn't have heard an arm reaching around, for all this necessary sharpness.

I didn't want to think what came next.

"I'm sorry," I said back to Tabby, not really loud enough, and stepped past the counter, thinking only of the backdoor, and all the wide-open world past that door.

That was where I was going, this was where I was going to live, where I was going to hide, what I was going to appreciate like I never had before.

Until a pair of eyes were watching me, the doggie door flap resting on top of its head.

A raccoon. I was ninety percent sure.

Maybe eighty.

I flinched to the side, backed up to the sink, and held on to the counter.

And now Tabby's phone was buzzing on the floor, skittering on the tile.

Slowly, I looked at this caller, dread welling in my throat: Aunt Cyn.

Yes yes yes: she could call the authorities, she could fix this somehow.

I punched the call open to establish some sort of lifeline, some tether she could pull me out of this with, but what I heard instead was that same moaning Alice had been making, in the master bathroom.

Only—it wasn't only coming from the phone.

It was also coming from Tabby, the house phone stretched across from the dining room wall, pressed to her face.

She'd bitten something in her mouth. Black blood was seeping past her lips. Past her smile.

Migration.

The other Alice had been in our Alice. Now it was in Tabby.

I dropped her phone, fell back into the farthest corner of the kitchen from her, then slid down to make myself smaller.

This was it, then, I told myself.

I should have run. I should have done a thousand things. I scratched hard enough at the tattoo on my calf to draw blood. What was happening to me?

"But what's the third part?" Tabby said, actually in the voice I knew from her. Which made it all worse. "That is what you're thinking, isn't it? You're a smart boy. You should go to graduate school, do something with yourself."

That last bit had been my whole family's chorus, four years ago.

When I shook my head no, like this was all cobwebs I could break free of, Tabby laughed, then began winding the phone cord around her neck, tight, watching me the whole time.

I closed my eyes, kicked my feet out like I could break free from all this, and, in doing so, thunked into the stainless-steel dishwasher. Evidently right where Aunt Cyn had told me to.

The water in there stopped, and the door clicked open, fell forward like a drawbridge, belching days of rotten steam up.

Tabby stopped strangling herself. She was just watching, now.

"You are a smart boy," she said, her voice half-choked. "Part three . . ."

I followed her eyes.

There were no racks in this dishwasher anymore. No dishes at all.

Just a pale, naked body. One not quite ready yet, it didn't look like. The skin was still loose, the hair pale, the fingers too spindly.

Without the door to hold it, it leaned over, falling halfway out, a right arm hanging over the door.

And—the face.

I kicked back hard, harder.

The face was me, minus the scruff, minus the bloodshot eyes.

The first step had been inhabiting one of us. The second was moving from one of us to the other—from Alice to Tabby.

The third step, it was this. It was *replacing* one of us. It was being the lone, wasted survivor in a house of dead people. The one coddled out into the light by emergency personnel, into the world. To infect it.

Except I'd opened the door too early on it. I'd opened the door before I'd been dealt with. Corollary to this, I had to think, was that to repair this situation, *I* now had to be dealt with.

I came back around to Tabby like to ask her why, like to reason with her, but then my whole body spasmed. Starting with my left leg. With my tattoo.

It was alive. The cat there, it was motile, it was moving, it was scratching. It was trying to break free.

I sucked in air to, I don't know, scream, cry, die, but ended up making zero sound at all. I couldn't. My cat tattoo was reaching one bloody paw up from my skin, feeling for the ground.

Then the rest of its blue-lined self birthed through, and I knew what this was: whatever was happening, it could grow a me in the dishwasher, from stray hair or skin or whatever. But it couldn't ink a tattoo.

So it would just call mine across.

"Take it!" I screamed, pushing back again, slipping in my own blood. I pulled myself up, stood against the counter, knew I could rush past Tabby. That I could still make it. That I had to.

When I finally pushed away from the counter for my big rush, I saw that the steam from the dishwasher had fogged the glass of the kitchen window. Written there all along, probably from when she first came through the television screen, was *ALIS*.

I could almost see the wonder on her shadow face as she wrote it—surprised to be granted corporeality again, after all those years behind the mirror. Relishing the way the glass pushed back against the pad of her finger.

Or—did she have to mark each place she came to, as fair warning?

Was *ALIS* written all over the house, on every reflective surface, to ensure we couldn't leave?

I shook my head no, please, and, keeping one hand to the counter, I crept away from the dishwasher, away from the doggie door, away from the window, ready to dive past the dining room table the instant Tabby looked past me.

Except then she *did* look past me. Without smiling.

I closed my eyes, opened them again, and turned around to what she couldn't look away from.

Standing on unsteady legs behind me—it was *me,* naked and starved down. New, born again in steam, from a box I was only just now realizing was shiny enough on the inside that it must have been like living in a mirror.

No, behind a mirror. For years and years. Seeing only yourself.

Of course, if you ever got out, you would want a new face. A series of new faces.

Crawling into the back of the other me's calf was a blue and bloody cat with a smile forever wide, and sharp. The sounds—no, I told myself. Don't remember those sounds. Or the smell.

When the other me raised a hand to touch my shoulder, or my neck, like to balance from this thing that was happening to it, I fell ahead, only Tabby was standing in my way.

I juked to the side. Into the hall.

And of course, like you do when you're a weak, weak human, I looked to the deep end first. To the dark end of the tunnel.

Dimly, there was a shape down there. A bleeding, raw shape.

Alice.

Just seeing her wavering there like she was injured, like she was failing, like she was about to fall, I understood.

She hadn't sneaked the basket of blades back to her bedroom like I'd thought.

There'd been another. There *was* another.

Tabby. She hated what happened to Lewis, and she knew Alice was a cutter, so, she'd delivered her some cutting *tools.* She'd walked the basket right down the hall, opened the door, and pushed them in, then come back to me in the living room like nothing had happened. Like she'd wimped out.

I should have seen it. I should have listened closer. I should have known.

I took a limping step across the hall, planted my shoulder into the wall, kept my eyes on Alice.

Every part of her was bleeding, each cut tiny and precise, just like she needed. There were a hundred, a hundred and fifty small, triangular flaps curling up from her. Like when your shoulders are sunburned and the dead skin is all peeling off. Only, her skin wasn't quite dead yet. Just the rest of her.

She held her hand out to me, the razor blade shiny in her palm, a tiny mirror I could probably see myself in, if I came close enough.

Or maybe I was already seeing it in me.

I could—if I cut just a small, nothing-line in the already-open meat at the back of my calf, then it wouldn't even matter, would it? It wouldn't even count. It wouldn't be backsliding; it wouldn't be starting anything all over again.

Alice, she could even hold her hand over mine, couldn't she?

We could do it together. Line after line in that new meat.

I sucked my breath in with the deliciousness of it, and when Alice's face back in the shadow cracked into a smile, I felt it spreading to my own face.

Never mind what had happened in the kitchen, at the dining room table, on the floor in the living room.

This was the hall.

This was a long corridor I could feel my way down. A tunnel I could walk down.

That's the thing about tunnels—they go both ways.

We were all so worried about what might crawl up. We should have seen that long hole in the mirror for what it was, though: an escape hatch.

A story indeed, Mr. Carroll.

And then it came to me as it must have to him—that soft flash of insight I was always waiting for in the math classroom, in the math basement. That eureka moment I'd been planning to build my future on, once upon a time.

Lewis, my *friend* Lewis, would appreciate this. Tabby would scoff. Alice just cocked her head at me.

There *is* a way around the Dichotomy Paradox, Lewis, Zeno—that paradox where, to cross a distance, you first have to go half that distance, and then half of *that* distance.

All you have to do is hold your wrist out, for the delicate girl at the end of the hall to open it with her handful of jagged brightness.

The red strings she exposes, she can pull you ahead with them, pull you to her bit by bit, slowly, so that you seem to be standing still, stuck in time.

Stop me if you've heard this one before.

ALL THE KING'S MEN

Jeffrey Ford

All the king's men and all their horses showed up one night at my estate some months ago. It was late, I'd already retired, and it was raining quite fiercely. A pounding at the door and I heard my butler get up to answer. A few moments later—hinges squealed, light from the hallway fell across my face and then was blocked by Brazzo's hulking silhouette. "My lady, the king's men are here to see you."

"All at once?" I asked. "Show them in."

"Very good," he said, and closed the door behind him.

I got up and put on my short silk robe, white peonies on an indigo background, and went out into the parlor with my hair a fright from the pillow. There sat three of the king's men in their uniforms, caps resting on their knees. As I entered, they stood and bowed. I gave them a flip of my hand, and sat in my own seat next to the glass table.

"We're here on important business from the King," said Montcrief, captain of the king's men. I'd known him for years, spent many excruciating hours with him at royal functions. A total blowhard. His two porridge-faced compatriots nodded.

I lit a cigarette and pulled the ashtray closer to me. "To what do I owe this disappointment?" I asked.

"This is top priority. Top priority!" he said.

I couldn't help but smile. "Get on with it."

"Seriously, Cinder, you can't breathe a word of it."

He spoke my first name, and it startled me. The dolt wouldn't think of calling me by any other moniker than Lady Syres. I realized he must really be warning me about something.

He put his finger to his lips in a sign of conspiracy, and whispered, "Humpty Dumpty."

Right then, I should have realized how twisted and off-putting the story that followed might be. Dumpty was an enigma. No one knew his origin—the clouds, beneath the earth, or if he crawled fully formed from the king's own backside. A nightmare hatched into daylight—a four-foot creamy blue egg in short pants, blue jacket, and red bowtie. Pipe cleaner arms ending in white gloves, legs in loafers. A wide mouth, one side turned up in a sneer, the other, down. Shell jowls that waggled without cracking, a high-pitched chuckle, and a pair of droopy eyes.

"Humpty Dumpty," whispered Montcrief, "met his end this evening."

I was heartened by the news. No matter how many times I'd been in that creepy wanker's company, he never seemed to belong to reality. The impossibility of him made me feel like too many rides on the carousel. "How could he exist?" was definitely the question at hand, but there was no reasonable answer.

Beyond the feverish fact of his existence was his personality, which was deeply unpleasant. He never shut up—pontificating, gossiping, sniping at the weak and downtrodden. He was protected by the King. When asked by my sister, the Queen of Hearts, why he kept the perverse egg in his court, the king's response was, "Where will I find another?"

Dumpty had free license to run wild in the streets. Whatever mess he made or trouble he got into, the king would make a decree and all would be made right again, no matter the effort or expense. But these acts became increasingly outrageous. Citizens were harmed, property was destroyed, and children were put in harm's way. One misadventure ended in fire, half of the business quarter turned to ashes. Dumpty's only response was a shrill chuckle. Those who threatened to break his shell were eventually found in darkened alleyways, a porcupine needle shoved deep into each eye. I knew a woman who'd slept with the egg/man. She said he rubbed her the right way, burrowed deep into her heart, but left her gagging on a rancid, runny yolk.

"Was it at the Wishing Wall?" I asked.

Montcrief nodded. "Yes, he perched atop it, as is his wont every evening, and made miserable the lives of those who traveled there to make wishes. Hurling at them epithets and accusations. Sometimes when the pilgrims reached out to touch the wall in order to make their appeal to fate, Dumpty undid his zipper, removed his snowflake pizzle, and rained insolence down upon those desperate hands."

I laughed aloud at "his snowflake pizzle" and Montcrief looked put out.

"You're as dramatic as a schoolboy, Montie," I said.

"Obviously, Lady Syres, you underestimate the seriousness of these events," he said.

"What events?"

"Aren't you curious, my lady, as to how the egg-cur died?" said the king's man to the left of Montcrief.

"Assassination," said the one to the right of him.

"By whose hand?" I asked.

Here's what Montie recounted in a whispered voice so annoying I wanted to set his mustache on fire. An hour before dusk the king's carriage came down the Pellham Road. While passing by the Wishing Wall, it stopped. The king stepped out and saluted Dumpty up above. The egg remained seated atop the brickwork but kicked his legs out in front, clapped his hands, and gave a high-pitched chuckle.

"And how art thou, Citizen Dumpty?" inquired his highness.

"Where's our lovely Queen?" asked the egg.

"At the chapel."

"Wrong, your blindness. She's making the beast with two backs on the floor of a stable with one of your most trusted councilors." The crowd of bystanders gasped in unison at the revelation.

"What?" said the King, obviously enraged. Dumpty got up carefully, his balance a tenuous affair, and danced trippingly across the top of the wall, all the time chuckling and singing "La-la-la, the Queen of the realm is rutting."

"Lie," yelled his highness, but Dumpty danced and chuckled. The King soon reached the end of his amusement with the oddity and went back in his coach for his dueling pistols. He had his attendant load one of the guns for him and then told the young fellow to load the next and to keep them coming until Humpty Dumpty breathed his last.

"Are you sure he breathes?" asked the attendant.

Dumpty stuck out the index finger of each hand and put up his thumbs, pretending to be shooting the crowd.

The King aimed the first pistol with a wavering hand, fired, and chipped a piece off of the top of the wall at the egg's feet.

"Shitty shot, shitty shot," said Dumpty.

The king took the other pistol from the young attendant and aimed up at the prancing figure. He fired and the bullet went wide of its mark.

"No good with the gun. That's what she said." Dumpty turned and shook his bottom at the king.

This time his highness waited until both pistols were loaded. He took them and drew closer to the wall, standing right beneath where Dumpty danced. "I should never have allowed your existence in my realm," he yelled, and fired. The left pistol again shot wide, but the right pistol's lead ball grazed the side of Dumpty's shell head. It was a minor scratch, not causing so much as a hairline crack, but the impact was just enough to throw him off balance. He spun his arms and twirled on one foot, swaying forward and back. Amid a storm of chuckling, the ridiculous dance went on for whole minutes as he tried to regain his balance.

All watched the fall without breathing, and it seemed to take forever. The mad egg/man landed directly atop the crown on the head of the head of state, shell caving in, yolk and the secret bodily juices of Dumpty spewing out in all directions. The king cleaved the egg, each side falling further to the cobblestones and smashing into a hundred pieces. His highness was laid low, bathed in the ichor of life, and all his men assisted him to his feet.

Montcrief's doltish companions nodded. I lit another cigarette.

"So why did you wake me? I couldn't care less if Dumpty's a broken heap somewhere. Good riddance to the abomination," I said.

"There's more," said the man to Montie's right.

"Quite a bit," said the man to his left.

Montie carried on, telling the rest. "The king went into a rage and yelled, 'I want this shit heap swept up. Every last insidious bit of it. Put it in a burlap sack, toss it into the blacksmith's furnace, and then put the ashes in a sealed box containing three rocks. Take the box to the bottomless lake, row out to the middle, and toss it in.'

"My men and I set to our assigned task, combing the cobblestones for pieces of Dumpty. Most of the shards were sizable. I found the bit of shell with his droopy left eye, which shifted its gaze even though it was no longer attached to anything. Yes, the mouth still chuckled, until the king pounced on it with the heel of his boot and silenced it. His highness then got in his carriage, yelled, 'To the chapel,' and the driver let the horses run.

"When we had every crapulous scrap in the bag, we took it to Harbrough's smithy and ordered him to get the furnace piping hot. We were just about to toss the sack of shell into the blaze when the king stepped through the doorway near out of breath as if he'd been rushing to get there. Still, he managed to yell, 'Don't burn those remains. I want that horrid imp reassembled.' He gave no explanation, but put me in charge of the task. 'Whatever it takes,' he said."

I laughed so hard the cigarette fell out of my mouth and I had to retrieve it from the floor.

"Enjoy your moment of jocularity," he said.

"Well, Montie, I'd like to know who's a bigger dolt, you or my brother-in-law. Of course, he's bringing him back to find out who my sister's sneaking around with," I said.

"Maybe. Are you through laughing? I'm here to tell you that I have authorization from the crown to enlist you in the effort to reassemble Humpty Dumpty."

"Why me?"

"You repair things, invent things. You've no equal in that respect. That flying carriage with the flapping wings was ingenious. You're just what this undertaking requires. And why? Because this is one of those instances where shit is running downhill. In fact, it's an avalanche."

"I refuse."

"Refuse and you'll be sent to the Isle of Misery."

"If I fail?"

"Then we'll all be accompanying you."

"I'll get my sister to intercede."

"If anyone finds out about this, you'll lose your head."

"Get out," I told them.

Before leaving the parlor, Montcrief looked back at me and said, "Let me know if we can help. We'll hand the sack of shell over to your man, Brazzo."

How could I sleep? I ordered Brazzo to take the sack of Dumpty to the workshop. Back in my room, I dressed in a full-length gold lamé evening gown and extra-high heels. Loved that golden gown—it gave me a sense of power, and I knew I'd need it for the task at hand. The heels weren't the best but they allowed me to get up above the problem, so to speak.

Crafting weapons for war, giving life to my daydreams, flying machines and perpetual motion was one thing, but reassembling a broken egg was the ultimate puzzle. I'm certain my jackass brother-in-law had never once considered the fact that even if Humpty Dumpty could be put back together, it didn't necessarily mean he'd be alive.

I pondered that very dilemma until I took the sack and emptied it on my largest work table. Spreading the heap of pieces out across the surface, I noticed that both of those shards holding eyes showed pupils still moving, and the three dozen or more pieces of lip that I readily spotted still twitched. A theory came to me and I went to the wall shelf to take up the hearing trumpet I'd bought for one of my early inventions. With the bell of the horn above a fragment of lip and the other opening to my ear, I could hear, like the cry of a flea, a voice screaming, "Help me." I listened again intently and shivered at the possibility when I heard a pin prick of chuckling.

By the time morning finally arrived and Brazzo had brought my coffee, I settled down to strategizing about the task the way I normally would with any project. My initial plan was to draw grid work upon the three large tables in my shop, number each piece of shell and organize them, one to a square. I was convinced I needed to see the problem from above. I wanted it laid out before my eyes.

It was later, during the day's first gin and a cigarette that my mind made an incredible leap and I saw a radically more direct approach. I reasoned that if the lips could still speak and the eyes perhaps see, why not reconstruct Dumpty's face first, in hopes that upon seeing the pieces of himself, he might be able to tell me where they each go.

I settled on a type of paste I'd invented for the repair of the very delicate furniture of a doll house—a concoction of swift's eggs and volcanic ash. The sheerest swath of it on Dumpty's backside when the king came by the Wishing Wall, and he'd never have been able to fall. I summoned Brazzo and sent him off to speak to Montcrief about mobilizing all the king's men to go afield and gather as many swift's eggs as they might. I told my man to make it clear that the sooner I got the eggs, the sooner I could start the reconstruction.

In the meantime, over the next few days, I sorted out as many of the shell pieces that were part of the mouth and put them on a separate table, fitting them in approximately the right places to create a pair of puzzle lips. When all was said and done only two or three very small pieces were missing. Bringing them into close proximity of their original form, as it was before they'd shattered, had them mumbling with one louder voice. I knew it would not speak clearly until all was affixed.

The feel of those shards of shell with bits of the lips on them was slimy and warm, as if I was holding a slug picked straight from a paving stone on a bright summer day. The effect made my skin crawl. My solution? Opera gloves made from lamb intestine—Black. I matched them, of course, with a simple black dress, low cut, and a string of pearls. Nothing daring, but serviceable for workshop toil.

I found the two rather larger pieces holding Dumpty's eyes. They were peering left and right. I set them above the mouth and then went in search of pieces of nose. I noticed that every time I leaned over the table, the scurrilous Dumpty was shifting his glance to look down my dress. The next time he did it, I stuck my thumb in his left eye, and a chaotic muffled scream leaked out from behind the lips.

The following day, Montcrief and the king's men arrived with a wagon load of swift's eggs. They assisted me in the production of the paste and with their help the process took only a day. I was ready to begin the reconstruction, half full of excitement, half of dread. I was curious to see what I could learn in trying to restore a magical entity to life. As the king had said, "Where will I find another?" But the fact that it was Dumpty being restored felt to me like committing a sin.

Gluing and fitting shell pieces together is the tedious work of Purgatory. The opera gloves got hot beneath the bright lamp and the microscope/goggles gave me a headache. It took me three days to glue the lip puzzle. On the last day, Dumpty's incessant chaotic mumbling entered the realm of clarity, and I could make out what he was saying. "You'll be richly rewarded for your efforts, my dear," was what I heard. I wasn't sure if he could hear me, but I spoke to him and slowly explained my plan to get him together again. For a long time, he recited what sounded like a prayer in a language unknown to me. I reconstructed the nose and found those pieces of shell that reattached it to the mouth.

Days later, after I'd successfully solved the jigsaw puzzle of the face, eyes, nose, mouth, all connected by the appropriate shell, I took the goggles off and blinked. My eyesight had been strained, and the aroma of the paste had me reeling in the heat. By then I'd stripped down to a sheer sarong the color of sunflowers. My next move was to work naked, which was my inclination, but Dumpty's half-alive leering and shoddy comments put me off.

"Lady Syres," said the freshly glued mask of Dumpty.

I swooned back into the chair, exhausted.

"I suppose I don't have to tell you that the king murdered me."

"I've heard," I said.

"Why'd you rescue me? I'd no idea you were so fond of the old egg."

"I'm not. The king requested that you be reassembled. The job was given to Montcrief and he shoved it off on me."

"Montcrief, tedious as dripping water. The king wants me back together after killing me? What a simpleton."

"I think it's that he wants to know who of his councilors my sister is having an affair with."

You can imagine the chuckling that followed. I wanted to strike with a sledgehammer that which took me days to assemble. When Dumpty finally calmed down, he said, "I'll tell you, but not until I'm back together."

"I'm working as fast as I can. I thought maybe you could tell me where certain pieces go and save me the guesswork."

"I'll do better than that," he said. "Lift me up and take me to where I can see all of the pieces."

I dragged myself out of the chair. The paste had already dried, one of my favorite aspects of its properties. I lifted him by a ridge of brow that ran just above his eyes, and a fragment of chin below the lips. Three steps and we stood amid the tables with the pieces of shell spread out upon them. When he finally saw what his shell had been reduced to, a grievous cry leaped from him and he slowly began to turn like a globe in my hands. An instant later, it became clear that the mask was floating in the air of its own volition and every second spinning more rapidly. Astonished, I backed away and watched it hover.

Pieces of shell from the two tables lifted into the air and then shot at the spinning Dumpty as if attracted by a magical magnetism. As he rotated, his shell of a body reformed itself a few pieces at a time. There was this otherworldly light, sky blue, glowing from within the forming shell. The entire thing was too overwhelming for me. I fell into the chair and shaded my eyes against the glare.

A string of chuckling wound round and round and finally, when every crumb of shell had found its proper niche and was affixed by enchantment instead of paste, he leaped to the floor and strode toward me. I didn't want him near but was too tired to run. He stood leering and announced, "You shall be richly rewarded, my dear."

I felt sick to my stomach and tried not to look at him.

"I've no idea who your sister is having an affair with, but all I need do is imagine someone. I just wanted to get the old man's goat."

I held my hands out in front of me to ward him off, but he didn't lunge as I feared he might. His newly set shell began to undulate with waves beneath the surface. Then I heard the cracks forming, sounding like ice on a spring river, loud snaps and pops. The disgusting thing farted loud and long accompanied by a swiftly dying chuckle that turned into the cry of someone falling from a high place. In a flash, Dumpty's eyes imploded, his lips crumbled, his arms snapped, and when they did, I had to wonder for a second when and from where he'd acquired arms . . . and legs?

He turned completely inside out. There was a bang and puff of smoke, and when I'd managed to clear the air, I saw what remained. In Dumpty's place there stood a large bird made of the clearest crystal. It captured the lights of the workshop and glimmered like an enormous diamond. There's no way to explain my confusion and dread, leaping from the impossible to the sublime, breaking every natural law. In the end the bird was so beautiful, so gentle in its bearing, I saw it as a gift. Weighing Dumpty against the crystal bird, the shell head lost every time. The sound the creature made was a soft, throbbing music, the purr of an angel.

The bird moved around the workshop, pecking here and there, catching a moth in mid-air with a lightning move of its head. The tips of its talons tapped-tapped light as rain upon the stone floor. "Dumpty, are you there? In the bird?" I called. But the tone and tune remained the same. It flapped its wings in a shower of sparkling light and leaped up from the floor to perch on the windowsill. When it tapped the glass, I knew it wanted out.

Believe me, I understood the problems I would face if I opened the window and let the thing fly off, but I couldn't stop myself. It flew into the dusk's pink clouds, shimmering with the last rays of reflected sunlight. Watching it flap away gave me a deep feeling of relief and a deeper feeling of regret. When the king found out I'd released Dumpty's incarnation into the world, it would cost my head. It didn't matter. Denying the impulse to free the precious creature was to defile the universe, and that rankled my soul.

For the next two days, I watched the skies around my estate, and spotted the bird many times. Every morning I'd see it fly out of the King's forest to the East, very often with other birds following it. It wasn't always easy to spot from the ground. You had to catch it in the sunlight. To assist, though, there was also the distinctive chuckling call somewhere between the snicker of a laughing thrush and a seagull's guffaw. As I tried to go about my business and work on other projects, I had a sense it was watching me, flying over the realm and watching us all. I pointed it out to Brazzo one day and he said, "A bird in the hand is worth two in the bush."

His words were prophetic. The following day, Montcrief arrived with the king's men in order to inspect the progress on Dumpty. He found me naked in the workshop sanding the rust off an old broadsword I'd found by the riverbank in the summer. I called for Brazzo to bring my robe, but Montie and the king's men were already scandalized by my body. I laughed at them till they all finally turned away.

I received the robe from my man and put it on and dismissed him. In the pocket were my cigarettes and matches. I lit one and told Montcrief what had happened. When I was done, he stood with his mouth gaping. A few moments later the anger turned his face red. "What do you mean, you let it go?" he screamed.

"I let it go," I said. "It wasn't Dumpty anymore. It was something beautiful." My revelation appeared to make him nauseous and, for a brief time, speechless. "Well," he finally said, "we've got to arrest her. Take her, gentlemen." They came for me from all sides, and Montie stood back, his arms folded and a look of resignation on his face. I picked up the rusty weapon and started swinging. Blood spurted and bone cracked as I waylaid the first five of the forty. "Brazzo!" I yelled, and a moment later, he was at the door to the workshop.

He fired his blunderbuss. The explosion, the smoke, and the grapeshot in their legs and asses distracted them. His massive form weighed into the depths of the remaining thirty-five and his ham fists cracked jaws and bequeathed concussions. In the end, though, we were simply outnumbered. As three of them twisted my arms behind my back so hard I dropped the sword, and two others grabbed my ankles, I watched fifteen men swarm over Brazzo like the ocean swallowing a mountain.

Every one of the fifteen paid a dear price, but my man slowly sank beneath a brutal beating from cudgels and clubs. Between the two of us we'd killed maybe ten of them. My last sight of Brazzo was of him lying in a fetal position on the floor, shuddering, his prodigious head cracked open like a ripe melon. Blood was pooling around him.

As for my fate, I fought the whole way to the palace's tower prison, and at least managed to kick Montie in the balls twice. They carried me like a sofa up the winding stone steps and threw me into the cell. The bars clanged shut and a large key turned in the lock. I scrabbled to my feet, still brimming with fight. Montie ordered the king's men away, save for one, who now sported a beauty of a black eye, compliments of Brazzo's fist. "Get Lady Syres something to wear."

"What?" said the fellow, glaring my way.

"Something decent. Where her ass isn't hanging out," yelled the captain of the king's men, and the fellow fled.

Montie lit a cigarette and handed it through the bars to me. I took it.

After lighting one for himself, he paced back and forth for a few moments. "Don't worry, I'll not let his highness execute you."

"Don't do me favors, you nipple prick."

"Here's what I'm going to tell your brother-in-law: Before Dumpty escaped, he revealed to you the name of your sister's lover. I will choose one of the councilors to be the culprit. I'm thinking of giving up Arnold Nershlir. He seems more an organic obstruction than a person. No doubt his advice to the crown is pale and weak like him."

"You're sick, Montie. I'll tell the king the truth. You can't accuse Nershlir of something he's innocent of."

"It's no problem at all," said Montie. "Whether it's true or not, once that worm is burned at the stake or made to sit on a spike till his weight pushes it up his ass and out his mouth, the king will be completely satisfied. Your sister can help me with your appeal and you'll go free."

"I don't want your help," I told him.

"I have plans for you," he said. "When all this is over, I thought perhaps we might come to an . . . understanding, so to speak."

He left the tower before I could answer. "You'll come to an understanding with my spike heels in your eyes," I screamed after him.

Immediately I set about trying to pick the lock with the wooden matches in the pocket of my robe. It was easier putting Dumpty together. All a failure, I slumped into the corner of the cold stone cell and worked to clear my thinking.

Days dragged on into weeks as everything, even the mechanisms of justice, moved at a glacial pace. I exercised on a daily basis, ate the slop they gave me even though it was toad shit. Every now and then Montie would show up and slip a cold roast leg of chicken or a block of cheese and loaf of bread through the bars to me. I accepted his gifts in order to remain in fighting condition, so that I might drive a dagger into his heart at a future opportunity.

Besides my exercises and meditation, my only way to pass time was peering out the small barred window at the back of my cell. I probably had the best view in the kingdom, high above the palace complex. I could see down into the marketplace, out over the king's forest, and even beyond to a sliver of sparkling blue that was the inland ocean. Nearly every day, from my perch, I spotted the crystal bird moving from tree to tree in the forest. Seeing its brilliance always made me feel momentarily free, and although I was trapped in stone, I felt a wind at my face and the exhilaration of flight.

At night, I occasionally noticed a slow lumbering form moving past the torches by the gates of the market. It stood, patiently looking up to my prison. I knew it was death, waiting to claim me. An antidote to those midnight terrors was for me, come morning, to look off at the sparkling water of the inland sea, and remember the strange girl, Alice, who told me one lazy afternoon as we lay abed, she with the Carpenter and me the Walrus, of another world just the opposite side of the looking glass.

One day, Montcrief came to visit and told me that he'd successfully implicated Councilor Nershlir in an affair with the queen. "Oh, Cinder, you should have seen the king. He was livid. When your sister played along to implicate the drip in order to keep concealed the secret identity of her real lover, who, by the way, turns out to have been me, his highness moved up the date of the fellow's execution to next week. Nershlir has been abandoned by his wife and family. He spends his days in irons wracked with lamentations. A sight to behold. As far as I know now, you, Cinder, are to be released after his death."

"Did I tell you you could address me by my first name? Liberties like that, and I'll make you suffer first instead of just killing you outright when I get the chance."

Montcrief laughed low and slow, the opposite of Dumpty but equally as annoying. He pulled something shiny from his pocket and held it up to me. "The king's gamekeeper keeps finding these little gems in the swift nests," he said. It was a crystal egg quite a bit larger than a swift egg. "I think your magical bird has been busy. I shouldn't have doubted you. I saw the creature the other day flying over the down. A stunning sight."

And then, before I knew it, the day of Nershlir's execution was upon us. The marketplace below me was set up to accommodate the official function. Stalls had been disassembled and a dais with thrones for the king and queen was set up. I watched like an eagle as the prisoner was brought out and each of his limbs was chained to a horse facing one of the four points of the compass. I could barely hear the charges being read. My sister, as devious as a fox, asked forgiveness from his highness, and it was granted, seeing as no one could be sexually jealous of Nershlir. Her affair was to be excused as a brief mental illness from what Montie had told me. The crowd hummed in anticipation of the execution, murmuring approval when necessary and cheering like mad to placate the crown.

I thought about poor Nershlir, so alone, falsely accused, not really knowing what had become of his life. Then Montie gave the command, and the horses ran away, separating the poor councilor from himself and himself. I thought his scream would split the stones around me. At the first splash of blood and sign of dangling tendon, I looked away. The crowd cheered, not because they had any lust for Nershlir's death, but in order to convince the King of Hearts that his justice was righteous.

The noise died down, and there was no sound but the hoofbeats of the horses as they returned to the king's men, dragging pieces of Nershlir through the dirt. It was then that a strange din arose from the direction of the king's forest, just beyond the marketplace. There was a rustling of leaves, a swaying of branches as if the forest was full with an enormous flock of blackbirds gathering for a murmuration. It was nothing of the sort, though.

I spotted them as the peripheral members of the marketplace crowd did. They climbed down the trunks of trees, climbed, I assume, from their nests. Miniature Dumpties the size of a fist, descended in waves. The first to see them froze, too stunned to cry out. But then their fear cut through the paralysis and they ran toward the middle of the marketplace. The tiny Dumpties surrounded the citizens of the realm, hemming them in and overwhelming them with magical numbers.

The king's men, all but one, drew their weapons and charged the charging weirdness. Cudgels and clubs made an omelet in the marketplace and still more of the biting, grasping egg/men came in their short pants, red bow ties, and white gloves, to devour and suffocate all. The collective riot of their mirth made it seem as if the very universe was chuckling.

The king was eaten a diminutive bite at a time, allowing for maximum agony, and my poor sister, the Queen, was hastily trampled as the diners rushed her husband. The sole king's man who did not charge into the fray and meet his end was, of course, Montcrief. I saw him run for the door of the palace tower. He was coming to me, fleeing for his life, and bringing the wave of death with him. All was lost.

Until a cannon ball blew a hole the size of three people in the side of my cell. The dust and smoke cleared quickly with the wind rushing in while outside, hovering next to the tower, a product of my own "magic," the flying carriage was flapping its wings under the power of Brazzo's pedaling. "All aboard, my lady," he said. There was a wicked scar across the hemisphere of his head, and it was impossible to miss his broken nose and missing right earlobe.

"Brazzo, I thought you were dead," I yelled above the wind of the wings. I had tears in my eyes.

"Kill Brazzo? Never! I thought you saw me, late at night by the market gate."

As I moved to the edge of the wall in order to leap out into the back of the flying carriage, I heard something behind me. I turned and saw Montcrief using his key on the lock to my cell. Only yards behind him was just the very tip of the wave of Dumpties flooding into the room. With all my training for a moment just like this, I was ready. I made the jump without incident, landing in the back of the flying carriage. "Fly, Brazzo," I yelled, and he pedaled harder and harder, working to get the craft away from the tower. In the meantime Montie sprang from my cell in a poor leap and merely managed to grab on to the carriage's running board. Dumpties rode his pants legs and coattails, and two lines of them trailed back to the tower where more were climbing out over those and heading for us.

"Help me, Cinder," he screamed. The fear in his eyes was as clear and black-hearted as the soul of Humpty Dumpty.

For his frantic beseechment, I gave him a big left foot to the face. His grip loosened, Brazzo swung the carriage up and away, and Montcrief, captain of the king's men, plummeted to earth and upon impact was buried in a flood of Humpty Dumpties. I must say, the sight of it was richly rewarding.

"To the inland sea, Brazzo," I called over the wind. "I need a vacation from kings and their men and the nightmares they hatch."

RUN, RABBIT

Angela Slatter

Rabbit has been running from the Queen for so long he's almost forgotten what he did.

Almost.

Such a small indiscretion, really. Just a teensy-tiny step out of line, really. On this side of the worlds a rabbit's foot is considered lucky, but he's sure folk would rethink that if they knew his many travails and trials. Missteps. He wiggles toes, all seven of them; inside the big black boots he's obliged to wear here, he seems to still feel the one that's missing. Feels the absence of the left little one; it doesn't upset his balance too much anymore. Besides, there was so much to adapt to when he fled, it was the least of his worries. It barely registered beyond the pain when it was taken off, the portal closing its teeth a little too soon, a little too late.

I'm late, I'm late, I'm late.

Rabbit looks around. The place is dimly lit, darkly decorated with striped wallpaper that's trying to make a break for it where wall meets ceiling, and small reddish-orange lanterns sit on sticky laminate tabletops; the leather-buttoned benches are tacky, too, both physically and decoratively. He prefers to sit at the bar, likes the stools because they make him feel taller, and he's less likely to be trapped against a table or in a booth. It would have been stylish, he supposes, back in the day, but he can't hazard a guess on precisely when that might have been. Still, he likes it, feels relatively safe there, the stuffy closeness is like the hugging safety of a burrow and there's an earthy smell, too, that almost reminds him of home.

Safe.

Safe-ish.

Not so safe that he doesn't keep glancing at the door whenever it opens. Not so safe that he doesn't already know he can exit quickly through the back office, the kitchen, the tiny men's room, and even tinier Ladies'. He knows what to look for in newcomers.

When he'd come through—and come through properly this time, not just jumping over the border then back again like a child on a dare or defying a parent who'd said *This far and no further*—he'd changed. Changed his shape to become like one of the humans. However, he wasn't entirely *solid*—not entirely three-dimensional, but flimsy, weightless as a playing card, feeling as if he turned side-on he might disappear. Not that the humans noticed—such a subtlety was beyond their blunt perceptions—but he knew this strange flatness, lightness, thinness afflicted the Queen's assassins, too. He could pick the bounty hunters from the way they moved, as if fearful a strong wind would carry them away.

"Another?" The barman's voice startles Rabbit, but he does his best not to show it; he smiles at the young man who wears a plain black shirt and matching jeans, no nametag, for this is a not a place where names matter. He's handsome in a rough sort of fashion; a good bath and some styling and he'd pass for civilised. Just the sort Rabbit used to like, over on the other side, although he finds he prefers the women here.

"Yes, please," says Rabbit softly, wistfully, "same again."

The barman has large hands, black hairs curl across the backs of his fingers; Rabbit imagines it's on his chest, too, a densely tangled inverted triangle, and thinks of the line of it that will surely travel from his belly button down to the loins. Not very muscular, slender, with ropey veins in his forearms that remind him of the Ace.

Oh, but he's melancholy tonight! Perhaps he should slow down on the whiskey. Perhaps not.

Rabbit watches the barman surreptitiously at first, then realises the youth isn't interested, doesn't care if he's sized up or not; isn't the sort to take offence at being found attractive by another man. He's new here, Rabbit is certain, but he's not sure if he's feeling anything genuine or just an echo of once-upon-a-time.

When the door opens about an hour later, it lets in a rush of cold air and driving rain, and Rabbit tenses. He unhooks his heels from where they've been propped on the lower bars of the stool, ready to run.

It's just a girl.

Then he realises she's got a heart-shaped face, and for a moment his pulse quickens. But she's not a feeble thing, not a fragile card person, not one of the Queen's ladies-in-waiting or hunting hounds or assassins or executioners, or any of the range of professional murderers that woman employs. This girl is solid, walks with a weight on the earth as if she belongs there.

A heart-shaped face, thinks Rabbit, almost sadly. Thinks of the card-courtiers with their tattoos to mark out their belonging; that they are *owned.* Thinks of how pretty they were, embracing their servitude yet adding their own twist to it: changing their designs every week (although not the shapes—always hearts) to stay in fashion or ahead of it. He remembers the legions of artists kept to undertake such artwork, the best ones bartered away to the highest bidder for ever-more ridiculous favours (a cake frosted with fairy breath, a dress of sunlight embroidered with moonbeams, a necklace of a child's new teeth).

And he, moving amongst them—hadn't he been a perfectly good courtier and procurer? Obedient and biddable and loyal, bringing new toys as per the Queen's commands. All those fresh amusements and oddities, children from the other side, sometimes to cosset, sometimes to hunt, depending on Her Majesty's whim. And all he'd requested in return was that his foibles be overlooked, his peccadilloes go unpunished. Was that so much to ask?

The last one he'd brought through—just doing what he was told, mind you—that girl! Such trouble; how could he have known? They'd never been like that before. The child was everything the Queen had demanded—a challenge!—yet she'd not been prepared for the consequences.

Hadn't he said? For years. Hadn't he warned? All those times. He'd told her in his most polite, courtly manner how wild the creatures were, no matter that they looked like butter wouldn't melt in their mouths. *So much the better,* the Queen had shrieked. *Adds spice to the day, the hunt, the night!* And so it had, though more than anyone could have expected. It took ages to put the kingdom back together again, to re-establish order. And in the wreckage, all of Rabbit's sins were brought to light.

"Do you mind if I sit here?" A voice at his elbow—*what a stupid phrase,* thinks Rabbit—pulls him back. Not the barman this time, though he's gone and refilled the glass again at some point without asking. Rabbit could afford better booze; he makes good money trafficking just the way he did in the other world, but there's something louche about the cheap hooch that appeals.

He looks at the girl—woman, really, though young, youngish—a little blearily. Green eyes, muddy brown hair, unkempt eyebrows that are almost a single entity, freckles sprinkled across a nose that's been broken and healed not as well as it might, and the trace of a scar on the right cheek, a fine raised line old enough to have turned white. Perfect teeth, though, and pretty mouth. Her dress is brown, a strange sack of a thing, some kind of coarse linen with a wide deep pocket across the belly, almost like a pouch; perhaps something so haute couture that it doesn't need to worry about being pretty. Comfortable in its ugliness.

Rabbit doesn't know enough about fashion to make an informed decision. He only knows he misses his stiff collar, starched shirt, and tidy waistcoat. And the gold watch, which was the first thing he sold off when he came through, the only thing of value he managed to bring, and something he misses like a limb (even more than the toe). Something he's never been able to find again, no matter how many pawn shops he visits. He thinks regretfully of the treasure rooms of Wonderland, all the gold coins and gemstones stamped with the head of the Queen, their eyes following you everywhere. Then again, the idea of carrying those around . . . might they not act as spies? As beacons for

Her Majesty's assassins? Something that would help the hunters find him?

"Is it all right? If I sit here? I shan't bother you, only I don't like the booths, they always feel like a trap!" She giggles and the sound is infectious. Rabbit laughs, too, in spite of himself.

The girl-woman is nothing like his type, the female type at least. He prefers them more matronly and wonders if he still yearns for the aloofness of the Queen, the untouchableness of her, and the mysteries hidden forever beneath her voluminous skirts. But the laughter is like a sudden drug, a drink from a quick silver stream, a ray of sunshine breaking through clouds.

"Of course," he says with rusty grace, a shyness not common to him. Rabbit ponders that—usually he's *smooth.* Usually, he doesn't have to try too hard; he's short but pretty with thick white-blond hair, pert nose, rosebud mouth, and muscular body—he's going soft around the belly, beneath the chin, but he does okay, can still attract women to his bed and children to points of sale. He's fine for now.

The girl smiles, no idea of what's going on in Rabbit's head. She offers her hand, which bears many healed scars, fresh scratches. She notices his gaze and says, "I'm Pleasance and I work as a gardener." By way of explanation she adds darkly, "Roses."

"Ah. I'm Ned." *Tonight* he is Ned; he has a range of identities, different ones in each city he inhabits. "Can I buy you a drink, Pleasance?"

He assumes this is what she wants. She could have sat anywhere, there are plenty of vacant stools, but she came to him. His nerves are soothed, his confidence firms. *She wants.*

"Why, yes you may, Ned." She leans close, maintains eye contact. "The cheaper, the better."

He laughs in surprise.

"A place like this requires cheap booze," Pleasance says, eyeing the faded velvet wallpaper, and Rabbit can't help but smile with delight.

They chat and flirt and laugh. Rabbit talks about his import-export business but doesn't mention the true nature of the goods. Pleasance confesses that while she loves gardening, she does hate the roses; they're beautiful but treacherous, not to be trusted. They move closer and closer without seeming to do so, and at some point Rabbit realises their arms and hips are touching and he can't think how long they've been like that. He can feel her every breath, every tremble, every giggle shivering through her. She smells like some exotic blend of tea.

It's almost an hour before he notices something strange about the pocket of her ugly dress. He looks down, cocks his head, and watches. Every few seconds there's a jerk, a twitch, in the right-hand corner, sometimes it bumps against his thigh; a small rhythmic pulse, like a frog in a sock. Pleasance, reaching for yet another drink, courtesy of the barman, sees the direction of his gaze and follows it.

She smiles suggestively and says, "Do you want to see what I've got?"

He's nodding when the door opens again, and the rain and wind blow in, far too easily, three thin men. Rabbit knows them immediately for what they are; with barely a thought he grabs the girl's hand and yanks her from her stool. She doesn't fight but follows, crouching down as he does so they are concealed by the bar. Rabbit's credit card is by the cash register, but he doesn't care. It's one of many in an identity he'll easily discard; there are more pieces of plastic in his wallet. They make it into the Ladies', and soon Rabbit is offering his interlocked hands so Pleasance can use them as a step and slip out of the small window. He watches her backside wiggle and is momentarily distracted from his panic.

In the alley, they lurch, then run like naughty children, fingers entwined. Perhaps Pleasance thinks it a game; they've had a lot to drink and Rabbit knows that inhibitions and caution are the first things to flee in the face of the alcoholic flood. When he detects no sign of pursuit after four blocks, he slows; his lungs are burning. He's out of shape, but the girl isn't puffing, she's laughing that joyous laugh again. She leans against a wall, still holding his hand; he swings in, presses his lips to hers, she responds, curls her arms around him, her hands up to the back of his neck—and then there's a sharp, unconceivable pain and he passes out.

* * *

"Rabbit? Oh, Rabbit? Wake up."

The voice sing-songs but cuts right through him. His headache is so great that he doesn't pause to consider who might know his true name. His mouth is dry, blood pulses hard in his ears; he feels fractured. The voice comes again, sharper this time, impatient. Rabbit opens his eyes with an effort that's like prising open a window with a crowbar. The light is blinding and he blinks, blinks, blinks until its bite lessens. Until the pain recedes and objects begin to resolve themselves into pieces of furniture: stylish sofas, an architectural coffee table, framed paintings that look suspiciously expensive, light fittings cleverly recessed into the walls, a fireplace with copper screens and blue-orange flames in the hearth licking obscenely at each other. Rabbit tries to move, but he's tied to a chair; beneath his mutilated now-bare feet is a plush rug, Kandinsky-patterned.

He'd have expected to wake—if he woke at all—in some abandoned warehouse in a bad part of town. He'd have expected to be cold and wet and uncomfortable; as it is he's warm and not completely uncomfortable, but he smells very bad indeed. No blood as far as he can tell. Not yet.

His field of vision expands beyond his immediate surroundings. There is an enormous patio outside the sliding glass doors, and a silhouette blocks his view of the Manhattan skyline where dawn is threatening. The outline is blurred at first, then firms up, comes into focus.

A girl.

Pleasance, but not.

The girl.

But not as she was, or not most recently.

The girl as he first saw her when he lay in wait; when he first hopped across her path as she curled on the riverbank beside her bookworm sister; hopping and tutting "Oh dear! Oh dear! I shall be late!" knowing that children can't resist either a bunny rabbit or a mystery.

A blue flounced dress with a white apron, the pockets of which are trimmed with red, black shiny shoes and white stockings, waves of golden hair held in place with an ebony velvet band. The same outfit, but the girl is taller now, just a little, strangely grown, strangely childlike. The scar on the cheek remains, the bump in the nose; she wears her markings with pride. She's human, she never looked like the playing card people, had the right weight, the right heft to fool him.

"Rabbit," she says almost tenderly. "Rabbit, do you remember me?"

"Alice."

"After all these years! Very good." She smiles but there's no true mirth in it.

"What are you doing? Here? Now? You escaped. You went back to the other side."

"Oh, yes, I did, but time moves differently between the worlds, Rabbit, as you well know. When I got home too many years had passed, everyone I'd loved was dead or almost so, their memories crumbled to dust and cobwebs. There was nothing left for me. So, I returned to Wonderland."

"You destroyed the kingdom," he says, then runs his tongue along his teeth to see if any are broken. He wasn't hit; perhaps a Taser—that would explain how fast he went down, why he lost control of himself, why his brain feels so scattered.

She shakes her head, the golden hair shimmering. "Disrupted, that's all. An easy thing to rebuild. Anyway, after what *you* did my sins were barely remembered. Besides, your Queen and I found we had a common goal."

"Alice . . ."

"She wasn't happy about you and her son. You should have known better."

"The Ace. My Ace."

"Not actually yours, the Queen's lovely boy, her bargaining card, a pristine husband for the King of Spades' daughter, an alliance that might have settled much of the infighting. But you dirtied him up, didn't you? Took that lovely virtuous shine off him."

"They'd never have found out but for you, never come looking for me at such an inopportune moment if you'd not wreaked such havoc. Wasn't that revenge enough?"

"No," Alice says quite simply. "I lost everything. How many other children over the years have you led astray, you shitty little bunny? Why do you deserve compassion when you showed none yourself?"

"Please, Alice."

The left-hand pocket of her apron judders again and again. She notices him noticing once more, and digs her slender scarred fingers into the fabric depths. "Do you want to see? Do you want to know how I found you?"

He nods reluctantly.

Alice pulls out the end of a golden chain. She keeps pulling, pulling, pulling until his precious lost gold watch is revealed and, hanging from the end of the links, is his severed toe. Still furred, the cut end pink and fleshy as if it had only been removed an hour ago. The thing twitches and jumps, trembles and thumps against the watch casing.

"You left this behind. The Queen was reluctant to let me have it—she's fond of wearing it as a pendant—but I told her that if she parted with it I'd bring back your entire skin and she could do with it what she wanted."

Rabbit closes his eyes in relief; he'll be dead before he reaches the Queen of Hearts. It won't matter what she does with his corpse. He won't feel it, he won't care.

"But," says Alice, and Rabbit cringes at the glee in her tone. "But I think she won't mind so terribly if I bring you back alive and in one—well, two—pieces and let her watch while I skin you. I'm a dab hand, nowadays." There's a moment when it seems she changes, back to her sack-like linen dress, which is now made of fur, the pocket *is* a pouch, something she's harvested from another such as he—how could he not have noticed? "But sometimes it takes a while. A long while before you die, Rabbit."

Alice listens to him weep. She wonders if he'll cry as many tears as she did when she was small and lost and so far from home. She doubts it, but she'll do her damnedest to make sure he comes close. She looks at his thick white-blond hair and nods.

He'll make a fine cloak; the Queen will be pleased.

IN MEMORY OF A SUMMER'S DAY

Matthew Kressel

He's twelve, yes?" I say to the smiling couple from Kyoto as their child looks up at me fearfully.

"Yes," his mother insists, flashing me a toothy grin. "Just last week!"

I'd bet fifty quid and my last Chesterfield the kid's not even nine, but I just smile and pull the rope aside to let the boy and his parents leap down the rabbit hole together. Their screams and laughter fade as they fall, while the queue presses ever closer to me. The languid river beside us glitters prismatically in the afternoon light, sending a flurry of rainbows across their anxious and eager faces. Among them I spot half a dozen kids of questionable age, but I've got orders to let everyone in now. Old, young, disabled, senile, deranged. Everyone but infants. And sometimes even them.

They come from all over: Japan, Brazil, Norway, China, Nigeria, Russia, Singapore, Yemen, South Korea, the States, the UK, plus lots of elsewheres and elsewhens. Wonderland has become one of the Things to See Before You Die, like the Matterhorn and the Grand Canyon and the Great Wall of China. They come in dusty coaches, packed to near-bursting, that pull right up to the River Isis and befoul the once-sweet air with carbonized exhaust. The coaches vomit out dozens of people onto the riverbank, once so quiet you could hear the delicate sound of leaves brushing the ground in autumn. Now there's a franchise cafe selling sandwiches and espresso, fifty sets of metallic tables rusting under towering elms, and two dozen bright kiosks offering everything from

Cheshire Chocolates to CDs with studio-recorded tracks of "Beautiful Soup" and the "Lobster Quadrille." The garbage cans always overflow.

After de-busing, a few kids inevitably cry. Adults and children rush to the lavatories. Pinafores are purchased and donned. Mediocre coffee is bought for exorbitant prices. Parents wrinkle their noses as they examine free maps (which are less maps than warnings), while spouses look on uneasily.

Are you sure you want to do this? You've heard the stories.

Don't worry. Don't worry.

Tickets are £186.40 per person, adults and children alike, sold only on location, on the day of arrival, discounts unavailable, admission never guaranteed. And all must sign a waiver absolving Wonderland of any harm, physical, mental, or otherwise, that might befall them while there.

The wise read the waiver first, but everyone always signs. None can resist the lure for long, because even though they think they know what awaits them down the rabbit hole, it's never quite what they've imagined. And after, no one's ever quite the same.

I go down there twelve times a day.

I've been leading tours of Wonderland for forty years, though it feels like twice that. And though my bones ache and my knees throb, my retirement's a distant ship on the horizon that might just be a floater in my vision. A lucrative job this isn't, and I've got spousal maintenance payments, a crushing amount of debt, and various court orders to consider. Plus, the boss has, let's just say, more *pressing* things keeping me here. In other words, I'm trapped.

I predict one day I'll just keel over in the middle of the Croquet Ground or collapse into the Duchess's manger. I wonder if they'll take my body back to Earth, bury me in Wonderland, or just flush me down the Pool of Tears. Some days I'm convinced the entire realm will suddenly go up in flames with everyone inside, myself included, like some virtual particle evanescing. The thought is not entirely unwelcome.

* * *

I'm on tour nine of twelve, we're in the Hall of Doors, and I'm so bloody knackered I could fall asleep standing up. But the show must go on. I yawn and cross my arms and lean against one of the hundreds of locked and mismatched doors, checking the time on my mobile (no signal), as my group of thirty-nine grows and shrinks and laughs and shrieks as they sample the food and drink on the table.

Back in the old days, we used to take hundreds at a time. But now we cap it at forty persons so we can more or less keep an eye on everyone, this ever since that poor boy guzzled all of the Drink Me fluid, even though we have signs in twelve languages warning people to take but a sip. He howled as he shrunk and vanished, and though we scoured the hall for days, his body was never found. To this day I still sometimes hear a faint squeal when I enter the Hall of Doors, and while I suspect it's Mouse having a laugh, I always look twice before I step there.

It tastes like rosewater! one says.

Gingerbread! says another.

In runs the White Rabbit, saying, "Oh, the Duchess, the Duchess, she'll be savage I've kept her!"

Damn. Rabbit's mussed the line, and though I doubt more than a handful have noticed, a few among the tour wrinkle their noses and frown. If the boss finds out, she'll be livid. I can't manage another inquisition. Underneath Rabbit's layers of makeup and dye, he's a little ruffled around the ears. The edges of his coat are tattered, and as he scurries past, dropping his fan and gloves, he smells strongly of whiskey. During today's lunch, he told me he's down to three flasks a day from upwards of seven, lauding himself as if this were great progress. But, I thought, what happens after zero? Beyond lurks only a great void, like Wonderland's starless sky, and when Rabbit wasn't looking I took a deep draught from his flask.

When he vanishes down the hall, saltwater trickles in from under the door frames to pool around our ankles. My group giggles nervously at first, but when the water reaches waists, their faces turn sober.

It's cold! they shout, smiles fading.

By the time it reaches the children's shoulders, out swims Mouse, paddling furiously. Some shriek. (Mouse is a mouse, after all.) And just like the story, a few wags try their French on him, and he feigns fright and darts off before returning. The kids, floating easily in the salt-water, adore him. And though Mouse is masterful with an audience, I watch him closely. He's on parole for petty larceny, and though he's been nothing but kind to me all these years, I keep a tight hand on my wallet as he swims past.

The water keeps rising, and by the time Duck and Dodo swirl by, you can see in the people's eyes they're thinking on the rumours again, the ones they've heard but didn't believe or conveniently forgot. But now they're worrying that maybe they should've read that map of warnings a little more carefully, and really, what *had* they gotten their families into?

Hold on to me! parents shout, scaring the kids, and their sudden burst of tears feeds the pool for my next tour.

As they shout and slosh and flail, the Eaglet pauses before me. Without words, I slip him fifty quid under the rushing waters, and he slips me two grams of the finest psychedelic mushrooms Wonderland has to offer, before swimming on.

Few seem to know or remember that Mouse will soon dry them on the riverbank with a lecture about *William the Conqueror,* because the parents are still panicking. The kids are still crying. With this, at least, the boss will be pleased.

I have a thousand rules I must follow, but the paramount one is this: *Under no circumstances must one ever stop the show.*

One afternoon many years ago, my tour came upon the Mock Turtle, who had somehow rigged up this enormous boulder to come crashing down upon his shell. It was meant to kill him—and it did, but only after his smashed body bled crimson soup all over the rocks for the better part of a day. The Gryphon, upon seeing the bloody mess, snorted and said perhaps it was best if the Mock Turtle died, because, really, everyone was so damned tired of his empty sorrow anyway.

I panicked and ran off to find help and left my frightened and bewildered tour to the vagaries of Wonderland. Some wandered away to drown or be eaten. Some were found naked and laughing in the forest, pulling out tufts of their hair. More than a dozen went missing and were never found.

The boss sat down with the ones we recovered and had what she termed "deep conversations" with them all. None of us heard what was spoken, though we had our intimations, because each emerged from their meetings with a curiously confused expression on their faces, as if they weren't quite sure what had just occurred, and as we escorted them back to their coaches and cars they seemed not quite sure even *who* they were.

And when the boss got finally to me, let's just say I *wish* I could forget what she'd done. But she made bloody well sure I remembered. Seldom a night goes by where I don't wake up screaming, dreaming of her teeth.

A few decades back I was still married, had all my hair, and my daughter had just turned seven. I'd finished my last tour, had a newly lit joint dangling from my lips, and was pulling out of the car park when a playing card suddenly appeared on my dashboard, causing me to swerve. There were too many people left waiting, the boss had scrawled on the back of the Queen of Hearts, and I was to do a thirteenth tour. I cursed and screamed as I pulled my car back into its reserved rectangle by the riverbank, and I punched the steering wheel so hard my knuckles bled. (I still have the scars.)

It was late afternoon and the rays of the blazing orange sun cut the forest into ribbons. It wasn't yet autumn, but the air was crisp and held an early chill unusual for the season.

I remember noting the shine of her black hair, her faint freckles, but most of all the way her blue eyes shone like translucent marbles. She clutched a natty grey stuffed-animal cat to her belly, and she approached me and the rabbit hole only after severe coaxing from her parents.

But I'm scared, Mummy. I'm scared.

Thinking back now, I wonder if she sensed the menace waiting below. But down they went, and it was only after the tour had reached the Caterpillar on his toadstool that I noticed she was missing. Her parents chuckled at the Caterpillar's witticisms, and politely waited their turn to sample the body-altering mushroom, but they seemed otherwise unaware of their absent child. I looked around, thinking she might have wandered off, but there was no way I would stop the tour, not after what the boss had done to me the last time. And so I led them on.

By the time the tour awoke from the shower of playing cards to wipe their groggy eyes and find themselves on the riverbank, the sun had set, the cafe had closed, and two idling coaches and a handful of cars waited in the once-full car park. Each person was given a pocket mirror, a discount voucher for the *Through the Looking-Glass Tour,* and a firm shove. The people wandered off, stunned and disoriented. Had the world changed, or had they?

It stood beside her parents, unsteady in the wind, a patchwork girl fashioned from mouldy leather and fraying twine, with marbles for eyes. I waited for her parents to wake and say, *This is not our little girl.*

Instead, with beatific smiles, they drifted away, holding the thing's hand. And I knew that in a week or a month this patchwork thing would disintegrate like cardboard in rain, and they'd come to think their child had died from some unknown and incurable disease, when she would be elsewhere alive and very much unwell. If Wonderland wants you, it takes you, and there's nothing you nor I nor anyone can do. And though I knew this well, my heart broke as I watched them go, and so I turned back and jumped down the hole.

Wonderland's checkerboard forest was already dark, the horizon limned with overlapping waves of purple and emerald, and the locusts were making an unholy racket by the time I reached the Caterpillar in his treehouse at the edge of the forest. Patron saint of all pot-smoking college students everywhere, the Caterpillar has been sober since the late '70s (he smokes an inert herb mixture on-shift), and he hasn't liked me very much ever since he discovered how much I partake of Wonderland's chemical fruits. So when I asked after the missing girl, he was less than forthcoming.

"She's just a child," the Caterpillar snapped, "and therefore perfectly expendable." Then he went back to reading his Dostoyevsky in reverse and would say no more.

But I couldn't accept this, and so I darted off in search of her. I scoured the Croquet Ground, the Duchess's house, the Queen's Court, and soon found myself in the murky woods, calling for her. I didn't know her name, but I knew she was here, lost and terrified, and that I was the only one who could find her.

Animals answered my calls: birds, rodents, insects, and other things I could not name, but which made me think that making loud noises was maybe not such a good idea, and that wandering into these dark woods, alone and without a light or weapon of any sort was perhaps the stupidest thing a man might do. I fell quiet, but I went on searching.

The woods were so dark that soon I couldn't see ten inches in front of my face, and the air was so thick and humid it felt as if I were not walking through a forest but swimming at the bottom of a deep and lifeless sea. I held up my hands so as not to slam my nose into something, and my ankles and shoes grew waterlogged from traipsing through the dewy grasses and puddles of mud.

I heard her cry faintly at first, but it grew louder as I followed it, stumbling as I went over twigs and stones and soft, wet things the size of small dogs that slithered away unseen in the dark. The air smelled thickly of mouldy earth and fragrant roses and a not-too-distant salty sea.

I stumbled again, and it felt as if someone had stuck out their leg to trip me. I lay on the ground staring up at the empty sky as my body slowly sank into the warm mud.

"It's me," someone whispered softly in my ear. And though I had only heard her voice once, I knew it was the missing girl. "Will you stay with me?" she said as a small, cold hand gently lay on my forearm. "We can stare up at the stars together."

But there were no stars. I wanted to rise, but could only lay there as her hot breath fell upon my cheek. I heard a massive gurgle of wet slithering in the mud nearby, as if an army of giant slugs were fast approaching. Warm, wet creatures crawled onto my feet and legs, covering them. They climbed onto my chest, enwrapping me in their wet warmth, and when they finally closed over my face, I tried to scream. But I could only lay there like a rotting tree.

"They want to be our friends," the girl whispered. "Can they be our friends, Daddy? Can we play with them, forever and ever?" She giggled and whispered things to me I couldn't quite hear, while the things on my body shivered warmly, and my head was filled with dark dreams.

I don't know how long I lay there before I rose from the ground. I grabbed the girl's arm and stumbled with her through the dark forest toward home. It wasn't until I had reached the riverbank, under the sickly light of Earth's crescent moon, that I realized I didn't hold the girl's arm, but the leg of her grey stuffed-animal cat. Its eyes were gouged out, and it was covered in pearlescent slime.

I'm on tour twelve of twelve (at last), we're in the Duchess's house, the Baby Pig is weeping, and I'm leaning against the door frame, barely able to stand. I was saving my last Chesterfield for the end of my shift, but bloody hell, I can't wait anymore. I light it and blow smoke out the door as the Cheshire Cat goes through his shtick and vanishes, leaving behind his trademark smile.

Like the call-and-response of church, the group recites, *Well! I've often seen a cat without a grin, but a grin without a cat! It's the most curious thing . . .*

They laugh and rub their children's heads, as if to reassure them that the terrible frights they've had today, the bizarre and growing sensation that they've become something not quite themselves, that they will never be the same person again, that something small and very much alive has niggled its way into their minds and will live there, growing, festering, forever, was all worth it just for *this* fleeting moment. And here it's always the children who notice first, who ask about the one who's been missing all along.

But, Mummy, where is she? Where is Alice?

Then all eyes turn to me, hopeful, expectant, with a twinge of fear. *Yes,* they ask with a hint of desperation, because they cannot fathom why they haven't considered this very obvious question themselves. *Where is Alice?*

I flick my cigarette away and pull out a pocket mirror. I hold it up to their faces and make sure each catches their own distorted reflection within it. "To find your Alice," I say, "look no further than a glass. For if you ask yourself, 'Where might she be?' the answer, quite plainly is, 'She, it seems, is me.' "

This satisfies some and frustrates others, the girls in their blue-and-white pinafores most of all, these poor kids who have been told endless tales and have read countless books, and have bragged to all their friends about this impending moment, only to realize it wasn't anything like what they had expected, that there's a curious emptiness at the heart of it all, that just maybe they've been lied to all along, or at the very least have been told countless exaggerations, none of which could ever approach the empty truth: there is no magic here, only chaos.

Some look sickened. Others cry. Still others become lost in a faraway dream they might never fully wake from.

We move on to the Tea Party (it lasts a small eternity), the Croquet Ground (the hedgehogs' screams make my flesh crawl), the Mock Turtle (brought back from the dead, don't ask me how), the Lobster Quadrille (where some show off their dancing), the Queen's Court (in which everyone on my tour is sentenced to death, then immediately pardoned), and at last the Pack of Cards (which sends them flying back to Earth, forever changed and bewildered, but with discount vouchers for the next tour) and, hallelujah, I'm done at last.

Seven of Diamonds lights a fag and I bum one from him. He's all creased and worn, and his painted colours have long-since faded to grey. "Come for a drink?" he says, exhaling smoke from the back of his paper frame. He tends We're All Mad Here, a small pub on a blue-grass checker of the forest beside a bubbling brook. "Three-C's playing tonight," he says as he takes a drag, and by this he means Three of Clubs, who's a mean guitarist and an even meaner drunk.

I know I should go home. But there's nothing there but my mouldering bed sheets, an empty fridge, and a picture of my daughter on the dresser that's slowly turning ashen like Seven of Diamonds. I'd just go home, eat some take-out, and pass out watching TV, only to wake up from yet another nightmare, only to return tomorrow to do this again. So I go to Seven's for some drinks and listen to Three-C jam for a few hours, until I can barely keep my eyes open.

Eventually I leave Seven's bar and stumble along the dark path that will take me back to Earth. Along the way, I pass the familiar stone house set high upon the hill, its windows flickering with orange light that sends long, foggy beams deep into the evening mist. My feet turn before I know where I'm going, and soon I'm climbing through the corkscrew path through the flower garden set alight by a million swarming glow bugs. I shouldn't be here, not without her permission, but I just can't stop. There is a stone underneath one of the flickering windows, and I step upon it to ever so carefully peek through the glass.

The fireplace is bright with flame, though there are no logs to burn. Above the fireplace, on a decorated mantel, are several glass-domed clocks, all ticking, and a large, flawless mirror that perfectly reflects the room. A girl in a blue-and-white pinafore paces on a circle of carpet before the fire, and every so often as the light plays across her face it's clear she's not quite a girl but a woman much, much older.

Above the circle of carpet, about waist high, held aloft by nothing at all, is a crystal sphere about the size of a grapefruit. And inside the sphere is a flickering nebula, neither jade, nor rose, nor teal, but a swirling mélange of all three colours that changes shape and shade continually.

"Tell me again," she says, and hers is the voice of a little girl, of an elderly woman, of one who holds utter contempt and the deepest admiration for the man whom she addresses. "Tell me the story again one more time."

And from inside the floating sphere comes a faint, wheezy voice, the sound of a sick man near death and perhaps beyond it, a man who wishes his soul could fly off to the next world, but is prevented from doing so by forces I don't even pretend to understand.

Slowly, he begins, "Alice . . . was beginning to get very tired . . . of sitting by her sister on the bank, and . . . of having nothing to do . . ."

At this, the ancient little girl rubs her hands together. She giggles and skips, and Kitty, curled on the rocking chair, stirs awake, then goes back to sleep. And it's this small motion that crushes me with despair. Despair for Kitty, so inured to this abhorrent sin she can only sleep. Despair for poor Mr. Dodgson, imprisoned in his floating sphere for all time. Despair for myself and for all of us trapped in this dreadful place. But most of all I despair for old Ms. Alice Pleasance Liddell. Because though she wears no chains, everyone knows she's imprisoned too.

After a time, I step down from the stone and slink away from the window. My buzz has faded, and I want a fag more than anything in the world. It's late, and I'm more tired than I've ever felt. I really should be getting home and getting to bed.

And it's about this time every night when I start to wonder if I even have a home or a bed to lie in, if I was ever married or had a daughter. Maybe these are just stories I tell myself to get through the day. But I brush aside these thoughts as if I'm swatting away smoke. I really have to get some sleep. I've got work early tomorrow.

SENTENCE LIKE A SATURDAY

Seanan McGuire

Doors
    Doors swing
  Doors swing both ways.

Doors swing both ways, yes, that's physics, that's *logic,* nasty creeping crawling clinging *logic* that gets into all the cracks and crevices of a concept like sand inside a swimming suit. If something doesn't swing both ways, it's not a door. It's a hatch, it's a gate, it's a barrier, it's an accident of space and time and cruel causality. It's not a *door.* Doors. Swing. Both. Ways.

Doors can look like something that's not a door, because doors are tricky. Doors are traps masquerading as opportunities. So a little girl tumbles down a rabbit hole or stumbles through a mirror and ah! That's the door, that's the trap snapping shut, jaws of the Jabberwock claiming its prey. That's the story starting. Stories are doors, you see. Stories swing both ways. Can't trust stories. Can't trust doors. Can't trust anything, not once logic gets involved.

So *snap!* go the jaws, and *slam!* go the doors, and a little girl falls down a hole, and something else falls up, because doors swing both ways, and if something has gone in, something else must come out. There are rules to these things. Wicked, awful rules.

The rules say "cats do not speak."

The rules say "if a thing can think for itself, why, it must be a person, and to be a person, a thing must look like *so,* and stand like *so,* and tie ribbons in its hair like *so,*" and suddenly the something that came out of the hole is a little girl, because the rules say it must be, and the rules are not to be denied, however much they should be. However much they burn to be.

Doors swing both ways.

The little girl who should not have been a little girl sat in the dust in front of the burrow, trying to sort through what had just happened. It was all very perplexing, and she did not care for it, no, not at all. Where was her fur? Where were her claws? It occurred to her that they might have gone off on an adventure together, seeking her whiskers and tail, which were equally missing, and equally missed.

"No," she said petulantly, and clapped her hands over her mouth, which was entirely the wrong shape, and entirely lacking in proper teeth, or a proper tongue—or, it seemed, a proper yowl. She was accustomed to speaking as the humans did. All things in Wonderland could speak as the humans did, when they so chose. But she was also accustomed to having a strong meow at her disposal, and it seemed to have absented itself along with the rest of her.

"This will not do," she said, and stood, wobbling on unfamiliar legs, feet pinched by unfamiliar shoes. The sunlight shone through the leaves above her, casting dappled shadows on her skin, where the stripes should have been. She attempted to brush it away, and it refused to go, behaving more like light than like syrup or molasses or any of the other things that afternoon sunlight should have taken after. She scowled.

"This will not do *at all,*" she said, and turned to peer into the hole she'd toppled out of. It was quite small, large enough for a curious cat, but not for the most curious of little girls; her head alone would have been sufficient to block all passage. Still, she got down on her knees, unforgivably mussing her tights, and scrabbled at the dirt. The hole remained a hole, which was something different than a door, and might not put her where she needed to be.

"Might" was not the same as "wouldn't," and so she stuck her head into the hole, which rewarded her, not with passage home, but with a great deal of loose dirt. She recoiled, hissing and spitting in a way which would have been quite sensible in a cat, and was quite unreasonable in a little girl. She clawed at her head, blunted fingernails doing no damage as she dislodged clots of earth from behind her ears.

She glared at the hole. The hole did not respond.

"Why is a raven like a writing desk?" she demanded, before climbing back to her feet and walking briskly away. Let the traitor hole know the pain of a riddle unresolved, and see how proud it would be *then*!

Really, she felt quite cruelly revenged, and did not look back, not once.

It was quickly apparent to anyone with eyes that this world ran entirely and unreasonably on logic, and hadn't the sense to speed things along when it would have been narratively appropriate to do so. She walked across the field with locusts buzzing in her ears and dried grass whipping at her ankles, and it was dreadfully dull, and nothing of any importance was happening, and yet the scene didn't skip ahead. Time stretched out like a string, rather than compressing like an accordion, and she was quite done with walking, and her destination had yet to conveniently appear.

This wouldn't do. This wouldn't do at all. She stopped walking and sat down where she stood, giving the story the opportunity to catch up with her. Surely it would realize its error and begin misbehaving properly, getting to the interesting bits.

A bumblebee buzzed past, off on unknowable insect errands. Its body was fat, furry, striped in a way she could only envy. It did not sing. It did not speak. It did not stop to dance for her, or to challenge her to a game of riddles.

Fear twisted in her gut, unfamiliar as a needle in a butterscotch pudding. The rules of this world, whatever they were, seemed to be consistent and cruel: they were not nonsense, no, not nonsense at all. Why, she could sit here forever, and the story might never realize the error of its ways and come back to get her! She could grow up, grow old, grow forgotten, and all for what? For a sunlight sulk on the wrong side of a door. It was *quite* unfair.

Unfairness was only proper if someone else knew about it. That was what unfairness was *for.* It was to be brandished, advertised, bragged upon, shown off, because if the world was being *un*fair, then surely you were a personage deserving of better treatment. Why, this might even be enough unfairness to buy her a dish of cod and cream! The thought was enough to get her feet back under her, and then moving besides, until she was striding across the field with a newfound sense of purpose. She was going to find someone. She was going to Make a Complaint. Yes! And once it was made, everything would be sorted. The hole would be taught the error of its ways and would become a door once more, and she would be able to go home, where things were sensibly senseless, and no one insisted she be anything but what she was.

The field went on for quite some time, persistently refusing to yield to narrative pressure, until finally, with neither barrier nor battle, it ended at a close-cropped expanse of green. She paused before cautiously tapping the new surface with her foot. It proved to be solid, and not a swamp, or a discolored lake, or a very large frog lying in wait for an easy meal. She stepped onto it.

On the other side of the green was a house. It was small, and tidy, and altogether boring, with a roof on the top and a porch around the bottom, and windows gleaming in the sunlight. Bunting hung on lines behind it, white and flapping in the wind. It was dull enough to become interesting, for houses this straightforward were virtually never seen in her homeland, and so she started toward it, sniffing the air, shoulders hunched, obeying the instincts of a body she didn't currently have.

A door at the back of the house opened. She shied away, suddenly afraid. Doors swung both ways, after all. What if she found herself pulled through this new door to balance the load, and wound up one step further from her home, from her stripes and whiskers and proper place?

A woman emerged. The door swung shut, apparently content to serve as egress only. The woman took a few steps before she stopped, spotting the girl on her lawn.

"Oh, my," she said, and her voice was soft and gentle, and her words were straightforward and plain, impossible to tie into ribbons. "Hello there. Are you lost?"

"Are you lost?" echoed the girl. Sometimes that was the proper thing to do with riddles, and this *must* be a riddle, because clearly, she was not lost at all: clearly, she was standing exactly where she was, and if anything, she was found.

The woman looked perplexed. "No, sweetheart, I'm not. This is my home. What's your name? Where are your parents?"

Too many questions and too many answers and none of them made proper nonsense. The girl decided she wasn't going to play this game until she knew the rules. Drawing herself up straight and tall, she said, "I am a Cheshire cat, and my parents are far away, doing whatever pleases them."

"You're from Cheshire? Why, that's a hundred miles from here! They just left you on your own?"

The girl preened. "They knew I was clever enough to survive, and so they washed their claws of me. I might see them again someday, but then again, I might not. Who you'll meet each day is one of the greatest riddles of them all."

"You poor dear. Come inside. There's cold beef from last night, and lemonade, and bread. I can feed you."

"Is there butter?" the girl asked hopefully.

The woman was surprised into a laugh. "Of course there's butter, silly girl. Come inside."

The girl, who knew many ways of spotting danger, but not all of them—not enough to spot a door in the shape of a hole, or a trap in the shape of a farmwife—nodded and trotted across the green, toward the farmhouse, toward the door that looked like a door, and nothing else. Nothing else at all.

That night, belly full, body swimming in an old shift of the woman's—whose name was Agnes, and wasn't that a solid, sensible name for a solid, sensible person—the girl lay drowsily in the spare room, struggling to keep her eyes from closing. They didn't want to listen to her. Fighting sleep was not a feline thing to do; she had no practice at it.

But Agnes, in the other room, was speaking with a man, whose name was Wesley, and they were talking about her. It seemed better to stay awake than to go to sleep. It really did.

Oh, but she was yawnsome.

"—just a little girl. Her parents left her."

"So she says, Agnes. Do you want to go to prison for kidnapping?"

"It's not kidnapping if we take her in until her parents come for her. She's a pretty thing. Surely *someone* will come looking, and she's safer here, with us, than she is out wandering the world, where anyone could take advantage of her."

Those words, "take advantage," seemed ugly somehow, like they, too, hid a door that swung both ways, one which led into a room she would not like to see. The girl allowed her eyes to close. She would be safe here, until the door opened. Until she could go home.

She would be safe.

The next morning, the little girl who was not a little girl woke to the smell of pancakes and frying eggs. She rose, untangling the sleeves of her borrowed shift, and moved toward the bedroom door. It held no terrors for her now. Either the other side would be farmhouse and farmwife and kitchen filled with breakfast, or it would be the route home. There was no in-between, not once *logic* had come to the table. Why, in a world ruled by logic, tadpoles would always grow into frogs, and never once into dragons, or Jabberwocks, or clerical assistants!

It must be very dull, living in a logical world. The desire not to be in one any longer was nearly stronger than the urge toward pancakes as she opened the door and stepped out into a very ordinary, logical room.

Tears sprang to her eyes, burning hot and altogether unfamiliar. She blinked them away hard, moving toward the promising smell of breakfast. Her stomach rumbled. It might not be cod and cream, but it would do. It would do.

Agnes was standing in the farmhouse kitchen, next to the farmhouse stove, and she was smiling, and the little girl who was not a little girl adored and feared her all at the same time. "Good morning, sleepy-head," she said. "Can you set the table?"

A riddle! That was a fine start to a morning. "A table's proper setting is in the kitchen," she said slowly, "and it looks to weigh more than I do. So no, I cannot set the table, for it is already settled, but I can sit, and having done, will have sat, and I a cat, which means to take a chair is to set the table." She beamed, confident in the quality of her answer.

Agnes blinked. "I mean for you to lay out the dishes and the cutlery, dear, so we can eat," she said. "Move smartly now; Wesley's leaving for the fields soon, and he needs his breakfast."

Feeling chastened, the girl began placing plates and forks in their proper spots. She knew how to set a table by logical rules: the Red Queen insisted on everything being *just so* when she was hosting a banquet, and it was impossible to throw things into proper disarray without knowing what array was.

Agnes turned away from the stove and blinked again, this time in amazement. The nameless child had set the table as perfectly and precisely as if she expected the Queen herself to come to breakfast. "Well," she said. "Someone taught you manners. Are you sure you don't remember your name?"

"I am a Cheshire cat," said the little girl.

"Kitty it is, then," said Agnes, and then the door opened—doors, damned doors—and Wesley appeared, and breakfast unfolded around the three of them like a flower opening in the sun, leaving farmwife and farmer well content, and a little girl who was still not a little girl, but who now bore a little girl's name, staring in dizzy confusion at the wall.

The pancakes smelled delicious. She took a bite, despite her confusion, and then she was eating in great gulps and swallows, while Agnes and Wesley smiled over her head, suddenly content with their world.

Doors swing both ways.

The rabbit hole, which had been a door, was still in the same place, nestled snug among the roots of an old oak tree. Kitty heaved a sigh of relief. It had been a week since her arrival at the farm, a week of increasing chores and questions shaped like riddles, but which somehow seemed to have a right and a wrong answer, as if each one were a door, to be opened by only one key. Seven days. That was how long it had taken for her to get an afternoon to herself, to convince Agnes she wasn't running away, merely going for a walk.

The hole seemed very small. Kitty knelt and peered into it. "Hello?" she called. "Little girl, little girl, where have you been? I seem to have found your life. I don't want it."

But that wasn't right, now, was it? Agnes and Wesley had no children of their own, only three little crosses in a thicket well behind the farmhouse, each marked with a name and two dates, terribly close together. Logic was such a cruel Queen to serve. The little girl who *was* a little girl, who had opened a door and consigned Kitty to this place, had come from a different farmhouse, a different life. Somewhere, another Agnes, another Wesley, waited for their daughter to come home.

The first thread of doubt wove its way through Kitty's heart. If she left now, if she walked out, walked away, found a door, Agnes would cry, wouldn't she? Surely she would, yes, surely she would weep and weep, thinking her foundling snatched up by bandits or devoured by a Bandersnatch. Wesley wouldn't cry, but he would attack the fields like they had wronged him, tilling rocks from the soil until his hands bled.

This wasn't her life. She didn't want it. But with every day that passed, it held on a little harder, holding her in place, holding her down.

"Come back," she called into the hole. "Come back and let me leave."

No doors opened; no little girls appeared. Kitty stood, shoulders slumped, and began the long, narratively static trek back across the fields to the farm, where Agnes would be waiting for her to come and set the table for dinner. It was getting late. She didn't want them to worry.

The cat, it is said, was not domesticated: the cat domesticated itself, out of laziness and hunger and pragmatism. Cats had to be somewhere, so why shouldn't they be where there was food, and milk, and warm places to sleep? Why shouldn't they be where there were people to pet them and tell them they were good, yes, they were the very best cats the world had ever known? It was dry inside. It was comfortable inside. So the cats came inside of their own accord, swearing all the while that they were not domesticated at all: that they were still wild things deep down, under the stripes, under the skin.

For the first few months, Kitty walked to the hole every Saturday without fail, turning ritual into riddle and back again. Why was a sentence like a Saturday? Because it had to be survived to carry any weight at all. She didn't really notice when Agnes brought her shoes that failed to pinch her growing feet, nor understand the importance when Wesley taught her to weed the gardens, picking out the bad, leaving the good behind.

One day, Agnes slipped and called her "Katherine," and when she asked what a Katherine was, Agnes replied that it was a Kitty, only more so.

"Like a cat is a kitten, only more so?" asked Kitty, who still looked for riddles everywhere, could not stop looking for riddles everywhere, any more than she could stop herself looking for doors.

"Exactly that," Agnes replied, relieved. Their foundling girl was an odd one, prone to whimsy, prone to idleness, but oh, she was a sweet child, and she was a lovely child, and she must have been a gift, to pay for what they'd lost. Nothing could replace her given children. Kitty—now Katherine, a good Christian name for a good girl—came close enough to ease the aching.

"Very well, then," said Katherine, and went about her business, not seeming to understand that she had been belled, and most decisively so. A cat without a proper name may still think itself a stray. A cat with a name, and a bed to go back to, and a bowl to lick clean, well . . .

Domestication comes in small steps, little kindnesses, simple things. Katherine went about her chores, not seeming to notice that they were *her* chores now, and not merely what she was asked to do to pay for her supper. Agnes watched, and smiled, and felt the ice around her heart give way.

* * *

Summer yielded to fall. The crops came on in the field, and the leaves changed colors on the trees, and Katherine ran through them, laughing, as they tumbled down, down, down, falling from what they knew into something new, something different. She dove into leaf piles, seeking the doors she was sure must linger at their bottoms, and when she did not find a tunnel, or a hole, or any other such entrance, she laughed again, and kept running. The world was finally abandoning its logical lines! Anything could happen again, and she would be gone soon, yes, yes, she would be going home!

She ran out of the yard at the sound of Agnes's voice, and stopped to see the farmwife standing side-by-side with the farmer, a bundle of books in her hands. Suddenly, logic seemed closer than ever, and dreadfully dangerous.

"What is this?" she asked—the greatest riddle of them all.

"There's not much work on the farm during the winter," said Wesley. "We think it's time to get you some proper learning."

"Learning?"

"School."

Katherine recoiled in horror. "I'm no fish, to school in silver seas! I'm a cat, and I already know everything there is to know about being as I am."

"You'll need your numbers and your letters."

"I can count my stripes, and spell the name of everything I care to claim!"

Wesley heaved a heavy sigh. He was, in many ways, less forgiving than his wife of Katherine's strangeness, and this had been his idea. Some good thoughts in that airy mind might bring her feet to the ground, and keep them there where they belonged. "You don't have any stripes, Kitty. You're a person, and people need to go to school. Classes start tomorrow. You'll go, and you'll learn, and you'll come back here and tell us what they've taught you."

Katherine frowned, trying to work her way through this puzzle. She could run away, of course, run back to the hole and camp in front of it, waiting for it to let her through—but it was cold outside, and it had been raining recently, and she was still, above all else, a cat. She had no desire to be cold or uncomfortable, just because she was waiting.

"Is this a quest?" she asked finally. She knew about quests. Some of them involved vorpal swords and terrible beasts. Others involved waiting for ages outside of hidden caves, until the moment to pounce arrived.

Quests could open doors. Completing them could change the world.

"Yes," said Agnes, relieved. "It's like a quest."

And so Katherine went to school.

The schoolhouse was small and plain, nestled on the outskirts of the village, where the shrieking of the children on the playground wouldn't bother anyone. So many children! Katherine had never seen so many human children, had never *imagined* there could be so many, had always thought them to be something of an endangered species. They wandered in from time to time, tumbling through mirrors or the like, and they did terribly dangerous things with terrible enthusiasm, and then they left, and were never seen again. Between that and the three crosses behind the farmhouse, human children seemed impossibly fragile, the sort of riddles that could only be told once before they fell apart. But now . . .

Dozens of children, maybe even as many as *hundreds,* all running and screaming and kicking balls back and forth between them. Katherine hung back, properly shy in the face of so much chaos, until Agnes urged her forward, saying, "I'll be here when the bell rings. I'll see you then."

"Don't go," said Katherine.

Something softened in Agnes's eyes. She leaned forward and kissed the crown of Katherine's head, quick as anything, before she whispered, "I do love you," and fled, back down the road, back toward the farmhouse, back toward *home.*

The hours passed like honey with Katherine gone. The house seemed too quiet, the yard too empty. When Agnes walked back down the road to the school, she half expected the teacher to come out and ask what she was doing there, when she had no children left in her home to go to class.

Instead, she was greeted with an indignant armful of little girl, complaining wildly about how the alphabet wasn't supposed to have an order—you needed letters, yes, absolutely you needed letters, otherwise how could you write acrostics? But they needed to be free to visit their friends for tea and conversation, not locked into an ABC of unnecessary orderliness—and how the youngest children had been given naps while the older children hadn't. Be consistent in all things or be consistent in nothing, that was her motto.

Agnes laughed all the way home, as much with relief as with delight, and the dinner table that night rang with tales of school, all the mischief to be made there, all the tricks to play, all the riddles yet to be written.

"I think we get to keep her," she whispered to Wesley after bedtime, with their heads on their pillows and the covers pulled to their shoulders.

"She's not a stray cat," he replied.

Agnes smiled. "But that's exactly what she is."

That was the first time—that was the last time—she saw Katherine for what she was. She saw the girl with eyes of kindness. She saw the girl with eyes of love. She never saw the girl in stripes and whiskers.

Perhaps that was a blessing.

The meat of a riddle is in the beginning and the end: in the *why* and the *what,* not in the linguistic tricks the riddler will play to try to stretch as much distance as possible between the two. The goal of a riddle is to trip you up, you see, to take the logical and turn it into the nonsensical. So here, then, is the what: a Cheshire cat—Cheshire kitten, by the way humanity would mark such things, but a cat in her own mind, for she walked alone, stalked alone, talked to wandering children alone, and did not suckle at her mother's breast, nor cower at her father's tail—

fell through a door, and into a world where the rules were wrong. Where what she thought was chaos became order, and vice-versa.

Doors swing both ways. In the cat's home, in her nonsense world of unordered alphabets and conversational flowers, a human girl found the rules just as wrong as the feline one did; found the sky to be too bright, the roses to be too argumentative. That girl found her door home quickly, for she was following what she knew to be true, and while logic is not stronger than nonsense, nonsense is often more patient. It knows its day will come again, and so it yields before the insistence that this is that and that is this, that water must be wet and fire must be dry. Nonsense knows that logic crumbles. Nonsense does not require it to stay.

Logic, though . . .

Logic likes to consider itself inviolate, as much as it likes to consider itself anything at all: anthropomorphism is a form of nonsense, if only a very mild one, and to flirt with personification is to flirt with disaster. Still, when Katherine attempted to nonsense her way through her trials, she was confronted again and again with reason, with reliability, with the Rs upon which a logical world is built. Most of all, she was confronted with time, with Saturdays like sentences and sentences like Saturdays, stacking each upon the other in bulwarks of months, in castles of years.

One day she looked around and realized she wasn't a little girl anymore, even in outward appearance, even if she'd never been a little girl in the first place, for the face in her mirror belonged to a woman grown, and the body in her plain cotton dress was a woman's as well, long of leg and full of breast and strange in ways a cat's body would never have been strange. Agnes no longer saw to the chickens or planted the garden; that was her job now, and had been for several years. Wesley still worked the fields, but there was less acreage planted with every season.

She went to them now, these people who had become her parents, and she asked them the most important riddle of all: "What can I do?"

They told her.

She started walking out with James from school a week later. He was a farmer's second son, and he never looked to inherit if he stayed in his family home. But her family home, ah—there was something there.

The wedding was held in the spring. It was not a church wedding. Katherine had never quite cottoned to church. Instead, it was held outside, in view of an old tree that had once held a rabbit's hole among its roots, a rabbit's hole that had been a door, when the circumstances were right. Katherine watched it closely all through the ceremony, thinking it would be a small, mean trick if the door were to open now, in view of everyone she knew, when she was unprepared to run.

The door did not open. The wedding continued its set, logical course, and James moved to the farm with his new wife and her parents, and the days passed, one after another, Saturday sentences forming paragraphs, pages, volumes.

The first child came some ten months after the wedding. There was pain, and blood, and a remarkable amount of screaming. Agnes knew some of what it was to play the midwife, and both James and Wesley were adept at boiling water and looking stoic. Katherine shrieked like a Bandersnatch the whole time, her hands snarled in the sheets, cursing every name she could think of, and a few she hadn't considered in years. Birthing wasn't supposed to be like this. Birthing wasn't supposed to *hurt.*

Then she heard her daughter cry, and the pain didn't fade, but it transformed, becoming something terrible and strange. They set the girl at her breast, still slick with blood and mucus, bald and ugly and terribly *hers,* and it made no sense, no sense at all, and it made all the sense in the world. A mother was a kind of door, she realized: a mother was the door through which tomorrow passed.

"Babies are where nonsense and logic collide," she said, and she closed her eyes, and went away for a while, into a clean dark place where nothing, not love nor fear nor pain, could touch her.

They named their daughter Edith, after one of the crosses behind the house, and Katherine was disappointed, in her own way, when she walked outside a week later and saw the cross was still there. In a proper world, a *narrative* world, rather than a causative one, the cross would have disappeared as soon as someone else held the name. Agnes's pain would have been symbolically lessened, and the grave wouldn't have been needed anymore.

There were parts of this adventure that were terribly trying, and she was trying terribly hard.

Two more babies after that, James Jr. in a year and Margaret two years later, and the house was filled to bursting, until it seemed that it was never quiet, nor still. Katherine thought of those as her favorite years. The babies were young, youth stacked on youth, and they were never calm, leaving her fighting an uphill battle against nappies and bottles and bedtimes, but Agnes was there to help, and Wesley worked the fields with James, who kindly never said a word about how slow his father-in-law was becoming.

Time passed. The babies became children, and she sent them off to school as she had been, kissing them fiercely, whispering, "They'll tell you lies, but learn your letters," before she pushed them down the road. They came back with heads full of questions, and she fed them riddles like candy, encouraging them to run, to question, to dream as brightly as they could. They were her kittens, even if they stayed kittens far longer than she expected—and perhaps that was something humans did better than cats, because oh, she loved them so, and oh, they knew her so much better than she had known her own parents, striped and scarce and silent as they had been.

Time passed. Wesley was the first to go, falling in the fields at the height of summer, dead before he hit the ground, and it made no sense at all, for it served no story, answered no riddle: it simply *was,* implacable and pointless as a stone. Agnes followed a week after, heartbroken and unable to see the way to go on, and two more crosses joined the three behind the house, newer, the names easier to read.

Katherine stood before them for an entire day and night, silent, dry-eyed, and did not cry until the people who had become her family failed to come back and tell her it had all been a silly, stupid game.

Time passed.

* * *

Edith was visiting with her children and her husband, a sour-faced, complicated man who did sums for a living and doted on his bright, perplexing wife like she had hung the moon. He did not get along with his mother-in-law, and had been locked in the living room with James since their arrival, going over the farm's accounts. Katherine found herself, for the first time in years, in the position of caring for children who were still more nonsense than logic.

It was refreshing, in its own way. It couldn't take the bend from her spine or the ache from her joints, but it put some sparkle back into her eye, reminding her of what life had been when everything had been for a reason, when a sentence had been like a Saturday and a Saturday had been like nothing at all.

"Tell us a story, Grandma," said the youngest—Agnes, her name was, and wasn't that a kindness? One by one, they stripped the crosses away.

"Well," said Katherine. "A long, long time ago, in a place that was nothing like this one, and everything like itself, a young cat was looking for an adventure when she saw a door where a door shouldn't have been."

"Like that one, Grandma?" asked Agnes, all in innocence.

She was pointing.

Katherine felt her tired old heart stutter in her chest, like a pocket watch going out of true.

Slowly she stood and slowly she turned, following her granddaughter's finger to the trees behind the house. The branches threw a wicker pattern on the ground, laced and interlaced, like fingers clasping tight. There, in the place where they came together, was something that could have been a stepping stone or could have been a door. There was even a toadstool where the doorknob ought to have been, ready to be turned.

Her shawl fell away, landing in a tangle of yarn at her feet, and she was running, oh, she was running like the kitten she had been when she tumbled from one kind of story into another, when she had fallen from nonsense into sense to balance out a little girl who had done the same, dared the same, in the opposite direction. She was running faster than she thought possible, reaching for the stripes waiting on the other side of an impossible door.

The screams drew Edith out of the house. She fairly flew down the steps, convinced she was going to find her mother—who was getting on in years, even if she never seemed to want to admit it—lying face down in the yard.

Instead, she found four children. Three of them were shrieking and confused. The fourth, little Agnes, was standing in front of a web of shadows, staring at a shattered toadstool.

"Mother?" called Edith. *"Mother?"*

There was no reply. She turned to her children.

"Where's your grandmother?" she demanded.

Peter, Jason, Abigail, none of them gave any answer.

"I think she went home," Agnes said. Then, in a speculative tone, she asked, "Do you think I could go and visit?"

When is a sentence like a Saturday?

When it's something that can't be avoided, when it's something that's over far too soon.

WORRITY, WORRITY

Andy Duncan

My dear Dodgson.

I think that when the jump *occurs in the Railway scene you might very well make Alice lay hold of the Goat's* beard *as being the object nearest to her hand—instead of the old lady's hair. The jerk would naturally throw them together.*

Don't think me brutal, but I am bound to say that the 'wasp' *chapter doesn't interest me in the least, & I can't see my way to a picture. If you want to shorten the book, I can't help thinking—with all submission—that* there *is your opportunity.*

In an agony of haste

Yours sincerely
J. Tenniel.

Portsdown Road.

June 8, 1870

Sir John—for since his elevation by Her late Majesty, he routinely thought of himself thus, to his mingled pride and shame—had attended many a dreadful testimonial dinner in his long career, but surely the worst was this one, his own.

Somewhere in the third hour, stunned into near-insensibility by the strenuous regard of strangers, Sir John found himself wishing he had something to draw with. That whiteness of tablecloth, between the dessert-plate and the port, looked so inviting. If he just had pen and ink, he could insert a porthole, or a trapdoor, and vanish through it like a hare.

Instead, he sat motionless, a slumped and wizened figure, cured and hardened by cigar-smoke, not quite dead but visibly eroding beneath the punishing waves of oratory, as platoons of grim-faced volunteers marched to the dais to pay their respects to the man of the hour. Who knew the room, the city, England to hold so many after-dinner speakers? Surely even the footmen would be persuaded to say a few words.

Sir John roused himself a bit when the grey-haired, grey-faced, grey-mannered man beside him rose to speak. As the highest-ranking person in attendance, surely the Right Hon. Arthur James Balfour, MP, DL, Leader of the House of Commons, signalled that the end was near. But Sir John's attention wandered when Balfour displayed a downright parliamentary inability to get to the point. The Leader's route to the subject of Sir John Tenniel was serpentine, led over boulders into thickets of nettles. He expressed himself on multiple topics, including Parliament's raising Edward VII's salary to 470,000 pounds per annum, which the Leader called "a small enough acknowledgement of the large debt owed His Majesty by grateful subjects the whole world round." This occasioned much cheering, and drinking of toasts, and further delays, as Sir John stared grimly at the few sheets of dispensed-with manuscript face down to the Leader's left, and the much thicker stack of yet-to-be-heard-from pages to the Leader's right. He wished he could draw a cricket-bat and smash Balfour's head with it.

When Balfour finally began talking about Sir John, the subject of his remarks nearly missed it, having become distracted by a stain. Sir John found himself strangely fixated on the single blemish on the Leader's immaculate shirtfront, too irregular and ill placed to be a button or a stud.

"For the past fifty years," intoned the Leader, "no political issue, no world crisis, no chapter in the history of our empire has escaped the witty and knowing attention of Sir John Tenniel, who in the pages of *Punch* has made himself an icon of an era second only to our late Queen, who bestowed upon him the first knighthood ever granted a popular cartoonist. Like many of you, I know the experience of being immortalized by his pen, and no subject of his ever laughed the louder at seeing himself made foolish on the page."

Coals to Newcastle, Sir John thought, to the extent he could think of anything but the Leader's shirt-stain. What *was* he looking at, precisely?

Had this been a black-tie *breakfast,* Sir John would have assumed a spot of marmalade. Given the hour, it was more likely a dab of mustard, or a smear of butter from a tumbling roll. Gravity was the foe of etiquette. The stain was yellowish-orange, at any rate. It was also—Sir John blinked and rubbed his good eye to confirm this—moving. The whatsit was notably nearer the great man's lapel. It seemed to expand—no. It was a live thing, shaking itself and unfurling its wings.

The Leader droned on, oblivious. Sir John fought the urge to reach over and brush aside the wasp (for surely it *was* a wasp), or to pop his napkin at it, like a schoolboy at target-practice during prayers. Surely this was simply not done; or, if 'twere done, surely the Leader had aides, trained public servants, to do it.

But no trained public servants appeared, and the Leader seemed untroubled. No one else seemed to notice them, either—not the first wasp, the vanguard, the one now inscribing arabesques on the Leader's shirt-front, not the demolition-wasp rubbing its forelegs together with satisfaction in the ruins of a pudding, not the Alpine wasp scaling the champagne flute, not the Magellan wasp pacing the circumference of the Leader's great bald head, not the explorer wasp tickling a route through the hairs on the back of Sir John's drawing hand.

Stifling a cry, Sir John flapped his hand. The evicted wasp rose lazily, like a balloon ascending, and hovered at eye level but beyond a napkin's reach. The wasp regarded Sir John, and Sir John regarded the wasp.

Twoscore wasps darted and circled and crawled everywhere Sir John looked, over and amid and upon the seated, smiling guests, who might have been waxworks for all they cared. A waiter emerged from the kitchen bearing a round tray that held a swarming pile of wasps in the rough shape of a coffee-urn. These began to peel off from the mass, disperse all over the room, and Sir John was bracing himself to stand and scream in revulsion and outrage when he felt his shoulder seized in the too-firm, too-familiar clamp of the Leader's hand.

"Zir John Tenniel," said the Leader, "I hope you will not take it amizz, old friend, if we all zzzing the zzzzong that befitzzzzz you zzzzzzo well."

The hand on Sir John's shoulder was no longer a hand, but a single bristled, insectoid claw, its grip chitinous and sharp, and the Leader was no longer the Leader, but a monstrous man-sized wasp in evening wear. Sir John saw his open-mouthed horror reflected a hundredfold in the faceted serving-platters of the creature's compound eyes. The Leader-wasp wore as best it could—at an indifferent angle between its antennae—a yellowing wig, the sort worn by old men when Sir John was a boy.

Pinned and unable to move, Sir John registered the rumbling, rushing sound of the floor falling away, but it was only two hundred dignitaries pulling back their chairs and standing as one, to roar out lustily as the Leader-wasp led the chorus.

"For he'zzz a jolly good fellow,
For he'zzz a jolly good fellow—"

Each table held at least one man-wasp, and an especially drunken table in the back held eight Fleet-Street wasps, swaying perilously as they sang, "And zzzo zzzay all of uzzzz!"

The din was frightful, half human bellowing, half a buzzing like a plague of Egypt. The Leader's voice was gone entirely over to buzz, as it frantically jerked its free claw in wild mismatch to anything resembling a tempo. The back of its dinner-jacket surged as its constrained wings struggled to break free.

In the front row of banquet-tables, a man-wasp shed its dinner jacket, its cummerbund collapsing around its impossibly narrow waist. It rose, wings a blur, trousers too short for its dangling, multijointed legs as it ascended headfirst into the chandelier and hung there, nestled and half-hidden as if feeding, its legs kicking in lazy joy.

"For he's a jolly good zzzzzz,
Zzzz nobody zzz zzzz!"

"Dropping the Pilot."

The once-great Bismarck, builder of modern Germany, descends the gangplank for the last time, noble in humiliation. The fingertips of his left hand brush the hull as he passes. The hand does not bear his weight, just reminds the old man of the rough timbers he planed and polished, the wheel that will be steered by others forevermore. Behind and above Bismarck, amid a cross-hatch of pen-and-ink shadow, lurks the Kaiser, who leans on his elbows and watches the pilot go, his own waxed moustache looking pasted-on, part of a child's costume at a summer fete, a faint echo of Bismarck's walruslike bristles. Behind the Kaiser's mummer-moustache, beneath his bejewelled crown, is the face of a wasp—an elderly, querulous, wholly un-drawable wasp. Beneath its crown oozes a yellowing wig, like butter-icing that melts during a long mayoral speech and slides off a plum-cake in the sun.

"But, Father," said young John, "can't we stop for today? I'm tired."

He knew instantly that he had said the wrong thing. In speaking so rashly, he also had proven his fatigue, beyond all doubt; but this was no comfort.

After a pause, Father smiled. A stranger would have thought it a kindly, forgiving smile—but John, at age twenty, was no stranger.

As he raised his epee once more, Father seemed to stand even straighter, if that were possible. His moustache was splendid, his carriage impeccable, his muscles taut beneath his Arctic-white shirt. He was every inch the Huguenot dancing-master of Kensington. If he ever sweated, his eldest son had yet to cause it.

"Another hit, I think," said Father, and waited.

John's bottom was against the courtyard wall as he leaned forward, hands on knees, sucking in air, almost spent. Seeing Father's resolve, he tried to breathe normally, and mostly succeeded. He gathered his thoughts, then stood, picked up his epee, which seemed heavier than before.

"If you need quick energy," Father said, "I suggest a sugar cube."

John tried to ignore this. A sugar cube! As if he were a skittish horse. Above him, in the eaves, wasps came and went from what must be a hidden nest a-borning. John envied the wasps their purpose, their freedom.

He walked in a circle, flexing his sore arms, cleaving the air with his blade. He felt uncertain, awkward: a right-hand foot in a left-hand shoe.

This was, in theory, only a practice round, impromptu, because Father was home early—from some country earl's London house—and was bored, and so both father and son were in shirtsleeves and street pants, and barefaced. A trunk in the stable held the padding, the jacket, the breeches, the masks.

"Come on, come *on,*" said Father. He underscored his impatience by whipping his blade up and down. Neither man noticed the faint *ping* of something tiny hitting the corner of the yard: the button off the tip of Father's sword.

"*En garde!*" cried John, and made the first lunge. Father parried easily. Then, a painful but familiar routine of thrust and parry, riposte and attack, disengage and circle parry and counterattack.

To John's astonishment, he was backing Father into the far wall. John pressed his advantage, pleased to see Father losing his poise. But Father also was losing his temper.

Lunge by Father, riposte by John—but Father wasn't where John expected him to be, and Father's blade—

John's right eye bloomed in agony. He stumbled, dropped his blade with a clatter, clutched his face. Pain drove all thought from his head, but somewhere below thought, he was sure his eyeball had been sliced in two.

"Son! What's wrong? My God, what have I done?"

"No, Father! It's quite all right!" John blinked back tears, managed—after several tries—to hold his eyes open. The world looked flooded and melting. "It's only . . . it's only a sting."

"Let me see," Father said.

Feeling Father's hands on his shoulders, Father's hot breath on his face, John wrenched away, and lied without thought.

"It wasn't you," he said. "It must have been a wasp. Yes, I'm sure of it. It was a wasp."

He tried to turn away, but his Father's face, ever before him, looked monstrous, was flowing into a worse shape yet. John knew that his life was over, that he would never be an artist now.

"Those damned wasps!" he cried.

"The Reform Bill, 1866. Frantic Excitement!!!"

A parlour scene. John Bull and his missus, his great gut straining his waistcoat buttons, her ample bosom straining the front of her dress, sit dozing over their evening papers full of the transcribed debate in Commons, rendered inert by Mr. Gladstone's latest riposte to Mr. Locke, or was it Mr. Locke's latest sally against Mr. Lowe? Untouched tea cools on the table between them. His hand is limp, the newspaper it barely grasps puddling on the hearth-rug. Her newspapers are spread nicely across her knees, as one squares and straightens in one's lap something that one has resolved never to read, only to admire in all its stately grey splendour. She hunches forward, intent on her inner eyelids. Will she concentrate so hard that she jerks herself awake? Their deep, gentle breaths, not yet coarsened into snores, are evident from the darkening ink that pools around the snoozing couple. The ink seeks purchase, demands entrance. At their feet, lying on a newspaper all his own—the *Illustrated Police News,* perhaps; or, worse yet, *Punch*—is the bull-pup, himself dozing, his multifaceted eyes staring in all directions, his pincers folded beneath his chinless lower face. His wig sits awkwardly atop his head, as if pasted there late in the production process, and his own snore is a buzz.

"How you go on!" the Wasp said in a peevish tone. "Worrity, worrity! There never was such a child!"

Worrity, indeed, thought Tenniel, who'd had quite enough of this chapter.

"Your jaws are too short," the Wasp went on: "but the top of your head is nice and round." He took off his own wig as he spoke, and stretched out one claw towards Alice, as if he wished to do the same for her, but she kept out of reach, and would not take the hint.

Tenniel snorted. Without lifting his eyes from the manuscript, he groped one-handed for the teacup, or more precisely for its handle. Finding it, he lifted the tea and took a sip: ice-cold. He blew on its surface and sipped again, and found it better, if only for the disturbance.

"Then your eyes—they're too much in front, no doubt. One would have done as well as two, if you must have them so close—"

"Nonsense," Tenniel said aloud, smacking the manuscript decisively onto the desk as if hoping to kill something small. Inviting children to go one-eyed! The idea!

Tenniel would give much to have two functioning eyes again. He had kept from his father the extent of the fencing injury, which eventually had claimed the sight in his right eye. Why had he done that? Why had he protected the old man?

Tenniel shook his head like a horse, to drive away the bites and darts of memory. Having learned precisely nothing helpful from re-reading, he picked up his pen, dunked it, *tink-tink-tink*ed it against the side of the ink-pot, and resumed his attempt to draw the impossible.

Before him, splayed beneath velvet-covered bookweights, were open copies of Spencer's *Introduction* and the relevant volume of *The Entomologist's Annual,* the bottom margin of which was spattered by Tenniel's growing indignation. The pages on display featured labelled anatomical sketches of order Hymenoptera, suborder Apocrita, family Vespidae. Everywhere Tenniel started was clearly the wrong place to start. The head was wrong, especially the mandibles; the wings were wrong; the abdomen and thorax were wrong; the obscenely tiny join between them was wrong. Tenniel's habit was not to crumple his failures, but to sail the flat sheets off the desk, so all around him were straggling lines and gaping crosshatches. They did not add up to a wasp.

As he sketched his fourth outstretched leg of the afternoon, his housekeeper bustled in.

"Goodness, Mr. Tenniel, ain't you closed your window yet? I warned you, all the little beasties are swarming to-day."

"Yes, thank you, Mrs. Cabot, you may leave it anywhere," murmured Tenniel, who while drawing attended to nothing else.

"Shoo!" said Mrs. Cabot, swatting flies from the cream-pitcher as she leaned across the tea-table to bring down the sash with an emphatic *bang*. As she straightened, she brushed her palms together and squinted at the drapes. She disliked these busy William Morris patterns, as all manner of vermin could hide against them. "Aha!" she murmured: A largish wasp was crawling up one of the drapes. Had he paid the slightest attention, Tenniel would have been astonished by her quick production from an apron-pocket of a horsehair fly-swatter with a foot-long braided leather handle. Mrs. Cabot liked to play the crone of a workday, in part to fend off employers more attentive than Mr. Tenniel, but she was barely thirty and full of life, and at home she and Mr. Cabot had many tools at hand. As she edged nearer the winged intruder, she spoke calmly and slowly, as if to soothe the creature.

"I never did hold with opening one's house to the elements," cooed the creeping Mrs. Cabot. "Before you know it, the outside has come inside, and then where *are* we, I ask you?" With a lunge, she brought the swat down on the precise spot formerly occupied by the wasp, which now sailed toward her face. "Go on!" she cried, slashing the wasp's vicinity with the horsehair. "Get away!"

"About six o'clock, I believe, Mrs. Cabot," replied Tenniel, without looking up, "and in the parlour. No need to bother with the dining-room." Tongue slightly protruding from the corner of his mouth, he was placing a human face on the wasp, as he had done years before with the Caterpillar—but the result was looking too much like Mrs. Cabot to suit him.

The housekeeper stopped flailing. She glanced about, eyes wide. From behind her right ear, tendrils of reddish-blonde hair plumed from her bonnet, as if electrified. With a rustle, another castoff sheet from Tenniel's desk sailed to the floor, landing near Mrs. Cabot's toe. The zigzag line Tenniel had drawn meant nothing to her, but she looked in the direction it seemed to point. There lay the stunned wasp, upon a plain woven coconut-mat blessedly free of Mr. Morris's curlicues. It was on its back, one wing crumpled, kicking its last.

"Hah!" Mrs. Cabot said, and smashed the tiny creature beneath her sensible heel. "That's for you, Mr. Gillie Wetfoot," she added, grinding its remains into the weave with force and satisfaction.

Sadism, thought Tenniel, inscribing an arc that never would be abdominal, *was an unseemly charge to levy against a fellow Englishman, yet the malign hurdles Dodgson had set him suggested at least a borderline case.*

"I'll return this mat directly, Mr. Tenniel," said Mrs. Cabot, bustling from the room. "I'll just give it a bit of a wipe-down."

"Why, thank you, Mrs. Cabot," murmured Tenniel. "I'm rather proud of it myself." He savagely scratched out another failed wasp-face, his nib tearing the paper.

To be sure, being a professional, Tenniel somehow had parried all Dodgson's challenges. He had managed to avoid, without Dodgson's noticing, having Humpty Dumpty's "legs crossed like a Turk." While drawing legs on an egg was no great leap, to draw those legs *crossed,* in Turkish fashion or any other, was an anatomical impossibility.

At Dodgson's insistence, Tenniel had redrawn the King's Messenger in prison—but why should the man *not* have been staring at his hat, Tenniel still would like to know? What else had he to stare at?

Tenniel had managed to draw the Rocking-horse-fly, the Snapdragon-fly, and the Bread-and-butterfly. He had drawn the toves, which were "something like badgers, something like lizards, and something like corkscrews"—a fine description, that! At his lowest ebb, Tenniel had even drawn a leg of mutton taking a bow.

But *this* was the last straw! He cast his pen point-first, harpoonlike, into his desk-sponge (where it stuck, quivering), opened his stationery-drawer and drew forth a single creamy white sheet, which he placed in the precise centre of the desktop. He would draw many things in his career, Tenniel vowed as he worked his pen free from its Arthurian depth, but *never* would he draw a wasp in a wig!

My dear Dodgson, he began.

Against the windowpane, a wasp, identical to the one Mrs. Cabot had killed, bumped softly once, twice, three times, unnoticed.

"The Haunted Lady; or, 'The Ghost' in the Looking-Glass."

The lady of the house, resplendent in a shoulder-baring, narrow-waisted dress, its hoop skirt filling the frame and threatening the adjacent columns, looks in horror at a mirror that reflects, not her beauty and newfound finery, but the corpse of a needle-woman, her head lolling and jaw slack, dead in a garret of exhaustion and starvation. "We would not have disappointed your Ladyship, at any sacrifice," buzzes the dressmaker looming behind the lady's shoulder. She pats her pincers together in what may be satisfaction, clacks her mandibles together in what may be a smile. Her fashionable headdress is perched atop an unfashionable wig. She continues to buzz, clack, buzz, as the ink lines sharply converge on Milady's shrieking mouth.

"Pat? Where the devil are you, Pat?"

The doctor had opened the first-floor window of his consulting-room and stuck his head out, to somehow yell both up and down at once.

"I say, Pat!"

Sir John, sitting patiently before the doctor's desk—having already been told, as he was told annually, that he was in surprisingly fine health for one so near death—heard a crash of broken glass, from which he concluded that someone had fallen into a cucumber-frame, or something of the sort.

Next came a voice he had never heard before: "Sure, then I'm here, yer honour!"

"Pat, what is all that noise out there? Don't you know I have patients, man?"

"And yer good to be patient with us, yer honour, and no mistake," said the unseen Pat. "We're trying to clean yer chimney, we are, but we've reached what you might call an impasse."

"Well, what's wrong, for God's sake?"

"Sure, it's a wasps' nest, yer honour. Got to knock it down, we does, afore we go another step closer to that chimney, yer honour. And so we're bunging shingles and cobbles from below, yer honour, and apples, whatever projectiles come to hand, only we got wasps all amongst us, and spiling our aim."

"Well, keep the racket down, will you?"

"Sure, I don't like it, yer honour, at all, at all! But what's to be done, yer honour? It's a worrity, it is, and no mistake. Oh, it's coming down! Heads below!"

Screams and crashes ensued just as the doctor slammed the window closed, reducing the aftermath to a hectic murmur. "My apologies," said the doctor, resettling himself. "Where were we?"

"You noted that I'm still alive," said his patient.

"And delighted to say so," said the doctor. "But tell me, Sir John. Do you ever find yourself, well . . . seeing things?"

Sir John cocked his head. "Seeing things? Such as?"

"Oh, anything that, how shall I put this . . . anything that's, ah, not there."

"You mean hallucinations."

"Exactly. It's not unusual in men of advanced age, who have some form of visual impairment. Blind in one eye, for example." He winked, which Sir John found tasteless in context. "Bonnet syndrome, it's called. Named for a Frenchman. Quite sound, though, for all that."

"Oh, I'm sure," Sir John said, brushing imagined lint from his knee.

"Do you have 'em, then?" asked the doctor. "Hallucinations?"

Sir John considered his answer for a few moments. "I cannot say that I have," he finally said, truthfully.

"Glad to hear it," the doctor bellowed, and stood, extending his hand. "Always good to see you, sir. *Punch* isn't the same since your retirement, no indeed." Hearty blather propelled them into the outer office, where the attractive nurse dimpled a greeting. "Oh, that reminds me," the doctor said. "My nurse has a request—if you're willing, of course."

"Oh, yes, sir," said the nurse. "If you could just sign a book while you're here, I'd be so awfully grateful."

"I'd be honoured," said Sir John. As she unwrapped the book, apparently a new purchase, he found himself preening his moustache, and felt ashamed.

The book was *Alice,* of course: both novels under one cover. He couldn't recall when he last had seen them published separately. He supposed Dodgson's text did well enough, if you liked that sort of thing. His own illustrations were trivial—yet, he conceded, strangely popular with children.

"And your daughter's name is . . . ?" asked Sir John, accepting the pen the young woman proffered. The doctor had fallen silent but was standing too close to him, a looming, jovial, intrusive presence.

"I have no children, Sir John," replied the nurse. "This is for me, if you please. My name's Alexandra. Oh, no, not there!" She flattened her hand atop the title page, to which he automatically had turned. He watched, perplexed, as she flipped the pages to Chapter Eight of the second book, to his drawing of Alice and the White Knight: the young girl astonished, the old man toppling comically over the bowed head of his chesspiece-horse. The nurse tapped the page between the two figures. "*This* is the spot," she said. "I'm nothing like Alice—I'm too dark—but you're quite like the Knight, I think. Tell me, was it a self-portrait? Did you use a mirror?"

"It was *not,*" Sir John grumbled, "and I *did* not." *And my God, woman, that was forty years ago!*

He signed hastily, neither his name nor hers being, in his view, quite legible. He did not so much resent this silly girl, as resent the fact that she was quite right: He *was* an old man with an absurd moustache, likely to fall at any moment. Dodgson had intended the Knight as an author surrogate—Sir John was quite sure of that—but in illustrating the scene long ago, Tenniel had drawn his own future.

Ah, well, Sir John thought, *it could be worse.* Alexandra could have asked him to sign the drawing of the Knight's two feet sticking out of the ditch. Still looking at the drawing, wondering where the years had gone, he absently handed the pen back to the nurse, who claimed it with a clawed insect-hand.

"Thank you zzzo much," said the not-nurse. "But tell me thizzz. When will you draw *my* picture, Zzzir John?"

Aghast, Sir John turned his back on her, just in time to see the doctor, wings a-blur, fly out the window.

"The Nemesis of Neglect."

Floating through a filthy alleyway, its unseen feet not touching the cobbles, is a hideous, hooded, taloned figure with the word CRIME inked onto the shroud that almost covers its staring, bulbous eyes. A butcher-knife is raised and ready in its right hand. *Finally,* Tenniel thinks, as the loathsome spectre drifts past like an odour, *here is one I finally got right the first time.* As if hearing Tenniel's thought, the dread figure slows, stops, turns to face the artist. The eyes grow even larger; the jaw retracts until the mouth is gone, not merely closed but folded inward; the chin protrudes and separates into mandibles. The wraith advances on Tenniel, the knife raised even higher in that single fingerless inhuman claw. Tenniel falls backward in horror, stumbles across something at knee height: lines of poetry, typeset precisely to the artist's forgotten specifications:

> *There floats a phantom on the slum's foul air,*
> *Shaping, to eyes which have the gift of seeing,*
> *Into the spectre of that loathly lair.*

The other lines all have turned to Zs, unreadable, and Tenniel's vision is filled by the buzzing not-face, its wig-locks crawling forth to frame the horror, like pale corpse-fingers fondling a skull. Choking, helpless, Tenniel paws the slum's foul air, and screams. His hand rends the phantom's rotting shroud, and a Londinium of wasps pours out, swarming into Tenniel's hair, eyes, mouth.

* * *

He thrashed awake, in his own bed, surrounded by doctors and nurses.

"Eazzzy, Zzzir John! Eazzzy-steady, now."

"You've juzzzt had a nightmare."

Sir John's mouth was ropy and dry, but empty. He felt vast relief, and shame: They all were staring at him, as if he were dead already, a specimen on exhibit. He swallowed, lifted his head, peered about. The room was too close and hot, the fire in the grate too high. He saw wheeled carts, and bottles, and those stinking flowers from the Palace. But where was his desk?

A nurse produced a glass of water, which Sir John gulped with relief, ignoring the spiked claw that held it. "You gave uzzz quite a zzzcare," said the wasp-nurse.

Handing back the empty glass, Tenniel tried not to look into the vast, prismatic eyes that gazed down all around. He would fight them no longer. He knew what he had to do—while the memory of that floating Whitechapel horror was fresh in his mind.

"Paper," he said, flinching at the toadlike rasp of his voice, "and pencil."

"What'zzz that, Zzzir John?"

"No deadlinezzz today."

"Are you hungry? Perhapzzz an egg? Or zzzome laudanum?"

"No food," Sir John said. "No drugs. Please, only paper and pencil. They're in my desk. Please."

He had them in moments, along with a lap-desk. Feeling better than he had in months, tongue protruding unnoticed from one corner of his mouth, he sketched with confidence: the bold, thick outlines, with the flat of the lead; then the sharp-tipped details; then the crosshatching. He stopped midway to demand a penknife, refreshed the point, and resumed.

In thirty minutes, he was done. He looked at the result. He nodded his head. He hadn't drawn the nightmare, not quite, but he *had* drawn an accurate caricature of it—as with Bismarck, or Balfour. A parody, like Dodgson's poems. He even had included the wig.

He had not bothered to draw Alice, though there was room enough, in that empty space, as the wasp reached for her hair. But Alice was never the difficulty, was she? Alice was easy.

He nodded and handed the drawing to the nearest doctor, who reached for it with a lightly haired, five-fingered, quite human hand, and looked at it with tiny, close-together, quite human eyes, his face displaying quite human bafflement. The other humans clustered around, looking at the sheet.

"What's this?" the doctor asked. Hearing no answer, he looked back at Tenniel. The old man lay flat in the bed, his head slightly off the pillow, his eyes closed. He looked peacefully asleep, but the doctor, who had decades of experience in such matters, knew that Tenniel was, in fact, dead.

"Remarkable. It's his final drawing."

"Sort of his last words, eh?"

"But what is it supposed to *be*?"

"Some sort of . . . insect?"

"Those certainly aren't hands."

"What's that on its head?"

"He was having us on, I expect."

"Joking? In his last moments?"

"He didn't *know* they were his last."

"*Punch* will want it," said a nurse. "They'll want to publish it."

This gave everyone pause.

"Perhaps," said the senior doctor, the one still holding the drawing. He paused. "Perhaps, Miss Price, it would be best that the public . . . not see this."

Almost everyone quickly agreed.

"Quite right."

"He couldn't give permission, could he?"

"Not his best work, anyway."

"We don't even know what caption he intended."

"*Punch* wouldn't mind *that,*" said Miss Price, who already contributed to *The Girl's Own Paper* under a pseudonym, and later would be a founding editor of the *Women's Dreadnought*. "They could do a contest. 'Write the Caption for Tenniel's Last Drawing.'"

"Oh, please," said the senior doctor, with a shudder. Before anyone else could speak, he turned and fed the drawing into the fire-grate, where it went to ashes on the instant.

You filthy brute, thought Miss Price.

With a cry, the senior doctor leapt back from the fire, one hand across his face. "My eye!" he cried. "Oh! Oh! My eye!"

His colleagues, save Miss Price, gathered around, concerned. When they pulled his hand away, his right eyelid already was swollen shut, an angry red welt spreading across his face.

"Some damned thing stung me!" cried the senior doctor. "Where is it?"

Of course, they couldn't find it. Miss Price opened all the windows, in hopes the whatever-it-was would have an escape, and thrive, and breed.

The mourners, crepe-swathed hats in hand, slightly windblown in the cold March air, watched in silence as the hearse jingled and rustled through the red-brick archway of Golders Green and turned onto Hoop Lane. The single layer of ostrich plumes atop the carriage, the single black horse drawing it, the practical, sanitary and compact inkpot-shaped urn within—all befit an artist who remained, despite his knighthood and other laurels, a precise and modest figure, a pen-and-ink draughtsman in a blurred and garish world. The horse nodded and nickered its respects as it clopped past the new Jewish Cemetery, en route to Tenniel's final resting place, of which Chesterton would write:

For there is good news yet to hear
And fine things to be seen,
Before we go to Paradise
By way of Kensal Green.

Not among the mourners, his absence remarked by some, was Tenniel's dear Dodgson, who had preceded his combative artist into the endpapers sixteen years before, to lie in a no-nonsense family plot in Surrey. As for a certain Oxford girl-child named Alice, now a respectable lady of sixty-one living with her cricketer husband in a distant wicket of Hampshire, her absence was noted by no one.

It was a normal Edwardian funeral in every respect but two. One was the incineration of the body, which was smart and of the moment but in no way traditional. The other was an unseasonal flurry of wasps. They droned among the crowd, neither attacking nor threatening, but swarming from all directions. As the hearse rounded the corner and passed from view, the wasps went with it, hovered just above and behind, like flickering yellow cinders from the Golders Green chimney—almost, said one onlooker (a fancier of children's stories), as if the tiny, fretful creatures were paying their respects to the dead.

Author's Note: The lost "Wasp in a Wig" section of *Through the Looking-Glass,* which Dodgson deleted from the page proofs before publication in 1871, surfaced from a private collection more than a century later, when the proofs were auctioned at Sotheby's. Tenniel's letter of 1 June 1870, which appears here verbatim, shows that removing the scene was a rare instance of the micromanaging Dodgson heeding his illustrator's advice, rather than vice versa. I would have known none of this but for the late Martin Gardner, as the missing passage, with extensive commentary, can be found in every edition of his *Annotated Alice* from 1990 onward. I take this opportunity to dedicate "Worrity, Worrity" to Gardner, a personal hero who humoured me in correspondence and phone conversations from time to time, and who encouraged all my obsessions.

EATING THE ALICE CAKE

Kaaron Warren

The dead man had been a great gardener, his front yard lush and green, but overgrown now, and wild without his constant care. Alice heard sobbing as she reached the front door and paused, trying to remember if the lawyers had mentioned a resident relative. No: The house should be empty.

Dunroamin, the dead man had called it.

As expected, the front door wouldn't open, so she pushed her way through a forest of red bottlebrush bushes on the left side of the house, making a tunnel through to the backyard. There, the light seemed different. A big tree overhanging the yard cast a shadow, and the autumnal leaves threw a tinge of colour over all.

The backdoor key was where they'd told her it would be, hanging off a hook on the worm farm, which stood blockishly on bricks. Alice had a worm farm at home. She liked the way you could tip your potato peelings in there, your broccoli stems, and before long the worms would writhe up through the dark, rich earth in the box and eat the waste, turning it into even better soil. This worm farm was an old, well-established one, many generational, hand-built using old Styrofoam boxes. The earth in there was almost black with nutrients and Alice took a moment to run her fingers through it before unhooking the key.

Pushing through the back door, she sniffed tentatively. That was always the sign of what sort of job it would be. A house that made you retch as soon as you opened the door was going to be tricky work. She'd seen some awful ones, houses so full of rubbish you needed to shovel your way in. Razors, rotting beds, broken glass, bags of shit, glass bottles filled with piss, newspapers piled to the ceiling.

She'd seen houses where the body had lain for weeks so you could see the outline of it in grue.

You can get used to anything.

She loved her job but was very glad she didn't have to touch any dead bodies, leaving that to the guys known as the body-lifters, who went through the houses before she entered. That job attracted a particular kind of man (they were all men), the kind whose senses were dull, almost null and void. She shuddered to think of the evening she'd spent with the one called Floyd, whose nasally speech patterns should have alerted her to the fact he had no real sense of smell or taste. And his touch . . .

She shuddered. Her uncle had dealt with Floyd directly, showing an uncharacteristic fury.

There was no smell in the house beyond the distant scent of burnt toast. Anything else would have surprised her; the owner, a quiet, habitual man, had died outside, while collecting his mail, so there should be no hint of death inside.

She pushed the door fully open and saw that the laundry was neat. There was a faint smell coming from the washing machine, usually a sign that a load was left in there, wet and beginning to rot. She looked in the cupboards and found plenty of cleaning supplies. Using these could provide a continuity of smell, a sameness, which she thought was a comfort to any loved one who came through the house once it was clean. Not for this man, though. He'd had nobody.

It also saved her from using her own products.

She tended not to take anything from the house except for food and cleaning products, to keep her record clean. She'd hate to lose this job because of theft or the perception of it; there wasn't another like it. She only had it because her favourite uncle owned the company. She loved the job, taking great glee when she told strangers what she did. *I clean up after dead people,* and they'd either recoil or be fascinated. Either way, if often meant she was the most interesting person in the room.

"Why do you do it?" she was often asked. She'd say, *for the money,* because the money was very good. But it was far more than that. It was the fascination of walking into a person's house who would never return to it.

The hallway was dim. She sensed movement to her right and turned, hands out, ready to fend off an animal or calm a person. Nothing; it was a full-length, ornate mirror at the end of the hallway. She saw herself and shadows, too, reflected in the glass. She squeezed her eyes to clear them, her vision blurred by the dust, because she thought she saw her uncle in the mirror, almost filling it with his bulk. He heaved a great sigh.

Of course he wasn't there.

Alice didn't have a mirror at home. While she loved the way she looked (especially on a good hair day), there were times, like now, when she imagined a whole different world in there. Not a place she'd like to be, but somewhere so dark and nasty she wouldn't want anyone to have to live there.

Her uncle always said she had a powerful imagination, and that imagination was the only weapon in the war against reality. He'd put his fingers up to show he was quoting someone, but he never said who.

She tapped the mirror with the toe of her left shoe, proving the surface was solid and that even if she wanted to, she couldn't step through.

Alice did a quick walk through the house, assessing what she'd need to do. One bathroom. Two small bedrooms, one of them used as a study and barely at that, with the desk neat and no papers left out to tidy. The lounge room. The kitchen.

Working methodically she cleaned, swept, vacuumed, and wiped. He really had been a tidy old man. While the towels in the bathroom were damp with mould, the rest of the room was almost spotless. She'd seen far worse. She'd flushed toilets filled with shit, she'd emptied bathtubs filled with dirty clothes, she'd thrown away baskets of used toilet tissue.

In the lounge room, the carpet was pale mauve, immaculate. Dark wooden armchairs with embroidered upholstery filled the corners, while an antique bookcase, neatly layered with leather-bound volumes, covered one wall. The TV hid behind a wooden screen as if the owner liked to pretend he didn't watch. Under the TV were rows of movies, numbered but not named.

She heard more quiet, desperate sobbing as she dusted the shelves. She didn't believe in ghosts, but given the emptiness of the house she wondered. This was too real, though. There was a buzzing noise also, usually a sign of something off and flies flocking around it.

She followed the sound into the kitchen, where she saw a small fish tank tucked into an alcove above a small fridge. Pressed up against the glass was a turtle, about the size of her two palms, waiting like a loyal dog for its owner to return, its face wet with tears.

It saw her and stopped crying with a deep, bone-shuddering sigh.

Her first reaction was irritation. Alice despised glumness. Morose faces made her want to shout, "Snap out of it." Sighing annoyed her because it was usually done with the intention of eliciting a particular response. A solicitation, an offer of help, or some sympathy. Certainly some attention.

The turtle somehow managed to sigh and cry at the same time, quite a feat.

There was a hand-lettered sign over its tank. "Mock Turtle. Genus: *saddus.* Feel Free to Mock the Turtle."

The turtle was looking at her mournfully, she thought. She wondered if that's why it was labelled *saddus.* The body-lifters should have taken it away when they took the dead man; it must have been overlooked. It wasn't the first time she'd found family pets. Dogs would die by their owner's side, or be so depressed they had to be put down. Cats would escape the moment a door was open; she'd seen one dash onto the road and be run over, a mercy, really, given the state it was in.

She'd never found a turtle before, though.

There was a thick sludge at the bottom of the tank. Flies buzzing around it, sinking into it. The dead man had been so tidy; why didn't he keep the tank clean?

"That's a lot of shit for a little turtle," she said.

"Go on, then, laugh," she heard. "I'm sitting here like a pig in shit, except I'm not a pig and therefore not very happy. You can laugh if you like. Millions would."

She turned around, looking for the prankster, the ventriloquist.

"It's me," the turtle said.

Her jaw dropped open, an unattractive trait her uncle told her he hoped she'd grow out of.

The turtle snapped his jaws at her. "Close your mouth, dear. Something'll fly in there, and I've seen the bugs in this place. Nasty nasty."

I'm dreaming, Alice thought. It wouldn't be the first time she'd dreamed of talking animals. "Very nasty, I imagine," is all she said.

"I know I am. Nasty as a nail gun and ugly as sin. No wonder the teachers always hated me. It's all right for you, Miss Blonde Hair Pink Cheeks. Your teachers must have loved you."

They didn't, at all. "Too much daydreaming," her teachers said. "Living in a fantasy world." That was true. What they didn't understand was that her fantasy world, her Wonderland life, was as real as their world. And it was safer. In Wonderland she was smart and fit and bright. There was no such thing as school in Wonderland.

"Why are you called Mock Turtle? You look like a real turtle to me."

"Because everyone makes fun of me. Even my dear, dead wifey did it."

"That's not nice," Alice said. "Nobody should mock another person!"

The mock turtle rose onto his back legs, reaching for her. "Go on, take me out of this glass box. I promise I won't run away!" He made a clicking noise Alice assumed was laughter. She lifted him out and placed him on the kitchen bench, which was covered with crumbs. There were half-empty jars of jam, honey, Vegemite, and peanut butter, with a knife resting across the Vegemite. She took a photo of this, the prep site of the owner's last meal. If there were relatives, they sometimes like to see this record of last movements.

She was glad there were none here. Relatives were an annoyance. They never wanted the food, at least, but they wanted to talk about that last meal, traces of which were often found in the kitchen and on the dining table, or on the arm of a sofa, or on a coffee table. Or they'd bore her with stories of favourite foods ("Tinned oysters!" as if that was the most astonishing thing) or they'd tells lies about the health of their loved one, say, "She always ate well," but Alice would find the cupboard full of cheap snacks, chocolate, fatty salty crappy food. She didn't mind any of that, though. It was the interfering relatives who insisted on helping her, who threw all the food out no matter how many times she asked them to let her do her job. Didn't they understand how much food was wasted?

She hated those ones.

"Let us see if there's any lettuce," she said to the mock turtle. *The half pun might have amused the dead man,* she thought.

She had to get to work, anyway. She set up her bags. One to take home and one for the rubbish. Not much went into that bag.

On the fridge, a sign said, "Give us this day our daily bread and butter and a slice of ham please."

The fridge held a plate of leftover roast lamb, some cooked green beans, a carton of milk that gave off a slightly sour stench, some supermarket cheese, three covered bowls of food she'd identify later, and a crisper full of limp vegetables.

There was half a lettuce there, soft but edible, and she tore two leaves off and placed them on the bench next to the mock turtle.

"M.T. is empty," she said, as if the ghost of the dead man whispered in her ear.

The mock turtle nibbled noisily, pausing only for breath.

While he ate she started on the cupboards. She found an old currant bun and would have added it to the bag to make crumb cake but realised the currants were actually small cockroaches. They'd formed the words "take me" and she was happy to find the message. She often found justification for what she did, even though she didn't need it. She knew she was doing the right thing. There was so much food wastage, why shouldn't she help lessen that?

She took a deep sniff at the roast lamb. It was dried up but not rotten. She didn't want to poison anyone. She wanted them to eat so much they could hardly move. She'd use some of that for shepherd's pie and some for soup. If she found jam tarts she wouldn't take them home, she'd eat the lot herself.

The mock turtle stopped eating the lettuce.

"All full?" Alice asked.

The turtle raised and dropped his shoulders. "What I really love are worms, but no one's ever fed me those. There's a whole world of them Outside." He lifted his head and jerked it towards the backyard. "There's everything back there. Before the old man turned nasty and left me in my tank he'd take us Outside to watch while he gardened. Such glory days!" the mock turtle said. "It was like a magic place where dreams come true."

"I call the magic place Wonderland," Alice said. She hadn't told anybody else the name.

"Oh, that's the perfect name for it! We just called it Outside."

"We?" said Alice, as she scavenged through the cupboard for more bags to carry food in.

"I had a friend once. My wife. You didn't think all that shit was mine, did you? Ended up as soup. I watched her being et, right before my eyes. She was a real turtle, not like me. I'm just a pretend one, really."

"What are you really?"

"I really am a mock turtle. Anyway. You've never felt pain until you've had a fish hook through your lip." He curled his lip down so she could see a small scar. She didn't want to get too close. She didn't trust those snapping jaws. "The old man threw me back in the tank, didn't he? Not wanted. He took my dearest friend, my lovely wife, reeled her up and over the edge, her dear little talons scratching the glass, and next I knew I could hear her screaming. Screaming as he plunged her into the pot. Oh, the cruelty. The terrible, terrible cruelty of it."

"That doesn't quite make sense. Why would your owner treat you so well only to eat you up? And why would he need to use a fishing line to take her out? I lifted you out easy as anything."

"You tell me, Alice. You tell me."

He began to weep.

"I've lost everyone I've ever loved," he told her.

Alice said, "I've never loved anyone, not so it hurt. My doctor says something happened to me as a little girl so I have barriers."

"Like what?" He sat back, nose twitching. Alice cleared her throat, clicked her jaw, sorry she'd spoken.

"What's that?" he said. "My hearing, you know. Louder, dear! Tell me your woes!"

He's one of those, Alice thought. The ones who loved the saddest stories. Who liked other people's suffering almost as much as they liked their own.

"Like nothing," she said. She felt nausea starting in the pit of her stomach and quickly ate a dry biscuit. Stale but bland; that's what she needed.

"I've been to Wonderland," she said. "Many times. I think I even met you there once," but that didn't make sense, because the mock turtle was real and her dreams of Wonderland were not.

"Did you now? Dreamt me up, do you think?"

"I thought I did, but here you are, in all your glory."

"No glory for me. Oh, the terrible things I've seen and heard and what's been done to me."

"Like what?" Alice said. Terrible things didn't happen to people like her, unless you counted having a family that didn't understand you. Her dad never forgave her for not finishing high school; he'd had high hopes for his moral little girl, his smart as a whip little girl.

"You'll remember."

But she couldn't, she wouldn't, not when there was Wonderland to visit, where the world was in her power.

"We'll find a box for you and take you to the animal protection people. Someone will want you."

"Nobody will want me," he sighed. "No one ever wants me. I'm abandoned again. Unloved. You can't imagine the sorrow I've seen." Alice kept sorting, piling tins onto the bench to check their contents.

She filled the next take-home bag and set up another. She filled that with tins, biscuits, and bags of coffee. There was frozen cake, too.

She patted her stomach, an instinctive action whenever she thought about her weight.

"You're a big girl, aren't you?" the mock turtle said.

"That depends on your perspective. To some people I look tiny. Sometimes I think I shrink or grow, depending on who's looking at me."

She gathered a pile of ingredients on the bench and pulled out a big pot. She liked to cook the soup while she was in the home; there was something about the taste of it that way. Finding a large pot sometimes proved difficult, but there was one in the pan cupboard, with a lid and all. She piled in ingredients as she found them in the fridge, the freezer and the cupboards; the lamb, the vegetables (those beyond use would go into the worm farm), the green beans, packets of lentils. She filled the pot to the brim. No one would mind if she took the pot away. She was doing them a favour.

The soup she cooked, turning waste to food, would last her a week.

"Is this what they cooked your wife in?" Alice asked, curious, knowing she was being rude.

"Who's that, then? I can't think straight, I haven't been fed in days. Weeks! I'm wasting away. Shrinking inside my shell." He'd had the lettuce but it seemed that wasn't satisfying.

She offered him cheese. Some soft apple.

"Never mind," she said when he refused. "I'll make a nice crumble with these apples. Cook them long enough and they turn to mash anyway. What is it you'd like to eat? The soup will be done soon. More lettuce?"

She knocked over the pepper as she reached for it to add to the soup. She sneezed, and thought, as she did every time, that a sneeze was like an orgasm.

"Oh, don't you just hate pepper?" the mock turtle said. "Sneezy breezy. Brings up all sorts of nasties for me. Oh, the nasty stories I could tell you about pepper."

Alice laughed. "You silly sad thing! Who has a bad memory about pepper?"

"You be quiet or I'll eat you up," he said, shaking the pepper pot at her using his two flippers.

"Silly sad thing," she said again, quiet now, because it wasn't the first time she'd heard those words, but the other time was best forgotten.

Alice closed her eyes and pictured the rabbit hole that led to Wonderland. She could feel the grass around her ankles, the breeze on her cheeks as she walked towards it, then the dark coolness as she stepped inside.

She imagined jam tarts, bread and butter. Unlimited food. She imagined not being hungry. Not having to beg for a meal. Not having to . . .

"You remember," the mock turtle said. "You remember the time your uncle cut off your arms and legs and you had to wait for them to grow back again?"

Alice laughed. "You're thinking of another girl's uncle. Mine is the kindest man ever. My dad says he spoils me but he says I deserve it."

"Oooh, that must be nice. That must help."

"You're like a hypochondriac but for emotions," Alice said. "Any emotion you can think of you feel and then you think everyone else feels it, too."

There was a whole cupboard full of different mustards.

"He called it the mustard mine. Wasn't he a funny old man?" The mock turtle looked like he was about to cry again.

Alice emptied all the mustard pots into the soup, and some frozen vegetables she chipped out of the freezer.

As the soup cooked she finished cleaning the rest of the house, with the mock turtle for company. She carried him from room to room, setting him down where he could watch and tell her stories and keep her amused.

She liked the atmosphere of this house. It was quiet. The dead man lived alone so there was a sense of peaceful solitude, from the single toothbrush in an ornate mug to the single bed beautifully made. The idea of living here was seductive. Alice wondered how long she could stay, away from home. Overnight? She flicked a switch; the power was still connected. She could stay a night at least, keep the thick, heavy curtains drawn. There was plenty of food. She could bake some bread to go with the soup or make croutons from the loaf she found in the freezer.

The mock turtle felt dry and soft in her hands, like old leather. He was heavier than she expected, his shell weighing more than the rest of him.

"Aren't you good?" he said. "Trained by the whip, weren't you? Like a good whipped dog serving her master."

She turned him upside down and carried his shell like a soup bowl, as if she was Oliver Twist begging for more, until his complaints got too much to bear and she flipped him over again.

She turned all the lights on so she wouldn't get caught out by the mirror again, but "Who's that, then? Who's a pretty little pink girl?" the mock turtle said, his voice so familiar she had to dash into the bathroom and splash her face with water, swallow a cupful, to stop herself from being sick.

"Tell me about your Wonderland, if you had one," she said, and he told her of tall majestic towers and deep green pools.

Back in the kitchen she found a roast chicken in the back of the fridge, eaten down to the bones. These she put into a pot of water to boil off the remnants of meat.

Then she opened a packet of pretzels and they ate those.

"What's for dessert?" the turtle said.

"I'll make a cake at home."

"Ooh! An Alice Cake! Make it now!"

"You never know with other people's ovens. I have to be sure the cake rises." She added flour to her take-home bag. "I've got a houseful of hungry mouths to feed."

The turtle weaved its head from side to side. "Now who's telling stories! You don't have a soul at home! Not one person!"

"I do!" she said. She fitted the last box of cocoa into a bag and she was done.

The pot on the stove screamed and she turned around to attend to it. The soup was cooking well. Her uncle and her parents would enjoy this. She'd feed them and feed them and feed them until they couldn't move, then she'd feed them Alice Cake covered with whipped cream until they screamed for mercy.

Alice found a cardboard box under the sink. There were remnants of something at the base, vegetable waste rather than animal, and she said, "If you hop in I'll take you out of here."

"To Wonderland? Where the worms are?"

"And beyond," she said.

The look on its face was so tragically grateful she had to laugh.

"Come on," she said. "Let's go look at the worm farm." She piled the worst of the vegetables into the box, then nestled the turtle on top before carrying it outside. That strange light still bathed the backyard and she saw now there were pathways ornately laid, set with tiny pebbles looking like cake decorations, albeit ones that would break your teeth.

The vegetable garden was overgrown and gone to seed, with the tastiest stalks like zucchini eaten to the ground by snails and other pests.

They walked around the lemon tree that had a sign saying "Number Ones Welcome Here" with the picture of a man pissing.

Next to the lemon tree was a gnarled rose bush hanging over a small headstone the size of her thumb.

"Will you look at that?" the mock turtle said. "He gave her a proper burial. Maybe he deserves the same after all, even if he did near starve me to death."

The headstone said "Beryl, neck broke by her husband."

Alice read it aloud to the mock turtle.

"He didn't, did he? Why'd he write that?" The mock turtle looked away, his shoulders shaking with sobs.

"Oh, poor turtle," Alice said.

"He couldn't handle the truth, that man. Wouldn't come near me in the end. Weak! I'm only telling it as I see it. When you've suffered like I have you realise the truth is the only way. Not my fault he was a lonely old man with no friends and never did."

This was true; the old man had no one to collect his belongings.

"You know the tender feel of fingers around your throat, dear. I know you do."

She put down the cardboard box. The turtle peered over the top as she tipped over the worm farm, adding the vegetable waste to the mound of dirt and worms.

The mock turtle stared mournfully at worms writhing in the hot sun.

"Go on," Alice said.

"I'm not sure I deserve them. Do I? I'm not sure I do."

"They're only worms."

She felt better tipping the worms out, whether or not they'd be eaten.

She hated the idea of them being trapped in the worm farm, slowly starving to death.

A clucking alerted her to the arrival of the chickens, round with feathers, but, she thought, probably starving.

They came quickly for the worms but quicker still was the mock turtle. Up on its back legs he took them one by one, using its strong jaw and teeth to tear off their heads.

"Off with their heads, just like that?" Alice said. He'd done it so easily. She wondered if a grown man would die as easily, if your grip was strong enough.

"There'll be eggs in there," the mock turtle said.

"In the hen house? I'll check," Alice said.

"In there, too." He pointed at one of the decapitated chickens. "Unlaid eggs. You could make us an unlaid egg cake. Slice her down the middle, that'll do it."

Leaving the turtle to gorge on worms ("I'll eat the chicken once it's cooked," he said. "Roast a chicken fresh as that and you'll be dreaming of that meat the rest of your life.") she went back inside for a sharp knife, some freezer bags, and the egg carton she'd seen under the sink. She turned the soup down while she was there, then back Outside to slice open the chickens. She did find eggs inside. Bloodied and a bit soft. She placed them carefully in the egg cartons and cut the chickens into manageable pieces, leaving the guts behind for the neighbourhood cats, who'd appeared like magic to devour.

She packed the car, unlocking the house's front door from the inside. The handle was sticky and there was a dollop of jam on the carpet. It wasn't blood. She felt momentarily sad then, but it was a good way for the owner to die; jam toast in hand, collecting the mail from your own letterbox.

She was waiting for her uncle to die, to own a home. Self-made man, rich man, generous man, looking after his family that way. When he died she'd make her parents move out, though. They'd never done anything for her. Her uncle would leave his business to her and she'd throw her parents out of the house and she'd be set.

The chicken bones were clean, so she fished them out of the boiling water and placed them on a tea towel to dry.

"Not for me, I hope," the mock turtle said after she'd collected him from Outside. "Not keen on bones myself."

"For my uncle's wine. He likes a nice glass of wine. He says it puts bone in his bone if you know what I mean."

"And you'd know what that looks like. Ay? You've known for a long time."

"Should have left you Outside," she said, and placed a cake tin over the turtle to keep him quiet for a bit. "You're too ugly for me to look at for now," she said. She set about wiping the benches and other surfaces.

Eventually the tapping on the tin annoyed her enough so she set him free. "We can't all be beautiful like you are," he said. "Take a look in the mirror. Glowing, you are. Glorious."

She picked up the turtle and took it to the mirror at the end of the hall. "I wouldn't say I'm glorious," she said, but she was lovely, she knew it.

"A little compliment makes it all better, doesn't it?"

She hated him for being right about that.

If she lived here she'd get rid of the mirror. It was flawed, covered with bumps and welts. Scabs. When she touched it, it felt smooth, but underneath and in the shadows she could see a different self. One who'd broken her arm three times. One whose first boyfriend when she was fourteen knew she wasn't a virgin but she wasn't saying how. And she could see back home as if she could step into the mirror and be there in a flash. Her uncle there with his mouth open, his jaw dropped, mocking her.

In the kitchen, the soup pot screamed.

Her uncle and her parents would enjoy the meal. She'd feed them and feed them and feed them until they couldn't move. Feed them soup and cake and milk. Feed them and feed them and feed them.

The mirror uncle leaned forward as if to poke her in the solar plexus and she'd be out of breath for minutes. "Can't speak? That's a pleasant change! Too busy flapping your gums to make your poor uncle happy." He wore loose pyjamas with a drawstring because he could flop himself out at a moment's notice.

"You've got nothing to be sad about," she imagined her uncle said to her in the mirror.

"You've got nothing to be sad about," she said to the mock turtle.

"I have, you know. I've been cursed with empathy to the nth degree. What you're feeling, I'm feeling. I can read your mind. I know what's hiding there. I know what he did."

"Don't believe what you see in the mirror," Alice said.

She picked up the turtle and carried him back to the filthy tank. "We'd better clean this tank up," she said, but she wouldn't bother.

"Don't put me back!" he said. "We don't need to take the tank with us. You can carry me in a backpack, or you can put me on your car seat. I won't budge an inch, or if I do, I'll budge so slowly you won't see me move."

She placed him upside down on his shell in the sludge in the base of the tank and he started to cry. "Carry the tank, then. We'll clean it out when we get home. Ay? We won't talk about the past anymore, not unless you want to. Oh, the lovely times we had," speaking through his tears. "Oh, such a good childhood you had, luckiest girl ever!" he told her. "I'll bite your uncle's cock off and we can watch him bleed to death. We can!"

It was too late, though. She couldn't trust him to leave her in Wonderland.

"You're not coming with me," Alice said. She stood, hands on hips, listening to his great gulping sobs. Then she carried the tank up the backyard and put it down behind the shed, where no one would see it. Right in the hot sun.

"Not this," he wept. "I'll turn to soup."

"Yes, you will," Alice said. Already she was back in the beautiful oblivion of Wonderland where, if she wished very hard, there would be jam tarts for supper.

THE QUEEN OF HATS

Ysabeau S. Wilce

I. Into the Trunk

The poor tamale girl, her tamale pail empty, but no coins tucked safely in her sash. Just before Northern crossroads, she'd been set upon by stealie boys. They'd slid down the sand dune screaming like sirens, knocked her over, stomped her hat, and rolled her until the coins fell from her sash into their graspy paws. Then they'd disappeared into the dune grass, their victory shrieks swallowed up by the gusting fog.

So now she sprawls in the sand, grit in her teeth, grit stuck to her wet cheeks, grit grating her bare knees, ribs burning, thinking of home. "Oh, what shall I do? If I go home with sash and pail empty, Papi will spit on me, and whip me with my own sash. My sibs will hiss like snakes and give me the ole stink eye. And Mami will make me sleep in the woodpile. I shall get splinters!"

The little tamale girl wiggles her tongue against her teeth, feels no wobbles, spits a mouthful of sandy blood. A cold wind is blowing in off the water, and the ground is wet and hard. Fog, and dank, and darkness, and maybe the stealie boys are not the only ones out tonight, hoping for a victim. Grimacing, the little tamale girl sits up, thinking to herself: "Oh, I should go home, and take my whipping, for surely that is better than lying in the sand all night and being preyed upon by coyotes or fleas. Fike those stealie boys, and—oh, no, do I hear a voice? Someone is coming! Perhaps it is the stealie boys returning, or perhaps it's Springheel Jack, or even the Man in Pink Bloomers come to drag me to Hell . . ."

Scrambling to her feet, the little tamale girl snatches up her pail and hightails it into the scrub. She should crawl deep into hiding, but if she's unseen, she'll also be unseeing, and curiosity has got the little tamale girl in its claws. She flattens herself into a pancake and peers through the ice plant to see a dark shape trundling down the road, muttering to itself.

". . . oh why did she have to pick this wasteland so far out of town, and with all this blowing sand? Where am I going to find actors out here? There are crossroads in the city good enough, but this was the only crossroad to suit, blast her!"

"Well," thinks the little tamale girl, "I have never seen such a large rabbit before, and why is he carrying such a heavy trunk? Surely he knows there are no hotels out here, nor either boarding houses or stage stops along this road, neither? And why is he putting the trunk down in the middle of the crossroads? Doesn't he know when the Presidio horse car comes in the morning the trunk shall be smashed to bits, or run over by the milk cows being driven to the Shiner dairy. . . . Should I warn him? See something, say something, my mami always says? But also mind your own business. What ever shall I do?"

Having deposited the trunk into the middle of the intersection of the Presidio Plank Road and the Northern Cut, the Rabbit fishes a large pocket watch from his weskit and, after consulting it, unlocks the trunk. Its sides hinge open like a butterfly's wings, but away from the little tamale girl's view. She can only see the back of the trunk, which is speckled with transfer stickers: *Ticonderoga, Arkham, Cibola, Porkopolis, Belegost, Goblin Town, Eboracum, Sunnydale, London.*

"Queer and queerer," thinks the little tamale girl, as she creeps forward for a closer look. "Porkopolis and Ticonderoga I have heard of. But London? That sounds like a made-up place to me. I do think I should warn him; clearly he is a visitor to the City, and does not realize how busy this crossroad can be during the day. Sometimes it gets two or three carts an hour! Hey, sieur! Hey sieur!"

The rabbit doesn't answer, and when the little tamale girl peeks around the side of the trunk, he is not there. But the inside of the trunk is a wonderland. One side is like a little closet, stuffed with hangers of glorious costumes gleaming with gold aiguillettes, silver soutache, and glittering galloon. The opposite side, all drawers, each filled with marvels. The first contains maquillage: pots of rouge, fat black eye pencils, trays of fluttering eyelashes, palettes of shimmering eye colors: sangyn, gris, ebon, celadon, octorine. The next drawer contains neat rows of gloves: satin, velvet, dogskin, crocodile leather. After that it's hair pieces: curly, straight, braided, puffed, fringed. Then whiskers, some long and flowing, some small and militaristic, some like bristle brushes, others soft and fuzzy.

The little tamale girl reaches for the wig-box on the bottom, so rapt in the spangles and sparkles she doesn't notice the skeletal hand slowly emerging from the tangle of garments behind her. It grabs the back of her pinafore and yanks.

"Oh, dear," thinks the little tamale girl as she plummets downward, "I seem to have fallen into the trunk. And nothing good can come to girls who fall into trunks, mami would say. But then I never heard of a girl who fell into a trunk; perhaps I am the first and shall buck the trend. Really it can't be much different than falling into a hole, though I suppose a trunk is less likely to have a lion in the bottom of it, or six feet of water, or be a portal to Hell. I wish—ooo, marmalade—" The little tamale girl grabs the jar of marmalade off the shelf as she plummets by it and, after wrenching the top off, shovels the sweet stuff into her mouth quickly as she can. She's famished, and the fall might end before she has time to finish. But she's still falling when the jar is empty, so she tosses it away, heedless of who it might land upon.

Down down down the little tamale girl goes. The drawers and shelves are done, and now it is ropes, and pulleys, and a canvas backdrop painted like a hallway full of closed doors. Another backdrop showing a two-dimensional courtroom, and one painted like the seaside, with frozen waves and glittery sand. Still, down down down she falls, past huge arc lights, lenses covered with colored paper, swaths of red velvet curtain, and a clutter of props: a plaster mushroom, pots of roses, giant papier-mâché oyster shells and an enormous soup tureen.

She thinks: "This fall is going on for quite some time. Perhaps I can twist like a cat and land on my feet. I certainly have the time to try." So she tries to twist and turn herself, but all she does is upend her pinafore, and blow air up her nose, tangle her hair, and lose her hat. "Well, that did not work, so perhaps I shall have to make my own cushion—" She's passing more racks of costumes now, so she snatches at the hangers as she plummets by, and soon her arms are heaped with kirtles and basques, garibaldi shirts and pelerines, manteaus and polonaises, sack-cloth and sables.

"Now I am ready for this fall to be over," the little tamale girl says to herself. "It was charming at first, but now it's just tedious, I wonder how far I shall fall, out of the bottom of the trunk, and through the sand, and the rocks beneath, and right into the arms of the giant squid sitting in the center of the earth and that, I suppose, will be that. At least no more woodpile—"

II. The Wardrobe

And then the fall is over, and the little tamale girl has landed not on the costumes, but under them, so she is smothered in ribbands, bows, velvet, fustian, taffety, lace, calico, brocade, sarcenet, grosgrain, cypress, and all other manner of textiles. This is a considerable weight to struggle out from under, and doing so takes her some time.

"But it's better than drowning in six feet of water, or being eaten by a lion," the little tamale girl says when she finally emerges. Despite the thud, she has not suffered at all in the landing, in fact, the aches left over from the stealie boys' thumping have disappeared and she feels wonderful. She's standing in a long hallway lined with doors, each inset with a small gold plaque that says, respectively: *Wardrobe, Dressing Room, Wig Room, Prop Room, Wings, Proscenium, Orchestra Pit, Office, Stage Door, Snack-bar, Canteen.*

But the doors are all tiny, only as tall as the tamale girl's knobby scabby knees. "Perhaps if I hold my breath long enough, I shall shrink down," the little tamale girl thinks, but before she can do so, a furious voice assails her.

"You, what are you doing! What a mess you've made—pick up those costumes extemporaneously!" A rotund figure wobbles toward the little tamale girl, waving a long pair of scissors in one glove and flapping a measuring tape in the other. "Immediately, independently, absolutely, intravenously, right now!"

The little tamale girl laughs. "Why, you are nothing more than a dress dummy!"

"Dummy! I am the wardrobe mistress of this troupe, capiche, comprende, don't you know?" the wardrobe mistress says indignantly. Her eyes are made of buttons, and her mouth picked out in straight pins. Her lack of hair is hidden by a blowsy lace cap that looks like an exploded cabbage.

"I cry your pardon, madam," the little tamale girl says, dipping into a curtsy, "but I wonder how you can talk through that mouthful of pins!"

"Better pins that are useful than those nasty bits of bones you call teeth!" says the wardrobe mistress. "Now, look what you have done to this gorgeous frock—" She has picked the garment in question out of the heap at the little tamale girl's feet. "It's the Leading Lady's favorite dress—designed by Schiaparelli; she wore it in the role of Rosalind, for which she won a BAFTA. You've got some of the duck feathers off—quick, take it to the wardrobe and get those feathers back on before she notices, and has your head chopped, chapped, chipped!"

The little tamale girl is so alarmed by the thought that her teeth are nothing but bone (which had never before occurred to her), she sweeps the dress away from the wardrobe mistress and rushes down the hallway. Either she has shrunk or the door has grown, for when the door opens, she fits through exactly. Inside, the room is packed full of garment racks, thick as corn in a field. The wardrobe mistress thrusts a needle and a duck into the little tamale girl's hands. Ignoring the panicked quacking, the little tamale girl begins to sew frantically. But soon her fingers are sore, the duck won't stop flapping, and the dress itself is beginning to complain about the little tamale girl's rough stitches. The wardrobe mistress has disappeared.

She throws the needle down; the duck snatches it up in its beak. It and the dress hurry away before the little tamale girl can stop them. The little tamale girl says to herself: "By the pricking of my thumbs, I don't see why I should sit here and sew feathers forever. Let the feathers sew themselves! After all that work, I'm thirsty. I saw a door marked *canteen* in the hallway. Canteens hold water, so surely I can get a drink there."

But the wardrobe door has disappeared into the racks of costumes, and soon the little tamale girl is disappeared, too, lost among the gaudy outfits that seem to go on and on forever. She fights her way through a covey of quail costumes, a fantasy of unicorn costumes, and a whole lamentation of swan suits. Regiments of military uniforms, and rude mechanical fustian. Chorus girl outfits covered in coins; white chitons; beetle-like armor made of pressed leather painted silver. The deeper into the wardrobe she goes, the more the drooping costumes seem sinister and watchful, as though they are just waiting for the proper moment to stand up and stride out upon the stage, declaiming a war speech in iambic pentameter, or fighting a swashbuckling duel up a flight of stairs, or hoofing a soft-shoe dance routine.

"Oh, this is so tiresome," the little tamale girl cries out, frustrated, after what seems like hours and hours. "I've been wandering through this wardrobe forever. Shall I ever get out? Or shall I just dwindle until there's nothing left of me but my clothes, and then they shall be a costume, too, and I shall be gone? Bother these fiking clothes. I wish I had some candy."

"Candy is dandy but liquor is quicker," a cheerful voice says from somewhere beyond the row of hanging wolfskins and double-horned helmets.

III. Advice from a Skeleton

And there, in a clearing of the costumes, sits the Man in Pink Bloomers upon a plaster mushroom, bony legs crossed. The long stem of a corn-cob pipe is clenched between his shiny white teeth, and pink smoke curls out of his nasal septum.

"Please, sir, do you have any candy?" the little tamale girl asks politely.

"I do not."

"Liquor?"

"Not that, either."

"Then why did you get my hopes up?"

"I have lots of hope; you can have as much as you want."

"But I want candy."

"Don't we all? Have you got any?"

"I don't," the little tamale girl says crossly. "And I don't see why they call you the Man in the Pink Bloomers when you are a skeleton. They should call you the Skeleton in Pink Bloomers."

"I am the bones that flesh is heir to, little morsel. And you are very rude."

"I am not rude! I'm just lost. Can you tell me how to get out of this fiking wardrobe? I've been here for hours, and it's growing quite tedious."

"The only way out is through," the skeleton says, smoke puffing out of the chinks between his thoracic vertebrae and his clavicle. The little tamale girl chews on this baffling comment for a few minutes; it's a tasteless phrase and makes her teeth ache. Finally she gives up and spits it out.

"Are you here to drag me to Hell?" she asks.

"What makes you think this isn't Hell?"

"It seems as though Hell would be colder."

"Oh, no, my dear, Hell is other people. Perhaps, since I am another person, you are there now."

"That's mad!" says the little tamale girl, bored of the conversation now that it is clear she is neither getting dragged down to Hell nor getting any candy.

"I'm not mad, but *she* will be if you don't hurry up. You are very late."

"Late for what?"

"Late for a hiding, I think. Are you hiding from a hiding?" The emeralds inset in the Man in Pink Bloomer's teeth twinkle like little bats.

"Or perhaps late and lamented is what you shall be if she orders your head off. What did the big tomato say to the little tomato, as it dawdled—"

"Tomatoes can't talk!"

"*Hurry and catsup,* of course! And so you had better!"

The Man in Pink Bloomers knocks his pipe against his bony knee, and the sparks in the bowl swirl like stars, dazzling the little tamale girl's eyes. He tosses his pipe into the air; it turns into a tea tray and flaps around his cranium. The pink bloomers, the lanky bones, the shiny skull, the diamond inset eyes are blinking out like a drying puddle of tea, until only the jaw remains, hinging like a gate, growing wider and wider, while the rest of him fades until the lower mandible has become a threshold, and the upper mandible a lintel, and through this toothsome gate hurries the little tamale girl, saying to herself: "He needn't have been so rude; I am going as quickly as I can!"

"But not as quickly as you could," says the tea tray, fluttering besides her.

"How could I go quicker when I am going as fast as I can?"

"How can you be quick when you are late?"

"But what am I late for?"

"I know you are, but what am I?" the tea tray asks. The little tamale girl tries to grab it; a bit of tea or a biscuit would be most welcome right now. But the tea tray winks away, and now another strange figure is rushing toward her down the hallway, a figure made of folded paper, all angles and edges, and every inch covered in marching black lines of type.

IV. The Audition

"You are late!" the stage manager shouts. "The audition is about to begin!" The paper woman pulls the little tamale girl into a room crowded with actors, all of them looking anxious, clutching their lucky charms and sheaves of scripts. Some are warming up by standing next to the fire; others are limbering up by pulling on cart shafts. In one corner, a lory and a mock-turtle are trying to untangle the lines they've been tossing back and forth, which have gotten all twisted up. In another, a small school of whiting are polishing their scales.

"What is the audition for?" the little tamale girl asks a dodo who is anxiously fluffing its feathers.

The dodo looks annoyed at being interrupted but answers: "*The Oxford play,* of course."

"Oxford play? That's a strange name for a play."

"It's not the actual name of the play, just what we call it."

"Why don't you call the play by its real name?"

"Oh, terrible bad luck to call it by its real name. Theater people are terribly superstitious, you know. So we call it the Oxford play instead."

"Where's Oxford?"

"I don't know. I think it's mythical," says the dodo. "Or maybe existential."

"It doesn't exist?" The little tamale girl is confused.

"It doesn't want to exist, that's what existential means, silly girl. Don't ask me why, I'm hardly a philosopher."

"Is the play a tragedy or a comedy?" the little tamale girl asks.

"Both!"

"How can it be both a tragedy *and* a comedy?"

"Everyone gets their heads cut off, but it's funny," explains the dodo. "I'm trying out for the dormouse."

"But you are a dodo!"

"I am an actor," says the dodo indignantly. "Are you suggesting I be typecast?"

"No," says the little tamale girl hastily. "I'm sure you are very good at being a dormouse. And I would never cast type at you."

"Well, I'm sure you are very good at being a girl. You certainly look the part," says the dodo generously. "You should try out for the duchess, I should say, for you are so tremendously ugly, but since you are quite obviously green, let me give you some advice."

"Am I green?" cries the little tamale girl in distress. "When did I turn green?"

"Oh, you silly girl," says the dodo. "I mean, inexperienced, of course."

"Then why didn't you say so?"

"I did say so!"

"But you said I was green!"

"It's the same thing."

Now the poor little tamale girl's head is spinning. Nothing here makes sense, and she's growing quite faint with hunger and exhaustion. "But one thing is a color and the other is a state of being."

The dodo flaps its tiny little wings. "I am only trying to help you, girl. Say so if you don't wish it."

"I do. I'm sorry, please, what is your advice, dear dodo?"

The dodo looks around to make sure they are not being overheard and then whispers into the little tamale girl's ear: "Don't upstage the leading lady. She'll have your head off."

"How can a stage have an up if it is flat? Shouldn't you say: don't sideside stage or overstage instead?" the little tamale girl whispers back.

"In the theater right is left and left is right," the dodo said indignantly. "Honestly, you seem to know nothing about the theater. I don't even know why you are here at this cattle call."

"Cattle call?" The little tamale girl looks around. She sees a lizard, and a white rabbit, and a lory, and a mock turtle, and a caterpillar, a cove of little oysters and a whole flamboyance of flamingos milling around, but no cattle. "I don't see any cattle."

"Oh, you are too tiresome! I must go talk to my agent! Break a leg—" And with that bewildering command, the dodo flounces off.

The little tamale girl says to herself: "Actors are so queer, and touchy, too. But I do not want to be a little tamale girl all my life, so perhaps I should be an actor instead, a little faery star, and dance upon the boards, and have miners throw gold-dust upon me, so I shall be famous, and I can retire a rich old lady and leave all my money to animal welfare. I wonder if I should audition for the dormouse, too? It would be a start; anyway, I don't know what other parts there might be. I hope the dormouse has not many lines, as I have a terrible memory. Sometimes I cannot even remember my own name!"

The actors are now clustering around the end of the room—growling, barking, chirping, howling, bellowing, and quacking excitedly. The stage manager has returned, and with her the rabbit the little tamale girl had seen placing the trunk in the crossroads. She sees now it's not an actual rabbit, but someone wearing a rabbit costume. The rabbit's eyes glow with a coldfire pink light.

"That's the spirit of the theater," says the dodo, who has returned to the little tamale girl's side. "He hardly ever comes to auditions. What an honor!"

"The audition is about to begin," the stage manager shouts, and this causes the flapping, stamping, shaking, stomping, and wiggling to start all over again.

The stage manager says, in her papery voice: "As you know, we are putting on the Califa premiere of the Oxford play. We shall be casting today for the dormouse, the mock-turtle, and the dodo."

"What about the axe?" squeaks a lizard.

"That part has already been filled by the Man in Pink Bloomers," the rabbit replies, and the lizard puffs its throat out in disappointment.

"What about Alice?" shouts the lory.

"Of course, our lovely leading lady shall play Alice."

There's a nervous shuffling among the actors, and a voice, the little tamale girl can't tell whose, says: "Bit old, ain't she? Alice is a just a girl."

"It's the lead," the stage manager answers nervously. "And she's the leading lady."

"But she's too old for the part—"

"Now, now," says the rabbit, consulting his pocket watch again. "The decision has already been made—" His speech is interrupted by a sudden rattling drumroll. The actors gasp and begin to look at each other uneasily. The stage manager begins to crumple and the rabbit's ears flatten.

"Oh, no," says the dodo. "She heard, and now she's coming. Heads are going to roll."

The dodo clutches the little tamale girl, who whispers: "Who is she?"

But before the dodo can answer, the drumroll ends and a fanfare begins. The actors fall flat on their faces.

"Well, I shan't do that," thinks the little tamale girl, "or I shan't be able to see who is coming, and perhaps ask for an autograph. Besides, the floor looks awfully dirty." So she remains upright, even as the dodo tries to pull her down.

The press agent, carrying a megaphone, steps through the door. He assumes a power posture and shouts through the megaphone: "She's the four-time winner of the Margo Channing Award for Theatrical Excellence, two-time Ticonderoga Critics Circle Award winner, three-time Oscar nominee; official face of Madam Twanky's Maquillage; Member of the Order of the Beamish Empire; United Factions Ambassador; star of *Diamond Legs, Daddy's Boy* and the Tony Award–winning musical *The Road to R'lyeh* . . . YOUR LEADING LADY!"

But first her entourage: A newsprint of reporters, fedoras pushed to the back of their heads, scribbling furiously in their notebooks; the critic, swaggering his cane back and forth, and stroking the Persian lamb collar of his velvet coat; four little pages rolling out a red carpet, and a personal assistant carrying the leading lady's coat, purse, and several shopping bags; a handler with four pink Labradoodleborgies in jeweled collars, yapping furiously; three nannies herding six children, all of whom look spoiled, surly, and jaded; two hulking bodyguards, bulging with muscles and tattoos; another assistant with a latte in one hand and a green juice in the other; a personal trainer carrying ten-pounds weights in each hand; the husband, carrying an album of press clippings. And finally the leading lady herself, wearing black stockings and an oversized black tunic with the words TEAM DESMOND printed on it.

"Who spoke? Who said I was too old for the part?" the leading lady demands furiously.

The actors grovel, looking sheepish, all but the sheep, who looks terrified. The stage manager has crumpled into a wad, and even the rabbit looks worried.

"I shall cut off ALL YOUR HEADS if the guilty party doesn't come forward at once—" To show she means it, the leading lady takes off her sunglasses. The assistant snatches them out of her hand, cleans them quickly, and then hands them back. She points the sunglasses at the quivering throng. "Do not test me! I will have all your heads, just as I had the head of that blasted Bosley Crowther when he called me more overrated than a porno at a children's film festival!"

The actors grovel a bit more, then the group parts and the lizard is ejected. It grins nervously and wrings its hat in its hands. "I cry your pardon," the lizard says, "I didn't mean anything by it—" The poor thing drops its tail in distress.

"OFF WITH HIS HEAD!" the leading lady cries, and puts her sunglasses back on. The bodyguards step forward.

"Nonsense!" bursts out the little tamale girl, before she can stop herself.

The leading lady turns in the little tamale girl's direction and takes her sunglasses off again. "Who are you?" she demands. "And what business is this of yours?"

"Now, now, dear," says the leading lady's husband timidly. "She's only a child, dear."

"Get off, Norman!" the leading lady says. "Do you think I am too old to play Alice?"

"I haven't the slightest," says the little tamale girl. "For I have never even heard of this play, so I don't know anything about this Alice. But you are only as old as you feel, as they say, and with age comes wisdom, as they say, and age before swine, as they say, and age makes waste, as they say." Although that last one didn't sound quite right.

"I feel sixteen if I am a day," cries the leading lady, who looks more like thirty-five to the little tamale girl. "So you see, this clever girl agrees with me! Can you sing, clever girl?"

"Yes," the little tamale girl shouts.

"Sing out then, sing out!" the leading lady orders.

The little tamale girl folds her hands over the front of her pinafore and sings:

"Sweetly braise the baby in the frying pan
Oh, it's so delicious, the little milk fed man
Sauté it with some mushrooms
Stuff it in a bun
Squirt it with some catsup, yum yum yum!"

"And you can cook, too!" declares the leading lady. She turns to the rabbit. "Give her a part, do you hear me?"

"Of course, of course, dear," the rabbit says, wringing its paws nervously.

While the little tamale girl has been singing, the other actors had taken advantage of the distraction to scarper, and now the room is empty, floor littered with torn paper, dropped gloves, fans, banana peels, sandwich wrappers, pencils, and the poor lizard's dropped tail, still wiggling. The leading lady doesn't notice the mess; she storms away, the entourage falling in behind her. The tamale girl follows, wondering what will happen next, but all that happens is that the leading lady chatters on about a dishwater cleanse, and then she gets into a row with her press agent over an article in *The Califa Police Gazette* alleging that she dyes her hair (which is patently true, unless she was born with purple hair), which ends with the press agent being dragged away by the bodyguards.

"If I stay here, I shall be next for sure," thinks the little tamale girl, and she takes advantage of the ballyhoo to pursue the bear exiting stage left.

"She's going to demand *his* head soon enough, and then without any good press, no one will be safe," says the bear glumly, when they are out of earshot. "I've heard there's a troupe in Ticonderoga putting on a revival of *The Road to Bali*. You can come with, if you want; I heard your voice, and we'd make a good team. We could work up a 'Hoot Mon' routine, and I bet we'd have Hope and Crosby sewn up. Do you play the bagpipes?"

"What are the bagpipes?"

"That's a no, then. Good luck," says the bear, and is gone.

V. Queen of Wigs

The little tamale girl is back in the hallway again, and the leading lady and her entourage have vanished. So has everyone else. She is wandering up and down, feeling a bit lost and lonely, wishing she had a nice cup of tea, when she smells a glorious smell, a sort of mixed-up aroma of cherry tart, custard, pine-apple, roast turkey, toffee, and hot buttered toast. Her tummy rumbles like thunder. Sniffing and sniffing, she follows the scent to the door marked WIGS. Inside is a small room lined with shelves, and these shelves lined with heads—

The little tamale girl shrieks before she realizes the heads are actually wig-stands, hundreds and hundreds of wig-stands, each displaying, of course, a glorious wig. Wigs shaped like shark-fins, wigs shaped like snapperdoodles, wigs frothy as frappes, and shiny as silver foil. Wigs with ships riding their crests, and zeppelins hovering among their curly clouds. But the disappointed little tamale girl doesn't see any cherry tart, or custard, or turkey dinner, or even one small piece of hot buttered toast.

"There you are!" The wigger pops out from behind a wig shaped like a sleeping tuxedo cat. There's a wig on his head, and another on top of *that,* and another on top of *that,* and another on top of *that,* so he looks exactly like an ice cream cone that is piled too high and in danger of dumping its load.

The little tamale girl laughs, for he looks so silly.

The wigger scowls at her: "You need not laugh; your hair wants brushing."

"At least I have hair of my own!" the little tamale girl says indignantly.

"We shall soon fix you up—hurry, hurry—your entrance is in five minutes—"

The little tamale girl is whirled through the crush of ribbands, hair swatches, switches, braids, and fringes, into a chair, and draped with a sheet.

"Now, now, let's see, what shall we do with her hair?" the wigger cries. He waves about a pair of clippers; he must be a barber, as well. His cuffs are brown and crusty, so a surgeon, too.

"Give her a buzz!" cries the glover, who has come in from the back room. She's wearing gloves on her hands, and gloves on her head, and her dress is made of gloves sewn together, and she herself may be a large glove, with a face drawn on the top of the extended index finger, and the other fingers curled under.

"A high-top fade!" the cobbler shouts, clomping in, tongue wagging.

"The Farrah!" shouts the glover.

"The Pompadour!" suggests the wardrobe mistress, popping out from behind the glover. "A poof, a pouf, a puff, a plover!"

"I don't want my hair cut," cries the little tamale girl, and she twists and turns in the chair, trying to escape the snippy blades of the barber's scissors. "I will wear a wig instead!'

"A lovely idea, lovely idea!" the wigger cries. The cobbler claps his heels together, and does a little clog dance. The glover slow claps and the wardrobe mistress wobbles back and forth, grinning a glittery gray grin.

"The hedgehog!" the wigger cries, slapping the wig on the little tamale girl's head. This wig is all over prickles and curls up into a little ball when the little tamale girl tries to scratch her head.

"Ooow!" she cries.

"The dormouse!"

"It's snoring!" the little tamale girl complains, looking at her reflection in the mirror.

"The wasp?"

"It's buzzing, and I fear the tail will sting me. And yellow and black don't suit me."

The hatter whisks the wasp off and throws it in the jumbled pile of discards.

"The Cheshire cat?"

"It's nothing but a smile."

"Pepper pig?"

The little tamale girl sneezes.

"The hare?"

"I already have hair!"

"I know just the thing!" the wigger says. "Perfect for the part. Ta-da!"

The little tamale girl groans in horror. The wig he dangles before her is long and blonde with a silly fringe held back by a black velvet band. "That's way too silly! Who would wear their hair done up so? There—I shall have that one!"

The little tamale girl points at the glorious gable hood sitting in pride of place on the wigger's dresser. It is peaked at the top like a chalet roof, and has long velvet lappets which will swing enticingly around her shoulders. "That one!"

"That's a hat, not a wig!" the wigger protests. "It's the last hat my cousin the hatter made before he went mad."

"I want that one!" the little tamale girl shouts. "None other! Or I shall—"

The rabbit appears behind the wigger, shouting: "TWO MINUTES!"

The wigger whisks the gabled wig off its stand and onto the little tamale girl's head. The edges of the hood completely cover her short spiky hair, and the point at the top perfectly complements the square of her chin.

"You look lovely, loquacious, lavish, linguistic!" screams the wardrobe mistress.

The little tamale girl has to agree.

"ONE MINUTE!" shouts the rabbit, looking at its watch.

The wardrobe mistress tips the little tamale girl out of her chair and flings a parti-colored gown over her. The cobbler fits her feet into black character shoes, and the makeup artist dabs her cheeks with red, and her lips even redder.

Just in time.

"YOU'RE ON!" shouts the director, and darkness descends.

For a moment there is nothing but the little tamale girl's fluttering heart. "Oh, what if I can't remember lines, what if I shall freeze, and they shall all laugh at me, oh dear, sleeping in the woodpile is seeming awfully charming now. But no, this is my last moment as an unknown. I'm just a little girl with a big dream, and greasepaint in my blood. Now is my big break; tomorrow my picture shall be on the cover of every newspaper in Califa. I've struggled and suffered, but I've gotten back up again. Never shall I have to worry about stealie boys or the woodpile again—tonight, tonight, tonight, a star is born!"

A spotlight comes on, and here is the little tamale girl center stage. Behind her stand the dodo and the lory, both dressed like playing cards.

The Man in Pink Bloomers' grin hovers to her right and the rabbit stands to her left, fishing its watch out of a red velvet weskit.

In front of her, the leading lady, wearing a white pinafore over a blue dress and the silly blonde wig, is saying: "Stuff and nonsense! The idea of having the sentence first!"

"Hold your tongue!" the little tamale girl shouts.

"I won't!" the leading lady shouts back.

"Off with her head!" the little tamale girl orders, and the lory and the dodo, the Man in Pink Bloomers glimmering between them, step forward to obey.

A COMFORT, ONE WAY

Genevieve Valentine

Author's Note: In *Alice's Adventures in Wonderland*, the White Rabbit mistakes Alice for his maid Mary Ann. Mary Ann, who apparently resembles Alice, never appears in the story. As if to confuse things even more, Alice briefly assumes the "Mary Ann" role herself by trying to bring him his fan and a pair of gloves. From a character so righteously angry, in a story so concerned with how hard it is to hold on to identity in the face of the hostile and ridiculous, this feels like a telling concession. After all, Mary Anns come from somewhere, too . . .

The kitchen is boiling hot, clouds of pepper everywhere, and her invitation to play croquet has just arrived; her chin pains her, and an Alice will be here any second.

Be what you would seem to be, that's the trick. She pushes at the bundle in her arms until it screams, and she waits for a girl who's done as she's told and brought some gloves and a fan to a rabbit who left her to die, a rabbit whose house she staved in because she couldn't curb her appetites.

The Duchess's mouth tastes like salt, and her neck aches from the executioner.

* * *

She doesn't blame any of the girls who visit Wonderland for what happens. You're either a Queen or a Duchess, eventually, and it's not like anyone else can be the Queen.

She can always tell when Alices are coming because their voices boom so loud it scares the bread-and-butterflies right off the branches. Alices have appetites. Mary Anns show up at the door a little sooner; they don't eat cakes and cordials that are just lying around. Mary Anns skip the sea of tears and never wash ashore anywhere near the Dodo. They show up prompt and get to work. They never get out.

Alices sob an ocean and stomp out the doors and throw the baby into the woods and shout at the Queen until they break free. Mary Anns stay right where they are and fetch and carry for the Rabbit. They don't think anything is particularly wrong; the Duchess watches them frown at the Rabbit a bit at first, but it fades. He's flighty; what employer isn't?

They all start out Alice, back in the world at the top of the tunnel, but something happens, and she doesn't know what. There's no chance to understand it, either; Alices leave, and Mary Anns get so quiet. It's awful.

"You're thinking about something, dear," she warns every Alice, "and that makes you forget to talk." There's no point in trying too hard to shake a girl loose from the branch—she's a Mary Ann or an Alice and you'll know soon enough—but still. Here, if a girl stops talking, the mice will do it instead. Rabbits will. The flowers will. If you ever stop talking, you'll never get a word in edgewise again. That's the moral of that.

This Alice scowls. Her mouth pinches shut, more pointed than a chin. Duchess lets her go. As Alice passes by, the roses lean in with their mouths open; whatever they're breathing on her, she won't last the night.

The trick is that the Mad Hatter never wants you at the tea, so if you're looking for your pig to collect him from the woods and want to catch them unawares, you have to wait until Alice has just left. They'll all be distracted, then; no one can resist an Alice.

She can't always manage to sneak off for long enough—the kitchen requires her attention, and the invitation to croquet is due, and then she has to die—but sometimes she gets so lonely she could scream, and even a Mad Hatter and a March Hare are better than a nose full of pepper and a door that's always got a little girl behind it.

When she sits, the Hatter howls, "Great galloping goodness, who asked you?"

"Nobody at all. Two sugars," she says, dumping the dormouse out of the spare cup and banging it once on the table.

"You were much nicer before," the Mad Hatter says, which is true, if he means who she used to be before she was the Duchess. It's a lie if he means she was different just before the last time the axe came down. She was the same then. Not much point explaining, though—the Hatter's not very good about changes unless he's the one making them.

The March Hare won't even look at her anymore. She killed him for the stew once, just to see if it would make anything different for the next Alice through the door. It didn't (that girl turned out to be a Mary Ann, and that tea party went on for six weeks because she was too polite to run), but for someone who forgets so much, the Rabbit's got an awful long memory about some things.

If the Duchess stayed at the table, time couldn't touch her, either. But someone's head has to be cut off to make room for the next, like pruning a rosebush ahead of the spring. Sooner or later, she has to grow older and older, until her face sags past her pointed chin, and the little girls that barge through the door freeze in their tracks seeing someone so old with a baby so young.

The tea party gets along without the Duchess. They pull the wings off the bread-and-butterflies, and knock the vase of murdered flowers sideways so the dormouse can imitate what it's like to drown. "Move down!" the Hatter shrieks from time to time, but she never does, and the rhythm of the party breaks when everyone edges past her as quick as they can. She's sure of it, though. If you move every time someone barks that you should, you end up horribly far from where you started. She has a chair that creaks under her and wobbles when she peers around, and that'll do her just fine from now until the last Alice.

Hatter claims the view is finer here, or the chair is softer there, but what she has is well enough suited. No point being curiouser.

It's a horrid party, but it's something, and she stays until eventually the edges of the garden start to smear. Time is getting on without her, too.

"Best go, old girl," says the Hatter quietly. "Time and tide are waiting."

She doesn't mind, usually. She's clung to the table once or twice until the cards had to come and get her, but most of the time she mutters her goodbyes and gets on with it. The tea's made of saltwater anyway; nasty stuff. The Alices'd hate it, if the Hatter ever let them drink.

Mary Ann is waiting in the kitchen when the Duchess comes home to change for croquet. Mary Ann eases her into her five skirts, and her fine jacket, and the collar that stretches tight around her sagged face and her violent chin. Though she wouldn't know why if you asked her, Mary Ann's fingers tremble as she fastens the collar buttons. Alices storm through so much they never need consider; Mary Anns have the time to fetch gloves, and listen to the stillness of the nighttime here, and see what will become of them all.

"The ones who make it out are all right, of course," the Duchess says, at tea with the Queen of Hearts. She often has tea with the Queen before she's doomed to execution; the Queen has enough sugar to drink it, and it's nice to have a bit of conversation.

The Queen looks her over. The Duchess knows the Queen hates questions, which is why she'd been careful not to ask one, but even if you avoid that, the Queen loves to find the eye in every potato. In the silence, Duchess reaches under her hat for another of the biscuits. (The Queen can't be expected to provide them—who would bake in that house? Those cards go up in cinders—but the Duchess finds that a tea that has no biscuits is like a hat that has no biscuits: all right if you must do without, but vastly improved with.)

"I dare say they seem to be." The Queen is staring at some of the flamingos nearby; it will be croquet after this, then. Sometimes she wonders if the Queen has secretly liked croquet all along.

Then, as if she's been wanting to tell a secret, the Queen says, "Alices *seem* to be a lot of things. They never stop *seeming.* Very few of them manage to *be.*"

The Duchess can't decide if being an Alice like that is better than being a Mary Ann. It must be worse, she decides. Mary Ann grows old, but she has duties that no one expects her to guess, and it's pepper stew every night.

"Oh, bother," sighs the Queen. Duchess follows her gaze. Over the maze of garden hedges, a hundred doors; at every keyhole, an Alice. "Too early. It will be croquet for days, now."

They already have an Alice going; she's a hundred times the size of the White Rabbit right now, splitting his house in two as she considers giving in. The Duchess takes a breath, but waits until Alice's voice rolls booming up the hill: "That'll be a comfort, one way—never to be an old woman—but then—always to have lessons to learn! Oh, I shouldn't like that!"

The Alices at the gate don't hear her; they're all talking to themselves. The Mary Anns hear her, but that's when the despair sets in, and after that there's no climbing back out where you came from, and you might as well come inside.

"You gonna behead some of 'em?"

The Queen looks over, and the Duchess flinches and curses herself for a fool—a question, a question, a cup of tea with a biscuit drowned in it.

"The woods will claim a few," the Queen says finally, with some relief. "One or two will drink so much they disappear. One or two, the Cat will play with. That leaves one for you, if you want her—I shan't have one today."

Of course; Alice tomorrow and Alice yesterday, but never one today. That's how she's stayed Queen so long. There have been a thousand Duchesses. Their heads are always coming off—the Queen doesn't like biscuits, or questions, or being late, or being foolish, or being old, and she is so tired and so easy to anger—and then the Duchess grows again in the kitchen, chin-first, remembering it all and already looking to the kitchen door for a little girl who will be coming through at any moment.

(What she never quite remembers: When she becomes the Duchess again, does she swallow those little girls? Is she like the mushroom that grows on the corpse? Do Mary Anns just vanish between one breath and the next into the body of an old woman who has a child she didn't want and a soup she can't eat? Do Alices come back to the house to tell the cook that the Duchess won't be coming home, and sit by the table to cry, and then stay right where they are until age begins to pull at the body that used to be magic, and then all at once they wake from a dream of falling and she's taken them over?)

"I'll not want one today, Your Majesty."

"Mm. Are you sure? If you get any older my executioner won't be able to saw through your neck. A ring thicker every year, you know."

"Perhaps tomorrow, Your Majesty."

"Perhaps I'll call my guards right now and let one of these Alices through while I polish the axe," the Queen says, taking a great long slurp of tea, but the Duchess knows she doesn't mean it. She has to go back home and meet Alice in the kitchen before she can be beheaded. If an Alice got to the palace grounds this early, she might see the Queen and the Duchess having tea and ask to join them. The Duchess might have to look her in the eye.

"With Your Majesty's permission," the Duchess says, and lumbers upright and off home. She'll pick up a pig from the woods on her way. For a little girl who's smart enough to make it to her doorstep, they don't half like what she holds in her arms; by the time an Alice reaches her, that girl is only thinking of escape.

(They all can, and most of 'em do.)

"I've a right to think," says an Alice, and she does, of course, they all do, but to get here at all means a girl is eating and drinking suspicious things and breaking into other people's gardens, and listening to foolish people and taking bad advice, and taking orders from the first fellow she runs across.

By the time a girl makes it to the doorstep, they've been angry enough to push past the footman after nearly drowning in their own tears and giving away the last things they have, but they've been stupid enough to get this lost.

The Duchess pulls Alice closer, feels like the mushroom on the corpse. "What a clear way you have of putting things," she says.

She was a little girl once—she's almost sure. It's awfully hard to tell with the Hatter's parties making sure no one ever has a birthday, and time has a way of moving past her so quickly that she might have been a hundred all this time and never known. Years just vanish.

How she hates the Mary Anns! How she hates the Alices!

"I must go," the Duchess says to every new one, "you may nurse it a bit, if you like," and then she has to run up the stairs and slam the bedroom door behind her and press her hands against her mouth until the urge to scream has faded.

It's impossible to warn them. You have to see what they do. A Mary Ann stays in the kitchen and takes the baby downwind of the pepper and listens to it screaming until she cries and still she never moves; an Alice runs away with it and realizes that little boys turn into pigs if you're not paying close attention. She doesn't know what happens to the pigs. One of them's probably Mayor by now, and the Mary Anns will never meet him; Mary Anns are meant for the house.

But Alices are meant for fighting—Alices get out, the Duchess reminds herself over and over, sneezing pepper out of her nose. The Queen promises it's true.

Imagine being Queen, she thinks, swinging her flamingo as hard as she dares. It's an awful hard swing—she's held that wriggling piglet still for a long time, it makes you tough—and the hedgehog lets out a little moan as it sails across the lawn, scattering cards in its wake. Red paint drips onto the lawn, in the panic.

Game play is paused briefly so several cards can be executed.

The Queen orders it, her voice filling like a sail, and watches over it all. She has the arms of a baker and the face of a butcher and stands a good foot taller than anyone else in Wonderland. (When she gets a good swing, the hedgehog can fly as far as the eye sees, and strike the doors at the edge of the garden, past which there's no world left at all.) And in all of Wonderland, only the Queen plants her fists on her hips and stares right at the executions all the way through.

It might be because she's so tall, and never has to see the look on the Ten of Spades as the axe comes down. When you're a Queen and so much taller, you only see the bowed heads, and that must feel awful nice. The Duchess watches three Hearts fold to the ground. A girl gets quite tired of being such a tiny little thing.

Someday an Alice will break the whole deck, the Duchess thinks; *they're all so angry, those girls, and one of them will have to be angry enough, someday.* She'll call for the Queen's head and someone will give it, and the Cheshire will crown her, and then it will be her turn to nibble on cakes and cordials until she's taller than the rest, and to swing flamingos until her arms are heavy, and to look across the garden slopes and see the edges of the world surrounded by girls lurching to get in, and scream and scream and scream for the axe.

The cards beg for mercy every time; they cry so hard the paint runs off the roses at their feet. The Queen signals the Ten of Spades. The Duchess makes fists, feels the sinew of her arms, the strain of her collar.

"You could spare them," she says, once, when her courage is up. "They'll only be back. Might as well leave it be and let their heads alone."

The Queen pulls back for the swing, says, "I could." The hedgehog goes flying.

The night she spends in her house, waiting for Alice, is short. She's counted. It's three dreams long, and very quiet. It's the same night every time, which she knows because somewhere deep in the rattle of her mind is the idea of snow up to her knees, and there are no seasons here. There isn't even rain. Far away, they tell her, there's a chessboard, and so many brooks and streams you can't count them all, but Wonderland's all saltwater, even the tea.

The night is so still she can hear the cards as they paint the roses red. She can hear the ticking of the White Rabbit's watch as he sleeps longer than what's good for him. The soup is simmering; it will be ready for more pepper in the morning.

When the wind picks up at last, just before sunrise, it's in her favor—the air is fresh, and the pepper and the paint blow past her and away, and for a moment the path outside the door looks open, as if it actually leads anywhere. It doesn't—she's tried a thousand thousand times, and that path spans all of Wonderland and brings you right back to the kitchen door. Better just to look through the keyhole and dream.

The pig snores in his dreams. The Duchess's hair pains her. Out past the garden, an Alice is saying, "It might end, you know, in going out like a candle. I wonder what I should be like then?"

THE FLAME AFTER THE CANDLE

Catherynne M. Valente

> "She tried to fancy what the flame of a candle is like after the candle is blown out, for she could not remember ever having seen such a thing."
>
> —Lewis Carroll, *Alice's Adventures in Wonderland*

A Melancholy Maiden

Olive was beginning to get very tired of going down to Wales with her mother on holiday every year and having nothing to do. It is a difficult trick to be tired of anything much when you are only fourteen and three-quarters years old, but Olive was just the sort of girl who could manage it. She would admit, if significantly pressed, that once or twice a summer it did *not* rain or drizzle or mist or thunder moodily, but never for long enough to do anyone a bit of good, and anyway, what is the use of having rain at all if the sun does not follow after? And now, Father Dear had left them for that pale, rabbity little heiress in London who they were only allowed to refer to as the Other One, and some damp, sheepy madness had taken hold of Darling Mother. She meant for them all to *live* here somehow, herself and Olive and Little George, mixing, presumably, among the scintillating society of shire horses and show-quality cucumbers.

Olive could have complained for England—it was her chief occupation in those drowsy silver afternoons and sopping woollen mornings.

It was dreadful here. Even the potatoes and the ponies were depressed. There was only one pub and you weren't allowed to dance in it. Her school friends got to go to Rome and Madrid and Mykonos on *their* holidays. If this place ever hosted so much as a knitting circle, the whole population would suffer simultaneous apoplexies from the scandal of it. She couldn't even pronounce the name of the village in which Darling Mother had insisted on shipwrecking them. Pronouncing the name of the house was right out, and a more cramped and dreary paleo-lithic hut Olive had never dreamed of. It had never been *planned* nor *built* so much as *piled up* and *given up on several times,* leaving nothing anyone could properly call a house, but rather, a sort of rubbish bin full of bits of other houses lying on top of each other. Somebody had clearly once thought there was nothing so splendid in the world as Victorian moulding and crammed it in anywhere it would fit, and rather a lot of places it wouldn't, including three hacked-off marble capitals meant to crown pillars in a grand bank or a Hungarian cathedral, which instead had to make themselves content with being mortared to the parlour wall without a single column to spare between them. The faucets leaked. The electricity could best be described as "whimsical." The staircase groaned like it meant to give birth every time Olive so much as thought about mounting an upstairs expedition.

Worst of all, there were only twenty-one books in the library, and the landlord never changed them out because he was a perfectly slovenly old duffer who never could get all the buttons on his waistcoat closed at the same time. If they got fresh linens every fortnight, they ought to get fresh books, as well. It was only logic. Anything else was unhygienic.

Lingering in the Golden Gleam

He sees her first in the corner of Butler Library at Columbia University. It is late afternoon and it is 1932 and it is so hot the books blaze like a great knobbled furnace. He just rounds the corner and there she stands among the nonfiction stacks, adrift between The Rise and Fall of the Roman Empire *and* The Golden Bough. *She is wearing a long, unfashionably conservative blue dress and smart black boots. Her still-thick white hair huddles in a knot beneath a brown velvet hat. The skin beneath is pale and wrinkled as a crumpled page. He is also wearing blue, which he takes as a good omen. They match. They should match. Her dress is expensive, well-preserved, the sort of dress only brought out for occasions. Her hat is not. It is very shabby, with shabby silk violets clinging pessimistically to its shabby rolled brim. The soft, comforting sounds of idle chairs squeaking across polished floors and idle coughs squeaking out of polished lungs punctuate the long sentence of his silence, waiting behind her, waiting for her regard, waiting for her to notice him, as though he has not had his fill of being noticed in this life.*

But suddenly he has not had his fill of it. He longs for her to turn around. He wills it to happen now. All right, then now. No matter. NOW. He is desperate for her to see him, desperate as thirst. She will know him at a glance, of course, as he knows her. They will talk. They will talk wonderfully, magically, their words spangled and glittering, sodden with meaning, a conversation worthy of being recorded in perfect handwriting, printed lovingly in leather and vellum, preserved like that blue dress, down to the last quotation mark. Unless she is not as he wants her to be. She might be awful, awful and bitter and angry and stupid and a dreadful bore. Anyone worthy, anyone special or sensitive in the least, would know by now that he was standing here like a bloody fool, would have turned around minutes ago, would feel the shape of him behind her like a shadow. Shouldn't she glow? Shouldn't she burn with the light of who she is? But of course, he does not. He never has. He scolds himself for his own expectations.

It does not happen the way he wants it to. Nothing ever does anymore. He clears his throat like a stage.

Now, Peter!

"Mrs Hargreaves," whispers the youngish man in the blue tie, "pardon the intrusion. My name is Peter. Peter Llewelyn Davies."

She turns her back on the books and meets his eyes with a cool, sharp expression. She's rather shorter than he imagined. But her eyes are far, far bluer than his dreams, bluer than her dress, his tie, the June sky outside the tall library windows. She holds out her hand. He takes it.

"You must call me Alice, Mr Davies. Everyone does, whether I invite them to or not."

I Am Not Myself, You See

Olive dutifully kept up her soliloquy of despair during business hours, with short breaks for lunch and tea. But she didn't mean more than an eighth of it on any given day. It was all a kind of avant-garde improvisational theatre staged for the benefit of Darling Mother.

The unhygienically unchanging books were a real problem, but she knew very well that the village of Eglwysbach was pronounced *egg-low-is-bach*, which always made her imagine the German composer running around a chicken pen in a powdered wig and speckled wings, crowing for his lost babies. The house went by the name of Ffos Anoddun. As that was nearly too Welsh to bear, Olive assumed it was something to do with fairies or a hillock or a puddle or all three together, and fondly referred to it as Fuss Antonym, which sounded reasonably similar, and comforted her, for to her mind, the opposite of a big fuss was a small contentment. Olive loathed all her school friends and most other people, and couldn't have given a toss where they went on holiday, even if they'd ever think to confide that sort of thing in her direction. She felt rather affectionate toward the quiet, as it meant hardly anyone came round insisting on being other people at them. Olive *liked* knitting, and shire horses, and electricity was rather a lot of bother, when you thought about it. It was 1948. People had gotten along well enough without lightbulbs for nearly the whole history of everything.

And she especially loved the three capitals on Fuss Antonym's parlour wall. She would sit beneath them of an afternoon in the big musty mustard-coloured wingback chair with silk horseradish-green cord whipping and whirling all over it and imagine the poor odd stone wolf and wild hare and raven heads in their curling pale ferns were holding the whole world up, and herself the only person ever to have guessed the truth.

It was safe, you see, to complain around Olive's sole remaining parent. It was the expected thing. Darling Mother was a complainer in good standing herself. Misery was, she always said, the natural resting state of the young. It was only the old who could not bear unhappiness. Only the old who buckled beneath the hundred million pound weight of it all. As long as Olive kept up her whitewater torrent of disinterest and disaffection and discontent, Darling Mother judged her a Normal Girl, and therefore safe to abandon, never once asking what she was *really* thinking, or feeling, or wanting, or doing with her time, which suited Olive like a good coat. Little George never complained a bit, even when a sheep ate all his paintbrushes, and Darling Mother practically *murdered* him with concern and attention.

But she did guess at the shape of her child's actual innards, occasionally. When some change in the weather troubled the meagre seams of maternal ore that ran deep within the mine of Darling Mother's heart, she did grope after some connection. She changed the books once. She left a Welsh dictionary on Olive's bedside table. And once, when she returned from one of her hungry scourings of antique dealers and auctions for more gloomy Victorian rubbish to weigh down the house, she paid a couple of the local boys to drag something silver and heavy and covered with a stained canvas into the parlour. She waved her thin, elegant hand and they left it leaning against the sooty mantel.

"I snatched it up just for you, Daughter Mine. I know you love all this sort of crusty ancient knick-knackery deep down, don't let's pretend otherwise. It's a looking glass. I found it down in Llandudno at an estate sale. Give the old dear a good seeing-to, won't you?"

Child of Pure Unclouded Brow

"Alice, then," he says.

The New York sun lights up his untidy brown hair, turns it into a golden cap, the opposite of Perseus, the opposite of himself.

The old woman touches her hat self-consciously. "Alice then; Alice now. Alice always, I'm afraid."

"And I'm Peter."

He is repeating himself, and feels foolish. But repetition is a very respectable literary device. As old as dirt and debt and Homer. She will forgive him. Probably.

"Aren't you just?" laughs Alice. "Well, let's have a look at you. One head, two shoulders, a couple of knees, rumpled suit, and half a day's beard. Honestly, Peter, how could you come calling on me without a fetching green cap and pointed shoes? I think I deserve at least that, don't you?"

Peter looks stricken. His throat goes dry and in all his days he has never wanted whiskey so badly as in this awful moment, and in all his days he has wanted whiskey very badly and often indeed. She did know him, then.

"Oh, I am sorry. I am sorry, Peter, that was unkind. Oh, I am a dreadful beast! It's what comes of not mixing in company apart from cats and cups, you know. Don't look quite so much like you've just been shot, dear, it doesn't become. People have done it to me so many times, you see. I couldn't pass up a chance to do it to somebody else, just the once! And who else in all this sorry world could I do it to but you? Allow an old woman her indulgences."

"It's quite all right. I'm used to it."

Alice Pleasance Liddell-Hargreaves squares her shoulders, bracing as if for a solid punch to the chest. "You may pay me back, if you like."

"Please, Mrs Har—Alice. I've quite forgotten."

"No, no, it was rotten of me. I won't accept your forgiveness, not one bit, until you've done me a fair turn."

"If you insist on making it up to me, I should much prefer you allow me to take you to dinner tonight," Peter demurs. He dries his palms on his tweed. "I know a place nearby that's serving wine again already."

The sunlight streaming through the library windows thins and goes silvery with clouds, darkening Alice's eyes. "And what do you imagine that will accomplish? That Peter and Alice, the Peter and the Alice, should share plates of oysters and glasses of champagne, quote each other's famous namesake novels with tremendous wit and pathos, philosophize about innocence, and achieve a kind of graceful catharsis whilst we malign the rather tawdry men who wrote us down for posterity?"

"Just that," Peter said with a smile that looked like a memory of itself. He held out his arm. "To talk of many things. Of shoes and ships and sealing wax—"

Alice clutches her heart in mock agony and staggers. "Oh, there's a clever lad! A palpable hit, Davies. I'll be wincing for days. Now we're quite even."

Peter sighs. This would be all, then. A library, a few sharp words, then nothing, a meal alone with his shadows.

"I think I shall allow you to drag this dreadful beast to a respectable supper, so long as it's not too far, and you pay for us both. I can't bear much of a stroll, nor much expense, these days."

She puts her thin, bony hand on Peter's elbow. When she leans against him, she seems to weigh no more than a pixie.

Every Single Thing's Crooked

Olive sat in the parlour of the house she called Fuss Antonym with her knees tucked up under her chin, staring at the looking glass. It was raining, because it was Wales and it was winter, and the raindrops against the old lead windows sounded like millions of tiny crystal drums beaten by millions of tiny crystal soldiers. The marble wolf and raven and hare on the misplaced capitals stared down at her in turn. Olive had spent the better part of the morning on her hands and knees with a tube of silver polish and a bottle of vinegar, coaxing the muck of ages out of the great heavy mirror. It was quite a lovely design, once you got down past the geologic layers of black tarnish and dust. The glass was still good, except for a little spiderweb of cracks in the lower right corner that no one but actual spiders would ever notice. The silver frame bloomed with curling oak leaves and pert little acorns and shy half-open violets, a perfect specimen of the typical Victorian habit of taking anything wild and pretty and nailing it down, casting it in metal, freezing it forever. Olive thought the violets probably had little polleny agates or pearls in their centres at some point. The prongs were still there, bent out of shape, empty. She touched them with her fingers. Those prongs were quite the loneliest and saddest thing she'd ever seen, somehow. They looked like her mother. They looked like her.

She and Little George had wrestled it up onto the mantel and snagged the thing on a couple of rusty nails. They hadn't any kind of level or ruler, so the poor looking glass hung up there at an unhappy angle that Olive informed Darling Mother was "unbearable," while privately thinking of it as "rakish." Little George had wandered off to beg the sheep for his paintbrushes back, and Olive coiled herself into the mustard-coloured wingback chair for a good long stare. She could see just the barest top of her own head from here, her dark bobbed and fringed hair, her white scalp like a pale road through her own head. She could see the back of the little brass clock on the mantel, the woebegone door to the kitchen cracked open a wedge, the bland pastoral paintings hanging against vaguely mauve wallpaper, all turned backward, and therefore slightly more interesting. The shepherdess on the moor was holding her black lamb in her left arm now. The fox was running the opposite way from the hounds and the horses. She could see the rain beating out a marching rhythm on the windows, and the green hills beyond disappearing away into a fog like forgetting. And she could see the broken capitals glued to the wall in the looking glass just as they were glued to the wall in the parlour, their faces turned the wrong way round, too, like the shepherdess and the fox, which was certainly why their eyes looked so odd and canny, the way your own eyes look when you see a photograph of yourself. *Very* odd and *very* canny. Really, awfully so, actually.

Olive stood up on the wingback chair. The upholstery springs groaned and complained. Now she could see her whole self in the looking glass: Olive, not much of anyone, in a shift dress the same colour as the wallpaper, with pearl earrings on. The earrings belonged to the Other One. She'd given them for Christmas, to curry favour. Olive wore them to vex and to vex alone.

She leaned forward toward the looking glass. She blinked several times. She opened her mouth to call for Darling Mother, which was pure idiocy, so she shut it again with a quickness. She glanced over at the capitals in the parlour, then back to the capitals in the looking glass. Back and forth. Back and forth.

"There you have it, Olive," she told herself aloud. "You've gone mad. I expect it happens to everyone in Wales sooner or later, but you've certainly broken the local speed record. Well done, you."

Before now, when she'd considered the idea of insanity, chiefly when Darling Mother came home from meeting with Father Dear and the barrister and the Other One and started drinking gin out of a soup spoon, all night long, one spoonful after another, like sugar, she had imagined that going mad would feel different. Wilder, more savage, more lycanthropic, more like a carousel spinning too fast somewhere inside a person's brain. But Olive felt perfectly Olive. She didn't even think of the gin bottle in the cabinet. She only thought of the wolf. One thing was certain—*she* had nothing to do with it. It was the wolf's fault entirely.

The marble wolf in the parlour had a noble expression on his face. His muzzle was smooth and gentle and sorrowful. It looked almost soft enough to pet.

The wolf in the looking glass had raised his stone muzzle into a fearsome snarl.

Phantomwise

Peter asks the man at the Stork Club for scotch on ice. Evening light turns the tablecloths pink and violet. The ice is his last bulwark against total, helpless nihilism. He rolls the oily ambrosia of the bog over the crystals.

Alice orders a glass of beer. It arrives quickly, dark and thick and workmanlike. She smacks her lips and Peter nearly calls the whole thing off then and there. He had imagined her drinking . . . what? Delicate things. Tea. Champagne. Rain filtered through a garret roof. She is a lady of a certain era, and ladies of that certain era do not drink porter. After the beer come oysters from some presumably dreadful, mollusc-infested swamp called Maine, which would not pair at all with her black beer. Peter found himself in an apoplexy of flummoxed culinary propriety.

Alice runs her fingertip around the rim of her glass and puts it between her lips, slicked with sepia foam.

"One 'drink me' out of you and I'll have your head," she scolds him, but her eyes shine. "My husband loved his beer. The darker the better. None of this prancing blonde European stuff, he'd say. Porter, stout, dubbel! I pretended that I had never met so curious a creature as a man who adores beer. That's how a girl makes her way in this world, Mr Davies. Pretending awe at the simplest habits of men. But beer has been the bitter tympani keeping time for the long parade of sad, strange, lonely men I've loved. My father and Charles called it 'our most ancient indulgence' and made a lot of noise about the pyramids while they poured their pints. Even our Leopold had barrels brought in from Belgium no matter where we were staying—imagine the expense! Nothing to a man of his station, of course. But to us? Impossible magic. Though he liked everything blonde, the rake."

"Prince Leopold?" It sounds absurd even as he says it, but he cannot think of any other fabulously wealthy Leopold she might mean.

"The very one. Didn't you know Alice had adventures in places not called Wonderland? Paris, Rome, Berlin, Vienna. All the lions and unicorns you could ever want. He never could decide between my sister and me, and in the end we were nothing but . . . well. Talking flowers, I suppose. He named his daughter Alice. That's something, at least." She strokes the silvery flesh of the oyster with a tiny pronged fork. "He died."

"The prince?"

"My husband. In the war. My sons, as well. Everyone, as well. My sister is long gone, a ghost in Leopold's locket. I've got one boy left and he doesn't visit anymore. It's too awful for him to face ruin in a blue dress. Oh, Peter, I live crumblingly in a crumbling body in a crumbling house and I burn my heating bills in the furnace for lack of coal and every so often I crawl out to tell a few people how wonderful it was to be a child in Oxford with a friend like Charles to teach me about all the sundry beauties of life so that I can buy another year's worth of tinned beef. And how are you coming along in the world, Peter Pan? How are you crumbling?"

Peter Llewelyn Davies flushes and eats in silence. The oysters taste like spent tears. His toast points stare back at him as if to say: what else did you expect?

"I'm in publishing," he offers finally.

Alice laughs sharply. "How hungry a thing is a book! Devoured you whole straight from the womb, and still gnawing away at your poor bones. Oh, but it was different for you, wasn't it? It was only ever that summer, really, with Charles and me and Edith and Lorina, punting on the river. But your James raised you, didn't he? Adopted the whole lot of Davies orphans. I can't tell if that would be better or worse. Tell me. Should I envy you?"

The soup course arrives. He frowns into a wide circle of pink bisque. His brain is a surfeit of fathers—his own, a-bed, rotting cancerous jaw like a crocodile, all teeth and scaled death, his older brothers, always running, fighting, so far ahead, so untouched, and Barrie, always Barrie, Barrie always kind and generous and ever-present, ever watching, his eyes like starving cameras freezing Peter in place for a flash and a snap that never came.

"He drank me," Peter whispers finally. "And grew larger."

Large as Life and Twice as Natural

Olive put her hand against the looking glass.

She was balanced rather precariously on the mantel, one knee on either side of a portrait of Darling Mother as a young girl, before Father Dear, before the Other One, before Olive and Little George and Eglwysbach and the sheep and the paintbrushes and all of everything ever. A book of matches tumbled down onto the hearth as Olive tried, somehow, to grip the brickwork with her kneecaps.

When she'd been cleaning it with vinegar, the mirror had felt cool and slick and perfect as dolphin-skin. Olive pressed her other hand against the glass. It wasn't cool now. Or slick. It felt warm and alive and prickly, like a wriggling hedgehog thrilled to see its mate waddling through a wet paddock. The marble wolf's head in the looking glass parlour still snarled. The one in Fuss Antonym's parlour still did nothing of the kind.

"Don't be stupid, Olive," she scolded herself. Darling Mother never did, anymore. Someone had to pick up the slack. "Really, you're such an awful little fool. Nothing's going to *happen*. Nothing's *ever* going to happen to you. That's just how it is and you know it. You've gone barking, that's all, and pretty soon someone will come and take you away to a nice padded room by the sea where you can't bother anyone."

The looking glass *writhed* under her hands. It spread and stretched and undulated like a great glass python just waking from a thousand years asleep. Slowly, the mirror turned to mist, and the mist stroked the bones of her wrists with fond fingers.

"Mum!" Olive screamed—but the looking glass took her anyway, scream and all, and in half a moment she tumbled through to the other side into a cloud of green glow-worms, and a thumping, ancient forest, and the hot, thrilling blackness of a summer's midnight.

Each Shining Scale

The salad course appears amid the wash of unbridgeable silence. Beets, radishes, hard cheeses as translucent as slivers of pearl, sour vinegars, peppercorns green and black. Peter sighs. The other diners around him simply will not *stop their idiotic noises, the belligerent scraping of silver against china, the oceanic murmur of inane conversation, the animal slurping of their food. The oysters begin to turn on him. He feels a pale bile churning within.*

"He said not to grow up, not ever," he whispers. "He made me promise. But I couldn't help it. Not for a minute. Even while he was telling his tale, scribbling away at his own cleverness while my father rotted away in bed, I was growing up. Becoming not-Peter all the time while he told me to stop, stop at once, hold still, keep frozen like . . . like a side of lamb."

Alice rolls her eyes and bites through a red radish. She has a spot of mauve lipstick on her teeth. "Oh, how very dare those precious old men prattle on and on to us about childhood! The only folk who obsess over the golden glow of youth are ones who've forgotten how perfectly dreadful it is to be a child. Did you feel invincible and piratical and impish when your father died? I surely did not when Edith passed. You simply cannot stop things happening to you in this life. And do you know the funniest thing? An Oxford don, living in the walled garden of the university, with servants and a snug little house in which to write nonsense poems and puzzles and make inventions to your heart's content—that's more and more permanent a child-

hood than I ever had. He used to moan and mewl over me about the horror of corsets to come, the grimoire of marriage, the charnel house of childbirth, the dark curtains that would close over me upon some future birthday—well, for goodness sake! What would he know about any of that? He never married, he never had a child, he never so much as scrubbed his own underthings! How dare he tell me four years old was the best of life when I had so many years left to face?"

"Eighteen months."

"Pardon?"

"When Peter left for Neverland. He was eighteen months old. In a pram in Kensington Gardens. An eighteen-month-old child can barely speak, barely walk without falling. But that was the best I had ever been, in his eyes. The best I ever could be. And all those people went to see the play and clapped their hands and agreed he was right, and all the while I was twenty, twenty-five, thirty. Thirty. As old as Hook. Watching myself fly away. Watching from the back row while my bones screamed, all in quiet: That's not what I was like, that's not how any of it goes; Christ, James, I was never heartless, I wish I was, I wish I was!"

Alice frowns into her beer. She rubs the glass with one fingertip.

"It's not children who are innocent and heartless," she says—bitterly? Pityingly? Peter has never had the knack of reading people. Only books, and only on good days. "Only the mad," she finishes, and goes after her beets with a vengeful stab.

A Life Asunder

The very first thing Olive did was look behind her. There was dear, familiar, batty old Fuss Antonym's wall—but it was no longer dear or familiar at all, and quite a bit battier. Instead of storm-slashed white-wash, the house sported a shimmering blackwash, roofed with over-turned tea-saucers, and crawling with a sort of luminous ivy peppered with great, blowy hibiscus flowers in a hundred comic-book colours. She had come through the middle window in a row of three. On the other side of the window, she could still see the parlour, the mustard-coloured chair, the painting of the shepherdess and the black sheep, the peeling moulding, the chilled grey afternoon peeking in past the curtains on the ordinary wall opposite. *All right, yes, fine,* Olive told herself, half-terrified, half-irritated. *This sort of thing happens when you've gone mad. It's nothing to get in a tizzy over. You've sniffed too much silver polish, that's all. Might as well enjoy it!* The other side of the looking glass was a window, and the other side of the house was a deep night, and a deep summer, and a deep forest, deep and hot and sticky and bright.

Olive's knees abandoned her. She tumbled down onto a new, savage, harlequin earth. She was going to have a tizzy, after all. *For God's sake, Olive!* She plunged her knuckles into the alien ground. Even the soil sparkled. Hot mud squelched between her fingers, streaked with glittering grime like liquefied opals. An infinite jungley tangle spread out before her, and it simply refused to not be there, no matter how Olive tried to make it *stop* being there. A path tumbled down the hillocks and shallows, away into rose-jet shadows and emerald-coal mists. Delicate wood-mushrooms curled up everywhere like flowers in a busy garden: chartreuse chanterelles, fuchsia toadstools, azure puffballs.

Something was moving down there, down the path, between the mushrooms and the ferns and the trees no prim Latin taxonomy could pin down. Something pale. Something rather loud. And, just possibly, not one *something* alone, but three *somethings* together. There is nothing for a tizzy like a *something,* and before she could tell herself sensibly to stay close to home, no matter how odd and unhomelike home had suddenly become, Olive was off down the path and through the garden of night fungus, chasing three hard, pale, loud voices through the dark.

"You're such an awful brat," growled something just ahead. "I don't know why we trouble ourselves with you at all."

"And *deadly* boring, to ice the cake," sniffed something else. "Why even tell a riddle if you don't have any earthly intention of answering it for anybody? It's not sporting, that's what."

"I think it's jolly sporting," crowed a third something. "For *me.*"

"A raven *isn't* like a writing desk. You can smirk all you like, but that's the truth and I hate you. It just *isn't,* in any sort of way that makes sense—" the second something spluttered.

"The farthing you go for sense, the furthing you are from the pound," the third something said loftily.

"*Do* shut up," snarled the first something.

Olive rounded a bank of birch stumps and mauve moss wriggling in such a way that she absolutely did not want to look any closer—and yet she did, for that was a something, too. The moss wasn't wriggling at all, rather, hundreds of silkworms wriggled while they feasted on it. Only these were *actually* silkworms—not ugly blind little scraps of beef suet, but creatures made up entirely of rich, embroidered silk brocade, fat as a rich lady, writhing greedily over the bank. Olive shuddered, and in her shuddering, nearly toppled over the *somethings* she'd been after.

In a clearing in the wood stood three hacked-off marble capitals, the sort meant to crown pillars in a grand bank or Hungarian cathedral. Her capitals. The very ones that hung so stupidly and dearly on her parlour wall. Only these were hopping about on their own recognizance, as if they were really and truly the wolf, hare, and raven that had been carved into their fine stone blocks.

The wolf's head, surrounded by carved fern-heads and flowers, the very one that had snarled *within* the looking glass and snoozed *without,* looked Olive up and down. The hare wriggled her veiny marble nose. The raven fluffed his sculpted feathers.

"Bloody tourists," the wolf snipped.

Seven Maids with Seven Mops

Alice watches another couple without expression. The man cuts the woman's meat for her. The woman stares into the distance while he saws away silently at her pork. A repeating face, turned away, a woman watching a woman watching nothing. Staring and sighing and gnawing, the great human trinity. Peter has a strange and horrible instinct to lean over the table, the salads, the beer, the scotch, the candles, the world, their whole useless strained, copyedited lives and kiss Alice. To make himself cheap, as Wendy did in that cruel first scene in the nursery. He has always kissed first in his life. Always tried to redeem that little viciousness in the other Peter, whose heart was an acorn and whose kiss was a jest. She is so much older than he, but Peter loves older women, since he was hardly yet a man. Guiltily, and to great sorrow, but who could ask more of the most famous motherless boy in all of history?

He doesn't do it. Of course he doesn't. He, too, is of a certain era, and that era does not clear dining tables for the madness of love.

"At least your man stayed to look after you," Alice says finally, without turning her face back to his. "It's a kindly vampire who tucks you in and puts out the milk by your bed once he's drunk his fill of your life."

Her lips are red with beet-blood. He supposes his must be as well. Peter orders a second scotch.

"Are you angry, Alice? Do you hate him? I can't think whether I should feel better or worse if you hate him. I can't think whether I hate mine or not. I can't think whether he is mine. I am his, that's for certain. His, forever. A shadow that's slipped off and roams the streets hoping to be mistaken for a human being. For a while I was so flamingly angry I thought I'd char."

"Not angry . . . angry isn't the word. Perhaps there isn't a word. Charles came back to see me once, after that summer. I was a little older. Eleven or twelve. A little was enough. He looked at me like a stranger. Like any other young woman—a slight distaste, a tremor of existential threat, a very little current of fear. He could hardly meet my eye while I poured the tea. Like a robber returning to the scene of the crime." She stopped watching the other woman and turned her blue eyes back to Peter. Their cold, triumphant light filled him up like a well. "He came to my window and saw that I'd grown old and he wanted nothing more to do with me."

Alice's Right Foot, Esq.

"You're going to spoil it," snapped the hare. "Oh, I *know* she's going to spoil it, it always gets spoiled, just when we're about to have it out at last."

"I won't spoil anything, I promise," Olive whispered, quite out of breath.

"You can hardly help it," sighed the wolf's-head capital. "Any more than milk can help spoiling outside the icebox."

"Raven was *finally* about to tell us how he's like a writing-desk when you came bollocking through! I've been waiting eons! There's no sense to it, you know. We've said a hundred answers and none of them are at *all* good. But he won't say, because he's a stupid wart. I'd advise *you* to tread more quietly, young lady, if you don't want to alert the authorities."

"What authorities? It's only a forest inside a looking glass. The constable is hardly going to come arrest me on my way from Nowheresville to Noplace Downs."

"The Queens' men," the wolf whispered. His whiskers quivered in canine fear. "All ways here belong to them."

"Which Queen? Elizabeth? She's all right."

"Either of them," answered the hare with an anxious tremor in her quartzy whiskers. "Twos are wild tonight and they're the worst of the lot." The pale rabbit tilted onto her side just as a real, furry hare would if it were scratching its ear with a hind leg, only the capital hadn't any hind legs, right or left, so she just hitched up on one corner and quivered there.

"All right, I surrender," cawed the raven's head suddenly. "I'll say it. But only because our Olive's finally going places, and that deserves a present."

"Oh, don't be silly!" Olive demurred, though she was quite delighted by the idea. "It's quite enough to have properly met you three at last! And to think, it would never have happened if I hadn't gone totally harebrained just then! It was all that silver polish, I expect."

The marble hare went very still. "I beg your pardon? What is the trouble with a hare's brain, hm?"

"Oh, I didn't mean anything cruel by it," Olive said hurriedly. "It's only that I'm . . . well, I'm obviously not playing with a full deck of cards this evening."

"Only the Queen has a full deck at her command," the marble wolf barked. "Who do you think you are?"

"Nobody!"

"Then we'll be on our way!" The hare huffed. "There's no point in talking to nobody, after all. People will say we've gone mad!"

"Oh, please don't go! I only meant . . ." She looked pleadingly at the marble raven, who offered no help. "I only meant that *I* went mad a few minutes ago, and as I've only just started, I'm bound to make a mash of it at first. I've no doubt I'll improve! The most dreadful sorts of people go mad; it can't be so terribly hard. But I only ever wanted to say that darling Mr Raven hasn't got to give me a present, it's present enough to make your acquaintance!"

"Would you prefer a future?" the hare asked, her pride still smarting. "It's more splendid than the present, but you've got to wait three days for delivery."

"Of course, the past is particularly nice this time of year," the wolf grinned.

"No! All we've got is the present, and not a very pleasant one at that." The raven snapped at a passing glow-worm. "Rather cheap, honestly. I'm only warning you so you won't be disappointed."

"Oh, stop trying to impress her! You haven't got the goods. Admit it!" The wolf howled from within his thicket of carved Corinthian leaves. "You just made up that bit of humbug because it sounded clever and shiny and it alliterated you never had the tawdriest idea of how to solve it. Confess! Perjury! Pretension! Petty thief of my intellectual energies! *Hornswoggler!*"

"I *have* got the goods, and the bads, and the amorals, too! But if I'm to give up my present, after all this time, we must have a proper party for it! You lot have abused me so long that just handing it over in the woods like a highwayman won't do—no sir, no madam, no how nor hence nor hie-way! I will have a To-Do! I will have balloons and buttercream and brandy and bomb shelters! And one good trombone, at minimum!"

The marble hare rocked from one side of its flat column-base to the other in sculptural excitement. "Shall we, shan't we, shall we, shan't we, shall we join the dance?"

The three capitals leapt off down the forest path, bouncing and hopping like three drops of oil on a hot pan. Olive raced after them, ducking moonlit branches and drooping vines clotted with butterflies that seemed, somehow, to have tiny slices of bread for wings. But no matter how Olive ran, she seemed only to go slower, the wood around her only to close in thicker and deeper, darker and closer, until she could hardly move at all, and had lost sight entirely of the talking capitals. At last, she found herself standing quite still in a little glen, staring up at the starry sky and the starry leaves and the starry massive skeleton sheathed in moss so thick it could keep out the cold of a thousand winters. Tiger lilies and violets and dahlias and peonies grew wild in the skeleton's teeming green ribcage, its soft, blooming mouth, its sightless eye sockets. It lay sprawled on the forest floor propped up against a tree as vast as time, arms limp, legs bent at the knee. A galaxy of green and ultraviolet glow-worms ringed the giant's dead green head like a crown, and the crown spelled out words in flickering, sparkling letters:

THE TUMTUM CLUB

No Thought of Me Shall Find a Place

A violinist, a cellist, and an oboist begin to set up their music stands in the corner of the Stork Club. They are nice young men, in nice new suits, with nice fresh haircuts and shaves. The violinist rubs his bow with resin as though he is sharpening a sword.

"I always felt . . . Alice . . . I always felt I was two people. Two Peters. Myself, and him. The Other One. And the Other was always the better version. Younger, handsomer, jollier, bolder. Of course he was. I had to bumble through every day knocking things over and breaking my head open. But the Other One . . . he got to try over and over again until he got it right. Until he was perfect. Dreamed, planned, written, re-written, re-re-written, edited, crossed-out, tidied up, nipped and cut and shaped and moved through the plot with a minimum of trouble. Nothing I could ever say could be as clever as the Other One's quipping. How could it be? Everything I say is a dreadful cliché, because I am alive and human, and live humans are not made out of dust and God's breath, no matter what anyone says. They're made out of clichés. So there are two of me—what a unique observation for a muse to make! No, no, it isn't, it can't be, because I only said it once, I didn't get to decide it was rubbish and go back, erase it, add a metaphor or a bit of meta-fiction or a dash of theatricality. So I just say it and it's terrible, it's nothing. But the Other One would be delighted with

two Peters, you know. What adventures they would have together. Nothing for mischief like a twin."

Alice's eyes narrowed with concern. "Peter . . . I'm not sure I follow, dear."

"Yes, well, no one does. I don't, when it comes down to it. If you don't mind a confession before the main course . . . I . . . I went . . . well, all this about two Peters and suchlike . . . wound me up in a sanatorium. For a while. Not long. But . . . well, yes. Er." He finished lamely, flushing in shame—shame, and the peculiar excitement of sharing a secret one absolutely knows is unwelcome and untoward.

"Oh, Peter!"

"Oh, Peter, indeed. It's such a funny thing. Nothing in the world so much like Neverland as a sanatorium. The food isn't really food, no one's got a mother, there's a great frightening man in a waistcoat who harries you night and day, and you keep fighting the same battles over and over, round and round in circles, forgetting that you ever fought the minute it's over and the next one begins. All of us lost boys in that awful lagoon, dressed as animals, wailing for home."

She puts her hand on his. The tableware shifts beneath their fingers.

"Did you ever feel . . . like that? Like there were two Alices?" he whispers.

Alice laughs wanly. "Good heavens, no. There is only one Alice, and I am her. He only . . . took a photograph. One great, gorgeous photograph, where the sitting lasted all my life, and he sold that picture to the world."

Cinders All A-Glow

Olive found that, if she walked very, *very* slowly, as though she were dragging her feet on the way to some unpleasant chore, she could speed along quite gaily through the shadowy glen. It hardly took a moment of glum shuffling before she stood at a tapering, rather church-like door wedged into the giant's skeleton, just where its briary ribcage came to a Pythagorean point. It certainly *was* a door, though rather absurdly done. It made her think of all the overdecorated, slapdash rooms of Fuss Antonym, thrown up without reason or sense, for the door was spackled together out of pocket watch parts and butter and breadcrumbs and jam, and she felt entirely sure that if she were to knock, it would all come oozing, clattering apart and she should be billed for the damage.

"Hullo?" Olive called instead, for she had forgotten her pocketbook on the other side of the looking glass.

A slab of cold butter bristling with minute-hands like a greasy hedgehog slid aside. Two beady black rodent eyes peered down at her.

"Password," the Doorman whispered.

"Well, I certainly don't know!" Olive sputtered.

Oh, bad form, Olive! she cursed herself. *Haven't you ever read a spy novel? You're meant to say something extra mysterious, in a commanding and knowledgeable voice, so that the doorman will say to himself, "Anyone that commanding and knowledgeable has to be on the up and up, so it stands to reason the password's changed, or I've forgotten it, or I'm being tested by management, but any way it cuts, it's me who's at fault and not this fine upstanding member of our society." Now, come on, do it, and you won't have to feel embarrassed when you think back on this later when you've gone un-mad.*

Olive stood on her tiptoes and stared commandingly into those black rodent eyes. *Something extra mysterious. Something knowledgeable. Preferably something mad. Like a chicken in spectacles and a powdered wig.*

"Eglwysbach," she said slowly and stoically, fitting her mouth around the word as perfectly as possible, even tossing in a proper guttural cough on the end.

The eyes on the other side of the buttered watch-parts blinked uncertainly.

"Er. That doesn't sound right. But it doesn't sound *wrong.* It *sounds* passwordy. Am I asleep?" the Doorman whispered.

"We both are, most likely," Olive laughed.

"I'm not meant to sleep on the job. I'll be sacked for wasting time, even though time doesn't mind. He does need to lose a bit round the middle, to be quite honest. In fact, I wasn't asleep! I heard every word you were saying. Very naughty of you to suggest it."

"I won't tell. Now, if you heard what I was saying, then you heard me say the password very well and very correctly."

"Did I? That's nice." The creature yawned, but didn't open the door.

"Let me in!"

"Oh! Please don't beat me."

The pocket watch door wound open, leaving a slick of butter and jam as it swung. The Doorman was not a Doorman at all, but a Dormouse, standing on a tall footstool in a suit of armour bolted together out of pieces of a lovely china teapot with blue pastoral scenes painted on it. He stood rather stiffly, on account of the armour.

"I feel most relaxed and un-anxious snuggled into my teapot," the Dormouse said defensively, puffing out his little mouse chest. "So my friend Haigha invented a way for me to stay in it forever. In the future, everyone will be wearing teapots, mark my . . . mark . . . my March . . ."

The Dormouse fell asleep stuck upright in his armour. He leaned back against the door so that it groaned shut under his little weight.

Envious Years Would Say Forget

Peter takes off his glasses and rubs the bridge of his thin nose. The musicians begin a delicate, complicated piece that is nevertheless easy to ignore.

"I'm terribly sorry, Mrs—Alice. I thought I wanted to talk about this. I thought I wanted to talk about it with you. But I think perhaps I do not, not really. I'm an awful cad, but I've always been an awful cad. Even the best version of me is a cad."

Alice quirked one long white eyebrow. She leaned back in her chair and folded her hands in her blue lap.

"Am I doing something wrong?"

"Pardon?"

"Am I doing something wrong? Am I not behaving as you imagined I would behave? Ought I to have ordered the mock turtle soup instead of the cucumber? Or perhaps you'd like us to leap up and dash round the table and switch places whilst I pour butter into your pocket watch? I could curtsy and sing you a pleasant little rhyme about animals or some such—I'm told

my singing voice is still quite good." Alice's thin, dry mouth curled into a snarl. "Or shall we simply clasp hands and try to believe six impossible things before the main course? What would satisfy you, Peter?"

Beneath the table, Peter dug his fingernails into his flesh through the linen of his trousers. He felt a terrible ringing in his head.

"It's nothing like that, Alice. I wouldn't—"

"Oh, I think it's precisely like that, Mr Davies. You ought to be ashamed. It's disgusting, really. How could you do this to me? You, of all people? You didn't come snuffling round my skirt-strings so that we might find some pitiful gram of solace between the two of us. You came to find the magic girl. Just like all the rest of them. You're no better, not in the least bit better. Life has hollowed you out, so I and my wondrous, lovely self must fill you up again with dreams and innocence and the good sort of madness that doesn't end you up with an ether-soaked rag over your face. Well, life hollows everyone, boy. I've got nothing left in the cupboards for you. Oh, I am disappointed, Peter. Rather bitterly so."

A kind of leaden horror spread over Peter's heart as he realized he was about to cry in public. "Mrs Hargreaves, please! You don't understand, you don't. You can't."

Alice leaned forward, clattering the tableware with her elbows. "Oh—oh. It's worse than that, isn't it? You didn't want me to be magical for you. You wanted to be magical for me. In the library. Just like a nursery, wasn't it? And for once you would really do it, fly up to a girl's window and sweep her away to a place full of crystal and gold and feasting, and she would be dazzled. I would be dazzled. You tell everyone else that you're not him, to stop gawping at you and only seeing the boy who never grew up. But you thought I, I, of all people, might look at you and see that you are him. Or, at least, that you want to believe you are, somewhere, somewhere fathoms down the deeps of your soul. Only I'm spoiling it now, because an Alice makes a very poor Wendy indeed."

Peter Llewelyn Davies gulped down the dregs of his scotch and thought seriously about stabbing himself through the eye with his oyster fork. It would be worth it, if he could escape this agony of a moment.

"Very well, then, Peter," Alice said softly. "I am ready. I am here. I am

her. I am all the Alice you want me to be. Now that we've seen each other, if I believe in you, you can believe in me."

"Stop it."

Let's Pretend We're Kings and Queens

The Tumtum Club was a wide, round room carpeted in moonflowers. Wide toadstool-tables dotted the floor, lit by glass inkwells in which the blue ink burned like paraffin, and all the sizzling wicks were quills. Creatures great and small and only occasionally human crowded round, in chairs and out, dodos and gryphons and lizards and daisies with made-up eyes and long pale green legs and lobsters and fawns and sheep in cloche hats and striped cats and chess pieces from a hundred different sets, all munching on mushroom tarts and pig-and-pepper pies and slices of iced currant cakes and sipping from tureens of beautiful soup. The revellers were dressed very poorly and very well all at once. Their clothes were clotted with sequins and rhinestones and leather and velvet, but it was all very old and shabby and worn through, and no one wore shoes at all. Advertising posters hung all round the mossy bones walling them in. One showed a rose with a salacious look in her eyes and two huge fans over her thorns, promising a LIVE FLOWERS REVUE. Another had two little fat men in striped caps painted on it yelling at one another, which was, apparently, THE SATIRICAL SPOKEN WORDS STYLINGS OF T&T, TWO WEEKS ONLY. On one end of the club stood a little stage ringed with glowing oyster-shell footlights. A thick blue curtain was drawn across the half-moon proscenium. Olive could hear the tin-tinning sounds of instruments warming up backstage. Whatever happened in the Tumtum Club at night had not begun to happen yet.

On the other end of the room stretched a long bar made of bricks and mortar and crown moulding. It was manned, improbably, by a huge egg with jowls and eyebrows and stubby speckled arms and a red waistcoat and a starched shirt collar and cravat, even though he had no neck for it to matter much. An orchestra of coloured liquor bottles glittered behind him. A couple of chess pieces, a white knight and a red one, leaned past the empties to catch the eye of the egg.

"I'll take a Treacle and Ink, my good man," the red knight said.

"It's *very* provoking," the bartender answered, filling up a pint glass, "to be called a man—*very*!"

"I'll have an Aged Aged Man, Mr D," the white knight whispered. "Or should I spring for a Manxome Foe? Oh!" the knight fretted and pursed his horsey muzzle. "Just mix a bit of sand in my cider and don't look at me. You know how I like it."

The egg-man turned to Olive. "And you, Miss . . ."

"Olive."

"Ah, with a name like that you'll want a martini. With a name like that you'll be small and hard and bitter and salty. With a name like that you'll be fished out when no one's looking and discreetly tossed in the bin!"

The notion of being served a martini, no questions asked, rather thrilled Olive. Darling Mother was very strict with everyone's indulgences but her own. "I can't pay, I'm afraid. I haven't got half a crown to my name."

"No crowns allowed at the Tumtum Club, my dear," the white knight whispered, "Not even one." And before he was done with his whispering, a cocktail glass slid down the bar into Olive's hand. Whatever was inside was nothing at all like a martini, being completely opaque and indigo, but it did have an olive in it. Frosted letters danced across the base of the glass: DRINK ME. So she did.

A voice like a crystal church bell wrapped in silk rang out over the club.

> *"Will you all come to my party?" cried the Monarch to the*
> *Throng*
> *"Though the night is close around us and its reign is harsh*
> *and long?"*

A long, slim, orange and black leg slid out from behind the curtain. A rude and unruly applause burst through the room, catcalls, foot and hoof-stomping, snapping of fingers and claws, a great pot of hollering and whistling stirred too fast. A long, slim, orange arm emerged from the blue velvet, its elegant fingers curling and dancing with each new word.

"Gather eagerly, my darlings, tie your troubles in a bow
For the Tumtum Club is open—are you in the know?
Are you, aren't you, are you, aren't you, are you in the know?
Are you, aren't you, are you, aren't you, aren't you ready for the show?"

Olive stared. This was, perhaps, a naughtier show than she really ought to be seeing. But then, if the mad are naughty, who can scold them? She scrambled for an empty seat among the toadstool tables. Only one remained, far in the back row, wedged between a large striped cat and a thin, nervous-looking chess piece, a white queen, knitting a long silvery shawl in her lap.

A huge saffron-coloured wing spooled out over that coy leg like a curtain all its own. It was speckled with white and rimmed with jet black and veined with ultramarine. Finally, a head emerged: hair like a beetle's back, skin the colour of flame, eyes as green as swamp gas and cut-glass. The girl swept and twirled her massive butterfly wings like the fans of a harem-dance and sang for the roar of the crowd:

You can really have no notion how delightful is our art
In here there is no Red Queen and there is no Queen of Hearts
Only me and thee and he and she all in a pretty row
Alive as oysters, every one—now, shall we start the show?
Shall we, shan't we, shall we, shan't we, shall we start the show?
Shall we, shan't we, shall we, shan't we, shan't we set the night aglow?

"The Queen of Hearts?" Olive whispered. "I read a book with a Queen of Hearts in it once."

"You must be very proud," yawned the cat.

It Must Sometimes Come to Jam To-Day

The candlelight lights up her cheekbones ghoulishly. She has the look of a fox on the scent of something small and scurrying and delicious.

"I shan't stop," she needles him. "If you know any bloody thing at all about Alice, you know that she doesn't stop. She keeps going, all the way to the eighth square and back home again. She's the perfect English Girl, greeting the most vicious of things with an 'Oh My Gracious!' and a 'Well, I Never!' You haven't the first idea what sort of stony constitution it takes to go through life as the English Girl. At least your Other One got to be wild and free and rule-less. A man can aspire to that. My Other One cannot rise above charmingly confused, because no English Girl may be allowed to greet nonsense with a sword or else all Creation would fall to pieces. But you wanted to meet me. You wanted to compare notes. You wanted a sympathy of minds, so no Oh My Graciouses for you, Peter. Only Alice, and Alice will have her tea and her crown if it's the death of her. Alice is curious, don't you remember? It is her chief characteristic. Curiouser and curiouser, as the meal goes on. Tell me everything. Leave off this poor mad little me *act. What was Neverland* really *like?"*

Peter coughs brutally. His vision swims with liquor and humiliation and the violin and the cello and the love he had prepared so carefully for this person, only to find it spoiled in the icebox. With the perfect timing of his class, the waiter appears with steaming plates of beef bourguignon and quails in a cream-mustard sauce, ringed in summer vegetables glistening with butter.

"You're mocking me, Mrs Hargreaves. I never imagined you could be so vicious. I might as well ask you what Wonderland was like."

"You might at that. It smelled much better than New York, I'll tell you that much. But no more. I am operating a fair business here, young man. Show me yours and I'll show you mine."

"You can't be serious. Are you quite drunk? Does it amuse you to pretend to a silly clod that Wonderland was a real place?"

Alice blinks. She turns her head curiously to one side.

"Does it amuse you to pretend that Neverland was not?"

Did Gyre and Gimble in the Wabe

The acts went by like leaves blowing across the stage. Three young girls in shifts called Elsie, Lacie, and Tillie did an acrobatic routine, pantomiming any number of things that began with M: mouse-traps, and the moon, and memory, and muchness. Olive couldn't imagine how a handful of gymnasts could act out *memory* or *muchness,* but when they froze in their tableaux, Olive knew just what they meant, and applauded wildly with everyone else. A pig in a baby-bonnet stood in a lonely spotlight and belted out one long, unbroken oink of agony that lasted nearly two full minutes before he fell to his knees, scream-snorted MOTHER WHY DON'T YOU LOVE ME while tears streamed down his porky jowls, then sprang up and bowed merrily while roses flew at him from all directions. A lovely turtle with sad eyes sang a song about soup. It seemed to be a sort of communal thing—anyone could whisper to the gorgeous butterfly master of ceremonies and take the stage, if they felt inclined. There was a bit of a queue forming in the wings. Olive shrank back as a monstrous *thing* crept onto the boards. He had claws like a great hairy dinosaur and eyes like headlamps and a tail that coiled down over the footlights, casting broken shadows over his violet-green-scaled body. His dragon wings were so tall and wide he was obliged to bend and scrunch them to wedge under the half-moon shell of the stage. A couple of fawns pushed a little rickety pianoforte over to him with their dear spotted heads. The monster tinkled out a few experimental runs up and down the keys. Olive could hardly believe his horrid tarantula-talons could manage such graceful scales.

"It's only a Jabberwock, my dear. You needn't clutch my hand *quite* so hard," said the White Queen. Her face was so serene and crisply carved, like a jeweller had done it.

"A Jabberwock! Like *'twas brillig and the slithy toves did gyre and gimble in the wabe? Whiffling through the tulgey wood* and that? *The* Jabberwock?"

The monster at the piano began to play a mournful torch song. He fixed his moony headlamp-eyes on Olive and sang in a gorgeous tenor: *I never whiffled, I never; and it weren't even brillig at all. Nobody gave me no chance to be beamish; I could've been someone, if I'd been born small . . .*

The White Queen frowned at her knitting. "That's Edward. He's rather a war hero, don't you know? He lost his right foot at the Battle of Tulgey Wood, see?" Olive leaned forward—the Jabberwock worked the pedals of his pianoforte with only one crocodile-foot. The other was wrapped in gauze and seeping. The White Queen sighed like a tea kettle boiling. "He's going to lose the other one in an hour, poor chap."

Olive blinked. "What? What do you mean he's *going to* lose his other one? How do you know?"

Edward belted out: *You can take a Wock's head but you can't make him crawl!* He stopped, leaned his long, whiskered snout over the footlights into the audience, and whispered: "On account of my brain's being in my tail, yeah? Joke's on you, O Frabjous Brat!"

"It's the effect of living backwards," the Queen said kindly.

"Oh!" Olive whispered excitedly. "I know this part! Jam to-morrow and jam yesterday, right?"

"Will you please be quiet?" growled the striped cat. "Talking during performance is a biting offense."

The White Queen blushed pinkly. She reached down into the knitting basket at her feet and drew out a toasted crumpet spread generously with raspberry jam. She brushed a bit of wool fluff off of it and offered it to Olive.

"I have learned a few lessons since I was deposed," she said softly, and with such a tender sadness. "Very occasionally, it costs one nothing to bend the rules."

Dear Me! A Human Child!

Alice stares down at her four neat quails adrift in their sea of golden sauce.

"You can't be serious," Peter hisses at her. "This is . . . this is unkind,

Alice. Monstrous, in fact. Why are you doing this to me? What purpose is there in it?"

"I'm not doing any little thing to you, young man. Now, stop it. You needn't pretend. What was Hook like, really? I always wondered if his stump pained him, at night, in the cold of the sea air."

"For Christ's sake, this is madness. You ought to be locked up, not me."

Alice's face goes dark and furious and sour.

"Say that to me again, boy. Say it, and I'll whip you like the child you are, right here in this lovely restaurant. Don't think I can't. I raised three sons and a husband, you know."

Peter blanches. He feels his blood rebel, not knowing whether to flood his cheeks or flee them. He begins a deep study of his beef. After a time, Alice softens.

"I am sorry—it's a wonder how many times I've said it in such a short while! But I am, I am sorry, Peter, I simply assumed. It was only natural, to my mind. Only logic. I only thought . . . if for me, then for you. Goose and gander and all that rot. Oh, I never told anyone—my God, how could anyone be told? How could I even begin? But you, you of all people! The moment you introduced yourself I thought that we had veered toward this, careened toward it, that we would converge upon it long before dessert, and at last, I would know someone like me, and you would know someone like you, and what peace we should have then, at the end of it all. Peace, and something nice with butterscotch."

"Please. You mock me, Mrs Hargreaves."

"I do not, Mr Davies. I make you my confession. In the summer of 1862, something rather astonishing happened to me. I was ten years old. And naturally, when it was all done, I ran at full pelt to tell my best friend all about it just as soon as I could. To my eternal fault, in those days, my best friend was a mathematics professor with a rather large nose and a rather large anxiety complex and an interest in writing."

The beef tastes like nothing at all. The wine tastes like less than that. He gives up. "It was real," he says flatly.

"Well, of course it was. Who could make up such a thing?"

Everything's Got a Moral

The egg brought Olive another indigo martini.

"From the fellow onstage," the bartender whispered. "He was very insistent that it arrive as he was performing, not before or beside or behind."

The fellow onstage was an old-ish man in muttonchops holding an improbably large lavender top hat with the size-card still stuck in it. He watched the crowd solemnly as he drew object after object after object out of the hat: a croquet ball stained with blood, a pocket watch with a bayonet thrust through the fob, a silver tea-tray with a great, unhappy boot-print on it.

"Deposed?" Olive said to the White Queen, who went on calmly with her knitting. "But you're the White Queen! Shouldn't you be off Queening about with the other Queens?"

"I wasn't red, so I wasn't needed," she sighed. "That's what they said. There were four of us once. The perfect number for bridge. The Red Queen, the White Queen, the Queen of Hearts, and . . ." The White Queen suddenly clammed up, shaking her head in distress.

"The Other One," the striped cat purred. "We aren't allowed to say her name. The Queens have ears. Hush hush."

"She kicked down the Queen of Hearts' horrid cards and shook the Red Queen so hard she nearly broke her neck—more's the pity she didn't finish the job. Everything was going to be all right, you know. With the Other One here to keep those scarlet women in line."

The cat licked his paws. "I met her. She was rather thick, if you ask me. And she kept going on about herself, which I think is very rude, when you're a guest."

"But you knew it wouldn't be all right," said Olive, who had a little brother, and therefore was immune to distraction. "Because of how you live backwards."

"Yes, yes! What a clever girl! I knew, but no one listens to me because I'm always screaming about one thing or another—but you would scream, too, if you remembered the whole future of the world until

Judgment Day and past it! You'd scream and scream and never stop! I knew she'd vanish like a shawl in the wind and she did and just as soon as she did, the Red Queen and the Queen of Hearts would decide Wonderland needed taking in hand. Needed one crown. We were all conscripted. My Lily died on the Croquet Grounds. I wish I had. I wish . . . I wish a lot of things. The Other One came back, of course, nothing only happens once in Wonderland. But as soon as she was gone again, those red ladies holed up in their castles and started building their armies once more. We are not at war now, my child, but we soon shall be. Now, we simply hold our breaths and wait."

"Something like that happened in my world, too," Olive said softly. "*Is* happening. Germany and Russia and America and . . . well, everyone, I suppose."

"The Tumtum Club is the only place the Looking Glass Creatures are allowed to be mad anymore." The White Queen sighed. "Outside, we have to report for duty at dawn. In here, the Hatter can pull his heart out of his hat."

The gorgeous butterfly slipped out of the curtain again to master further ceremonies, twirling on her tiny black feet in a sudden cloud of stage smoke. She peered into the audience as though she were speaking to each of them in particular, as though what she said were more important than anything that had ever happened to them, and the whole of the universe waited upon their answering her.

I am young, little darlings, the Butterfly crooned
My wings have become very bright
The larva I was drowned inside my cocoon
Growing up really is such a fright!
I hardly remember the old mushroom now
I liked hookahs, I think, and fresh dew
Yet I'll still have my answer, I do not care how:
Who Are You?

Something knocked into their toadstool table and toppled Olive's drink. She tried to keep mum for the sake of the Hatter and shout indignantly at the same time, which is impossible, but she tried anyway.

The marble raven capital blinked up at her.

"Come on, then," he cawed. "This is our five-minute call. We're on, Olive, old girl."

Living Backwards

The trio of musicians wind down. The lights are dim now. The restaurant nearly empty, nearly shut. Peter and Alice toy with the notion of eating their slices of plum-cake awash with double cream, but neither can fully commit to it. They speak of Wonderland, of cabbages and kings, of riddles and chess and what sort of tea could be got in the wilds. It is pleasant, there is a joy in it, but it is unreal. It is like listening to someone try to tell you the plot of a radio play you missed. Peter feels a chill. Perhaps another cold coming on.

"I want to believe you," he says.

"Clap your hands and give it a go. Or decide I'm a barmy old woman and go on with your life. It won't change what I know. Oh, Peter, how disappointing for us both. You thought we were the same. I thought we were. But Alice in Wonderland could never take me from myself, because it was myself, it always was. We're both the victims of burglars, dastardly fellows who stove in our windows and bashed up our houses. But my robber only took the silver. Yours took the lot. Of course, Charles got it half wrong and put a great lot of maths in to amuse himself; and perhaps if I'd been the one to write it, I wouldn't have to sell my first editions to keep the lights on in my house; but losing Wonderland didn't ruin me. Losing . . ." and then she cannot continue. She grips her beer glass like it can save her, but it will not. It never has saved anyone. ". . . my boys . . . all my pretty boys . . ."

"My brothers, too," Peter whispers. There is nothing more to say than that, than that they are people of a certain era, and people of a certain era know an emptiness in the world, a place where something precious was cut out and never replaced.

"Coffee?" asks the waiter.

"Tea," they answer.

"What I don't understand," Peter ventures finally, "is what you're doing here."

"I beg your pardon?"

"If it was all real, why don't you go back? When the lights have gone out and . . . your boys have gone . . . why stay here, in this dreadful world?"

"I never went on purpose. It just happened. I saw a white rabbit one day. I touched a looking glass. I never decided to go. It decided to take me. It's never decided since. Wonderland is like my son, my last son. It's just so awfully awkward for him to see me the way I've ended up, it avoids me as much as it possibly can."

"I suppose I should scour the countryside for bunnies and mirrors," Peter laughs despite himself.

"I suppose I should," Alice giggles, and for a moment she is that child on the cover of a million novels, the English Girl, rosy and devious and brilliant. The check appears as if by magic, and Peter pays it, as good as his word. Alice stands and the waiter brings their coats. "No, Peter, it's best as it is. Whatever would I say to the White Queen now? Give me my bloody damned jam, you old cow? I gave up weeping for my lost kingdom years ago. I made my own, and if it crumbled, well, all kingdoms do. The world's not so dreadful, my dear. It is dreadful, of course, but only most of the time. Sometimes it rather outdoes itself. Gives us a scene so improbable no one would dare to put it in a book, for who would believe in such a chance meeting between two such people, such a splendid supper, such an unlikely moment in the great pool of moments in which we all swim?" She kisses his cheek. She holds her lips against him for a long time. When she pulls away, there is a thimble in his hand. "Oh, goodness," Alice says with a shine in her blue eyes. "What a lot of rubbish old ladies have in their bags!"

They walk arm in arm out into the New York street. People shove and holler by. The lights spangle and reflect in the hot concrete. The air smells like rotting vegetables and steel and fresh baking rolls and summer pollen. Alice stops him on the curb before he can cross the road.

"Peter, darling, listen to me. You must listen. You've got to answer the Caterpillar's question—you've got to find an answer, or else you'll never find your way. I never could, not until now, not until this very night, but you must. It's the only question there is."

"I can't, Alice. I want to."

Alice throws her arms round his neck. "I like you better, Peter. Ever so much better than him. Peter Pan was always such an awful shit, you know."

They start across the long rope of the street, but being English and unaccustomed to traffic, they do not see the streetcar hurtling toward them, painted white for the new exhibit at the Metropolitan Museum. Peter hears the bell and leaps back, hauling Alice roughly along with him, barely missing being crushed against the headlamps. When he collects himself, he turns to ask if she's all right, if he didn't hurt her too much, if the shock has ruffled her so that they need another drink to steady them.

There is no one beside him. His arm is empty.

"Alice?" Peter calls into the darkness. But no answer comes.

London Is the Capital of Paris, and Paris Is the Capital of Rome

Olive stood on the stage of the Tumtum Club in the brash glare of the spotlight. She could barely make out all the glittering scales and claws and furs and shining eyeballs of the Looking Glass Creatures in the audience.

"Go on," hissed the marble raven. "I'm not doing this alone. You do your bit, then I'll do mine. Mine's better, obviously, so I'll close."

"My bit? I haven't got a bit! I didn't even sing in the school concert!"

"Do something! You're sure to, if you stand there long enough!"

Olive felt like her heart was dribbling out of her mouth. Everyone just kept *looking* at her. No one had ever looked at her for so long. Certainly not Father Dear or Darling Mother who ignored her benignly, not Little George who was more interested in painting the sheep, not the Other One, who seemed never to notice her until they collided in the hall. She could hardly bear it. What could she possibly do to impress these aliens out of her own bookshelf? In the book, Alice always had something clever to say, some bit of wordplay or a really swell pun. Olive could never be an Alice. She wasn't quick enough. She wasn't endearing enough. She wasn't anyone enough.

Really, she only had one choice. She'd only ever practiced one thing long enough to get really good at it.

"It's . . . ahem . . . it's dreadful here," Olive complained. Her voice shook. Everyone liked the pig screaming about its mother. Would they understand her talent? "Even the toadstools and the cocktails are depressed. There's only one pub and you can't even play darts here. Alice got to meet a Unicorn and dance with Dodos and learn something about herself on *her* holiday." A great gasp ripped through the crowd. A tiger lily burst into tears. The White Queen looked like she might faint.

"It's not allowed!" the chess piece whispered. The cat grinned and began, slowly, to disappear.

Olive pressed on. "But what do I get? The saddest country I've ever seen! If any of you so much as breathe wrong, the government passes out from the scandal of it. I can't even pronounce half of the stuff the Jabberwock says! A more cramped and dreary place I've never dreamed of. It's clear no one ever *planned* nor *built* Wonderland so much as *piled it up* and *gave up on it several times.* Somebody obviously thought there was nothing so splendid in the world as Victorian allegory and crammed it in anywhere it would fit, and rather a lot of places it wouldn't. The martinis aren't even close to dry. How do you even have electricity? And the local politics are appalling, I'll tell you that for free. Stuff all Queens, I say! Except Elizabeth, she's all right."

Olive bowed, then curtseyed, then settled on something halfway between. A smattering of uncertain applause started up, growing stronger as the Looking Glass Creatures recovered from their shock. The smattering became a thundering, became a roar.

The raven hopped up into the spotlight to soak up a bit of adoration for himself. He coughed and shook his stone feathers. The audience quieted, leaned forward, eager, ready for more—so ready they did not hear the thumping outside, or the terrified squeak of the Dormouse in his teapot armour.

"How," said the marble corvid, "is a raven like a writing desk?"

"It's a raid!" a Dodo shrieked from the back of the Tumtum Club.

The club fell apart into madness as playing cards flooded in from all sides, grabbing at the collars of egg and man alike, shouting orders, taking down names. Looking Glass Creatures bolted, down rabbit holes and up through the mossy rafters, behind the posters advertising THE CHESHIRE CIRCUS and MISS MARY ANN SINGS THE BLUES. Olive froze. She saw the turtle who'd sung so beautifully being dragged off by a pair of deuces. A Knave of Clubs swung his rifle into the scaly ankle of Edward, the poor Jabberwock, who roared in anguish. Tears shone on Olive's cheeks in the footlights. But she couldn't move. The sound of the raid slashed at her ears horribly.

"We both devour humans, piece by piece," the raven finished his riddle into the din, but no one heard him.

Someone gripped Olive's arm.

"Come," said the White Queen. "I'll take you with a pleasure. Twopence a week, and always jam to-day."

"Come where?"

"Where you were always going, where you have already been. Where we are already friends, where we have already fought long and hard together, where we have sat upon the field of battle in one another's arms and looked out over a free Wonderland. Where everything is as it was before the war, before our world split in two, before the Other One, before anything hurt."

"Is that really what's going to happen?"

"No. It's impossible. But I believe it anyway. It's the only way I can bear to face breakfast."

Olive glanced offstage. There was a flash of light there, something reflecting in all the flotsam of the theatre. A pane of glass from some lonely window. And for a moment, Olive thought she could see, on the other side of the glass, Darling Mother in the parlour, asleep with Little George in her arms, a nearly empty bottle of gin on the end table and rain still pouring down outside. The shadows of the raindrops looked like black weeping on her mother's face. *Everything as it was. Before. Before anything hurt. Could such a thing ever be?*

She took the White Queen's white hand. They ran together through the wings and out through two mossy hidden doors back beyond the reach of the footlights. The two of them burst into the glen, into a river of folk running away from the Tumtum Club and into the Looking Glass World, running slow, and thus, streaming along so fast they could never be caught.

Olive looked back over her shoulder at the great skeleton covered in moss and flowers and briars and vines. She hadn't seen it when she came in. The glow-worms had dazzled her. The whole world had dazzled her.

"We loved her so," the White Queen said, not in the least out of breath as they ran on and on into the wood. "She came back, and she ate a hundred mushrooms so she could grow big enough to protect us. I was there when she died, hardly bigger than a pearl in her hand. She was so old—I hardly remember ever being so old! Living backwards makes it terribly easy to forget. She smiled and said: *oh my gracious!* and closed her eyes. And of course the moment she did, the Red Queen called her pawns to arms—but for a moment, when she was huge and high and here, for one tiny minute in all the world, almost everyone was happy. We loved her so; we never wanted to be parted from her. We wanted her to be with us forever. And she is."

The giant's skeleton was wearing a heavy iron crown, and the crown had two words lovingly etched all the way round it:

QUEEN ALICE

MOON, AND MEMORY, AND MUCHNESS

Katherine Vaz

I begin at three o'clock in the morning. There's a glaze over tonight's rind of the moon. Sometimes—this being a dense part of the East Village—I jump out of my skin at the sound of breaking glass, a quarrel; I almost cry out for Alicia. I assemble the adorable, tiny pots of lemon curd and mango jam and the comfits that my customers steal. I use a butter-cutter pastry tool on the best butter for the pumpkin scones. A *New York Times* food editor asked for my secret ingredient in the crystallized-ginger muffins, but I demurred, not because it is exotic but because it's frightfully simple: I add coconut extract. My walk-in freezer is packed to its gills, but everything is precisely labeled. Grief can do this: There's a ferocious desire to control and align the world, as if that stops or reverses the time. Mini-quiches, miniature tortilla molds for lentil salad. I fix roulade sandwiches with Russian dressing, turkey, and Cotswold cheddar. Does a person ever conquer an eating disorder? Everything screams, Eat Me, Drink Me. As a young wife and mother, I blew up two sizes, melted down three, over and over. Now I survive on toast and rose-hip infusions. Practically nothing. My Wonderland Tea Shop and its kitchen are downstairs, and I perch in small quarters above. After one day's prep, service, and clean-up, it's always time to start over again.

What is the "bargaining" stage of grief? Since I've never figured that out, I fear I'm in the grip of its unknowable rules. If I hold my temper when a customer spills clotted cream on the floor, will Alicia reappear?

If I smile as a woman changes her order from white tea to rooibos to the Zen Mix, will my child's ghost appear? If I throw out the news clippings about the two young madmen who tormented and murdered Alicia, will I get un-stuck in Time? (Is that even something I want?) My ex-husband, Bill, lives with a new wife and son (already a schoolboy!) in Phoenix, and we chat on occasion; we have lunch (I watch him eat while I can't finish my soup) when he returns for the parole hearings. I'm glad for him. He blamed me for Alicia, and I blame myself. At an arts and crafts emporium in Chelsea, while gathering holly and garlands for Christmas, I turned my back, and the earth swallowed her.

Above the shop, my rented rooms are so minute it's as if I live in the cutaway of a whelk shell. Painted on the face of the ticking tabletop clock is a girl on a swing, her Mary Janes frozen toward heaven. There's never wine on hand, because I'd drink it and then there'd be no wine anyway. Occasionally I resort to pills for sleep and glide in Technicolor dreams where flowers are talking and flamingos are playing a game, with me as the croquet ball. I maintain, intact, the pint-sized tea table that Alicia loved arranging for Mr. Bun, her stuffed rabbit, and Mabel the mouse, and Jackie the toucan. At each setting are plastic wands filled with water, glitter, and tiny keys. Bill joined the little parties we threw for her animals, mint in sugar-water and vanilla wafers; he was a warm father and husband.

I used to teach poetry at a small college on Staten Island, and those eager faces, even the ones ravaged by wild partying, blazed their hopeful innocence in my direction, nearly burning me alive. Bill was an accountant. We lived modestly, the three of us, in Murray Hill. After selling our apartment, he and I shared the profits after the two boys—rich, with a lawyer passionately loud about the burden of their privileges—were sentenced to only twelve years. Alicia died at age six. Eight years ago. It feels like yesterday.

Of course Kumiko Mori is the first employee to show up, clear-eyed, cheerful, with a red streak feathering her jet-black hair and her signature thick belt accenting a cinched waist her boyfriend likely spans with his hands. "Morning, Mrs. Dias."

I've told her to call me Dorrie. Or Doreen. Old-school, she resists.

I should return to my maiden name, Lewis—I'm a custard of Welsh, English, and Finnish—but then I wouldn't have Alicia's final name anymore. Bill Dias is of Brazilian and Irish stock.

Kumiko picks up the sign-up sheet at the counter to see how many people want to try a tea ceremony. *Chanoyu*. Zero. Her grandfather is at the ready, should we enlist enough takers. Sweets served to balance tea's bitterness. Everything spotless, arranged with flowers. Tranquility. The idea that the small things we think are meaningless have as much meaning as anything great or small. And therefore all meaning is equal. Who in searching for greatness in life can bear examining that?

I joke about how many entertainments vie for our attention nowadays, and tea ceremonies of painstaking slowness are a tough sell.

Kumiko grins and unwinds the eternity scarf from her neck. It's autumn; our décor is purple and gilt. She hangs her scarf and coat on the hook in the kitchen as she takes the teapots from the shelf, and she says, "I need to tell you something, Mrs. Dias."

Why does my heart skip a beat? All the servers eventually leave, but I hate giving her up. Her beauty, grace, and hard work. The faint promise of a ceremony of tea.

"Kumiko?"

But then in barrels Jason, sleepy, mild, a decent waitperson, good with card tricks at the tables while the tea brews. He wants to be an actor. The older man he lives with might be cheating on him. He's pleasant. Alex is less so, dragging himself in, a lean practitioner of the faint sneer, eager to convey that he's primed for better things when he graduates from Columbia. His financial-world parents—he lives with them—encourage his refusal to abase himself with a mouse-filled, starter studio apartment. I should fire him, but he keeps his disdain subdued, and it's hard to find help.

Kumiko unlocks the front door, and hordes on their way to work pour in for cinnamon rolls and croissants to go, and the mothers-at-ease trundle in their squalling children, babies wrinkled as piglets. I feed off the tumult of children, though Alicia was quiet. Why didn't she bellow and scream when those boys abducted her?

A girl in a fairy princess outfit tugs my apron and says, "I like apricots!"

I kneel to meet her eyes with mine, delighted. "Guess what? I made apricot tarts last night." All true! I treasure these unexpected little connections as victories.

The mother, a natural beauty in a ponytail, a child herself, says, "Wonderful."

Then laughs. Because *wonderful* and *wonder* belong in *wonderland.*

I rarely remember that Alicia would be fourteen now. I live for these girls who come with their mothers, a special treat. They're joyful in this make-believe realm I've made. Throwback to gracious times. Tea, gen-til-i-ty. Bite-sized salmon sandwiches. The pots warmed British-style, loose leaves if you have more time, an extra spoon for the pot. I'm not raking in a fortune, but I've kept my nose above water.

Kumiko carries a tray of Earl Grey. More customers sweep in. Morning rush. The walls offer murals of white and red roses, white rabbits. Fish-footmen. A queen, a chorus of humans as playing cards. A caterpillar on a mushroom, hookah in mouth; the college kids flock near that one.

I wave at Kumiko over the tables, the sea of speeding New Yorkers. She does a funny mock-dance of panic. Her red-and-white Wonderland apron is spotless. Crash! A child has dropped her fragile cup; an accident. Kumiko comforts her and sweeps it up. Alex checks his phone until he sees me glaring. Jason's sleeves are already stained with jam.

My child once found a songbird, egg-yolk yellow, with a head wound, during a walk with us in Central Park. She fed it with an eyedropper at home. Bill and I warned it wouldn't make it. She insisted that it would, or at least it wouldn't die alone. She was all of five, one year left to live. She named the birdie "Dodo." I'll never know why. Came the dawn that the bird flapped around her room, and Alicia opened the window and chanted, "Go now, go away. Fly! Go on," though she was in tears.

One night, as a prank, because Alicia was magical, she put crayons in Bill's and my bed. Her reason was that we seemed so drained she was afraid we were dreaming in black-and-white.

* * *

When I ask Kumiko, as breakfast cedes to the lunch crowd—more sandwiches, more tiered stands with savory items on top and petit fours below—what she needed to tell me, she says, "Mrs. Dias, I got that internship at Bellevue." Her smooth skin suddenly looks like satin balled up in a fist and then let go. "It's full-time."

No surprise, really. She wants to be a psychiatrist, and she deserves any portal that opens. Her future is unfurling before her. But as she gently gives two-weeks' notice, I drop into the chair behind the counter, because the purple room is spinning.

"Hey," she says. "Hey, Mrs. Dias. I'm so sorry."

I say I'm glad for her. And I am. I hiss at Alex to get off his phone and stop pretending he can't see the guests at Table Five waving their arms as if they're in a lifeboat. For a horrid moment, I imagine unlocking the drawer near the register, extracting my silver pistol, and scaring the dumb grin off his spoiled face.

"I'll come back with my grandpa if you get the sign-ups for a tea ceremony," Kumiko whispers, an arm around my slumped shoulder. Jason glances my way as he passes with a lethally large serving of éclairs. What is wrong with me?

There's work to be done, it never stops; I hug her, flooded with a vision of Kumiko in her late twenties, married, telling a depressed patient in a sea of tears that *there are endless reasons to go on*. Her office has bronze statues of naked bodies. On the wall is a picture colored by the son I figure she'll have, a smiling family with a cat, all bigger than their house.

Alex forgets the chutney requested by two grand dames at Table Three for their walnut bread. They declare, in ringing tones, that they did not ask for the jasmine teabags; they want the expensive Tienchi Flower, twelve dollars a cup.

Jason approaches them and says, "Shall I fix that?"

"Someone should!" trumpets one with so much plastic surgery that her nostrils are holes, her head a skull. She seems ready to start throwing the dishes.

"Where is the manager?" asks her friend, wearing an honest-to-God turban with a jewel on it, like the kind favored by fraud magicians who saw people in half.

Am I invisible? Alex stands helpless, a pleading expression trained on Jason for rescue. Much of my tearoom is staring.

"Shall I get their tea?" whispers Kumiko. "Or just kick their asses?"

She's brilliant at getting me to smile.

Because she knows what to do without being constantly told, Kumiko sidles into the kitchen, unlocking the cupboard where I store the expensive stuff. I have some Yellow Gold Bud—it sounds like weed—painted edible gold. $120 an ounce.

Turban Lady launches into a tirade about the city falling apart; I gesture at Alex and Jason to attend to the rest of the room, to distract it, as I force myself to coo at the women that we'll put everything right. Did they know Tienchi Flowers—a refined choice!—relieve pain and cure rashes?

They assault me with a barrage of nonsense: Is the water in my Wonderland Tea Shop drawn from the tap, or do I have a proper reverse-osmosis system? Did I bribe some inspector to grant me that "A" grade? Why do so many menu selections start with "M"—mountain mint, marvelous mango, mascarpone, macaroni, moon cakes, and much about melons? Molasses. They suggest I need a haircut. I venture they needn't be rude. Why is the Duchess on my mural so fatheaded? Why can't I say what I mean? Why is the clock on the wall five minutes fast? Are the macarons—another "M"—stale? Why are crumbs on their butter knives? Why is my expression blank; why am I trembling?

"Excellent, ladies, here's your tea," I murmur as Kumiko brings out a fragrant batch in the teapot painted with Dutch children skating on a pond. I want to gorge on a stack of pressed cheese sandwiches until my body threatens to resign.

After the imperial pair finishes and offers parting complaints and leaves nary a tip for Alex or Kumiko, I notice a mother and daughter tucked in the corner. The girl is black-haired like my Alicia, five or six; I wander closer to see that yes, her eyes are Alicia's green. She smiles, a tooth missing.

Alex interrupts my reverie with a rare apology; sorry he got that order topsy-turvy. His apron is off; he never stays a second past his shift. His lashes brush the lenses of his hip glasses.

I assure him it's not the end of the world, not by a long shot.

He's not accustomed to admitting a failing, to feeling bad. He's not used to making a slight mistake that someone pounds into the dirt with a sledgehammer.

Kumiko and Jason commandeer the room as I approach the corner table. The mother lights up and whispers at me companionably, conspiratorially, "Gosh, those ladies were something else. How do you stand it?"

"There are worse things," I say. The child is daintily eating the mozzarella—M!—flatbread, and her teacup, the artful scarlet-rose one, holds the Sweet Dreams and Citrus, which shivers when she brings it to her lips.

What else may I do for them; are they having a good time; what else may I bring?

The mother is around my age, nearing forty, though she is much more in the forty-is-the-new-twenty category, olive-skinned, mahogany hair with yellow highlights. Her bracelets jangle out music. The girl has a rhinestone barrette shaped like a spider, and she tells me proudly that her name is Charlotte.

"Did you spin any webs for Wilbur?" I ask; my blood flows as if gates have lifted in my veins. The child beams at me. "Yes!"

We chat about the places where *Charlotte's Web* made us cry, and the mother adds that she even gets teary-eyed in public when she recalls certain parts.

I almost say my little girl loves books, too. I wrote and taught poetry, once.

"I'm Betty," says the mother, "but my friends call me Bird."

The creature my child saved, brought back to life. Yellow feathers now yellow streaks in hair. Betty praises the butter's sweetness, and the apricot tarts, today's special. It's lovely to be here. Her clothing is pressed, high couture. Piercing her ears are diamonds.

"Look at us, enjoying high tea," she says to Charlotte. Because it's around twelve o'clock.

I explain that high tea is so-called because the *tables* are high. People at a social gathering wander and graze on food and drink set up for easy access. “High” doesn’t signal the hour. Americans think of high noon. Gunslingers! Time to settle scores.

“That’s amazing!” Betty proclaims. Her daughter nods. They’ve learned something, together. They probably dance at night, Mother making Baby giggle by offering to toss her into the stars. I’m dying to ask what Betty “does,” other than care for this smart, pretty, alert child. My skills in chatting with customers need sharpening.

Charlotte swings her legs and gazes with a devotion at her mother so profound that I glance away, because it’s not meant for me. Well-trained, a city girl, she thanks me for the tea, the cup, the mozzarella and desserts. Kumiko clears tables; Jason shines the coffee urn. My staff knows nothing about Alicia, nothing of my history. Charlotte near-shouts, “Could we have my birthday here, Momma? May I, please?” Her fingernails shine with dots of crimson polish still wet-looking.

Betty wholeheartedly agrees: Certainly! Charlotte’s sixth birthday will be here next week, at the Wonderland Tea Shop! We live only two blocks away! Sorry she must hasten now, she tells me, but she has a deadline. Her aspect clarifies as familiar, from the papers and from my long-ago, long-slumbering days as a poet. It’s Betty Lezardo, the novelist whose successes have been capped recently with a National Book Award.

A soaring career and the most darling child alive; a woman my age accomplished and kind.

When I inquire if she’s Betty Lezardo, she shyly nods and asks for my name.

Dorrie. Doreen Dias.

A hand extended to press against mine. Betty/Bird says, “I have a question about your murals.” She points—artist’s eye—toward the Hatter and March Hare, the crazy duo at their table, in leg irons. That, she avers, is odd enough. “But where is the Dormouse?”

Almost no one catches that omission. That absence.

“The Hatter and Hare pinched the Dormouse several times, in the original story,” I say. “Remember? The Dormouse had done nothing to warrant that. They used it as a cushion. They poured hot tea on its nose, to torment it. I don't want to stick it anywhere near those two."

Betty finishes her tea. Basic green, superior for weight-watching and longevity.

For fear of upsetting the child, I omit mentioning the other detail about the Dormouse that gets glossed over: When Alice left the table, the two madmen *were stuffing the poor tiny thing headfirst into the teapot.* Another reason I had the muralist clap the madmen in leg irons. *Were they trying to kill it? Or just escalate the torture?* The Dormouse appears at Alice's trial in the famous book . . . so it survived, unless its appearance is obeying the rubric of fantasy and it's come back from the dead. But the madmen, at the very least, must have watched it struggle for air.

Betty and Charlotte's tea and edibles are on the house, in thanks for wanting the birthday under my roof. My face is an unreadable mask over agony when Charlotte throws her arms around my middle to say goodbye and rests her head where I can hold it, that soft dark hair.

No reason to add that the two Princeton dropouts who drowned my child for kicks stuffed her headfirst into a drainpipe near the Hudson. She was not raped. The defense attorney cited this as cause for leniency. I hold my breath sometimes, to own the exact feeling she suffered. But I can't begin to fathom it. I'm not at the mercy of someone else.

The customers disappear, a breather before the late afternoon tide, and then nothing; we close at six; then prep for tomorrow and me under an afghan as I watch an umpteenth rerun of *Mad Men,* starving myself, alert to street noises. I should take my pistol upstairs, but I hate having it near Alicia's Mr. Bun, Mabel, and Jackie. Does Charlotte have a spider doll, a pig? Is Betty's book award in a frame?

The water runs hard in the kitchen; Kumiko is scrubbing the grill pan. Baking soda and boiling water clean the pots; no detergent to interfere with the delicate balance of tea. Jason is belting out lines from *Cats* because he's in the chorus; Kumiko groans and orders him to stop. She meets my eyes with sadness that she'll soon be gone. I let myself feel touched she'll miss me.

* * *

Some drunken fool is yelling as time-wasters spill out of a bar. Two in the morning. Scratchy blanket, gut like a drum. I awaken from my recurring dream of carrying a sleeping Alicia, her head on my shoulder. Since her death, I imagine her everywhere, and therefore everything *is* Alicia: flour, lightning rod in the distance, Mrs. Marcy's lapdog drowsing as she drinks chrysanthemum tea. Alicia is the blue of the caterpillar on my wall.

A prayer for her phantom to visit; a prayer I won't keel over of fright. A rattling of my shop's door! I should sleep with the gun near, though I barely know how to fire it.

The sound goes away. Probably they'd only invade my refrigerator. Zucchini frittatas tomorrow; hibiscus herbal tea on special.

In the week of planning Charlotte Lezardo's party, I get to know her and her mother better; they stop by for tea daily. Charlotte favors a brooch with a fake-emerald lizard. Momma allows her a hint of rouge, "just for fun." Betty wrings her hands about writer's block, and I say, Oh, that must be awful. Terrible.

Betty has ordered new living room furniture. I picture their high-ceilinged home, with bookcases and a kitchen in candy shades. The fireplace has tiles from her love affair with Art Deco. Tempera-painted pictures by Charlotte. Of jellyfish and friends, Mom and Dad, the aurora borealis she discovered on a nature show, leaving her stunned.

Betty/Bird splurged on a Carolina Herrera dress to attend an upcoming literary event and got a matching floral number for her child. Her husband, Vincent, is a corporate lawyer on business in Chicago and promises to be back in time.

"Beautiful Momma!" cries Charlotte.

"What do you think, Dorrie?" Betty says, showing me a picture on her phone of her modeling the dress. She gleams with pleasure. Is she ever scared or afflicted or desperate?

"Not bad," I say.

Yesterday my landlord increased my rent. I tuck Charlotte's hair behind her ears as she sips from the cup with a winking man in the moon. Kumiko makes her celebrated corn fritters, her last days drawing near.

* * *

A glorious truth about tea is that it's like that quote from Heraclitus, about not being able to step into the same river twice. No sip from a pot is like a preceding mouthful. The steeping deepens; the color mellows. A second pot aiming to recapture the perfection of an earlier one is doomed. It's itself, with its own intensifications.

We shut the restaurant for Charlotte Lezardo's sixth birthday. I am blurry with insomnia, puffy from succumbing to such lunatic, midnight cravings that I wolfed profiteroles drowning in chocolate sauce, a shameful sight, chin dripping, fingers smeared. In addition to my rent going up, I've received notice of a tax increase.

About a dozen girls and six of the mothers—and one father—show up at four o'clock. Jason finishes tying balloons to the chairs. We've shoved a few tables together. Alex has the day off. Kumiko is cutting crusts off the tomato-and-basil sandwiches. Charlotte is a vegetarian because she does not want to harm animals. My Alicia was the same. I'll never forget the evening she wept enough to smash me to pieces when she looked at a pork chop and realized it was from a piggy.

"This is fantastic!" declares Betty/Bird, gripping Charlotte's hand and surveying the streamers twisting from the ceiling's light fixtures to the sconces.

"Mrs. Dias!" the birthday girl cries, flinging herself into my grasp. Grateful. She's in a sparkly peach-tinted belted dress, and Betty/Bird wears a chic white shift. Does she never spill? She moans about the price of the blow-out she treated herself to. We exchange girlish asides about how women lie to husbands about the cost of salons. I haven't much focused on my good years flying by, without a real romance since my divorce. (One or two misfiring relationships, sex tales from the crypt, don't count.)

Another mother exclaims how terrific it is to discover this darling spot hiding in the Village. Everyone piles into seats, Charlotte in the place of honor. There's mint and orange tea, and Charlotte's Birthday Mix, rose and lemon. The grown-ups down mimosas as if they're on fire inside. Kumiko, Jason, and I cart out teapots, desserts, and finger food.

Jason offers to read tea leaves. There's squealing. Gifts stacked high are wrapped in neon papers with cascading, curled ribbons. I keep a tiara on hand for these events, and I crown Charlotte. She rewards me with her happiness.

Jason, reading her leaves, announces, "Well! This is incredible!"

"Tell me!" begs Charlotte.

"Mmm," muses Jason. "What'll you pay me?"

The birthday girl giggles. "Please?"

A dramatic pause. "Miss Charlotte. I believe I see—" and he scrutinizes the cup. "I hate to disappoint you. But since you're already *adorable,* you're stuck with growing up adorable. Since you're already smarter than I am, you'll get even smarter. Hmm . . . it's murky. I'm trying to read what you'll do with your life . . ."

"I'm going to be a writer like Momma," Charlotte offers, voice hushed.

"Don't tell her," he replies in a stage whisper, "but you're going to have so many fans, they'll mob you. Your picture's going to be everywhere! How does it feel, to be a star?"

Applause. Betty's the perfect vision of the proud mother. Charlotte reaches up to award him a kiss. She's not timid with strangers. Her mother should warn her about how that's good in one way but bad in another.

Jason moves on to a woman waggling her cup (violet sprigs) at him. The dipped strawberries and cucumber sandwiches vanish. Betty calls for champagne! Out come the flutes, and the red velvet cake with vanilla frosting and piping of a web cascading off "Charlotte." Happy sixth birthday, love. The gifts are abundant, T-shirts and a lacey dress that elicits sighs, and from me, *Through the Looking-Glass*. She contemplates the book in a hush, solemnly rises, embraces me again, and says, "Best present ever." Betty converses with a friend, slapping the table with glee over a story I can't hear.

Charlotte continues, her face upturned toward me, "One day, I'm going to paint you a picture, Mrs. Dias."

I tell her I can't wait.

And I don't know what comes over me, my sorrow at peak agony;

maybe my unrest is from cramming a surfeit of sickly-sweet junk down my gullet alone in the chilly hours after days of hunger. It might arise from something as simple as Kumiko and Jason having no clue about Alicia; what could they possible offer, were I to break down and inform them? They clearly haven't Googled me. Maybe I'll flat-out die if I mount those stairs to my bide-a-wee lodgings tonight where, under a waning moon with my memories, I'll tolerate another night of intoxicated dolts in shouting-distance putting their twelve-dollar drinks on their credit cards because, God knows, the hour of reckoning will never come. Maybe I've always been murderous about wanting to kill those guffawing bastards who took my Alicia. Or maybe I'm welling up with nothing, and everything, a formulating of an admission to the police: I thought my girl was gone, but she's come back to say hello, to tell me, using the tea party I prepared for a birthday numerically matching the last one she knew on earth, that she would have been sensible and strong, lovely and thriving, unafraid of the arts and other people, maybe, just maybe, like the mother I lost my chance to have been. She's come to my rescue. Or, rather, Charlotte has lightly muscled her into view.

A trance envelops me; a mist descends. The party's streamers sway. Kumiko gathers the ripped paper and puts the gifts in our Wonderland tote bags. She says softly, "Bellevue wants me to start tomorrow, Mrs. Dias. A few days early. What should I tell them?"

I smile and hand her an envelope with the bonus I've been saving, along with a set of blank books with ornate covers. She has mentioned wanting to take notes about patients by hand. Her head is bowed. Mine, too.

The first guests file out, profuse in their thanks, and Jason is rushing because he has an audition . . . I tell him I'll clean up. Go on.

Kumiko cries at the door. I hug her and say, "There, there. Going now isn't much different from leaving in a couple of days, right?" The children, as they begin to leave, want to know what's wrong, and I say nothing. Nothing; my friend is moving on. I watch her disappear, and the room clears, except for the guests of honor.

Betty is lingering over more champagne. As if it's finger-painting, frosting mars the table, floor, and chairs. Betty glances up as if she just noticed she's in my place. Empty now, except for her and Charlotte and me.

I'm behind the counter. While Charlotte heads to the ladies' room, Betty comes over, weaving slightly, to pay the bill. "That was memorable," she says. "So glad we found you." She adds that she's not sure when they'll be back, but hopes it's soon.

What possesses me? I'm calm. I take her money. The gratuity is twenty percent on the nose. I unlock the drawer that holds my silver pistol and take it out and put it on the counter, the business end pointing in her direction. Her eyes turn the size of saucers.

"I want to see your home," I say. I stick the gun in my large, floppy handbag. Exhaling in gusts, she says, "Dorrie? What are you doing?"

"I won't scare your girl," I say, nestling the pistol against the debris in my bag. "She won't see this, unless you refuse to do as I ask." I need to absorb the dwelling that might have been mine, what it looks like, feels like; I want to observe, via Charlotte's room, how Alicia might be enlivening her own space. The one upstairs is stuck in time.

Charlotte bounces back to us, haloed with the lavender from the bathroom's soap dispenser. There are three tote bags of presents.

"Good thing there're three of us!" I trill. "I'm free to help you carry the gifts to your house. It's a way to keep the party from ending." I keep one hand in my purse, as if I'm about to pull out my wallet. Betty's mouth stays open.

"Oh," says Charlotte. "That's nice." But she's watching her mother and says, "Momma?"

"Yes, my sweetheart," says Betty/Bird. A damp patch blooms on her white shift. She bends to kiss her daughter's head. "Let's go home."

Out we go, and I fumble with the outer lock, and as Betty glances around, I bring my purse around to face her, and she freezes. Charlotte is merry from the festivities.

I don't get out much. The air is crisp with fall, spiced and reddened and golden. People stride by, in a hurry. The sidewalk is cracked. "Slow down," I hiss at Betty.

After a tiny yelp, she starts shaking. She whispers, "I would have invited you. I don't understand. I would have invited you over."

"That's not true," I say.

Charlotte, carrying the lightest tote bag, stops to adjust it on her shoulder.

"Did you have a lovely birthday?" I ask her.

"The best ever, Mrs. Dias," she says. Her spider barrette catches a glint. "Thank you so much."

Betty, color drained, begins to hyperventilate and gasps at me, "I don't understand."

"Charlotte," I say, "didn't you promise me a picture? Why don't we get it, once we get home?" The child is slowing, staring at the grown-ups.

"But I haven't done one specially for you," she says.

"How about if you pick one you've already done, and I can have that?"

She weighs this and speaks with caution. "All right. Momma, what's wrong?"

My hand rides the pistol, cool, silver. The poor woman loses the starch in her knees and buckles. "Momma!" Charlotte shrieks.

"She's fine," I say, gripping her arm to help her along. "It's just a little too much champagne."

"That's right," croaks Betty. "We're almost home, honey."

They live close but at a remove from the racket of the bars. An Indian market offers its scents of turmeric, star anise, and cumin; the fruits on display shine like jewels. I'm a mite faint myself. A boy on a phone jostles Betty, and her cry is sharp and anguished. Charlotte becomes more puzzled. She pats her mother fondly on her back. Leaves scratch the asphalt, and the tips of midtown peer over the streets to watch. The fear in Betty's eyes has infected her whole being, saturating her. She's quivering. Charlotte puts an arm around her mother and seems to be humming, singing. I needed to witness a child giving comfort, a mother and daughter bound together to defy terror, while at the same time I protect the girl from the worst of it.

Their doorman in his cap and jacket with golden frog-closures leaps forward to help with the packages. I blurt, "No, we're fine!"

"Mrs. Lezardo?" he says.

"We're okay, Ralph. Thank you." Betty looks ejected from a wind tunnel, and her daughter guides her ahead. My hand trembles on the gun.

Betty collapses into sniffling in the elevator as we shoot up to a top—but not *the* top—floor. There are mirrors and elegant brass trim, and the unscratched wood is polished. I adjust the angle where I stand to keep the pistol in my bag trained on her. Charlotte hasn't registered how steadily I've kept my hand out of view.

And then at their threshold—her reaction is worse than I expected—Betty shoves the key in her lock after the fourth try and cracks, disintegrates into a shambles, weeping. She genuflects from trembling and drops her tote bag. I scoop it up. Charlotte bleats, "Momma, are you sick? What's wrong? What can I do? What happened?" Her pleading eyes on me, she beseeches, "Help us. Help me."

My turn to shake, rendered speechless. Did some disturbed part of me long to see a cheap imitation of my Alicia's fear and worry in her last hour, so I could heal it? "Let's go inside and get her some water." I can't look at Charlotte; I'm propelled forward despite knowing I should bolt.

Disappointingly predictable: It is in fact my dream apartment. Large and open, lined with books, flooded with light. The large kitchen at the far end has bar stools so dinner company can chat over appetizers as Betty watches the water boil for pasta. Corked bottles of wine display various levels, half, or a few fingers remaining, or three-quarters, rich purple-reds. How do Betty and her husband Vincent not hear them screeching *Drink Me*? Under one of those netted domes to deflect insects is a plate of cookies . . . don't they shriek *Eat Me*? In the adjacent dining area, the chairs are wrapped in beige cloth with ties behind them to resemble the backs on the dresses of bridesmaids. An office is visible off to the side, a laptop open. More rooms farther down a hallway. A spiral staircase to a loft.

Crayoned pictures on the living-area wall. I venture slightly out of Betty's range as I inspect them. A blue cat floats in a sea of red water. I fall in love. What's in Charlotte's childhood realm; what are her toys, dolls, books, paints? But I can't explore that and still keep Betty at bay. I can't maintain a gun trained on her from another room.

She's slight, but fear might impart the strength she needs to disarm me, or worse.

"I would have invited you in!" Betty shouts, dropping onto the plush red sofa. She unleashes a fresh wave of sobs.

"Momma!" Charlotte screams, and then it happens, what I've wanted to see, what I half-sensed—and didn't—was my reason for doing this worst thing of my life: Charlotte hugs her tight, and Betty clutches her as if she'll die if she doesn't and swings her daughter to a tucked-away point, to protect her. "Go to your room, Char," she whispers.

"Not while you're sad. I love you, Momma! Don't cry! What's wrong? I love you!"

"I'm good," Betty whispers. "Baby, don't you worry. I've got you."

I take my hands out of my purse and it's my turn to crumble, into a Lucite chair with a stylish decal of a teenaged girl with standing-up cobalt hair. There was a lot of pure hate in what I did, I'm aware of that: Such a perfect existence you have, Betty; it's a replica of the reel I starred in, inside my brain in my youth. What do you look like when you might be in danger of loss?

But mostly: How else can I enact some message to my Alicia that she's the only one I wanted to comfort me in those days and weeks and months when I sobbed and shook and couldn't face the terror? *What might it look like, my child holding me when I'm afraid, sickened by the world's violence? She holds me and begs me not to be shattered because she's here, here to stop my grief.* I've wanted her consolation.

Does anyone fathom what it's like to be scared every second walking down the street, afraid a monster will lunge? No wonder I seldom go out.

They're crooning together, guarding one other, clinging.

There's one thing—it should have been obvious—I didn't count on. Brilliant child, attuned, she's calculating that the only thing different in their home is . . . this virtual stranger.

"Why are you here?" Charlotte asks me, sitting next to her mother and holding her hand. Betty raises her head.

"I came to carry your gifts, and to look at your pictures." I get to my feet and calculate the distance to the door. "I should be going."

The green eyes study me; the sequins on her peach-tinted party dress catch dying light. "Did you make Momma cry?"

If the windows could open, I would leap out of one.

"Mrs. Dias wanted to make sure we got safely where we belong, bunny rabbit. Isn't that nice?" says Betty/Bird. She's sitting straighter, wiping her eyes, turning a hollow stare at me. "Sometimes grown-ups get a little sad."

The exit is perhaps a ten-second sprint. I'm not sure what she's doing, other than a masterful job of reassuring a child.

"What made you sad?" asks Charlotte.

"Oh," she says, gathering her daughter's hands back once again in her own. "I was crying because . . . well." Betty bites her lip, drawing a spot of blood. Her aura of stellar cheer roils with darkening shades, and she peers at me with downright tenderness. No wonder her writing wins prizes: She reads deep; she kindles; she is aware of others.

Her words float into the air. "Mrs. Dias once had a little girl, too, and some very bad things happened."

"What?" asks Charlotte, scarcely breathing; she turns her attention full at me.

I'm arrested, immobile, unable to inhale.

"Well, just some bad things," says her mother. "The little girl went to heaven. It's too bad we can't visit there, while we're here on earth. So this lady wanted to spend more time with someone who reminded her of—" and she stops. No need to finish.

It is my turn for water to stream from my eyes. I can't blink it away. Easy enough to Google my name and learn my nightmare. Betty did that. Like everyone who knows my story, she had no blooming idea how to bring it up or convey how she wished she could take away my pain: Surely the birthday party was her trying to share with me a fleeting memory of joy. And this is how I repaid her. Charlotte dashes to me, and I kneel, and the size of my baby when I lost her is in my embrace. Betty trembles on the sofa.

How long do I hold on?

Another shock awaits: As I rise to go, Charlotte patting my back as she did her mother's, a stirring, a rustling, happens above.

A girl aged about thirteen or fifteen appears at the railing cordoning off the loft. Her hair is tousled, as if from sleep. She's in those jeans ripped to shreds and a loose shirt, with a black bra strap drooping. "What's going on?" she asks.

"You're home from school early, Elsie." Betty's voice is subdued.

"Flu, I think." Elsie regards me and says, "Hello. Do you know my mother?"

My mouth opens, fish on the shoreline, last air, nothing coming out.

Elsie says, "Dad's at the airport, I think, Mom. He's on his way."

"I was just leaving," I manage, barely loud enough to be heard.

Charlotte tells her older sister that she had a great tea party thanks to me, and that I'm sad.

"No," I say to the birthday girl. "I'm happy I met you."

I run a hand through my hair. Elsie is the age my Alicia would be. Charlotte isn't my stand-in for Alicia; Elsie is. And it's like standing in the surf, when it drags its curling self back to the sea and a person feels she's sailing backward even though she's not moving. I've barreled through the worm-hole, speeded forward in the time machine, gone through the glass, lost my grip on make-believe: *This would be my baby now.*

They let me stumble away. I don't look back, not even at Elsie, rumpled and blossoming, self-possessed, appraising me from on high.

I ask Time to dash forward, and He obliges in spades; the months bunch up in heaps. The slightest crashes still startle me, either at work in Wonderland or in my upstairs rooms, with the compounded fear that the police have come to drag me off. This never happens: This is how thoroughly Betty and Charlotte—and Elsie—want to be shut of me. I should be glad for the immensity of Betty's forgiveness. No wonder her existence in the world-at-large is more vast and far-reaching than mine.

I've turned Alicia's shrine into a study, to write in. Mr. Bun sits on a shelf, watching over me. My spirit thanks Betty for reminding me that words matter. I touch the pictures Alicia did ages ago, so the colors enrich my blood. I eat and drink normally, or close enough. I speak less and less to Bill, my ex-husband. I'm happy alone. The stars over the city are pinpricks that soothe me. All the heavens do. When the moon shines in a curved rim at its bottom, it's called the Old Moon Holding the Young Moon in Its Arms.

An editor who read a story of mine in a small magazine asked if I'd write about The Real Thing That Happened to Me. I replied that it's bad enough those boys will be free in a few years; why do I want to bolster their notoriety? I'd submit page after page of:

Alicia Renée Dias, Alicia Renée Dias, Alicia Renée Dias, Alicia Renée Dias, Alicia Renée Dias, Alicia Renée Dias, Alicia Renée Dias, Alicia Renée Dias, Alicia Renée Dias, Alicia Renée Dias, Alicia Renée Dias, Alicia Renée Dias, Alicia Renée Dias, Alicia Renée Dias

The accent marks can serve as a guide to letting it be sung.

I won't turn my child or criminals into cash. To atone for my own violence, I'll do something that stays known only to me. Aid to a victims' support network, I'm thinking.

The serving girl who replaced Kumiko is exasperating. I fired Alex. It's a revolving door. We lack enough sign-ups for a tea ceremony, though I hope for a reason to contact Kumiko. One day I'll marvel at bumping into her by chance and confess I need her as my psychiatrist.

The Dormouse remains missing.

Now and then, I picture Charlotte growing, attending school. Does Elsie get in some harmless teenaged trouble? Vincent, their father, loses hair. At the dinner table, he entertains his wife and daughters with anecdotes that leave them hysterical with laughter.

One day, on Facebook, I note a picture on a friend's page and gasp. It's Betty Lezardo. In another fashionable dress, at a literary event. I enlarge the photo, clicking until I can better countenance her face. There's no mistaking it, and it's my doing, I'm sure: A slight but definite sidelong glance distorts her eyes, as if fearing what's behind or not trusting what might be gaining on her. She clutches a glass of white wine with a burning marble of fluorescence in it, from the lights overhead. Her face screams forty-ish more than when I saw her, like a time-lapse. She appears completely haunted.

Next to her is Elsie, in an LBD, a gateway garment to female adulthood. The skirt flares. Elsie Lezardo, the person who pried me out of fantasy and hurled me into the reality of forward history. Is she sixteen? Has that much time sped past? What are her crushes and career plans, her despairs so enormous she refuses to believe they'll subside with time? There's no Charlotte, because this is a grown-up party.

Once, thinking of Alicia as she'd be—Elsie-sized now—I fell asleep in Central Park in Sheep Meadow, on a sloping lawn, and leaves like crisp scuttling crabs walked sideways over my face. I sat up with a start. *I am alive,* I thought.

I'll never behold Charlotte, Betty/Bird, or Elsie again in the flesh. If we happen upon each other by accident, I'll cross the street unless they do it first. When I awaken in the morning, I put on a kettle and answer it when it screams. And then I open my front door to Wonderland, and the strangers come in, good and ill, and I serve them the best of what I've made from my hours in the night.

RUN, RABBIT, RUN

Jane Yolen

He left his hole for a whole new life,
spats and hats and chats with the queen,
ticktocking into the human world.

Such shocking developments, then,
when the dogs caught his scent.
He'd forgotten his wild.

Had no more tricks, just ticks,
caught soon after. The dogs devoured him,
with a good red wine, cigars, laughter.

ABOUT THE AUTHORS

Richard Bowes has published ten books and eighty short stories. He has won World Fantasy, Lambda, Million Writer, and IHG awards.

A new edition of his Nebula-nominated novel *From the Files of the Time Rangers* came out in March 2017 from Lethe Press. His 9/11 story "There's a Hole in the City" recently got a fine review in the *New Yorker* and is online at *Nightmare* Magazine. Recent and forthcoming appearances include *Fantasy & Science Fiction*, and the *Darker Realms* and *Black Feathers* anthologies.

Bowes is currently writing a novel about a gay kid with a bit of magic about him in 1950s Boston.

C. S. E. Cooney is an audiobook narrator, singer/songwriter, and winner of the World Fantasy Award for her collection *Bone Swans: Stories*. Her work includes the Dark Breakers series, *Jack o' the Hills, The Witch in the Almond Tree,* and poetry collection *How to Flirt in Faerieland and Other Wild Rhymes,* which features Rhysling Award–winning "The Sea King's Second Bride." Her short fiction and poetry can be found at *Lightspeed, Strange Horizons, Apex, Uncanny, Lakeside Circus, Black Gate, Papaveria Press, GigaNotoSaurus, Goblin Fruit, Clockwork Phoenix 3* & *5, The Mammoth Book of Steampunk,* Rich Horton's and Paula Guran's *Year's Best Science Fiction and Fantasy* anthologies, and elsewhere.

She can be found at csecooney.com and on Twitter at @csecooney.

Kris Dikeman lives in New York City. Her work has appeared in *Lady Churchill's Rosebud Wristlet, Year's Best Fantasy 9, Strange Horizons, Sybil's Garage, The Best of All Flesh,* and *Sympathy for the Devil,* among other places. Read more of her work online at krisdikeman.me.

Andy Duncan's short fiction has been honored with a Nebula Award, a Theodore Sturgeon Memorial Award, and three World Fantasy Awards, as well as a 2016 Individual Artist Award from the Maryland State Arts Council. His third collection, *An Agent of Utopia: New and Selected Stories,* is upcoming from Small Beer Press. An alumnus of Clarion West 1994, he is on the tenured English faculty at Frostburg State University.

Jeffrey Ford is the author of the novels *The Physiognomy, Memoranda, The Beyond, The Portrait of Mrs. Charbuque, The Girl in the Glass, The Cosmology of the Wider World,* and *The Shadow Year.* His short story collections are *The Fantasy Writer's Assistant, The Empire of Ice Cream, The Drowned Life, Crackpot Palace,* and *A Natural History of Hell.* Ford's short fiction has appeared in a wide variety of magazines and anthologies.

Ford is the recipient of the World Fantasy Award, Nebula, Edgar Allan Poe Award, the Shirley Jackson Award, the Hayakawa Award, and Gran Prix de l'Imaginaire. He lives in Ohio in a 120-year-old farmhouse surrounded by corn and soybean fields and teaches part-time at Ohio Wesleyan University.

Stephen Graham Jones is the author of sixteen novels, six story collections, more than 250 stories, and has some comic books in the works. His most recent novels are the werewolf novel *Mongrels* and the novella *Mapping the Interior.* Jones has been the recipient of an NEA Fellowship in Fiction, the Texas Institute of Letters Jesse Jones Award for Fiction, the Independent Publishers Awards for Multicultural Fiction, and three This Is Horror Awards. He's made Bloody Disgusting's Top Ten Novels of the Year.

He teaches in the MFA programs at University of Colorado at Boulder and University of California Riverside-Palm Desert. He lives in Boulder, Colorado, with his wife, two children, and too many old trucks.

He can be found on twitter: @SGJ72.

Matthew Kressel is the author of the novels *King of Shards* and *Queen of Static.* He's been twice nominated for a Nebula Award and once for a World Fantasy Award. His short fiction has appeared in such venues as *Lightspeed, Nightmare, Tor.com, Clarkesworld, Beneath Ceaseless Skies, io9, Interzone, Apex Magazine,* as well as the anthologies *Cyber World, After, Naked City, The People of the Book,* and many others.

He cohosts the Fantastic Fiction at KGB reading series in Manhattan alongside Ellen Datlow, and he has been a longtime member of the Altered Fluid writing group. Find him online at matthewkressel.net or @mattkressel.

Seanan McGuire lives, works, and watches way too many horror movies in the Pacific Northwest, where she shares her home with her two enormous blue cats, a ridiculous number of books, and a large collection of creepy dolls.

McGuire does not sleep much, publishing an average of four books a year under both her own name and the pen name "Mira Grant." Her first book, *Rosemary and Rue,* was released in September 2009, and she hasn't stopped running since. When not writing, she enjoys Disney Parks, horror movies, and looking winsomely at Marvel editorial as she tries to convince them to let her write for the X-Men. Keep up with McGuire at seananmcguire.com, on Twitter as @seananmcguire, or by walking into a cornfield at night and calling the secret, hidden name of the Great Pumpkin to the moon. When you turn, she will be there. She will always have been there.

Priya Sharma's fiction has appeared in *Albedo One, Interzone, Black Static,* and on *Tor.com.* She's been anthologized in several of Ellen Datlow's *Best Horror of the Year* series, Paula Guran's *Year's Best Dark Fantasy & Horror* series, Jonathan Strahan's *The Best Science Fiction*

& Fantasy 2014, Steve Haynes's *Best British Fantasy* 2014, and Johnny Main's *Best British Horror* 2015.

Her story "Fabulous Beasts" won the British Fantasy Award for Short Fiction and was nominated for the Shirley Jackson Award. The first collection of her short fiction will be published in 2018. More about her work can be found at priyasharmafiction.wordpress.com.

Delia Sherman has written numerous short stories, many of them for her current editor. Her collection, *Young Woman in a Garden*, was published by Small Beer Press. She has written three novels for adults: *Through a Brazen Mirror*, *The Porcelain Dove*, and *The Fall of the Kings*, with Ellen Kushner. Novels for younger readers include *Changeling*, *The Freedom Maze*, and *The Evil Wizard Smallbone*. Although she can recite all of "Jabberwocky" and large chunks of dialogue from *Looking-Glass* and *Alice* verbatim, she can't play chess. She can, however, knit, and does.

Angela Slatter is the author of the collections *The Girl with No Hands and Other Tales, Sourdough and Other Stories, The Bitterwood Bible and Other Recountings, Black-Winged Angels, Winter Children and Other Chilling Tales,* and *A Feast of Sorrows: Stories,* as well as the novellas *Ripper* and *Of Sorrow and Such.* With coconspirator Lisa L. Hannett she has written *Midnight and Moonshine* and *The Female Factory.*

Slatter has won a World Fantasy Award, a British Fantasy Award, one Ditmar Award, and six Aurealis Awards. She has an MA and a Ph.D. in Creative Writing and is a graduate of Clarion South and the Tin House Summer Writer's Workshop. She was an inaugural Queensland Writers Fellow in 2013, and the Established Writer-in-Residence at the Katharine Susannah Prichard Writers' Centre in Perth in 2016. Her work has been adapted for the screen.

Angela's debut novel, *Vigil,* was published in 2016, and the sequel *Corpselight* in July 2017. *Restoration* will follow in 2018.

Catherynne M. Valente is the *New York Times* bestselling author of over two dozen works of fiction and poetry, including *Palimpsest,* the Orphan's Tales series, *Deathless, Radiance,* and the crowdfunded phenomenon *The Girl Who Circumnavigated Fairyland in a Ship of Her Own Making.*

She is the winner of the Andre Norton, James Tiptree, Jr., Mythopoeic, Rhysling, Lambda, Locus, and Hugo Awards. She has been a finalist for the Nebula and World Fantasy Awards.

She lives on an island off the coast of Maine with a small but growing menagerie of beasts, some of which are human.

Genevieve Valentine is the author of *Mechanique, The Girls at the Kingfisher Club, Persona,* and *Icon*. Her short fiction has appeared in over a dozen Best of the Year anthologies.

In comics, she has written Catwoman and Batman and Robin Eternal for DC, and Xena: Warrior Princess for Dynamite; her short work has appeared in Vertigo's Strange Sports Stories and Kodansha's *Attack on Titan Anthology*. Her nonfiction and reviews have appeared in the *New York Times, The Atlantic, The A.V. Club,* NPR, and other venues.

Katherine Vaz is a former Briggs-Copeland Fellow in Fiction at Harvard University and Fellow of the Radcliffe Institute, and is the prize-winning author of two story collections, *Fado & Other Stories* and *Our Lady of the Artichokes,* and two novels, *Saudade* and *Mariana*.

Her work is often in the school of magical realism. Her children's/YA stories have been published in various anthologies, including as the title story in *Swan Sister*. Her latest book is *The Love Life of an Assistant Animator*. For years she has been a frequent contributor to anthologies edited by Ellen Datlow and Terri Windling.

Kaaron Warren has lived in Melbourne, Sydney, Canberra, and Fiji.

Her work has been nominated for the Bram Stoker Award and the World Fantasy Award, and won the Shirley Jackson Award.

She's sold more than two hundred short stories; four novels, including the multi-award-winning *Slights;* and six short-story collections, including the multi-award-winning *Through Splintered Walls.*

Her most recent novel is the multi-award-winning *The Grief Hole* and her most recent short story collection is *Cemetery Dance Select: Kaaron Warren.*

Ysabeau S. Wilce is a graduate of Clarion West and has been nominated for the World Fantasy Award, the James Tiptree, Jr. Award, and won the Andre Norton Award for the second volume in her Flora Fyrdraaca series, *Flora's Dare.*

Her short fiction has appeared in *Asimov's Science Fiction, The Magazine of Fantasy & Science Fiction,* and several year's best anthologies. Her most recent book, a collection of short stories entitled *Prophecies, Libels & Dreams* was published in 2014.

She may be found online, intermittently, at @crackpothall.

Jane Yolen, author of more than 360 books, is a master of disguise—sometimes a writer of delightful award-winning children's books, sometimes a punster of awe-filled jokes, sometimes a poet of depth-charged verse, sometimes a writer of Nebula Award twisted and twisting short stories and novellas, sometimes the author of Holocaust novels, sometimes the Grand Master of SFWA (the Science Fiction/Fantasy Writers of America). Try to keep up.

ABOUT THE EDITOR

Ellen Datlow has been editing science fiction, fantasy, and horror short fiction for more than thirty-five years. She currently acquires short fiction for *Tor.com*. In addition, she has edited about a hundred science fiction, fantasy, and horror anthologies, including the series *The Best Horror of the Year, The Doll Collection, The Monstrous, Nightmares: A New Decade of Modern Horror, Children of Lovecraft, Black Feathers: Dark Avian Tales,* and *Haunted Nights* (with Lisa Morton).

Forthcoming are *The Saga Anthology of Ghost Stories* and *Devil and the Deep.*

She's won multiple World Fantasy Awards, Locus Awards, Hugo Awards, Bram Stoker Awards, International Horror Guild Awards, Shirley Jackson Awards, and the 2012 Il Posto Nero Black Spot Award for Excellence as Best Foreign Editor. Datlow was named recipient of the 2007 Karl Edward Wagner Award, given at the British Fantasy Convention, for "outstanding contribution to the genre"; honored with the Life Achievement Award, given by the Horror Writers Association, in acknowledgment of superior achievement over an entire career; and was given the Life Achievement Award by the World Fantasy Convention.

She lives in New York and cohosts the monthly Fantastic Fiction Reading Series at KGB Bar. More information can be found at ellendatlow.com, on Facebook, and on twitter at @EllenDatlow.